TOM CLANCY

LINE OF SIGHT

ALSO BY TOM CLANCY

FICTION

The Hunt for Red October
Red Storm Rising
Patriot Games
The Cardinal of the Kremlin
Clear and Present Danger
The Sum of All Fears
Without Remorse
Debt of Honor
Executive Orders
Rainbow Six
The Bear and the Dragon
Red Rabbit
The Teeth of the Tiger
Dead or Alive (with Grant Blackwood)
Against All Enemies (with Peter Telep)
Locked On (with Mark Greaney)
Threat Vector (with Mark Greaney)
Command Authority (with Mark Greaney)
Tom Clancy Support and Defend (by Mark Greaney)
Tom Clancy Full Force and Effect (by Mark Greaney)
Tom Clancy Under Fire (by Grant Blackwood)
Tom Clancy Commander in Chief (by Mark Greaney)
Tom Clancy Duty and Honor (by Grant Blackwood)
Tom Clancy True Faith and Allegiance (by Mark Greaney)
Tom Clancy Point of Contact (by Mike Maden)
Tom Clancy Power and Empire (by Marc Cameron)

NONFICTION

Submarine: A Guided Tour Inside a Nuclear Warship
Armored Cav: A Guided Tour of an Armored Cavalry Regiment
Fighter Wing: A Guided Tour of an Air Force Combat Wing
Marine: A Guided Tour of a Marine Expeditionary Unit
Airborne: A Guided Tour of an Airborne Task Force
Carrier: A Guided Tour of an Aircraft Carrier

Into the Storm: A Study in Command
with General Fred Franks, Jr. (Ret.), and Tony Koltz

Every Man a Tiger: The Gulf War Air Campaign
with General Chuck Horner (Ret.) and Tony Koltz

Shadow Warriors: Inside the Special Forces
with General Carl Stiner (Ret.) and Tony Koltz

Battle Ready
with General Tony Zinni (Ret.) and Tony Koltz

Tom Clancy's
Line of Sight

MIKE MADEN

MICHAEL JOSEPH
an imprint of
PENGUIN BOOKS

MICHAEL JOSEPH

UK | USA | Canada | Ireland | Australia
India | New Zealand | South Africa

Michael Joseph is part of the Penguin Random House group of companies
whose addresses can be found at global.penguinrandomhouse.com

First published in the United States by G. P. Putnam's Sons 2018
Published in Great Britain by Michael Joseph 2018
001

Printed in Great Britain by Clays Ltd, St Ives plc

A CIP catalogue record for this book is available from the British Library

HARDBACK ISBN: 978–0–718–18929–7
OM PAPERBACK ISBN: 978–0–718–18930–3

www.greenpenguin.co.uk

Penguin Random House is committed to a
sustainable future for our business, our readers
and our planet. This book is made from Forest
Stewardship Council® certified paper.

Europe today is a powder keg and the leaders are like men smoking in an arsenal. . . . A single spark will set off an explosion that will consume us all. I cannot tell you when that explosion will occur, but I can tell you where. Some damned foolish thing in the Balkans will set it off.

ATTRIBUTED TO OTTO VON BISMARCK
AT THE CONGRESS OF BERLIN, 1878

PRINCIPAL CHARACTERS

UNITED STATES GOVERNMENT

Jack Ryan: President of the United States
Scott Adler: Secretary of state
Mary Pat Foley: Director of national intelligence
Robert Burgess: Secretary of defense
Jay Canfield: Director of the Central Intelligence Agency
Arnold Van Damm: President Ryan's chief of staff

THE CAMPUS

Gerry Hendley: Director of The Campus and Hendley
  Associates
John Clark: Director of operations
Dominic "Dom" Caruso: Operations officer
Jack Ryan, Jr.: Operations officer / senior analyst
Gavin Biery: Director of information technology
Adara Sherman: Operations officer

PRINCIPAL CHARACTERS

Bartosz "Midas" Jankowski: Operations officer

Lisanne Robertson: Director of transportation

OTHER CHARACTERS

Dr. Cathy Ryan: First Lady of the United States

Kemal Topal: Turkish ambassador to Bosnia and Herzegovina

Tarik Brkić: Commander, Al-Qaeda in the Balkans

Shafiq Walib: Captain, Syrian Arab Army

Aslan Dzhabrailov: Lieutenant, ground forces of the Russian Federation

Aida Curić: Owner, Happy Times! Balkan Tours

Emir Jukić: Happy Times! chief operating officer and tour guide

Dragan Kolak: Officer, Intelligence-Security Agency (OSA-OBA), Bosnia and Herzegovina

1

D r. Guzman rubbed her tired eyes. She became a doctor to heal the sick, not to file endless reports. But here she was, typing away after hours.

Again.

No matter. It was the price she paid to run the free clinic for the poorest of the poor in the area, mostly immigrants.

She checked her watch. The delivery was late. As soon as it arrived, she'd finish up this last budget report and head home for some needed shut-eye.

A noise in the back room startled her. She glanced up from her laptop, listening.

Nothing.

Probably just the rats again, she told herself. *Gross.*

She made a mental note to pick up some more traps at Lowe's tomorrow on her way in.

She settled back down into her spreadsheet, her bleary eyes

focused on the empty columns she still needed to fill with numbers. Her fingers froze.

She smelled the acrid tang of sweat and dope before she felt the blade against her throat.

The man stood behind her. Grabbed a fistful of her hair.

"The drugs are in the safe. I can't open it," she said in Spanish, her first language.

The voice behind her laughed. "Don't want the drugs, bitch," he said in English. "We gonna party."

Guzman whispered a prayer and cursed her stupidity. She'd left the back door unlocked for the delivery. That meant no alarm. That's how he got in.

And with no alarm, no help was on the way.

The man grabbed her shoulder and spun the chair around. He stood over her, flashing a gold tooth in a nicotine-stained smile. His bare, ropy arms were slathered in tattoos, but it was his shaved skull that shocked her. His entire head, from the neckline up, was a tangle of blue ink, with MS splashed across his throat and 13 emblazoned on his forehead.

She recognized him. He had come in last week, a wreck. Hep C and gonorrhea. He gave a name—Lopez—but no ID. She assumed it was fake. Didn't matter. He was sick, she was a doctor. She treated him. Even if he did give her the chills.

But now?

"You don't have to do this," she said, steeling her voice.

"Don't have to. Want to." He smiled. He stepped closer, thrusting his belt buckle close to her face. He laid the blade flat against her cheek. "So do you. If you want to live."

"Not like that."

A soft whistle from behind.

The gangbanger whipped around, pulling a chrome Ruger .357 out from beneath his shirt. Fast. A real gunslinger.

But a larger hand was faster. It grabbed the four-inch barrel and yanked it up toward the ceiling, then outward and away.

Fast, but not fast enough.

Tendons snapped in the banger's wrist, but his index finger smashed against the cocked trigger. A magnum round fired with a deafening roar into a ceiling tile, superheating the barrel in the big man's right hand. He didn't let go.

The big man's left hand crashed into the banger's jaw, buckling his knees. He crumbled to the floor, out cold.

It had all happened in a flash.

Dr. Guzman didn't have time to scream, let alone help. She stared wide-eyed at the man standing in front of her now. Six-one, one hundred and ninety pounds of lean muscle. Black hair, blue eyes.

Still in shock, all she could manage was, "Who are you?"

The man tucked the Ruger into his waistband.

"My sister Sally sent me. With those." He pointed at a backpack on the floor a few feet away, where he had set it down. "Antibiotics. Said you were running short."

"Dr. Sally Ryan?"

"Yeah."

"Then you must be Jack Ryan."

He shrugged and smiled.

"Junior."

3

IDLIB, SYRIA

The Syrian fighter stood on the roof of the apartment building, shielding his aging eyes from the western sun as he watched the children playing in the street seven floors below. They sweated and laughed in the long shadows of the fading light, swarming after the ball like bees chasing a dog, ignoring the calls of their anxious mothers to come in and clean up. He smiled.

Kids everywhere, the same.

The truce was a mercy. "Thanks be to God," he whispered to himself. He checked his watch, a nervous habit. By the fading light he knew the muezzin's voice would ring out over the loudspeakers, calling for the *maghrib*.

He had raged when his battalion commander, an Iraqi, first announced the truce with that butcher Assad and his paymasters, the godless Russians. But the last nine weeks had given them time to rest and regroup with smuggled weapons, food, fuel, cash. Now they were ready for anything up close, and their Stinger missiles kept the dreaded Russian jets and helicopters out of the skies. The senior Al-Nusra commanders were all stationed here; even the emir was living in Idlib, just three blocks away. This was the safest place in Syria, as long as the truce lasted.

The war seemed far away now. A distant, painful memory. So much blood. And for what? Life was better than death, was it not?

He craved a cigarette, even after all these years, but cigarettes were *haram*, and men in his unit had been executed for smoking them. But perhaps a strong coffee after *maghrib*, he thought, his eyes tracking the black-clad women scurrying into the street, clapping their hands and shouting, trying to herd the laughing children back to their homes.

The *adhan* began, a strong voice calling the faithful. Its familiar words warmed his soul. The mosque would be full tonight.

He picked up his rifle and headed for the stairs. Perhaps the war was indeed over and these children would finally know peace.

Thanks be to God.

NINE MILES SOUTH OF IDLIB

A bead of sweat trickled down the side of Captain Walib's face despite the A/C unit blasting overhead. The Syrian captain stared at the monitor in front of him, his right hand poised near the master launch button.

The monitor verified the ready state of the fire-control computers on the six TOS-2 Starfire launch vehicles stationed nearby, each composed of a seventy-tube box missile launcher fixed on a heavily armored T-14 Armata tank chassis, and all linked to his command console.

He and Major Grechko sat at their stations inside the cramped BMP-3K armored personnel fighting vehicle, Walib's mobile command post. Technically, the Russian major was only an adviser on today's operation. But in reality Grechko was evaluating Walib's combat command capabilities along with the new TOS-2 Starfire system.

Walib stole a quick glance at Lieutenant Aslan Dzhabrailov sitting near the doorway. The young, broad-shouldered Chechen was the platoon leader of the commandos guarding his unit. There was a fierce intelligence in the man's pale gray eyes and a well-used ten-millimeter Glock on his hip. The Chechens were savage, brutal fighters—a breed apart, the best in the war, at least on his side. Dzhabrailov was a man to be feared.

The major checked the GLONASS receiver—the Russian version of GPS—one last time, along with the laser guidance beam. "Targeting confirmed. Free to fire, Captain."

Walib smoothed his mustache with his thumb and forefinger, hesitating.

"Something wrong, Captain?" Grechko asked.

Walib was a Syrian patriot. He had no problem killing terrorists, especially foreign ones. The Syrian "civil war" was fought by everyone but Syrians these days. But they were all just proxies for the Americans and Russians, who happily sacrificed the Syrian people on the altar of their superpower ambitions.

He hated them all, especially today.

"There are no civilians in Idlib, Captain," Grechko said. "Only Al-Nusra bandits, the women who breed them, and the children who become either bandits or breeders. This is a war of demographics. We must fight accordingly."

This wasn't the war Walib had volunteered to fight. He never imagined the terrible weapons under his command would be used to slaughter innocents.

But if he disobeyed Grechko's order, the Russian would pull his nine-millimeter Grach pistol out of its holster and splatter his brains against the BMP's steel hull, and simply order one of Walib's lieutenants in the other vehicles to fire.

Nothing would be accomplished except that Walib would be dead in exchange for a few minutes of respite for the doomed civilians.

He hated himself. He hated this war.

But he hated dying needlessly even more.

"Just checking the spin on the number-eleven gyro," Walib said. A convenient lie. "Good to go."

"Then you're free to launch. Proceed at once." Grechko's drooping bulldog eyes narrowed.

"Yes, sir." Walib flipped the safety cap on the launch button and jabbed it before he could change his mind.

Instantly, the French-designed, solid-fuel motors on the 122-millimeter rockets fired. The roar was terrifying, like the shout of God himself, even inside the idling command vehicle. Each half second, another nine-and-a-half-foot-long missile screamed out of its tube. A full-throated chorus of death.

Thirty-five seconds later, all 420 missiles had launched, lofting nearly fifteen tons of thermobaric munitions into the air. The TOS-2 master fire-control computer coordinated the launch timing and trajectories so that all of the warheads arrived on target simultaneously, avoiding warhead fratricide and increasing the explosive effects.

Grechko stared greedily at his monitor displaying a live video feed from the Israeli-designed Forpost-M aerial drone circling high over Idlib, which also provided the laser guidance beam for the missiles.

"Any second now," Grechko said, grinning. "Time to burn out those cockroaches."

But Walib didn't want to see it. He was already outside, barking orders to his men, who were scrambling to prep for rapid "shoot and scoot" redeployment, the only defense against counter-battery fire, real or imagined.

Walib marched through the billowing clouds of exhaust and debris still swirling in the air, rage and shame welling in his eyes.

Lieutenant Dzhabrailov stood outside the command vehicle, studying the Syrian captain with keen interest.

IDLIB, SYRIA

The laser-guided TOS-2 Starfire rockets struck inside a kill box two hundred eighty meters square—about eight densely populated city blocks. A much tighter pattern was possible with the new guidance system, but it would have resulted in far fewer casualties.

The cascade of crashing warheads released clouds of combustible fuel mixed with finely powdered aluminum, PETN high-explosive, and ethylene oxide gas into the open streets. The incendiary clouds also penetrated through the cracks and crevices of nearly every mosque, apartment building, and shop in the eight-block area. Basements, attics, kitchens, toilets, and bedrooms filled with the toxic mixture in nanoseconds, leaving nowhere to hide.

Timed scatter charges of conventional explosives within the warheads detonated next, igniting the explosive fog into a blazing plasma cloud. The few people standing outside and nearest to the points of impact were instantly incinerated.

They were the lucky ones.

The shock wave produced by the explosion caused the first surge of destruction, producing thousands of pounds of pressure per square inch—enough to crush the hull of a World War II submarine. Those who weren't initially killed by the striking force of the overpressure waves suffered terribly. Limbs were torn away or broken; alveoli and bronchioles ruptured in the lungs; emboli formed in coronary and cerebral arteries; bowels perforated; inner ear structures were crushed; eyes were ripped from their sockets.

The crushing force of the expanding overpressure waves smashed walls, broke windows, shattered doors. The city itself became a form of shrapnel, hurling shards of burning brick, glass, wood, and iron through the fiery winds, lacerating soft tissues and exposed flesh.

Yet this still wasn't the worst of it.

The powdered aluminum in the expanding plasma cloud slowed its burn rate, resulting in the total consumption of the atmospheric oxygen. This created both a massive vacuum and a fireball of nearly 3,000 degrees Celsius—twice the melting point of steel. But it was the vacuum that caused the most destruction.

The buildings and other structures still standing held no protections against the fast-forming negative pressure, equal to its opposite in energy and violence, generating fiery, hurricane-force winds. Shrieking survivors were crushed beneath tons of crumbling debris, buried alive in basements, crucified on shattered timbers, impaled on twisted metal. Anyone still alive in the rubble spent their last few minutes suffocating to death, gasping like carp for oxygen that no longer existed.

There were no more laughing children in the streets.

The last of the thermobaric munitions burned out just as the explosions of gas mains, petrol tanks, and other urban flammables began, stoking the burning rubble and the still-living bodies beneath into an inferno of unquenchable fire.

Within seconds, thousands had died, and thousands more suffered. Within a few hours, many of the wounded survivors would perish as well.

It was the explosive equivalent of a tactical nuclear device, but entirely conventional, and perfectly legal, according to international treaties.

It was also Hell on Earth.

3

THE WHITE HOUSE, WASHINGTON, D.C.

Jack Ryan, Jr., spooned up the last of the Burgundy beef stew, earthy and rich, scraping the bowl as he fished out the last piece of savory meat.

"More, son?" Dr. Cathy Ryan asked.

"Always, but two helpings are enough," Jack Junior said. This was his favorite meal, and his mother made it better than anybody. It was just Jack and his parents tonight—the twins were on an ecological field trip to the Virginia wetlands for the next three days and his older sister was on ER duty at the hospital, so she couldn't join them.

Jack and his parents were seated at the round table in the First Family's private dining room, formerly known as the Prince of Wales guest room, before Jacqueline Kennedy converted it to its current function for her own young family. Cathy Ryan had redecorated it in a transitional Craftsman style, favoring the clean lines and sturdy functionality of an original American art form.

"I hope you saved room for the apple pie," she said, standing.

"Are you kidding me?" Jack said. His mother's apple pie was his all-time favorite dessert. His suspicions grew. "What's the occasion?"

"Does a mother need a special reason to cook for her son?" she said.

"When a mother is as busy as you are, yes, she does need a special reason."

"I haven't had a chance to see you in forever, and you're off to Europe soon. I knew the only way I could get you over here was to bribe you with a home-cooked meal. Besides, it's something I love to do." She glanced at her husband, a pair of reading glasses perched on the end of his nose, his mind buried in a file folder on the dining room table. "Isn't that right, honey?"

Senior grunted. "What? Yeah. Dinner was great."

Cathy fake-frowned. "Hey, bub. What's more interesting than us?"

Senior kept staring at the file. "I'd tell you, but you don't have the clearance."

Cathy Ryan leaped out of her chair and plopped into her husband's lap, wrapping her arms around his neck. She leaned in close to his ear, whispering heavily. "Vee hav vays of making you talk, Mr. President."

Senior laughed, shut his file, and pulled off his glasses, wrapping his arms around his wife's slender waist. The two exchanged a glance. He whispered in her ear. She giggled and swatted him. A lot of years, a lot of love. They were as steady and solid as the Stickley oak table they all sat around.

Junior watched them canoodling like a pair of frisky teen-agers. The most famous power couple in the world. His father was arguably the greatest president of his generation, exercising selfless leadership on behalf of the national interest through every crisis in a town notorious for ruthless, self-aggrandizing ambition. His mother was a brilliant physician in her own right, and bore the responsibilities of being First Lady with dignity and grace. She was his father's rock.

But to Jack, they were just Mom and Dad.

He felt like a little kid again sitting around the familiar table, but in a good way. Hard as they worked, family always came first for them. Whatever strength or honor or virtue he possessed, Jack knew, he got it from these two. He envied them. He and Yuki had to put a hold on their budding romance; their schedules and careers were both too demanding, and Skype just wasn't cutting it. It was becoming a painfully familiar pattern in his personal life. He already felt the void of Yuki's absence, brief though their affair had been. His mother and father were married by the time they were Jack's age. Hell, John Clark, the eternal warrior, was married and had been for many years, and one of his daughters was married to Ding. Even Jack's cousin Dom and Adara were together. Nobody on The Campus seemed to suffer performance-wise by being in a stable relationship.

So what was wrong with him?

All three Ryans stood and cleared the table, hauling the dishes to the kitchen. Senior made a pot of decaf coffee while Cathy served up the pie and Jack fetched the vanilla-bean ice cream out of the freezer. It was a small kitchen but perfectly adequate for the First Family on the few occasions they cooked for themselves. With some of the finest chefs in the country available around the clock, and the two senior Ryans working more than full-time jobs, cooking at home was a rare luxury.

Ten minutes later, Junior scraped up the last piece of Granny Smith apple from his plate and forked it into his mouth, savoring the sweet and tangy bite—just the way he remembered it.

"I wish you'd shave that awful beard," his mother said. "I miss your face."

"Just keeping it real," Jack said. He didn't tell her that he changed his looks just to keep people guessing. He was, after all, the son of these two famous people, and because they had worked hard to keep their kids out of the limelight, he wasn't nearly as well known as some might think.

But he wasn't completely anonymous, either, so he took the extra step every six months or so to comb his hair in another direction or grow it out long, or let a beard or mustache do the camouflage work. Sometimes he even wore contacts to change the color of his eyes.

After the last ragged op, he thought about going for the clean-cut look of a stockbroker, which he sort of was. But no facial hair made him feel a little exposed, even if it was sometimes safest to hide in plain sight. He decided to keep the beard, but trimmed it close.

Senior's attention was buried back in his classified file folder.

"Another piece of pie?" Cathy asked her son.

"No, thanks. I'm stuffed." Junior smiled. "It was perfect. Thank you." He sipped the last of his coffee and set his cup down. "Well, I need to get going. Got a plane to catch tomorrow."

"You're off to the former Yugoslavia, right?" Cathy asked.

"London first, then to Ljubljana, Slovenia."

"I've heard it's beautiful over there."

"It's on the southern border of Austria, near the Adriatic coast. You get the Alps and the ocean for one low price."

"Send pictures, for sure. I'm curious, though. What financial interest does Hendley Associates have over there?"

Senior again glanced up over the glasses perched on his nose. His wife didn't know about The Campus—the "black side" special ops team that Jack also served with. All she knew was that Jack was an analyst with the "white side" financial firm Hendley Associates, which funded The Campus special operations through its highly successful investments and fiduciary services.

"There's a company over there that wants to offer an IPO on the NASDAQ, and they hired us to do the preliminary financials."

"Sounds . . . boring," Cathy said.

"Numbers tell a story, if you know how to read them," Senior offered. He looked at Jack. "Financial analysis has its own particular rewards in that regard . . . and risks."

Junior smiled at the double entendre. Gerry Hendley was in charge of the personnel decisions, and he didn't always inform the President when his son was deployed on a dangerous op. Neither did Jack.

"The only risk in Slovenia, from what I hear, is eating too much cream cake."

Jack's father smiled. "Good to know." He returned to his reading.

Only a handful of people knew that it was the President's idea to create the firm, or that it was his friend, the former senator Gerry Hendley, who ran both sides of the company.

The Campus was a private intelligence organization created to carry out black ops missions that regular government agencies couldn't or wouldn't do, serving at the President's discretion.

In a perfect world, The Campus shouldn't have to exist, but the dysfunctional swamp of unscrupulous self-interest known as Washington, D.C., was considerably less than perfect, even in the estimation of its slimiest inhabitants. In the President's mind, D.C. was one giant Hungarian cluster dance, with occasional interruptions of clarity and purpose, but only when the national interest was properly communicated to and understood by the preening peacocks on the Hill.

"So, I was wondering if you might do me a favor while you were over there," Cathy said.

"Sure. Name it."

Cathy stepped over to a chair in the corner, where a brown leather folder was perched. She picked it up and carried it back to the table. She pulled out a file folder and set it down in front of Junior before sitting down herself.

"I was cleaning out some of my old medical files from Johns Hopkins and came across this."

Jack opened the file dated 1992. Inside the stiff green cover was a picture of his mother, twenty-six years younger, in her white doctor's coat, holding in her arms a little girl with luminous blue eyes and blond hair, grinning at the camera. Well, one blue eye. The other was heavily bandaged.

"Her name is, or was, Aida Curić. She was just three years old at the time, when they brought her to me for eye surgery for a shrapnel wound. It was during the war."

"Which war?" Jack asked. "From what I remember reading, Yugoslavia had several after the breakup in 1991."

Senior closed his file. "Your mother is referring to the

Bosnian civil war, when Serbs, Croats, and Muslims fought one another for independence—and survival. You know the term 'ethnic cleansing'?"

Jack nodded. "Sure. One group of people trying to exterminate another one. Evil stuff."

"Well, Bosnia is where the term was invented. Civil wars are the worst. It was the bloodiest conflict on European soil since World War Two—even worse than the Ukraine invasion a few years ago. By some estimates, one hundred and forty thousand Yugoslavians perished because the UN and the Europeans dragged their feet. It took NATO airstrikes to finally end it."

"If my two history wonks can spare a moment, I'd like to finish my story about Aida, if that's okay."

"Sorry," both Jacks said.

"Anyway, by some miracle I managed to save her eye and her vision. After the war her parents took her back home to Bosnia, but they stopped writing to me shortly afterward." Cathy began to tear up. "I've seen those blue eyes of hers in my dreams a thousand times, and I can't tell you how many candles I've lit for her over the years. Sometimes when I stared into your sister Sally's eyes, I saw hers. I don't know why Aida had such an effect on me, but she did, and I finally had to let her go. But seeing this file again yesterday stirred something up in me and I can't stop thinking about her."

Cathy opened up her leather folio again and produced a sealed envelope. "I was wondering if you had any spare time while you were over there, if you could find a way to get down to Sarajevo and look for her and give her this for me."

She handed it to Jack. Only Aida's name, written in his mother's graceful and meticulous hand, was on the otherwise blank envelope.

"Did you try Googling her for an address?" Jack asked.

Cathy shrugged. "Sure, but Curić is a common name, and it wasn't very helpful. Facebook wasn't any better—or Twitter, for that matter."

"The FBI is the world's greatest detective agency, and you're married to the boss. Why not call them?"

"This is personal business. I'm not going to ask my husband to deploy public resources for my personal benefit."

"Well, I'm not on the government payroll, so I'm happy to do it. I've always wanted to visit Sarajevo. I hear it's an amazing city with a lot of history."

Senior nodded. "Yeah, a lot of history, for sure."

As President Durling's national security adviser, Senior had seen the photos and read the firsthand accounts of the atrocities on all sides when the wars broke out in 1991. He'd urged Durling into action, but the Europeans told the Americans to back off, promising to handle things on their end. Three years later, a suicidal Japanese pilot slammed into the U.S. Capitol building during a joint session of Congress, killing hundreds, including President Durling, the justices of the Supreme Court, and many others, soon followed by a new Middle East war breaking out. By then, there wasn't anything the newly sworn President Ryan could do about the Yugoslavia situation. Still, many had suffered and died needlessly, and Senior still felt guilty that the United States hadn't tried to stop it unilaterally when it first began.

Senior repeated himself, almost in a whisper. "A lot of history."

"Are you sure you don't mind, dear?" Cathy asked her son. "I hate to be a bother."

"It's not a bother at all, Mom. It's going to be a lot of fun."

4

Lieutenant Dzhabrailov trailed Captain Walib as he circled the TOS-2 Starfire vehicle parked in a courtyard next to the mosque, shielded from prying American eyes orbiting in space overhead by computer-designed camouflage netting. The netting broke up the searing sunlight pouring out of the sky as well, a welcome respite. The big Chechen stood a head taller than the slight Syrian. Both carried holstered pistols. Walib dismissed the three Russian enlisted men for lunch break while the two of them conducted a security inspection of the vehicle.

"I've reviewed your proposal, Lieutenant."

"And?" the Chechen asked.

Walib knelt in the dust, checking one of the track plates on the tread. Or pretending to.

"Your . . . commander. He's reliable?"

"As reliable as you."

Walib stood back up, facing Dzhabrailov. "Meaning?"

The big Chechen glanced around. They were alone. He lowered his voice anyway, and shrugged. "Meaning, I haven't been put up against a wall and shot since we last spoke. So I trust you. And I assume that means you trust me. I'll vouch for my commander with my life."

Walib's eyes narrowed, taking the measure of the man again. "You're vouching with both of our lives."

"Understood."

"And there's no question in your mind we can pull it off?"

"If there were, I wouldn't be standing here." Dzhabrailov glanced around again. "And you are certain you want to do this thing? There is no turning back from it."

Walib's face hardened. "As certain as anything I have ever known. I will die rather than turn back. Do you doubt me?"

The Chechen shook his head. "I trust your hate, brother. And the will of Allah."

"Then we'll speak no more about it. And I am still your captain, not your brother."

"Yes, sir. When do you propose to make the move?"

"The sooner the better," Walib said. He turned around and continued with his halfhearted inspection. "Before the next fire mission, thirteen days from now."

"How about tonight?"

Walib whipped back around. "Tonight? How is that even possible?"

Dzhabrailov allowed himself a small grin. "Everything is already arranged."

"You are overly confident, Lieutenant. You couldn't have known what my answer would be. I didn't know it myself until an hour ago."

"I saw what happened to you at the launch, Captain." Dzhabrailov darkened. "I saw the same thing in myself not so long ago." But the Chechen brightened just as quickly. "And I also knew because Allah told me that this was His plan."

"You mean your commander's plan, don't you?"

"My commander is a servant of the Most High, as am I." The Chechen smiled. "As are you, Captain."

"Perhaps," Walib said. "We'll know soon enough."

"What do you propose for tonight, then, exactly?"

They spoke in measured whispers for the next fifteen minutes while they inspected the hulking tank chassis with its giant missile box affixed above, pretending to check for signs of damage or needed maintenance. Anyone watching them from a distance wouldn't have thought anything about them or paid attention to the short salutes they returned to the grateful guards as they resumed their posts.

The two conspirators parted ways, each in a different direction, their determined steps quickened with the urgency of the damned.

PRESIDENCY BUILDING, SARAJEVO,
BOSNIA AND HERZEGOVINA

The Turkish ambassador sipped a strong, black Bosnian coffee from a cup of fine bone china. His smiling eyes gleamed behind steel-framed glasses above a sharp, distinctive nose and a thick but well-trimmed mustache tinged with gray, as was his hair, though he was nearly bald now. This gave Ambassador Topal a rather agreeable but owlish appearance, which suited his reputation as a patient and thoughtful diplomat.

He sat across the desk from the Bosnian president, a Muslim, locally known as Bosniaks. In fact, the man was just one of *three* Bosnian presidents. If a camel was a horse designed by a committee, then the Bosnian presidency was a three-headed camel; a collective head of state. It was composed of three presidents: an ethnic Croat, an ethnic Serb, and a Bosniak. But such was the mystery, and compromise, that governed the enigma of this ethnically and culturally divided republic. At least the three presidential heads were of one mind—for now.

Topal had accepted the modest posting to the small but troubled republic for a number of reasons, one of which was his fascination with its complicated politics and governance. Bosnia and Herzegovina—"Bosnia" for short—was a nation comprising two political entities, like states: the Federation of Bosnia and Herzegovina, with primarily ethnic Croats and Muslims; and the Republika Srpska, with mainly ethnic Serbs. Bosnia was a creation of European design at the end of the Bosnian War to form a peaceful, liberal democratic republic between these three distinct but hostile groups. So far, the experiment had worked, after a fashion.

Yet in the last few years, just about the time Topal accepted his ambassadorship, ethnonationalist factions from each group began agitating for independence from one another. In recent months, small acts of insurgency had occurred across Bosnia, committed apparently by resurgent ethnic militias. Sloganeering graffiti sprayed on government buildings, smashed shop windows, burned cars. Fortunately, no people had been injured or killed by the hooliganism—at least, not yet.

Serbs, Croats, and Bosniaks were equally active on social media, airing current and historic grievances against one another while simultaneously claiming the moral high ground against the "fanatics" who "oppressed" them. Local and national politicians from all sides were beginning to pick up their respective ethnonationalist flags in hopes of taking advantage of the increasing friction. This occurred even as the national police and security forces stepped up their efforts to find and prosecute domestic terror operations.

The senior leadership of the national political parties, along with each of the three Bosnian presidents—the titular heads of their respective parties—came up with a unique plan to stem the rising tide last year. They ordered a national Unity Referendum to be held on the same day as the upcoming national elections, just six weeks away. The idea was to show that the vast majority of Bosnians—Orthodox Serbs, Catholic Croats, and Muslim Bosniaks—all preferred to remain a single, unified democracy. The hope was that a successful referendum would curb the rising nationalist forces and, not coincidentally, assure the easy reelection of the incumbent parties that sponsored it.

The initial announcement was greeted enthusiastically by liberal democrats of all stripes and widely supported in the public opinion polls, especially among the business community. If Bosnia had any hope of entering the EU in the near future, it would have to demonstrate that it was a stable, functioning, and pluralist democracy.

The religious leaders of all three faiths even signed a joint letter supporting the referendum, speaking in favor of continued national unity as a practical act of faith in God and in one another.

But in the months that followed, opinion polls began turning in the opposite direction, particularly as local violence escalated. There was now a real chance that the Unity Referendum would fail. If it did, Bosnia would undoubtedly break up. What seemed like a painless, thoughtful solution last year had become both a social and political crisis of the first order today.

This explained why the Bosniak president sitting in front of him was so animated this afternoon, Topal thought. The magnificent Ali Pasha Mosque loomed in the bright fall sun in the large window behind the president's desk.

"I don't care what they say. This isn't an act of religious renewal," the president said. He was referring to the recently announced Serbian Orthodox Renewal liturgy. The president's round, clean-shaven face reddened with each word. "It's a political act, pure and simple, meant to derail the Unity Referendum. And Ivanović"—the Serb president of Bosnia—"knows this. And yet he chooses to attend. What is he thinking?"

Topal set his cup and saucer down on the small table in front of him. "What choice does President Ivanović have? The bishop is his bishop, and his Orthodox citizens vote. If he steps away from the Renewal, it looks like *he's* the one playing politics. Besides, none of us thought this was a problem two weeks ago. I don't blame President Ivanović. I think other forces are at play."

"As do I. And we both know who."

The Serbian Orthodox Renewal service was just weeks away. When it was originally announced by Sarajevo's bishop for the local metropolitanate as an outdoor baptismal service and liturgy at Sarajevo's Olympic soccer stadium, it was assumed that no more than several hundred, or perhaps a few thousand at most, would participate. Like most Europeans, the average Bosnian—Serb or otherwise—was usually more passionate about his local soccer team than the practice of his religion.

But with the announcement by the patriarch of the Serbian Orthodox Church—a Serbian national from the nation of

Serbia, not the Republika Srpska within Bosnia—interest began to grow. But it was the announcement by the patriarch of Moscow, the head of the Russian Orthodox Church, that he would also be attending that kindled a fire of apparent faith renewal. The latest estimate was that thirty thousand Orthodox Serbs from around the region now planned to fill the stadium, many from across the Serbian border.

"There's no question in my mind that this is stoking Serb nationalism," the president said. "And if Serbs galvanize, so will the Catholic Croats, not to mention my own people."

Topal shook his head. "A democracy cannot survive identity politics. Bosnians must think of themselves as Bosnian, first and always. All religions are respected in your country, and everybody has equal rights, and there has been peace. But all of that is at risk if ethnic identity trumps democratic ideals."

The president leaned back in his chair, tenting his fingers. "If Bosnia breaks apart, there will be trouble again, like in the old days." His round face darkened, overwhelmed with painful memories of the genocidal war.

"My country stands with you, Mr. President, and with all Bosnians, especially our Muslim brothers and sisters. I believe we have demonstrated our commitment to you and your democracy." Topal was politic enough not to mention the hundreds of millions of Turkish liras his government had poured into Bosnia over the past decade, much of it under Topal's guidance.

"Turkey is our best friend, and we are grateful for your continued commitment. Both of our governments understand the existential crisis that a failed Bosnian democracy represents. The nationalisms here will only spread, and regional instability will be the inevitable result. If Croats and Bosniaks feel threatened, other nations—even NATO—might intervene against the Serbs to prevent another genocide."

Topal sighed. "Yes. And if the Serbs are threatened, the Russians will intervene on behalf of their Slavic brethren, to make up for their failure to protect Serbia from NATO during the Yugoslav wars."

"NATO versus Russia again?" The president sighed. "We're speaking of World War Three."

"That would be a disaster, which is why my government stands ready to serve you and the Unity Referendum in any way possible." Topal leaned forward, smiling. "Be encouraged, my friend. Bosnia isn't dead yet. I have confidence that the forces of democracy will prevail. And who knows? Perhaps the Renewal service will lead to something positive. A renewal of faith can be a good thing."

"Given the history of my country, I'm not as sanguine as you are. But I thank you for your assurances, and your friendship."

The president stood, as did Topal. They shook hands. The Turkish ambassador caught a glimpse in the window of a flock of redwing birds circling the tall minaret in synchronous flight. He smiled to himself.

A good omen, indeed.

5

HAMA, SYRIA

Grechko's heavy boot crushed the throttle of the tiny UAZ jeep, its poorly maintained suspension bouncing him around in his seat like a bean inside a Cuban maraca. The UAZ was throwing dust and granite chips in a rooster tail behind him, slewing around the snaking curves of the quarry road as fast as the straining four-cylinder engine would allow. He cursed violently, clutching gears in the sharp, spiraling turns, his headlights splashing across the twisting maze of steep quarry walls as he raced toward the bottom of the pit.

His boot smashed the brake and the jeep skidded to a tooth-rattling halt in front of the heavy steel doors of the ammo warehouse, cut deep into the thick walls of granite. It was a highly unusual location to store munitions and therefore not on American or Israeli aerial targeting lists, and well hidden from overhead surveillance. The steel-reinforced concrete walls were doubly protected beneath several hundred tons of quarry stone, creating a virtually impenetrable shield for the explosive contents inside.

Grechko leaped out of the jeep in a cloud of dust and stormed past the big covered 6x6 Kamaz cargo truck parked to the side. The jeep's headlights illumined dark blood spatter on one of the half-opened steel doors, confirming his worst fears. Walib's phone call had interrupted his evening with his favorite talented contract whore, a redheaded Ukrainian girl with high cheekbones and low self-esteem. But the captain's panicked voice quelled Grechko's rage and convinced him that the Syrian was out of his depth, and a firm, Russian hand was needed to take charge.

Grechko's eyes adjusted to the dim lights inside the warehouse. A long trail of blood and dust led from the doorway to Walib, who was kneeling down next to a body splayed out on the floor. Grechko knelt down beside the body as well, examining the young face. One of the Russian guards, a corporal. Grechko couldn't recall his name. The slit across the dead boy's throat was a wide, bloody smile beneath his clean-shaven chin.

"What the hell happened here, Captain?"

"This one dead, along with the other two, farther back." Walib stood as Grechko laid a soft hand on the young corporal's unblinking eyes and closed them.

Grechko sprang to his feet, his back to Walib. "We'll get the bastards who did this!"

He suddenly noticed that dozens of crates of 122-millimeter missiles were gone from the far wall. He pointed at the empty spaces. The rest of the facility was stacked high with crates of

220-millimeter thermobaric missiles needed for the TOS-1A Sunfire system still operating in country.

"Walib! The 122s!"

"Yes, I know. They're gone. One of the Shmels, too," Walib said, referring to the RPO-A Bumblebee, a thermobaric shoulder-fired rocket.

"Start an inventory immediately. I'll call security—" Grechko spun back around, reaching for his cell phone.

Walib's pistol was pointed at him.

"No need. I know exactly how many missiles were taken."

Grechko's eyes widened with fury. "You traitorous shit!"

Walib crashed the butt of his pistol in the center of Grechko's wide forehead, breaking the skin. Blood gouted from the wound. The Russian staggered under the blow but didn't fall. He wiped the blood out of his eyes with the back of his hairy hand, stunned and incredulous. His mind cleared, and he lunged with a shout at Walib's throat with his thick fingers. But the Syrian was ready for him, hammering the top of the major's skull again with the pistol's steel butt. Grechko moaned as his knees buckled, and his head hit the concrete with a sickening thud, like a ripe melon dropped on a hot summer sidewalk.

Walib holstered his pistol.

"Why didn't you just shoot him?" Dzhabrailov asked from the doorway.

Walib called over his shoulder, still staring at Grechko. "In here? You want to meet your virgins with your manhood cooked and your face fried like a falafel?"

The Chechen grinned. "We need to move."

Walib spat on the Russian. "One last thing, Lieutenant, then we can go."

D zhabrailov was driving the heavy truck west on a two-lane ribbon of asphalt when the moonless sky behind them erupted in a flash of blinding light.

Walib sat in the cab, riding shotgun. He checked his watch. The timer had worked perfectly. He imagined the bunker's thick steel doors melting like butter beneath the withering torch of the white-hot gases, and the explosive flames exhausting harmlessly through the quarry, scorching acres of nothing but granite and dust without a single civilian casualty.

Not only had Walib destroyed the rest of the thermobaric arsenal, he had also found a way to cover their tracks. There would be nothing left of the corpses—not even ash—or any hint that the crates of missiles they carried in the truck had been stolen. All of the missing personnel—the Russian guards, Grechko, Dzhabrailov, and him—would be presumed killed in an attack by Israeli Sayeret Matkal or Iranian Quds Force commandos. The Russians wouldn't allow the possibility of an accident.

For the first time in a long time, Walib was happy. Killing Grechko with his own hands had done that. That surprised him. He was an artillery officer, not an infantryman. He'd never killed in anger before, or at close distance. Before tonight he wasn't sure if he could do it. But it had been shockingly easy to kill the raging bastard, and satisfying to force the guards at gunpoint to load the heavy missile crates before Dzhabrailov's vicious blade dropped them like slaughtered lambs. Walib felt no guilt about them, either. Revenge had a sweetness he hadn't expected.

And tonight was only the beginning.

He smiled.

"Something funny, brother?" Dzhabrailov asked.

"The Russians will probably award us medals of valor for our glorious sacrifice."

"A medal would be nice," the Chechen joked. "Too bad we can't collect it."

"Neither can Grechko."

The thought of the Russian's head cracking on the concrete made Walib smile again. Perhaps Dzhabrailov was right after all. Perhaps they really were doing the will of Allah. Walib had never known a plan to survive first contact with the enemy. That alone was a miracle.

All of the pieces were in play now. So long as the checkpoint guards up ahead had been bribed as promised, they'd be home free. The foreign Chechen—a violent and unlikely ally—had proven as good as his word so far. Walib looked forward to meeting this mysterious commander of Dzhabrailov's when the real work began.

Walib was, no doubt, a changed man now. A man on a mission.

But did that make him a mujahid?

Walib checked his watch again. They were even ahead of schedule. "We'll make the coast before sunrise."

"*Inshallah*," the Chechen said.

Walib patted the heavy black Pelican case between them, an object of even greater importance than the other device they had stolen, or even the ordnance stacked in the covered bed behind them. "Yes, indeed."

Inshallah.

6

AHTOPOL, BULGARIA

I t was a modest house with a priceless view, high on the ridge
of a finger of land thrusting into the Black Sea.

Vladimir Vasilev owned many more houses far grander
and with even more magnificent views all over Europe, but
Bulgaria was home and he had wanted to die here.

Each morning, Vasilev woke to a shimmering sunrise above
a wine-dark sea, the light pouring through his plate-glass window. The dawn was not so much a promise of the day to come
as it was a sparkling reminder that he had managed to survive
one more fearful night. Another day to realize his last and final
wish.

The short Ghanaian contract nurse changed his catheter
with practiced economy, neither smiling nor frowning as she
completed the intimate task. Her large breasts strained against
her tight-fitting green scrubs, which were barely able to contain her enormous posterior. Exactly the kind of woman Vasi-

lev favored. Even just a year ago, he would have taken her with
a seduction of Ossetra sturgeon caviar and a fine champagne on
his yacht, or, if she resisted his charms, raped her as she wept.
But he felt no stirring in his loins this morning, despite her
gloved hands fingering his flaccid manhood.

She finished her work, removed her gloves, and cleansed her
hands with antiseptic gel before asking him if he needed anything else in nervous, lilting English.

Vasilev shook his enormous head, his withered jowls stub-
bled with white. His flesh was pale gray and mottled brown
with moles, like a mushroom cap. He had no appetite, only an
unquenchable thirst from the cannula constantly blowing oxygen into his nose. Drinking fluids directly nearly drowned him.
He could only soothe his parched throat with ice chips from
the large cup on the table beside him.

"Is he here yet?"

The nurse nodded. "He arrived fifteen minutes ago. I
thought you would prefer for him to wait until—"

"Send him in now." He was paying her too much to be
polite.

"Of course."

Vasilev elevated his bed with a remote control as his number two appeared, a tall Czech—Sudeten German from the
Ore Mountains, in fact—with brittle, yellowed skin like old
parchment. The lifelong smoker was only five years younger
than Vasilev, and despite his cadaverous appearance, healthy
as an ox. Never a day in hospital in all the years Vasilev had
known him.

The Czech took the chair near the bed, removing his felted
green Tyrolean hat. "Vladimir, how are you feeling this morning, my old friend?"

"I dreamed last night my body was full of crabs, clawing out my guts with their giant red pincers."

The Czech shook his head, frowning. "My wife died from cancer. I know how painful it must be."

"Drink a bottle of battery acid and then shit out a box of roofing nails, and then you might have a glimmer of an idea of how painful it is."

"I'm so sorry."

"No, you're not. You're relieved it isn't you in this bed and me sitting in that chair."

Vasilev winced with a sudden stab of pain. He jabbed the morphine button in his hand, dosing himself again. It was having less and less effect. When the pain finally eased, he asked, "What news for me regarding Rhodes?"

The Czech's eyes dropped for a moment, thoughtfully fingering the red-speckled feather tucked in the hatband.

Not a good sign, Vasilev knew.

"Still no luck, I'm afraid."

"Luck? Luck has nothing to do with it. How hard can it be to kill a man trapped in a prison cell?"

"An American prison cell," the Czech protested. "A federal one, at that. And he is a former senator, so he is closely watched."

"You don't need more luck," Vasilev said. "You need more money. Increase the bounty. Make it five million dollars."

"That's a lot of cash."

"I haven't much patience. I'm flying to the Paris clinic tomorrow."

"Then five million it is." The Czech raised an eyebrow. "How long will you be gone?"

"Two months, at least. But what choice do I have?"

"It's a smart move. And it's Paris."

"Bah," Vasilev said, waving a veiny hand. "It's a medical facility in the suburbs, trapped in a quarantined cage with no guarantees of success. Still, my doctor says without this new experimental treatment, I would be fortunate to last another six months." The old Bulgarian winked. "He nearly pissed his pants telling me that, so I suspect it would have been less."

"You'll make out just fine. I read up on this CAR T treatment. It's the very latest Western medicine has to offer."

The Czech's investigation caused him both despair and hope. Despair because the revolutionary treatment had proven wildly effective in pediatric blood-cancer trials. The treatment removed a patient's natural cancer-fighting T cells and genetically altered millions more into little homing missiles targeting the specific cancer when reintroduced into the body. Vasilev stood an excellent chance, theoretically. That meant more years of the old killer's tyrannical rule, and he himself was not getting any younger.

The Czech's only hope was that other clinical trials for solid, adult tumor treatments such as Vasilev required had been mixed. There was an even chance that the Bulgarian butcher wouldn't survive after all. Vasilev's kill-list madness would end, and the Czech's ascendancy could begin.

"For the half million dollars a month it's costing me? I should be more than fine," Vasilev said, wheezing with effort. He grinned mischievously. "With this 'miracle' treatment, maybe I'll live forever."

"Nothing would please me more." The Czech shuddered inwardly but hid his disdain with a smile.

Vasilev's fixation on the kill list bordered on insanity. It had cost the Iron Syndicate millions, the loss of several vital assets, and unnecessary attention from state authorities. Fortunately, their organization had penetrated the police and security agencies of most industrialized countries years before, scuttling investigations into Iron Syndicate activities. Otherwise, they might all be in jail by now, or dead.

If he were in charge, the Czech thought, he would have abandoned the kill list before it even began. Revenge for its own sake was bad for business. But the Czech was resigned to his fate. As long as the targets lived and Vasilev breathed, the list would drive everything to the exclusion of far more pressing business opportunities.

The Czech briefly considered killing his Bulgarian overlord when this madness fell on him, but quickly dismissed the idea. Vasilev had a personal security system that amounted to "mutually assured destruction." If Vasilev died of any suspicious causes before his time, a secret network of assassins would avenge his death, targeting first and foremost the Czech, the heir apparent to the coveted throne, even if he wasn't at fault. This incentivized the Czech to guarantee Vasilev's security at all costs.

The only other solution to end Vasilev's kill-list madness was to finish the job as quickly as possible before it ruined them all.

Vasilev grunted a laugh. "You're a good friend, and a good liar. The syndicate will be in good hands when you take the reins."

The Czech nodded his appreciation. "Thank you."

The Bulgarian darkened. "But know this: Rhodes must die before I do. Or else."

The Czech nodded grimly, and what little hope he had drained away. "I understand."

The death of Rhodes was clear enough. It was the "or else" that truly disturbed him. It was Vasilev's cryptic promise to reach out from even beyond the grave and slaughter him and everyone he loved if he failed this last assignment.

He feared Vasilev more than any other man he ever knew, living or dead, despite their decades of friendship. His dying boss was the former head of the "Murder Bureau"—the highly secret assassination division within the now defunct Bulgarian Committee for State Security. Vasilev's talent for killing was surpassed only by his raging vengeance against those who either betrayed or failed him.

Together he and Vasilev had formed the Iron Syndicate at the end of the Cold War, along with several other comrades in other security services in the former Soviet republics, transforming their murderous skills and intelligence resources into a vast criminal network that now included many Western colleagues. Vasilev had led them all from the start, and the Czech was now next in line.

But only if he completed this final assignment.

"And the last man? Do we have a name?" Vasilev asked.

The Czech leaned forward, smiling. "Yes. We learned of it just two days ago."

"Who is it?"

The Czech told him. Also the man's employer, and the direct connection to Tervel Zvezdev, Vasilev's adopted son, butchered and parted out like cat food last year. The Americans found pieces of his massacred body fermenting in a kimchi jar—some sick kind of joke.

No one connected to Zvezdev's horrific death was laughing now.

Vasilev had made a kill list of those he held responsible for Zvezdev's death, including the North Korean who was shot by firing squad by his own government on an unrelated matter less than a week after Zvezdev was found. The inability to wreak his own vengeance on the Korean enraged Vasilev, and only made the killing of the rest of the list more urgent for him and, consequently, the entire organization. Ten had been disposed of so far. Only two remained. Rhodes, and this last man.

Vasilev's eyes widened with hope. "And?"

The Czech hesitated, his smile frozen. "We have his place of business, his home, and even his favorite restaurant under constant surveillance."

"And he's still alive?" Vasilev suddenly coughed, the first of a long, jagged tear of seal barks and throat rattles as yellow sputum gurgled up out of his cancerous lungs. The Czech helped him sit up as Vasilev's face reddened, long strings of viscous spittle dribbling from his thick lower lip.

The Czech reached for a plastic tray near the bed and held it up to Vasilev's mouth, trying not to vomit himself as he watched the old Bulgarian spit up gobs of bloody mucus into the vessel.

The Ghanaian nurse suddenly appeared in the doorway, her eyes wide with worry. "Is everything okay—"

"GET OUT!" Vasilev screamed at her as he batted away the plastic tray, scattering the liquid filth across the floor, barely missing her.

"I'll come back later," she offered meekly, and dashed back out of the room.

Vasilev gasped for air with the exertion. The Czech gently lowered him back onto his bed, then reached for a tissue to wipe the man's mouth, but Vasilev pushed his hand away.

"I want him dead," Vasilev said, his chest heaving. His bloodshot eyes stared vacantly at the far horizon of the trackless sea.

The Czech carefully wiped the sputum from his own hand with the tissue. "The man travels. He could be anywhere—"

Vasilev's bloodshot eyes narrowed. He was still gasping for breath. "I want his head . . . in a box . . . in my hands . . . before I die."

"I have our best people on it."

"Fuck your best people . . . and fuck you . . . if you don't . . . do this thing."

"I understand."

Vasilev grabbed the Czech by the lapel with a liver-spotted hand, pulling him close.

"Do this thing for me . . . please . . . I beg you . . . and then . . . the Syndicate . . . is yours."

"You have my word."

Hatred narrowed the dying eyes again. He pulled the Czech even closer. "Yes . . . you will. Or you will suffer for it."

Vasilev coughed again, and jabbed the morphine button.

"I'll fetch the nurse."

The Czech sped for the door, secretly hoping this was the last of Vasilev, but he knew better. The man's unquenchable hatred was stronger even than his metastasizing cancer. The only course of action left to him was to complete the damned list.

Finish off Senator Rhodes.

And kill Jack Ryan, Jr.

NEAR VUČEVO, REPUBLIKA SRPSKA, BOSNIA AND HERZEGOVINA

The tour van was packed with eight happy Germans, out-doorsy twentysomethings, including two newlyweds. It barreled south down the two-lane asphalt road at the legal speed limit, towing a trailer carrying ten sturdy river kayaks. Forested hills were on either side of the asphalt road; the jagged peaks of the Dinaric Alps loomed in the distance toward the south.

The thirty-year-old driver, Emir Jukić, was a Bosniak from Sarajevo, and he'd been hauling adventure-seeking tourists to his favorite drop-in spot on the Drina River for several years. In fact, he was the principal driver for Happy Times! Balkan Tours. In his years with the company, he had driven passengers as far south as the Greek port of Piraeus near Athens, and transported tourists all the way north to Austria for ski vacation packages. He knew the roads and villages, the mountains and rivers of his native country like the back of his hand. His sparkling dark eyes, an infectious, bearded smile, and an encyclopedic knowledge of Bosnian history made him a favorite among tourists, with more repeat customers than any other driver working for the region's most successful tour service.

Emir kept a two-handed grip on the wheel but raised one hand to wave at the 4x4 police vehicle heading toward them—two young Serb cops he knew by name. Just last week he had taken them kayaking with a couple local girls, along with bottles of sparkling wine and grilled sausages on the hibachi he kept stored in the back. All free, of course. The two cops smiled and flashed their headlights as they passed, the laughing German tourists unaware of the friendly exchange.

A kilometer later, Emir slowed the vehicle onto a dirt track that led down to a wide flat bank near the river. It was the second day of their kayaking tour, and the group knew the drill. Everyone, including Emir, pulled out their gear; pulled on wetsuits, safety vests, and helmets; and began unloading the stacks of kayaks and setting them near the water.

Two of the German girls, tall and muscular, reached for the tie-downs on a kayak up on the highest rungs of the trailer. "Please, not that one," Emir asked politely. "I don't want you to get hurt." Shorter than both of them, he had a gentle voice that belied his stocky boxer's build. They happily complied as he helped them unload the one just below it, affirming what every tourist to the area knew: Bosnians were the friendliest people on earth.

Minutes later, they were all paddling in the gently flowing

turquoise water, Emir leading the way with promises of hot lunches and cold beer waiting for them at a beach six kilometers downriver.

As soon as they made the first bend, a battered green Škoda Octavia wagon pulled up next to the van. A young man in a blue Denver Broncos T-shirt and tan cargo shorts jumped out of the passenger seat and climbed into the tour van. Moments later he pulled the van and the trailer with the lone kayak back onto the asphalt and headed north for six kilometers to another dirt track leading to a village deep in the forest on the far side of the mountains bounding the road.

The man driving the Škoda was another Bosniak, well-groomed and in his thirties; a chemistry teacher who'd immigrated to Germany and returned in the past year, leaving behind his wife and two young daughters for safety.

He kept the wagon a discreet distance back from the trailer. The bricks of C-4 packed into the kayak on the back of the trailer wouldn't explode without a detonator, owing to the unique nature of the chemical bonds within the explosive and the high amount of inert binding agent. Bouncing the C-4 on the pavement or even setting it on fire wouldn't cause it to blow. Only a rapid infusion of high energy from an exploding detonator cord or blasting cap could break those chemical bonds, releasing the enormous stores of energy inside the compound in a violent eruption. The combination of stability and lethality in such plastic explosives made them highly favored by all freedom fighters everywhere, his group especially. It wouldn't be long before the shipment would be put to good use.

There was even less concern regarding the ten kilos of premium Afghan heroin also packed into the kayak. At fifty dollars a gram on German streets, that amounted to half a million dollars—a nice addition to their operating budget.

But still, he was a careful man, and he hadn't survived this long without taking precautions.

Inshallah.

HEATHROW AIRPORT, LONDON

Jack hadn't thought about Paul Brown in a long time, he realized, when he boarded the United flight from Dulles to London ten hours before, and now he thought about him again as he stepped into the terminal at Heathrow. He and Paul had landed here for a connecting flight to Singapore last year, and spent the better part of a long and frustrating day in this very terminal, waiting for mechanical repairs and a missing flight crew to finally resolve themselves.

Gerry had been right. Paul had been a guy worth getting to know. Jack was just sorry he hadn't known him longer.

The crowds of passengers shuffling past him on the way to baggage claim had no idea that the portly accountant sacrificed himself to keep the world economy from crashing that stormy night, and saved Jack's life. Jack firmly believed now that most of human history was composed of such unwritten chapters, full of nameless heroes known only to God and the privileged few who witnessed their sacrifices firsthand.

Paul deserved better than a passing thought from him. Jack recalled the wasted hours the two of them had spent at Heathrow. Jack wished he'd used that time last year to run into the city and see Ysabel, a former lover he'd met while on the Iranian assignment—another relationship doomed by the demands of their respective careers. Jack would always put his country first before his personal desires, but a wife, a home, and a couple kids someday were high on his list.

Jack thought about that when he was getting ready to board at Dulles. He had another long layover again tomorrow when he landed, and he was determined not to make the same mistake twice.

While the flight attendant lectured on the proper deployment of the seat belt, Jack pulled up Ysabel's Facebook page. What he saw felt like a punch in the gut. Ysabel cradled her newborn baby daughter in her arms as she stood next to her handsome Anglo-Iranian husband, both of them beaming. A striking couple. For a brief moment, Jack imagined that it was him standing next to her in that picture.

Jack scrolled briefly through her posts. His disappointment quickly faded. She seemed to have married a stand-up guy, a banker with impeccable credentials. The two of them appeared to be building an amazing life together. "Good for you," Jack whispered. He was genuinely happy for her.

He started to post a note on her page congratulating her on everything but thought twice about it. No point in putting her in an awkward position where she might have to explain something to her husband that obviously didn't matter anymore.

Jack clicked off his phone, feeling a little more than stupid for even looking her up. Why did he assume they could just pick up where they had left off?

A few hours and a few fingers of Maker's Mark into the long Atlantic flight, he got the bright idea of contacting an old professor from Georgetown now teaching at the London School of Economics. He shot Dr. Patrick Costello a text, and to his happy surprise, his former teacher responded eagerly. They set a place and time to meet in London.

As soon as Jack passed through customs, he shoved his carry-ons into a storage locker in the baggage area and grabbed a cab for the forty-minute ride into the city. He had six hours before he needed to get back to the terminal, and he was determined to enjoy every minute of it.

8

The narrow pedestrian street was packed with a slow-moving parade of protesters, chanting against tomorrow's visit by Scott Adler, the American secretary of state. Jack didn't realize that Scott, one of his father's closest advisers, was scheduled to lecture at the London School of Economics' prestigious Department of International Relations.

Jack checked his iWatch. He was right on time. He pushed his way toward the school's high-arched doorway where a phalanx of nervous police kept the belligerent crowd at bay. Protesters of every stripe and hue waved signs and shouted slogans against American imperialism, predatory capitalism, Thatcherism (*Really?* Jack asked himself), white privilege, and a host of other alt-left complaints.

Sloganeering like that was typical of college campuses these days, even in Europe. Some of them were true believers, but he'd seen his share of them at Georgetown, and most of them were poseurs who preferred protesting to the actual heavy lifting of making the world a better place. And for too many of these malcontents, especially the guys, that kind of virtue signaling was designed primarily to enhance their shaky social status and, possibly, even to get laid.

As Jack neared the doorway, a police sergeant showed him her palm to block his entry. "Business with the school, sir?"

Just then he saw the familiar smile and shock of silver hair of Dr. Costello as he stepped through the glass doors.

"Jack! So good to see you!" The professor touched the sergeant's shoulder gently with an "Excuse me," as he squeezed past her.

The two men shook hands.

"You look good, Jack. Staying in shape, I see."

"You look pretty dapper yourself, Dr. C."

"Comes with the job. And please, it's Patrick." Dr. Costello was in his traditional priest's black suit coat and white collar, both spotless. Besides being a visiting lecturer at LSE, the shorter, bantamweight priest not only served an inner-city parish church but also tutored neighborhood kids in math.

"Hope you're hungry," Dr. Costello said, pointing the way.

"Famished."

"Good. We're going to my favorite pub. Best shepherd's pie in the city. How's your father?"

"Great. Thanks for asking. He sends his best." Senior had taken a graduate course in international political economy with Costello years ago, and had recommended the professor to his son when Jack decided to attend Georgetown, too.

"Tell him hello for me, will you? And please let him know he's in my prayers."

They chatted briefly, dodging the protesters ambling down the sidewalk, many of whom seemed like only interested spectators. Jack caught sight of flags, banners, lapel pins, hijabs, and tattoos of communists, anarchists, fundamentalist Muslims, and symbols of a dozen other radical causes. Too many faces were covered by the black bandannas of Antifa for Jack's liking. Only cowards hid their faces at public protests. Or criminals. He tensed up a little, half expecting something to happen.

Just as they turned a corner, a large protester, three inches taller than Jack, shoved a flyer into Jack's chest. His long, dark hair was pulled into a ponytail. He had a plain, unremarkable face, but his towering frame and intense gaze intimidated most people. Ponytail's black T-shirt caught Jack's eye, emblazoned with bold white letters that read FUCK FASCIST AMERIKA! above an upside-down American flag.

"Hey, man. Careful," Jack said.

"Read that, dude. Join the revolution."

Jack recognized the man's California accent. He read the flyer.

Students for a Moral Order demand that American imperialism stops now! End racist American foreign policy! Impeach the fascist president Jack Ryan! Deport war criminal Secretary of State Adler!

"Interesting," Jack said, handing the flyer to Dr. Costello, who chuckled as he read it.

"What are you laughing at, old man?" Ponytail said.

"So I take it you know President Ryan personally," Jack said.

"Yeah, he's a fascist fuck. You're an American, so you know it's true."

"Trust me, he's not a fascist. His dad killed fascists with the 101st Airborne at the Battle of the Bulge. What did you ever do for your country?"

"Oh, Christ—you sound like you voted for that bastard!"

Jack's fists clenched and he stepped forward.

"Jack," Dr. Costello said. "Let's get some lunch, shall we?" He tugged on Jack's arm, breaking his eye lock with Ponytail.

Jack turned to the priest. "Sounds good, Dr. C."

"Yeah, go get some lunch with your pedophile friend."

Jack's eyes narrowed. "What did you say?"

"You heard me. We all know what the Catholic Church is all about. And Hitler was a Catholic, you know."

"Hitler persecuted the Catholic Church," Jack said. "Priests and nuns were killed in the Holocaust along with the Jews and a lot of other people who weren't politically correct."

The man sneered and pointed a finger at Dr. Costello. "He told you that? That's just a bunch of Vatican propaganda. Right, Padre?"

Jack felt the heat rise in his face. "You don't know who this man is, and I don't appreciate you insulting him or my faith."

A group of protesters gathered in a loose circle around them now. A few wore the cliché Guy Fawkes masks. Some were clearly high on something. Most were agitated, itching for a fight. Jack knew they were all out of eyesight of the police, who were back around the corner. The odds were stacking up in the wrong direction, but Jack didn't care.

"Religion is bullshit, dude. It's the Muzak in the men's room at Macy's. Wake the fuck up."

"You tell him!" someone said, and laughed.

Dr. Costello said to Ponytail, "If you want to change the world, son, meet me at Saint Luke's at four o'clock and help me teach algebra to some bright young minds."

"First of all, I'm not your son, and second, do we teach them algebra before or after we rape them?"

"You need to watch your piehole, ace." Jack stepped closer, his eyes focused on the man's throat.

Dr. Costello smiled at Ponytail. "I'm sorry you're so angry." He turned to Jack. "Come on, the shepherd's pie is getting cold." He tugged on Jack's arm, but Jack didn't budge.

"It's not worth it, son," Costello said.

Jack turned to him. "But he insulted you, and our faith."

"Our Lord suffered far more for our sake." He nodded at Ponytail. "And his."

"Yeah. You two go run along and find yourself a safe space— while you can. Some of us have work to do." The big man pushed against Jack, but Jack held his ground, jabbing a finger in the man's broad chest.

"The truth, you stupid bastard, is that if your fat ass got caught in a sling over here, it would be some God-fearing eighteen-year-old U.S. Marine who'd be laying it on the line to save your worthless hide. So show some respect for your country and your flag, especially over here."

"I don't have a flag anymore, Richie Rich. I wiped my ass with it this morning, and then I burned it."

Everything in Jack told him to take the shitbird down, honor most of all. But he also had responsibilities as a Hendley employee, and as his father's son. Dropping this sack of human waste hard onto the pavement with a smashing blow to the temple would feel mighty fine, and would render at least a small service to humanity. But a criminal and diplomatic incident wouldn't do anybody any good, least of all him, and the idea of turning this guy into some kind of hero-martyr wasn't very appealing. It took Jack all of half a second to decide to stand down.

About the length of time it took for Ponytail to start braying like a donkey at his own foul joke.

"Get out of my way," he barked, as he brushed past Jack,

who suffered the humiliating laughter and catcalls rolling through the crowd following in the big man's wake.

Jack stood fixed to the pavement, his blood still boiling.

"Free speech is a beautiful thing, isn't it?" the priest said with a snarky smile on his face.

"So's a well-thrown punch, Dr. C. You should try it sometime."

"I'm surprised you didn't."

"Me too."

"You had me worried for a minute, son. I prayed for you."

"I was never very good at that turning-the-other-cheek stuff."

The priest-professor tugged at Jack's elbow. "If it was easy, it wouldn't be a virtue." Costello's eyes crinkled with his impish smile. "How about a pint of Guinness and we talk about old times? First one's on me."

9

Jack and Dr. Costello spent the next two hours catching up over pints of Guinness and the best shepherd's pie Jack had ever eaten. Costello grilled him on his work with Hendley Associates, nodding approvingly as Jack explained the wide range of practical skills and fiduciary knowledge he'd acquired in the field after his stint in Costello's economics course.

"You ever think about going back and getting your Ph.D. in finance?"

Jack shook his head. "No, not really." For some reason he'd never considered it as a possibility. His dad had a doctorate, of course, and his mother was an M.D., but they were brainiacs. So was his older sister, also a doctor.

"You might consider it."

"Maybe later. I'm having too much fun now," Jack said. Between his duties for both The Campus and Hendley Associates, he just didn't have the time, and the idea of spending more hours behind a desk instead of in a HALO parachute didn't appeal to him at the moment. But he had to admit it was an intriguing thought, at least for later. Why not?

They finished up and Jack paid the bill for both of them. Outside, they said their good-byes, promising to stay in touch. Jack hailed a cab for the airport as Costello headed for the Tube. Neither paid any attention to the CCTV cameras posted on the lamppost just outside the pub; they were ubiquitous throughout the city. Second only to communist Beijing, London had nearly half a million of the surveillance devices monitoring the activities of visitors and citizens alike, including Jack, who, for a split second—against his training and better judgment—cast his open face upward to catch a glimpse of a jetliner roaring low overhead before jumping into the taxi.

Big mistake.

In a city with so many government and private closed-circuit television cameras already in place, the addition of still more of them in crowded public spaces was hardly noticed, let alone regulated.

The Iron Syndicate had installed more than five hundred such cameras in London but also operated similar networks in Beijing, Frankfurt, New York, and a dozen other cities. Whatever cameras they didn't own they were often able to hack through a variety of methods.

The first-level hack was commercial. The vast majority of CCTV cameras sold in the world were built in just three Chinese factories in Guangzhou, each of which was partly owned by a board member of the Iron Syndicate. That provided the organization a back door into every computer chip within those cameras, including the ones deployed on NATO military installations and ships, as well as police and intelligence offices.

The second-level hack was human. The Iron Syndicate exploited dozens of compromised individuals within corporate divisions and government agencies around the world, who provided restricted CCTV and surveillance database access, either for a fee or under threat.

The third-level hack was the Iron Syndicate's own world-class IT department, staffed with some of the most important private-sector and government scientists and technocrats who had originally designed these omnipresent surveillance systems. Whether through back doors they had left behind or simply through skill or brute force, there were few databases and live feeds that the Iron Syndicate couldn't access around the globe as needed.

The recent bonus, though, was the advent of the smartphone. Whether through live camera chat programs like Face-Time or through the new facial-recognition software required to access phone use, the smartphone companies had provided billions of new real-time and securely identified faces for the Iron Syndicate to exploit.

But the coup de grace was the Iron Syndicate's infiltration into the big social media platform databases—Instagram, Facebook, WeChat, Tencent. By posting billions of selfies every day, ordinary platform users were unwittingly contributing to the world's most dangerous facial-recognition and surveillance program on the planet.

In all cases, the Iron Syndicate maintained a central processing center in Bucharest, Romania, where images were monitored and evaluated with Dragonfly Eye software, recently acquired through their Chinese affiliates. Dragonfly Eye was an AI-driven facial-recognition program deployed by the

Chinese government, capable of processing up to two *billion* faces in mere *seconds*.

At the moment, the Dragonfly Eye algorithms were tuned to find a match for Jack Ryan, Jr., for whom current photographs were strangely difficult to come by, even by open-source intelligence, or OSINT. It was as if somebody was going to the extraordinary length of constantly scrubbing any digital facial reference to the handsome young American throughout all private and social media. However, after enormous effort, the syndicate had acquired a few degraded images. These were sub-optimal, but adequate for the task at hand.

By the time Jack's taxi pulled up to the departure gate at Heathrow, his image had been identified by the Iron Syndicate system, and the Code Red priority alarm triggered. The man on duty notified his shift supervisor by phone according to protocol, but he knew she would have already been alerted automatically. He'd seen only one other Code Red alarm in the last five years. Somebody wanted this guy badly.

The surveillance camera that had captured Jack's image was immediately identified and its footage reviewed by hand by the shift supervisor. In short order she acquired the license plate number of Jack's taxi.

As the Iron Syndicate reverted to its automated tracking system and tapped into its network of cameras positioned throughout London, as well as at the major airports and train stations, the taxi was quickly located and footage of Jack entering the airport secured.

It took only a few more AI-driven moments to track the American back with his carry-ons working his way through the security check and then toward his gate, where his flight information and destination—Ljubljana, Slovenia—were secured and transmitted to Unit Black, the field operations "wet work" team. The supervisor put her best analyst on the Ljubljana airport cameras, though the algorithms would spot Ryan faster than a human eye.

The shift supervisor shuddered. She worked for a vast international criminal enterprise to be sure, but she was a trained software engineer, not a killer. Even within the merciless Iron Syndicate, Unit Black's reputation was fearsome.

This Jack Ryan fellow didn't have long to live, and the manner of his death wouldn't be pleasant at all.

10

A light rain streaked the small windows as the Embraer 170 jet gently touched the runway. Jack powered up his iPhone as the plane taxied to a stop, a hundred yards from the terminal. A text message pulled up on his screen. "Meet you in the lobby."

Jack deplaned from the narrow-bodied Air France jet onto the tarmac, ignoring the spattering drops in the brief hop over to the wide bus that ferried them to the small terminal of the Ljubljana Jože Pučnik Airport. Heathrow International this was not, but it was perfectly serviceable—more like a regional American airport than an international hub.

Unfortunately, Jack's carry-on suitcase was two inches too tall and three kilos over the weight limit for his air carrier, so he had to check it. The time to retrieve his luggage seemed longer than the flight itself, but customs was little more than a perfunctory nod and a quick stamp of his passport, so it all evened out. The trick with commercial aviation travel, he'd learned over the past few years, was to keep your expectations low and to relax.

He was greeted in the airport's small lobby with a broad smile and a firm handshake by his host, Rojko Struna, the thirty-seven-year-old owner of the firm that had hired Hendley for the consultation. He had a runner's build and an easy gait.

"Mr. Struna, it's a pleasure to meet you."

"Only one bag?"

"I travel light."

"Good. I'm the same way. My car's close." Struna and Jack headed for the sliding glass doors and the temporary parking, which was just a few feet from the drop-off, another advantage to the sleepy little airport. There wasn't enough rain to bother with an umbrella. A security camera was perched on the lamp-post just above Struna's SUV, a blue BMW X3.

Jack loaded his carry-on and laptop into the back of the BMW, then climbed into the plush black leather passenger seat as Struna pressed the starter button. By the time they pulled onto the southbound two-lane E61, the sky had darkened considerably and the windshield wipers were slapping away a heavy rain. The light traffic sped along nicely, mostly German and Italian nameplates on the cars, with a few Škodas making up the rest.

"Sorry about the weather. We're due for rain the whole week. I was hoping to get you up into the mountains while you were here."

"I've got plenty to do anyway. At least I won't be tempted to leave the office."

"It still might clear up. Around here we say, 'If you don't like the weather right now, just wait ten minutes.'"

"If you don't mind my saying, your English is perfect." Jack couldn't detect any Slovenian accent—not that he knew what that would sound like anyway.

"Thanks. It's my first language. I was born in Newport Beach."

"What's a beach bum from California doing in the Balkans?"

"My parents immigrated to the States just after Tito died in 1980. They opened a pizza joint and a bar and did pretty well. You know, the American Dream and all of that."

"That's great."

"My sister and I both graduated from San Diego State. She went into nursing, and I studied computer science."

"Which explains your company." Struna's firm was pioneering some of the best medical robotics technologies in the industry. "What brought you here?"

"California is a great place to live, but it's a hard place to raise a family. Too crowded, too expensive, too many taxes. My wife and I have two small kids, and I'd come back here for vacations for years, so I knew the place well. Maybe it was my parents' nostalgia or something else, but I really wanted to make a go of it, so here we are."

"So far, so good?"

"As I hope you'll see from our financials."

"I've already seen the preliminaries. You're tearing the joint up. Based on those, I don't foresee any problem with you getting registered on the NASDAQ next year."

"I hope you're right."

"Well, that's what I'm here to find out, one way or the other."

Jack glanced out the rain-streaked passenger window. He saw low tree-covered mountains and green fields, dotted with the occasional farmhouse.

"Slovenia is a beautiful country."

"This? This is nothing. Wait until you see the Julian Alps and the Soča River. It will take your breath away."

Struna eased into the passing lane to get around a big Mercedes eighteen-wheeler. "And by the way, thanks for not calling it 'Slovakia' like a lot of Americans do. That's another country altogether."

"Not every American is geographically illiterate. But it's not like I know a whole lot about your country."

"I take it you've never been here before?"

"No, but the pictures I found on the Web were incredible."

"We used to be Europe's best-kept secret. I'm afraid our tourism office is doing too good of a job these days."

"Lots of tourists?"

"The euro goes a long way here, if you have a lot of euros."

"You joined the EU in 2004. How's that worked out?"

Struna smiled cautiously, uncertain if he should be completely honest with the American analyst.

"For me, and people like me, it's great. We have complete access to markets from here to the Atlantic."

"But if you have access to them, they have access to you, right?"

Struna nodded. "And therein lies the problem. Big European companies, especially the Germans, have moved in, and the euro is strong relative to our economy. Some of us are doing pretty well, but others are falling behind. It's hard to become middle class in a globalist environment unless you're very entrepreneurial."

"Same in the States," Jack said. Too many American companies were chasing cheap labor overseas and importing cheap goods. High-wage blue-collar jobs had been lost in the process, and too many blue-collar folks never made the transition to high-tech, high-wage jobs.

"Overall, it's been a net benefit. But at a cost. Foreign companies coming in, young Slovenes emigrating out to find better work. As a European, it's a good thing. But as a Slovenian, well, I sometimes wonder."

"Can't you be both Slovenian and European?"

"In theory, yes. But the reality is that European money and culture are overpowering. Small states like ours will have a hard time maintaining their national identities, which I suppose was the reason the EU was created in the first place."

"Hence Brexit."

"Exactly. Don't get me wrong. I still think we gain more than we lose, but the EU must adapt or it might not survive in its current form. The idea of 'Europe' is just that—an idea, beautiful and vague. But identity is deeply personal, specific, and concrete."

The rain lightened up. The automatic windshield wipers slowed.

"Do I sound like some crazy nationalist to you?"

"You sound like a man who loves his country, or, at least, his new country."

"I have dual citizenship, actually, and I still do love America and all that it did for me. But I have several hundred years of family history rooted in these mountains and valleys. That's hard to let go of. A man's identity is his destiny, don't you think?"

"Yeah, for sure." Jack scratched his chin. He wondered what that meant for his own country, when the definition of being an American was changing so rapidly.

"What do people think about Tito these days?"

"My grandparents—really, anybody who remembers the Tito days—wish they lived in the old Yugoslavia again."

"Communism is that strong here?"

Struna laughed. "Well, not communism like Stalin and those crazies. It was more like a really progressive social democracy. We could own land, vacation overseas, and had other freedoms that the Soviets didn't enjoy."

"But it was still a dictatorship."

"Sure, but a benign one. What my grandparents say is that everybody had a job, everybody got a long vacation, everybody had a relatively good life without having to work eighty hours a week. Nobody was too rich—well, except for Tito and the elites, of course—but nobody was starving. I'm not saying they're right, but it is a nearly universal longing among the older generation."

"A lot of American millennials think socialism is a good idea, too, mostly because they don't really know what it is. They just know it's really hard to make it in the current system, and they're looking for alternatives."

"You know Yugoslavia's history?"

"Only the rough outline. It was a communist state under Tito, and then he died in, what, 1980? Then the wars started in 1991 and didn't end until 2001."

"Very good. Yugoslavia was a federation of six republics and two autonomous regions, including Serbia, Croatia, Slovenia, and Bosnia-Herzegovina. We declared independence on June 25, 1991, along with Croatia. The Yugoslav Army, which was really the army of Serbia, controlled by Milošević, attacked us, and we defeated them in ten days and earned our freedom. The

Croatians had it worse, but in the end they won their independence, too. It was the Bosnians that suffered the most."

"I read over a hundred and forty thousand Yugoslavians died in the wars."

"Yes, but not here, thank God. Almost no Serbs lived here, so Milošević couldn't claim to be protecting anybody from our 'aggression' like he did in Bosnia."

"Why were the Yugoslavian wars so vicious? I read stories of lifelong neighbors killing neighbors, friends killing friends."

"It's strange, isn't it? The only good explanation I've ever heard was that for many years, everybody was a Yugoslavian and there was peace. But once people started saying, 'I'm a Serb,' or 'I'm a Muslim,' all of a sudden people started seeing their neighbors as 'others,' and all of their problems were because of 'them.' Democracy and identity politics don't work so well together."

"Is it really that simple?"

"Probably not. What's really crazy is that most families were mixed. I have a Bosniak friend—a Bosnian Muslim—whose grandfather was a Catholic Croat and his grandmother was an Orthodox Serb. Nobody cared about all of that until Milošević and the Serbs started causing trouble."

"So everything was caused by the Serbians?"

Struna shook his head. "Maybe they were the cause of the most recent troubles, but believe me, there are five hundred years of grievances in this part of the world. Nobody is innocent.

"The amazing thing is, someone did a genetic study a few years ago. Apparently, Serbs, Croats, and Bosniaks are genetically closer to each other than any other groups in the region.

We're just one big, happy Slavic family that keeps murdering each other. And that's just recent history. I won't bore you with the sixteenth-century Islamic Ottoman invasion."

"So today there is the Catholic country of Croatia, but many Croats still live in Bosnia. And there is the Orthodox country of Serbia, but many Serbs live in Bosnia, too. Is that about right?"

"Exactly, and the Muslims are the majority in Bosnia. Nice people, great food. You should visit Sarajevo sometime."

"I plan to, actually, when I'm done here."

"Business or pleasure?"

"Pleasure, sort of."

"Good. You'll love it. It's a beautiful country and the people are kind. More Americans should visit there, but a lot of them think the war is still going on even though it ended twenty-three years ago."

Struna hit his turn signal and eased into the right lane. "Your hotel is at the next exit."

"If you don't mind, let's go straight to the office. There's a lot to do and not enough time to do it."

"Are you sure you don't want to rest up first?"

"My grandmother used to say, 'There's no rest for the wicked, and the righteous don't need any,' and I learned a long time ago to never argue with her."

"She sounds Slovenian."

"German-Irish, but close."

Struna killed his blinker just as the sky opened up again. This time it poured.

Jack sighed. It was going to be a long, wet week stuck in an office.

TRIESTE, ITALY

Elena Iliescu loved her work, and she was good at it. She took particular joy in her profession, devoting laser focus and creative energy to each endeavor. Phone calls and other distractions simply had no place. But there was one ringtone the busty, girl-next-door blonde always answered.

Always.

She stabbed out her cigarette on the wall of rough-hewn stone, nude beneath her badly stained coveralls.

"Yes?"

"I need you." A man's voice. The Czech.

"When?"

"Yesterday."

She swore in her mind. Romanian, her native tongue. "I'm not finished here. I was told what I was doing here was a priority."

"This assignment is Code Red."

Elena's heart sank. She swallowed her fear.

"How long do I have?"

"Ten days, maximum. Preferably sooner."

"That isn't enough time for me to scout and plan the op."

"It has to be. Details to follow."

"At least tell me where I'm going."

"Ljubljana."

Not her favorite city. Quaint but boring. At least it was a short drive. A little over an hour by car without traffic. She checked her watch. It was just after midnight.

"I'll leave first thing in the morning. Photo and genetic sample, as usual?"

"No. You need to bring me his head, his face fully intact. That's straight from the top."

What the hell?

"Elena, you understand what I'm saying?"

"Yes."

"Ten days."

"I'll call you when I check in to my hotel in Ljubljana."

The Czech rang off.

Elena swore again, but this time audibly. She pocketed the phone and marched back into the other room in the dank cellar, lit by a dim bulb hanging from a frayed cord.

The naked man duct-taped to the chair was semiconscious and still whimpering beneath the gag. He shuddered when she entered, sensing her presence rather than seeing her through his blackened eyes, swollen and bloodshot. Brand-new jumper cables snaked from a car battery on the floor to the foot of his chair. Her plan was to attach the sharp teeth of the copper battery clamps to his ruined genitals, and then the fun could really begin.

Too bad.

Elena swept past a table, on top of which was a neatly ordered collection of specialized knives, forged in fire by her own hand. She snatched up the smallest one, her sharpest by far.

"It's your lucky day, Sanchez."

She drew a thin line across his throat. His neck opened up, spitting blood. He bled out quickly in a spasm of terror and pain, dead before she hit the stairs a few minutes later.

Lucky, indeed.

The ancient farmhouse flamed like a druid's torch in the cool night air, fueled by its three-hundred-year-old timbers. Elena caught a last, smiling glimpse of the towering fire in her rearview mirror as she made a turn.

Time for a hot shower and a stiff drink back at her hotel. She wasn't tired; in fact, every nerve in her body was on fire. Her work had a rhythm, and it had been interrupted. It had been an unsatisfying kill. That left an itch inside her that still hadn't been scratched. She needed to clear her head.

She checked the speed dial on her phone for the name of a man she knew in Trieste, a hard and angular Florentine. A few hours in the embrace of the violent, insatiable *signore* would be the best thing she could hope for before starting her next assignment.

11

NEAR ČITLUK, BOSNIA AND HERZEGOVINA

The night air cooled a little, but not too much, and the breeze off the mountain carried the sharp, sweet tang of the whispering pines. It was fall but not yet cool, the summer warmth lingering like a lonely cousin in the small, rocky valley. The inky black sky shimmered with stars bright in their courses.

It was the first September the four teenagers hadn't been in school, and none of them were going to college this year. The boys—fraternal twins—were heading for Split to work in an uncle's restaurant on the Adriatic coast in two days. Like other ethnic Croats in Bosnia, all four of them had relatives in the country of Croatia to the west, where there was more work to be had, though mostly for the tourist industry. It was long, grueling labor, but better than no work at all, and the new American tourists tipped like drunken sailors, unlike the Germans.

The girls were planning on leaving, too, as soon as they

could find something, somewhere—anywhere. They had their feelers out, but nearly half of all Bosnians were unemployed, and good, steady work with a decent paycheck was scarce, especially in the countryside. The taller girl was good with numbers but shy, and the fine-boned brunette spoke passable French. They were heading to Sarajevo at the end of the week to start their search.

But all of that was for later. The four of them had spent the last two days hiking in the hills and swimming in the Lukoć River, roasting river trout on open fires and drinking sweet summer wine, cheaper and better than weed, which was harder to come by, too expensive, and still illegal in Bosnia.

Tonight was their last night together and they turned in early to their respective tents, summer lovers soon separated, probably forever. They each finally fell asleep, spent and sated, the smell of salty sweat and campfire smoke in their nightclothes. Their deep, rhythmic breathing wasn't disturbed by the crunch of pine needles beneath eight pairs of heavy boots, and the tall girl woke only when she heard the muffled scream of her friend in the dark, followed by the zip of a blade shearing through her tent wall.

The camouflaged men hid their faces behind balaclavas. One of them, the unit commander, stood back in the shadows, his milky left eye glistening in the moonlight, watching the other men bind and gag the four teenagers. They tied the boys to the trees and forced them to watch the gang rape of the two girls, then forced the girls to watch them beat the boys with batons until their bones cracked, before raping them with the same heavy instruments.

The four broken bodies were tossed facedown onto the pine needles, whimpering and faint. Two men stepped forward, put heavy knees in the center of the boys' backs, pulled their heads up by the hair, and slit their throats.

The last thing the brunette remembered before she passed out was a rasping whisper in her ear.

"Croatia for Croats, Bosnia for Serbs."

On a bridge six kilometers north of the campsite, the man with the milky eye was dressed in civilian clothes again, as was his driver, their camouflage gear carefully packed and hidden in the back of the unmarked panel van beneath a stack of boxes.

His burner phone signal had just one bar, but that was enough to call the local police. He reported that he had heard screams in the woods west of Čitluk, and hung up before he could answer any further questions, then pulled the battery and pocketed it before tossing the remainder of the burner phone into the river below. He signaled the driver to head for home, careful to keep within the speed limit.

With any luck, the police would respond quickly. Violent crime was virtually unknown in the area, and cops didn't have much to do, especially this time of night.

The milky-eyed man couldn't take the chance that the girls might die from their injuries or exposure before they were found, or that somehow they might fatally harm themselves trying to get back to human habitation. They might even be tempted to commit suicide after such humiliation.

No, that wasn't acceptable at all. The plan required them to survive. He was confident the police would arrive in time, and the girls would be found, and their stories told so that the whole country would know what had happened to them tonight and, more important, who had done it.

The man with the milky eye had no regrets about the suffering of the two girls, even though he had three daughters of his own about that same age.

After all, what he had done was for them.

12

LJUBLJANA, SLOVENIA

Jack had spent eight days on his ass, his nose buried in financials and spreadsheets, three days longer than he'd planned. That would cut his search time in Sarajevo down to just three days, but he thought that might be enough. Gavin had generated a list of potential Aida Curićes, including those who had married and changed their names. Sorting by age and other factors had shortened the list considerably. Tracking them down wouldn't be a big deal.

Jack's office window overlooked the parking lot and another glass-and-steel building in the Technology Park, each of the last eight days marred by dark clouds and rain. Struna offered to take him on a walking tour of the small but charming Old Town, where cars weren't permitted, but he confessed it was mostly restaurants, bars, and small retail shops, so Jack politely passed. He'd rather spend the time finishing up his work as fast as he could, but he would allow himself one day to tour the Julian Alps with Struna, hoping that the weather would break by then.

He woke up sorely disappointed. It was still raining.

The night before, Struna took him to Pop's Place in the Old Town because Jack was craving an American-style burger and, frankly, so was Struna. The place was hopping with locals and tourists, with a friendly and animated staff. He and Struna sat at a communal table next to a quiet Belgian couple and a group of rowdy Aussies. The huge selection of local craft beers was amazing and tasty, especially the Bevog Ond smoked porter, an Austrian brew. The grass-fed Slovenian beef burgers were pretty damn good, too.

"You did a great job for us, Jack," Struna said, his red-rimmed eyes smiling, as he hoisted an oatmeal stout.

"You're gonna be a billionaire," Jack said, toasting his friend. "But you better get some shut-eye. You look pretty beat."

"No rest for the wicked, right?" Struna smiled and finished his beer, then paid the tab, and the two of them headed for Jack's hotel.

Jack was hardly surprised when his phone rang at five-thirty that morning. Struna's clogged voice apologized. His wife and kids were sick and he wouldn't be able to take Jack to the mountains. Besides, it was still raining.

"But if you still want to go, you can take my car. I preprogrammed the GPS for you last night and left a guidebook on the front seat."

"If you don't mind, sure."

He felt awkward borrowing the man's car, but what the hell else was he going to do? Stay in his hotel room and watch re-runs of *Say Yes to the Dress* with Slovenian subtitles?

TRIGLAV NATIONAL PARK, SLOVENIA

Struna's BMW was a joy to drive and, fortunately, Slovenians drove on the right side of the road, for which Jack was grateful, given the twenty-four hairpin curves he traversed on the narrow road to the top of the highest point in Triglav National Park.

The good thing about the rain was that almost nobody else was out but crazed mountain bikers and he seemed to have the place mostly to himself.

He listened to an audio guidebook he'd downloaded onto his iPhone the night before. This high country was hallowed ground in many ways, part of the four-hundred-mile "third front" in the holocaust known as the First World War, where invading Italian troops battled the forces of the Austro-Hungarian Empire to seize Slovenia for Italy. Jack passed battlefield cemeteries crowded with thousands of men cut down in their youth, and innumerable Catholic churches perched on seemingly every hilltop, bastions of faith that also served as fortified positions during foreign invasions.

It was hard to imagine the brutal tragedy of that mindless conflict in the middle of the stunning beauty of these snow-capped mountains covered in pines. According to the guidebook, the mountains had been utterly scarred and stripped away of all vegetation after four years of industrial warfare. But a hundred years later, the forests had returned, and the mountains, as always, remained.

Jack tried to imagine fighting in these steep, unforgiving mountains in the depths of winter under constant artillery barrage, hunkered down in frozen trenches or charging up the craggy heights into the teeth of withering machine-gun fire.

No wonder more than a million men bled and died in these mountains. And for what? The flower of Western civilization had perished on these stony slopes, and in the fields, swamps, and forests of a thousand other battles all across the continent.

And for what? Jack asked himself.

For what?

No wonder the Europeans feared nationalism, Jack thought.

As he finally reached the top of the road and the magnificent view of the Triglav mountains, the audio guidebook reminded him that this was also Hemingway country. The Julian Alps were the setting for his famous novel *A Farewell to Arms*, though the eighteen-year-old ambulance driver never actually served in the region.

Jack parked the car, pulled up his jacket hood, and headed out into the misting rain for a look-see, following the paper map in his hands. Despite the weather, he was anxious to get out and stretch his legs and breathe cool, fresh mountain air again.

It was so worth it.

He followed the muddy path to the top of the hill, where an abandoned concrete structure stood. A bunker? Maybe. But the walls weren't thick enough and the window frame was too large. Something else, then. The audio guidebook said that it was part of a tram for hauling hundreds of tons of ammo and supplies daily through the chain of mountains, dismantled for parts after the war.

Jack turned his attention to the view before him. The magnificent, snow-dusted "three-headed" Triglav was the tallest link in a chain of jagged limestone peaks piercing the wide, cloudy horizon. Jack stared in rapturous wonder at the enduring power of the timeless mountains before him. It made him feel clean somehow, especially after the human filth he'd experienced in Dallas and the human trafficking ring The Campus had helped break up.

He felt no guilt for killing evil men, but he didn't exactly feel like a righteous man, either, standing in this place where so many other men had died so long ago.

He took another deep, cleansing breath of the crisp mountain air. The bad memories receded in the spattering rain that washed over him in the quiet solitude.

No wonder the prophets of old went to the mountains to pray and commune, Jack thought. This place felt, well, *holy*.

Something from catechism bubbled up in his memory. *El Shaddai*. Wasn't that one of the Hebrew names for God? God Almighty—the God of the Mountain?

Hard to believe that such butchery could happen in a sacred space like this. The sins of empires had drenched these mountains with innocent blood. It was a kind of blasphemy.

Jack spent the next twenty minutes exploring the hilltop area, where he found a few other manmade remnants from the war. But for the most part, Nature had prevailed, and there was little evidence that any murderous humans had ever defiled the sharp contours of her magnificent body, or scarred her lovely face.

13

NEAR KOBARID, SLOVENIA

Struna had promised him that the hike to the Kozjak waterfall was well worth it, a real showstopper. He crossed the Napoleon Bridge high over the deep chasm of the Soča River and passed through the small town of Kobarid on his way to the trailhead. His was the only car in the lot save for a mud-spattered Jaguar parked on the far end bearing Italian plates.

The rain was still falling, not so heavy as to keep him out of it, but strong enough to still keep the tourists away, which was fine by him. He enjoyed the solitude, and when he found his thoughts drifting back to Yuki or Ysabel, he easily put them out of his mind by taking in the stunning views around him, not the least of which was the surging Soča River. Struna's guidebook featured the same photos he'd seen on the Web—a translucent turquoise, like a flowing gem.

But as he stood on the narrow hanging bridge that spanned the wide chasm, the rain-swollen Soča was altogether different today—opaque, and light green, like liquid mint. It was no less impressive and certainly beautiful. He supposed it was the rain that was washing limestone and other minerals into the otherwise crystal-clear water.

He took in the view, thankful for the solitude but mostly for the sense of awe and wonder the river and mountains inspired within him. What was there to fear in a world with this much beauty?

Jack checked his iWatch. It was getting late. He needed to push on if he wanted to get to the falls. His weather app said more rain was on the way, but no telling how much. At some point he would have to beat a retreat if the storm got too bad here in the mountains, and he was still two hours away from Ljubljana.

He crossed the bouncing bridge and worked his way up the rough-hewn trail, following close to the surging tributary Kozjak cascading down its own sharp chasms in the midst of the trees until he reached a narrow wooden walkway spanning the river and hugging a wall of rock.

He stepped up onto the first plank and worked his way carefully along the slippery boards in a curving ascent in the steadily falling rain. Even with the rain spattering his hood and the river roaring over the rocks, he could hear the surging falls ahead. A few steps more and he entered a towering cathedral of wet, green granite opening up to a small, gray sky. The roar of the waterfall was nearly deafening now. One boulder jutted out along the wooden pathway like the corner of a building. Jack couldn't see around it, but he knew the end of the walkway was near. He eased his way around the huge, slippery rock.

To his surprise, someone was already standing at the end of the platform. A woman in a green rainsuit stared up at the bridal veil of falling water tumbling from the lip high above. Strands of wet, blond hair spilled out from beneath her hood. A heavy daypack tugged at her shoulders, amplifying her curves.

Jack's weight on the rickety platform caused her to turn with a start.

"Oh!" She gasped, her eyes wide like saucers.

"Sorry, didn't mean to . . ." Jack held up his hands in mock surrender. "I mean, *govoriš angleško?*"—Do you speak English? He had to raise his voice in order to be heard above the thundering echo of the falls.

The woman sighed and smiled prettily, obviously relieved. "Yes, of course I speak English."

Jack couldn't place the accent. She didn't sound like the Slovenians he'd been listening to for the last week. Obviously not a native English speaker, though. "Good. My Slovenian is terrible."

The woman nodded up at the surging water tumbling from above. "Isn't it magnificent?"

Jack turned to look, his irritation at not being the only person here soothed by the beautiful image in front of him and the gorgeous young woman beside him, now nearly touching his shoulder with hers.

"Wow."

She smiled. "I thought I was the only one crazy enough to come out in the rain to see this."

"It's unbelievable, and we don't have to fight the crowds." He looked down at her, just a few inches shorter. She filled out her rainsuit pretty well, in all the right places. Her eyes were fixed on the falls, filled with childish wonder.

"Can you imagine being the first person to ever see this?" she asked.

"It's the first time I've seen it, so I can sort of relate," Jack offered clumsily.

She looked up at him, smiling. "First time here? Congratulations." Her smile faded. "Perhaps you want to be alone, then?"

"Uh, no. It's fine. I mean, please stay, if you want to stay."

She smiled again. "Yes, I would. I just arrived."

They both gazed back up at the falls. Jack lost himself in the moment, mesmerized by the natural wonder of the scene before him. The ancient rock and the endlessly flowing water felt pure and eternal in the dark, isolated cavern. It made him feel both small and finite, yet also alive and connected to the world around him.

Her voice broke his trance. "It's getting late. I should be going."

"Yeah, me too."

Since Jack was closer to the exit, he led the way out, traversing the big corner boulder, then working his way back down the walkway. He felt her steps just behind him, sure and steady.

When they reached the trail, Jack turned to say good-bye, but the woman interrupted him.

"Perhaps since this is your first time here, we should celebrate a little?" She tapped one of the straps of her daypack. "I have a little wine and sausage, and some cheese, if you like. Nothing special, but it's a kind of tradition, I think."

Jack had never heard of such a tradition, but he wasn't going to argue the point. He was hungry and a little wine wouldn't break his heart, and the mischief in her smiling eyes suggested the promise of something very interesting in the near future.

"Yeah, sure. Why not?"

She beamed. "Excellent. I know just the place. Follow me."

The shape of her amazing body was evident even in her rain

pants, and she moved with an athletic agility. Jack felt a familiar hunger. The woman was ruggedly beautiful, and the situation unfolding felt refreshingly familiar.

In his sophomore year, he'd had a torrid sexual encounter with a girl in a forest like this one, though it was warm and spring. They both had quite a crush on each other after that, but a summer internship took him across the country, and the two of them lost touch. When he came back to school in the fall, she had a new boyfriend. Jack hadn't thought about her in years. A pang of longing suddenly shot through him. Amy was awesome. Another one that got away.

The blonde led him off the public trail, which they still had all to themselves, and onto a narrow path that cut deep through the trees about twenty meters until they reached a small clearing. Jack felt a surge of lust and larceny welling up inside, and he tried halfheartedly to push it away. After all, she was just offering him a picnic, right?

In the middle of the clearing stood an old weathered park bench beneath an overhang of branches that provided a degree of shelter from the rain, which had suddenly stopped. Clearly there was no one else around and the woman felt comfortable enough with him to bring him to this place. A small plastic ice chest stood on one end of the table.

The blonde pulled off her pack and set it on the bench next to the ice chest, then motioned for Jack to take a seat.

The bench seat was wet, but Jack was wearing waterproof pants. He swept away a tiny puddle of rainwater and pine needles before sitting as the woman unzipped her pack.

She pulled out a bottle of white wine and handed Jack a corkscrew. "If you don't mind?"

"No, happy to." Jack jammed the bottle between his thighs

and grabbed the corkscrew as she set a styrofoam cup on the tabletop.

"I only have one cup. Is that okay?"

"That is *so* okay," Jack said as he stripped away the foil from the top of the bottle, his eyes focused intently on the task.

The woman reached into her pack again, and out of the corner of his eye Jack saw her pull out a finely hammered blade, no doubt to cut the cheese and sausage. She drew the knife out in a singular, deliberate motion, the muted sunlight glinting on the highly polished steel.

The gleaming blade flashed high in his peripheral vision. Jack twisted his upper body just as the razor-sharp tip sped past his left shoulder, the right-handed strike clearly aimed for his heart. Before Elena could draw it back for a reverse slashing cut across his throat, Jack seized her wrist in his right hand and yanked it back across the table, throwing her off balance despite her surprising strength. That didn't keep her from launching a punch at his face with her left hand, but there was no leverage behind it and she managed only a harmless glancing blow to his temple.

Jack drove all of his weight onto her trapped arm, hyperextending her elbow with a sickening crunch and twisting her wrist with both of his hands, snapping ligaments and separating the carpal bones from the ulna. Her hand released the knife and it fell into the wet grass.

Elena's face was close to his, and her wounded yelp barked in his ear. But the yelp morphed into a raging snarl and she lunged at him with an open mouth to bite his face. Jack swung a heavy elbow into her jaw that snapped her head back, giving him enough time to raise the same arm up and drop a crushing hammer blow to the side of her skull with his fist, slamming her head into the mossy wood, knocking her out instantly.

He leaped to his feet, gasping for breath, his body surging with adrenaline and fury.

What the fuck just happened?

14

THE MONTENEGRO-BOSNIA BORDER

The Happy Times! eight-passenger van pulled to a stop a few meters in front of the one-lane trestle bridge to let the southbound Volkswagen coupe with German plates exit, its tires thumping on the wooden planks. The white-haired driver snarled in aggravation, raising a withered hand to shield his eyes from Emir's headlights. Without so much as a thank-you, the old man gunned the engine and sped away.

Emir ignored the insulting lack of courtesy and bit his tongue, knowing his passengers were paying close attention now that they were about to cross the border. He assured them it was a quick and painless process that involved little more than waving them through or, at most, stamping their passport pages and driving on.

This was a little-traveled crossing, especially at this time of night, and Emir had done it a hundred times if he'd done it once. More important, he knew the customs officer stationed

here on this shift very well, and the man was on the organization's payroll. He was a good Muslim brother as well. No
worries.

But Emir was a cautious man and thumped across the bridge
a few kilometers slower than the speed limit permitted, then
pulled to an easy stop in front of the barrier arm, which, to his
surprise, was in the down position.

What surprised him even more was the customs officer who
approached his van. He didn't recognize the pinched, officious
face or the crisp uniform. The fact he was carrying a clipboard
was worrisome as well.

"Passports."

"Is there a problem, sir?"

The man glanced at the rear passenger window. "How many
passengers?"

"Six tourists, and myself. Is there a problem?"

"Not if you hand me your passports for scanning."

"Normally, we just get stamped."

The man's eyes narrowed. "Really?"

"Sorry, my mistake. Just give me a moment."

Emir turned around in his seat and the six passengers passed
their passports forward, two sleepy American teenagers in the
near bench, two Germans behind them, and two nervous
Greeks in the back, a hard-sided Pelican case wedged between
them.

While Emir was gathering passports, the customs agent circled the van, casting an inspector's eye on the vehicle and
scratching notes on his clipboard. He circled back around a few
moments later, greeted by Emir's forced, impatient smile.

"Passports," the man repeated.

Emir handed the stack of them over.

"I need to scan these. It will take a few minutes."

Emir swallowed his panic. The two Greek passports were good enough for the lax border controls he frequented in the region, but they almost certainly wouldn't pass a computer check. He had to do something.

"Sir, I noticed you were making notes about my van."

"Oh, yes. That. I found several problems. Your left headlight isn't properly aligned, and your right rear tire is nearly bald, a clear safety violation." He referred back to his clipboard. "I'm tempted to impound your van for violation of the commercial vehicle standards."

"You must be kidding," Emir blurted out. The man had spoken enough to reveal he was a Serb, probably from Pale, judging by the accent. It angered him. At least the two of them were speaking in Bosanski, the Serbo-Croatian language spoken throughout the region. Otherwise his passengers might have become alarmed, especially the two Greeks, and he couldn't be sure what they might do next.

"I think I'm going to issue you a personal citation as well. Two months of driver education, and a citation for careless operation of a commercial vehicle."

"That's a four-hundred-mark fine." About two hundred euros, Emir quickly calculated. A lot of money.

"So you do know the law?" The Serb officer allowed himself a grin.

Emir reached for his wallet. "Of course, I understand. But you know, I've been on the road for the last three days and I haven't had a chance to inspect the vehicle."

Emir knew that cops in this part of the world were grossly underpaid, and like almost everybody else in Bosnia, his salary probably couldn't keep up with the rising cost of living. So cops like him found other sources of income, including shaking down drivers desperate to be somewhere else. Corruption was corroding everything in Bosnia these days. It was more than annoying, but it was the cost of doing business. Soon that would change, Emir reminded himself. And he would remember this man when it did.

Emir pulled out a neatly folded wad of two hundred Bosnian convertible marks, the local currency. "I'll be sure to take care of all of those things as soon as I get back to Sarajevo." He slipped the folded cash to the officer. The Serb took the money without even looking at it and pocketed it while still staring at his clipboard. "Well, yes, I understand how it is. I'm not a harsh man. Just trying to keep the law, yes?" He glanced up at Emir.

"Yes, of course," Emir said, offering a smile. "It's very late. Perhaps we can leave now?"

The border policeman frowned. "Not just yet. I must first scan these passports." He pointed toward a cinder-block building behind him and the door marked "WC."

"There is a public restroom if your passengers have the need. I'll be right back."

The Serb turned on his heel and headed for his tiny toll-booth with the large glass window. He wasn't in any hurry, making a big show of taking his time, Emir noticed.

Bastard.

As soon as the Serb had turned his back, Emir snatched up his phone and hit the speed dial.

"What's the problem?" asked one of the two Greeks sitting in the back. The Syrian's English was good, better than the Chechen's.

"No problem," Emir said, lying. Walib's nerves were frayed. Emir couldn't blame him after the harrowing week the two

87

defectors had spent crammed into the backs of trucks and the trunks of cars crossing borders from Turkey to here, with rumors of Russian Spetsnaz in hot pursuit. It would be fatal to both men if the SVR—the Russian version of the CIA—were somehow alerted to their location tonight. Worse, the mission would fail, especially without the Syrian missile officer.

Emir watched the Serb slow-walking toward the booth, flipping through the passports as he went. No one was picking up on the other end of Emir's call.

Emir touched his waistband, feeling for the small-caliber pistol he kept in a banded polyester holster. Killing the Serb wasn't the best option. But letting the Serb scan the passports into the Interpol I-24/7 database clearly wasn't an option at all.

And failing this mission was impossible.

"I'll be right back." Emir climbed out of the van and headed for the tollbooth, trying to decide what he would do with the Americans and Germans after he killed the Serb, but three steps from his van his eye caught sight of a pair of speeding high beams curving in a violent arc onto the far side of the trestle bridge.

The bouncing high beams also caught the Serb's eye from behind the glass, causing him to glance up as he prepared to scan the first German passport.

The four-door Fiat sedan skidded to a halt on the asphalt in front of the customs booth. A bald man dressed in shorts, a tank top, and flip-flops jumped out, not even bothering to shut off the engine. He jogged over to the door of the booth and rattled the locked handle until the aggravated Serb reluctantly stood and opened it.

Emir suddenly recognized the other man as the border agent who should have been there in the first place. Emir approached the booth cautiously, uncertain as to what was unfolding in the blur of wildly gesticulating hands and muffled voices shouting behind the glass. By the time he arrived at the front of the booth the voices had lowered and the gestures were calmer. Emir relaxed a little. This was the time-honored ritual of negotiation, Bosnian style.

The Serb officer shrugged hugely and the Bosniak's head waved back and forth for emphasis. The Serb glanced at the ceiling and the Bosniak checked his watch. The Serb took his seat and lit a cigarette from the pack on his desk, clouding the cramped booth with blue smoke on the first exhale. Then he slid the lighter and pack across the desk and the Bosniak snagged one for himself and lit up as well, signaling the end of the negotiation.

The Bosniak came out of the booth with a wide smile plastered across his unshaven face, the cigarette dangling from his lips and the stack of passports in his hand.

"Emir, it's good to see you."

Emir smiled but lowered his voice. "Where the hell were you?"

The Bosniak's smile disappeared. He tossed the cigarette to the ground and crushed it under his flip-flop.

"My brother, I'm sorry. They changed my shift. I called you. Didn't you get my message?" He handed Emir the passports.

"For your wife's sake, I hope you fuck better than you lie."

The border officer quailed. He'd never known Emir to swear or to speak in any vulgar terms.

"I failed, obviously. But I have solved everything. See?" He pointed to the passports in Emir's hands. "No scans."

"Are you sure?"

"Yes, of course."

Emir stepped even closer. "As sure as your life?"

The Bosniak nodded. "Yes, I'm certain. He has no reason to lie. But unfortunately, it will cost you five hundred euros, cash. Now."

Emir glanced over at the tollbooth. The Serb looked up just at that moment, a thin smile creasing his narrow face. Emir nodded his unsmiling thanks and silently cursed the incredible greed of the Orthodox thief. He reached again for his wallet. All he had on hand was two hundred and forty euros in bills. He handed it to the Bosniak.

"Brother, this won't do."

"It's all I have."

"But I made him a deal. He says his mother needs a surgery." The claim was not unreasonable, Emir knew. Health care was free but of poor quality in Bosnia. The best medical services were privately provided, and expensive.

"If you don't pay him, he'll call those passports in and report you." The Bosniak lowered his voice for effect. "I know this man. He's not kidding."

Emir smiled. "I'm not kidding, either. That's all I have right now. You'll have to make up the difference."

The Bosniak pointed at his empty pockets. "I don't have any money with me—"

Emir's eyes burned like smoldering coals, cutting him off in mid-sentence.

The Bosniak swallowed hard. "No worries. I'll take care of it, Emir. I swear."

For a moment, Emir considered killing this fool and the Serb with the pistol in his waistband, but his rage cooled.

"Yes, you will. We're leaving now."

The Bosniak nodded. "Please tell our friend how sorry I am to have failed tonight. It won't happen again."

Emir's eyes softened. He laid a hand on the man's shoulder. "I know it won't. Thanks for showing up when we needed you."

The man sighed audibly. "Of course. Safe travels, brother."

Emir jogged back to the van, fired up the engine, and handed the passports back before driving away. *Everything is fine now*, he told himself, but he couldn't shake the feeling that the mission had nearly been compromised by that lazy idiot. Half of the money he handed over tonight would probably wind up in the Bosniak's pocket as well.

And the Serb? Who can trust a Serb to keep his mouth shut?

Emir picked up his phone again and hit the speed-dial number of a true brother he trusted completely. The man was local, and talented. Emir whispered in Bosnian and in code, though the tourists weren't paying any attention to him. By this time tomorrow, the Serb would be dead without suspicion in a car accident or a drowning.

The Bosniak would die within the week, but only after Emir found a suitable replacement.

15

Jack shifted uncomfortably in his creaking wooden chair, an empty styrofoam cup in front of him. More than anything, he needed to pee. But he was hoping the interrogation would be over in a few minutes and he didn't want to leave the room.

Detective Valter Oblak pushed through the door and sat down across the battered steel conference table from Jack with his notepad and pen in hand. He had a carefully groomed three-day growth of beard on his lined face and his close-cropped hair was tinged with gray. In jeans and an athletic shirt, he looked more like a coach than a cop. He opened up his notebook again and reviewed it.

"Just one more time, Mr. Ryan, if I may—"

"Sure."

"And you said here . . . you twisted at the very last second before the knife could strike you, *ja?* Very lucky."

"Yes, I said that before. About five times." Jack couldn't tell the man that hundreds of hours of training in close-quarters combat (CQC) had honed his senses to a fine edge. He wasn't even conscious of making the decision to twist out of the way. It was purely reflex.

Oblak looked up. "I'm sorry, I'm just trying to get the details right."

Jack knew from his own training in interrogation that the detective was just trying to catch him in a lie.

"I understand. Sorry if I sound impatient. I'm a little stressed."

Oblak set his pen down and leaned back with a sigh. "Well, there is one more thing. I just received a phone call from headquarters. The woman who you said attacked you? She's filing charges against you for assault, attempted rape, and attempted murder first thing tomorrow morning."

Jack's eyes bulged. "What?"

"She says that you attacked her with the intent of raping and killing her, and that she only tried to defend herself with the knife."

"That's bullshit. Like I said, she tried to stab me with that knife, which was hers. My prints aren't even on it. All I did was defend myself."

The detective checked his notes, shaking his head. "Breaking her jaw, wrist, and forearm in the process of 'defending' yourself." He looked at Jack. "You're a big, strong guy. Was that kind of force really necessary?"

"It was an instant reaction. I wasn't really thinking." Which was true, Jack thought. It was all adrenaline and muscle memory at that point. Fortunately, he'd calmed down enough while she was still knocked out to grab retina and fingerprint shots with his smartphone and get them to Gavin Biery, Hendley Associates' IT director.

"Lucky for her you didn't kill her, then."

"I never intended to. How can she claim I wanted to kill her if I didn't do it after I knocked her out?"

"And you claim it was she who was trying to seduce you before trying to kill you. But why would she behave in such a manner?"

"How the hell should I know? Check her Tinder profile." Jack instantly regretted the snarky comment, but he was exhausted and still highly apprehensive. He was beginning to regret his decision to not have his lawyer present.

Oblak's eyes narrowed. "We take sexual assault and violence against women extremely seriously in my country, Mr. Ryan."

"Not more than I do, Mr. Oblak. I was raised by a strong woman and a father who taught me to respect them."

Jack cast his gaze down at the worn blue indoor-outdoor carpet of the tiny conference room. Good old Gerry Hendley. He was the first person Jack called after he knocked the woman out. In his honey-baked Carolinian drawl, Gerry promised to take care of things on his end and not to worry, but he warned Jack not to touch anything, which turned out to be damned good advice. He further advised Jack not to say anything to anybody, but that if he did, to just tell the truth. Also good advice.

"I appreciate that, Detective, and I hope you appreciate the fact I didn't require my very nervous lawyer to be present in this room even though she's pacing downstairs in the lobby.

I've cooperated fully and answered all of your questions over her objections."

Oblak's eyes softened a little. "Yes, I do appreciate it, and your cooperation has been duly noted."

Jack leaned forward. "Do you really believe her accusations against me?"

Oblak set his pen down again. "Frankly, no. But I hope you understand my situation. Once she claimed you attacked her, the nature of the case changed entirely. She is presumed under the law to be telling the truth."

"In other words, I'm guilty until proven innocent."

"In effect, yes. You should also know she has contacted her attorney and has asked for police protection. She says she's afraid for her life."

"She's bluffing. If I wanted to rape and kill her in a secluded area, why in hell didn't I rape and kill her in the secluded area instead of calling the police?"

Oblak shrugged. "I don't disagree. In fact, her attorney has already communicated with my office and made an unofficial offer. Ms. Iliescu would be willing to drop her charges against you if you decided to not press charges against her."

"So that's her play."

"But her attorney claims that while her client is so traumatized that she would prefer not to press charges, she will do so if forced by circumstances."

"Unbelievable." Jack drummed his fingers on the table. "So, is there a chance I'm actually going to be arrested?"

"It's according to my discretion at this point."

"And how are you leaning?"

Oblak frowned. "Frankly, there are too many holes in her story that don't add up, including the most obvious one that you've pointed out. Why call the police if you intended to commit a crime?"

"So I'm free to go?"

"Of course, but please be advised that the state prosecutor may decide she has a case against you, and you might be subject to arrest in the future."

"How can that be?"

Oblak shrugged. "We have politicians just like you do in the States. If the prosecutor thinks the trial makes good publicity for her office, she might be tempted to do it, even if the case lacks merit."

Jack shook his head. "When will that happen?"

"Who knows? Could be tomorrow. Perhaps never."

"Humor me. If I were to be arrested and charged tomorrow, how long would it take to go to trial?"

"It will take several weeks to gather and process all of the forensic evidence and begin to put the case together. If the prosecutor decides to move forward, depending on the court calendar and witness availability, it could be two to four months before an actual trial is held. Perhaps longer."

"I can't hang around for four months for a trial. My employer won't allow it."

"Your employer must be a very important man. Your government has promised to my interior minister that you will make yourself available for any court proceedings should the need arise."

"So long as I can have a week's notice to make travel arrangements, I'll show up." Jack hoped that they didn't make that call in the middle of a Campus mission. But Murphy's law being what it was, that was the likely outcome. Did that mean

Gerry might put him on hold status from The Campus until the case was resolved?

"If you don't appear, a warrant will be issued for your arrest, and our two countries are signatories to an extradition treaty. Failure to appear for a summons carries a mandatory two-year prison sentence."

"You make it sound like it would make sense for me to drop the case."

"You might consider it. But it's up to you."

Jack started fidgeting. He now wished he hadn't had that third cup of coffee. His nerves were on edge and his bladder boiled. He couldn't tell if Oblak was trying to help him out or if he was just a bureaucrat trying to protect his pension.

"But if you are innocent," Oblak said, "that means she is the guilty party and I need to build a case against her for attempted murder. What I can't understand is her motive for trying to kill you. Any ideas?"

"None."

"Perhaps she is a serial killer of some sort?"

"I'm betting you've already run her passport and found out she's an upstanding citizen with no warrants, priors, or Interpol notices."

Oblak offered his first, small smile. "Very good. You are exactly correct."

"Maybe I reminded her of an old boyfriend or something. She never did tell me her name."

"Elena Iliescu. Romanian by birth, but she carries an Italian passport. Does the name sound familiar?"

"Not at all."

"And you think the attack was spontaneous?"

"I sure didn't see it coming."

"What if I told you that the ice chest on the table was empty, except for a block of dry ice?"

"I'm not sure what that means."

"She also had a pair of surgical gloves, a small bottle of bleach, and a bone saw in her backpack. She claims they aren't hers."

"A bone saw?"

"If I had to guess, I'd say she was going to cut off your head and store it in that ice chest."

Jack felt the blood drain out of his face. "Excuse me?"

Oblak checked his notes again. "You're a financial analyst, *ja?*"

"Yes."

"Perhaps in your line of work you have made some powerful enemies along the way?"

More than you can possibly know, Jack thought.

"Not that I'm aware of." Jack's bladder was about to commit its own crime. "Can I go now? I'd like to get back to my hotel and pack. I'm catching a flight tomorrow."

"To Sarajevo, correct?"

"Yes."

"Business or pleasure?"

"Pleasure."

Oblak stood, as did Jack. They shook hands.

"It's an interesting city. Be sure to try the *ćevapi*. It's quite good."

"I'll do that."

Oblak opened the door and waved Jack through. "We'll be in touch, Mr. Ryan. Safe travels."

"Thanks," Jack called over his shoulder as he bolted for the men's room.

Twenty minutes away from Kobarid, Elena Iliescu lay quietly in a hospital bed in the small medical clinic, her mind fogged with painkillers but her soul raging like a caged animal. Jack Ryan's face kept flashing in her fevered brain. She consoled herself with images of tearing out his eyes with her lacquered nails and pissing in the open mouth of his bleeding corpse.

But for now, she was trapped in a broken body, immobilized and feeble. Her fractured forearm had been X-rayed and stabilized in a sling but not yet cast in fiberglass because corrective surgery on the torn ligaments in her broken wrist was scheduled for the following morning. Her broken jaw had also been wired shut by a local dentist who thought she might need corrective surgery on that in the near future.

But if she was honest with herself, the raging hatred she felt for Ryan was only a mask for her unspeakable fear. In reality, she was already dead.

She'd failed her assignment for the Iron Syndicate, something that had never happened before. She was the Mantis, and no doubt called upon because of her unassailable record of kills over the last ten years. A Code Red assignment had the highest priority, as well as the highest penalty for failure.

Her only hope lay in the private phone call she had with her attorney, whispered through the clenched teeth of her wired jaw. The attorney had told her to be on the lookout for an Iron Syndicate contact. "Arrangements are being made for you, even as we speak," the attorney said. Had Elena the capacity, she would've cried for gratitude.

A contact could only mean the syndicate still had faith in her to complete her assignment once her injuries had healed. It was a great honor to be trusted in such a manner, she reasoned, but nothing would please her more than to slaughter the American who had injured her so badly and caused her such great shame.

Elena saw movement through the tiny window of her hospital door. The policeman who guarded her door was being relieved by another cop. A moment later, the door opened and a harried nurse with thick ankles and a dour look came in with a pressure cuff and thermometer to check her vitals. The cop stood in the doorway and glanced in her direction, then looked away as the nurse wordlessly cuffed her arm and began pumping the squeeze bulb.

Elena glanced up into the nurse's pinched face as the cuff gripped her arm. The nurse scratched the side of her nose with the tip of her nicotine-stained finger, an inconspicuous gesture. But Elena understood it perfectly. Nothing could be said, nor need be.

Contact made.

KOBARID, SLOVENIA

Detective Oblak watched the vehicles pull out of the police station parking lot from his private office on the second floor. Struna, Ryan, and his attorney would arrive in Ljubljana in a little more than two hours.

Oblak had a lot on his mind tonight, and not all of it good. He had Jack Ryan's contact information, and also his address in Sarajevo.

The detective picked up his encrypted cell phone and dialed the number of a colleague working in the Bosnian Intelligence-Security Agency (OSA-OBA).

"Dragan Kolak here."

"Dragan, it's Valter Oblak."

"Yes, of course. I didn't recognize the number."

"My apologies. A new phone. A precaution."

"I understand. But it's rather late for a call, isn't it?"

"A man is arriving in Sarajevo tomorrow. I thought you might be interested in him."

"If you're calling, Valter, you know I'm interested."

16

Ambassador Topal sat in the deputy director general's office, flipping through the documents and photographs in the intelligence folder on the table. Topal was homing in on the deputy's anxious tone of voice more than the content of his briefing, the substance of which he was already familiar with from his own sources.

The deputy director general of Bosnia's OSA-OBA was a competent but unimaginative political appointment in an underfunded intelligence agency tasked with the internal and external security of perhaps the most dysfunctional country in the heart of Europe. The Bosnian government itself seemed incapable of imagination or vision; why should this poor fellow be expected to exceed the limits of his political masters?

Topal understood the man's anxiety, however. In fact, he expected it, partly owing to the deputy director's own traumatic experience during the Yugoslav wars. As a younger Muslim man, he'd been trapped in the crossfire of the siege of Mostar, surrounded on both sides by Serb and Croat armies relentlessly pummeling the historic city with mortar and artillery fire. The man had every right to be nervous this morning, and his calling Topal into this private briefing was a good sign.

"As you can see, social media activity by the extremists has exploded in the last few days. Everybody is accusing everybody else of perpetrating this vile act," the deputy said. "But according to the police transcription of the two surviving witnesses, it was clearly an act of war by the Serb militia."

Topal read the last statement again out loud: "'Croatia for Croats, Bosnia for Serbs.'" He nodded grimly. "Any other evidence?"

"Turn to the next page. See the artist's rendering? Both girls confirmed that this was the shoulder patch on each of the uniforms of the men who raped them."

Topal turned the page. He recognized it immediately as both the national symbol of Serbia and the unit insignia of the infamous White Eagles, one of the most vicious of the many paramilitary units that fought in the genocidal Yugoslav wars. This particular unit included Orthodox Serb militia, armed, trained, and directed by the Serbian government to carry out its policies of ethnic cleansing in an attempt to create a pure Greater Serbia devoid of Catholics and Muslims. The White Eagles were forcibly disbanded after the war and some of the leaders tried for war crimes. The news that they had reassembled caused enormous concern among the other ethnic groups, who were now reconstituting their own militias in response.

"And if that wasn't enough evidence," the deputy said, "there's this." He slapped an ace of spades playing card in front of Topal.

The Turk picked it up and turned it over, revealing the same White Eagles logo.

"A death card," Topal said. He shook his head grimly. "This is bad news." He set the hateful thing back down on the table. "I'm surprised your government allowed this information to get out."

"Believe me, we tried to keep a lid on it. The police reports were sealed and the officers sworn to secrecy against their formal protests."

"Perhaps they leaked it."

"No. It was the Serb criminals themselves who took credit for it on Facebook and Twitter."

"Then you must be hunting them down."

"We are searching high and low, in cooperation with the Ministries of Security and the Interior, of course. But so far, we haven't been able to find them."

"What about tracing them through their social media?"

"Dummy accounts, untraceable e-mail addresses—these guys know what they're doing, or they have help from someone who does."

"Help?"

The deputy director stood and turned, jabbing the large paper map on the wall, his finger touching the capital city of Belgrade.

"I think it's the Serbians."

"The White Eagles were Bosnian."

The deputy director nodded. "Yes, Bosnian *Serbs*, but directed by Belgrade and the old Yugoslav counterintelligence service."

"Greater Serbia again?" Topal asked.

"Yes, of course. The 'dream' never dies, does it? Or maybe it's a nightmare."

Ambassador Topal shook his head. "It's hard to believe. I thought we were past such things."

"The past is prologue, my friend."

"But why jump to such a conclusion? If what you say is true, the Serbians are engaging in an act of war."

"Think about it. This is classic New Generation warfare, straight out of the Russian playbook, and you know how close the Serbians and Russians have become in recent months."

Topal was well aware of the growing alliance between the two countries. In fact, the Russians were holding the Slavic Sword and Shield military exercises just over the border in Serbia at this very moment, over the protests of Topal's government. It was the largest deployment of Russian Special Forces in a foreign country training exercise ever.

The ambassador was even more familiar with Russia's New Generation warfare concept, which they had deployed with devastating effect in Chechnya, Georgia, and even earlier in Ukraine.

New Generation warfare was a multidimensional, nonlinear strategy that engineered and exploited social, moral, ethnic, and political tensions within a target country. It included arming and training local civilians as paramilitary units, often seeded and even led by Russian Spetsnaz special operators posing as civilian fighters. New Gen warfare also appealed to ethnic unity, and against ethnic discrimination by the local government, and pushed those narratives out into the public arena through sophisticated mass media campaigns and "fake news."

False-flag events were also staged to reinforce that narrative with paramilitary factions armed and directed by Russian forces, resulting in further social division and political destabilization. Terrorism, extortion, and crime were also deployed as needed. Anything to disrupt and demoralize the social order.

Finally, sophisticated Russian electronic and kinetic weaponry were inserted to win the battle against organized government forces within the target country.

In short, it was the high-tech Russian version of the old Soviet Cold War model for Third World conflicts: exploit class and ethnic tensions through political propaganda, fifth column action, political subversion, and the support of armed insurgency until revolution was achieved.

"And your government believes the Serbians are engaged in this New Generation style of warfare? Or is that your own opinion?" Topal asked.

"Given the presence of large numbers of Russian Spetsnaz troops next door in a 'training' exercise with Serbian Special Forces, the interior minister and I have concluded that it's a strong possibility. He and I have a meeting scheduled with the security minister within the hour to discuss the matter."

"Perhaps you are correct," Topal said. "But I would be quite careful about taking any overt action against Belgrade."

"We aren't in any position to do that, frankly," the deputy director said. "But NATO is."

"But you know that NATO has lost interest in this part of the world. Brussels is far too occupied with the Middle East and Africa these days."

"That's why I was hoping your government would intervene on our behalf. As a member of NATO, Turkey has a great deal of influence in these matters."

"Not so much as you suppose." Topal didn't mention that the German armed forces had withdrawn entirely from Turkey over recent political tensions.

The Bosniak intelligence officer sat down again, folding his hands in front of him on the table. "As I'm sure you know, the number of NATO peacekeepers in the region has fallen from several thousand a decade ago to just a few hundred. A strong NATO presence here in Bosnia along with NATO resources to support our own security forces would be enough to stem this rising tide of ethnic violence."

Topal shrugged. "Of course, I will raise the issue with my superiors, but I fear the Europeans have no interest in coming back into a conflict that only confuses and frustrates them."

The deputy's neck reddened. "It was the Europeans who refused to act when the Serbs began their ethnic-cleansing campaign against my people, and thousands of us died." His clutched hands flexed. "And it was the Europeans who embargoed arms against us to keep us from defending ourselves. And when the Bosnian Army turned the tide and was finally on the verge of victory, it was NATO that threatened to bomb us—us! The victims! Why? To keep us from winning the war."

"I know the story well, my friend," Topal said, nodding in commiseration. Topal didn't need to remind him that Turkey illegally broke the NATO arms embargo and smuggled weapons in to Muslim fighters during the war.

"And all of that because the Europeans couldn't stomach the idea of a Muslim majority country on European soil." The deputy director sighed through his nose as if trying to vent his anger away. "NATO has a moral duty to prevent another war."

"Since when have we ever been able to count on NATO to protect Muslim interests?"

"Still, you must try. I know you have unofficial connections in Brussels."

"And I will do everything in my power to persuade them. But one way or another, my government will do what is necessary to protect the people of Bosnia, and our Muslim brothers here, just as we are elsewhere in the world." It was no secret that the Turks were expanding their military presence in the Caucasus, the Middle East, and Africa.

The deputy director nodded. "This I know well, Kemal. You have always been a good friend, and Turkey our great, strong brother."

Topal closed the file in front of him and slid it back across the desk. The deputy director reached out his hand to slide it toward himself, but Topal's hand didn't release it.

"One thing occurs to me," Topal said.

"Yes?"

"The Serbians may, indeed, be taking a page from the Russian playbook. But have you considered the other possibility?"

The intelligence bureaucrat frowned. "What possibility?"

"That it's actually the Russians who are behind all of this."

Judging by the deputy director's ashen face, Topal guessed that he had not.

17

General Sevrov, the stocky deputy commander of Russia's Electronic Warfare (EW) Forces, stood at the lectern, where his laptop computer was located. He stole a glance at the double-headed white eagles adorning the Serbian national and army flags that hung from the tall, wood-paneled walls of the auditorium. They were flanked by oil portraits of mustachioed Serbian generals from wars long past, glaring down at him with martial ferocity.

Sevrov's commanding voice thundered with the technical authority of a man with three advanced degrees in electrical engineering, but the fruit salad of medals and parachutist's jump wings on his barrel chest reminded the assembled audience of Serbian military staff and field officers that he was also an accomplished combat commander.

Sevrov's mission today was twofold. Certainly it was to convey his country's most recent advances in EW, but even more important was the political goal of stiffening the spines of the soldiers and politicians in the room, including a delegation from the Republika Srpska, representing the most nationalist elements among the Serb population in Bosnia.

To Sevrov's shame, some of the people in this room didn't trust his country to defend them during a crisis. He couldn't blame them entirely. The Serbs had expected the Russians to protect them against NATO intervention during the war, but his government made the strategic decision to leave the Serbs to their own devices, primarily out of weakness, having just emerged from the fall of communism.

Sevrov was a junior lieutenant at that time, and felt personally betrayed that his own government would allow NATO to kill Slavs in order to protect Muslims. Many of the men in this room had also been active in the war. Having experienced both NATO military prowess and Russian weakness, they were entitled to their doubts about the ability and willingness of his government to protect them in a time of crisis.

Sevrov intended to dispel those doubts today, once and for all.

Today's briefing, coupled with the ongoing Slavic Sword and Shield special ops exercises, was also meant to solidify the growing Russian–Serbian military alliance. Tomorrow morning, Sevrov himself would jump with five hundred other Serbian, Russian, and Belarusian paratroopers in the opening spectacle for the joint Serbian–Russian civilian air show being held at Batajnica Air Base.

Sevrov killed the lights as a giant projector screen slid into view.

"I don't need to remind anyone sitting in the room of NATO's power and reach across Europe," Sevrov began. "Or its abuses."

He used a laser/presentation combo remote to flip to the first PowerPoint image, a familiar sight to anyone of a certain age who lived in Belgrade. It was a picture of the former Yugoslavian Ministry of Defense building burning in the night. Despite their painful familiarity with the subject matter, there was still an audible gasp in the room.

Sevrov advanced to another picture of the same building taken last year. It still stood in the heart of Belgrade, a shattered remnant of its former glory.

The architecturally significant building had been smashed by NATO fighters in 1999 in response to Serbian aggression in Kosovo. Officially, the Serbian government left the remains of the ruined building standing as a monument to the unjust "cruelty and suffering" inflicted upon the Serbian people by NATO. Critics of the government said that the bureaucrats in Belgrade were either too poor or too incompetent to manage a proper demolition and reconstruction of the massive edifice, a view not shared by any of the nationalist patriots in this particular room.

Sevrov let the image of the bombed-out building linger on the screen to allow the moment to soak in, another reminder of the shame, humiliation, and outrage Serbians felt at the time— and still did.

The general then clicked through a series of short videos of NATO tanks, planes, missile launchers, and self-propelled howitzers in action.

"Nor do I need remind any of you of the history of NATO's combined-arms AirLand Battle doctrine."

He then flipped to an animated graphic representing the same battle systems, but now all connected to one another by electronic signals transmitting to and from satellites circling over Europe.

"The AirLand Battle doctrine has now evolved into NCW—Network Centric Warfare—which, of course, is merely following the lead of the Americans, who also use the term NCO—Network Centric Operations." Sevrov grinned and wagged his head. "But you know how the Americans are. They always have to put their own little spin on things, don't they?"

A smattering of laughter rippled through the room.

Sevrov continued with more slides displaying facts, figures, and quotes, all of which were presented in the voluminous notebooks sitting in front of each delegate. His job today was to summarize the presentation into easily digestible bites, not to regurgitate the reams of data in their hands.

"NCW/NCO relies on a vast array of sensors, everything from tiny RFID chips tracking shipping crates of MREs all the way up to orbiting satellite platforms.

"The essential theory of NCW/NCO is that massive inputs of data from all of these innumerable sensors, combined with faster rates of communications at all levels, increases the decision-making abilities and combat effectiveness of all units and commands, from the lowly soldier in the field to the general directing the war.

"The means of accomplishing this is referred to in the NATO literature as C4ISR—Command, Control, Communications, Computers, Intelligence, Surveillance, and Reconnaissance.

"In other words, the Americans and Europeans believe that they have enhanced, extended, and improved the speed and effectiveness of their combat capabilities by relying on the latest communications technologies."

Sevrov flipped to more images as he continued. "GPS, cell

phones, shortwave radio, radar, computers, satellites, laser-guided munitions . . . ships, planes, tanks, UAVs, soldiers, sailors, airmen . . . everybody linked, everybody connected, everybody seeing what everybody else sees. Building on the platform of NCW, their ultimate goal is to create a vast collective network of perfect informational awareness, command, and control."

One of the civilian Serbian politicians spoke up. "But General, is such a capacity even possible? It sounds like more American 'fake news.'"

Sevrov shrugged. "It's not only possible, it's inevitable. Perhaps you have heard of IoT—the Internet of Things? American corporations are proposing to connect every toaster, lightbulb, television screen, A/C unit, and food blender in their homes to an integrated network, so that everything is connected and monitored. You know, 'Alexa, buy a box of cereal' or 'Siri, turn the thermostat down.' That sort of thing.

"In the same way, the American war planners are proposing an IoBT—an Internet of Battlefield Things, where everything is both a sensor and a processor, from the rifle scope to the aircraft carrier. The Pentagon imagines that in the future there will be one giant central nervous system of combat operations, coordinating efforts between units, and across services—Army, Navy, Air Force, Marines. They have even envisioned squadrons of swarming drones—air, land, and sea—all connected to one another, engaging enemies as one AI mind, fighting as fast as quantum computers can think."

Sevrov let that idea wash over the audience. And then he winked. "Sounds pretty scary, doesn't it?"

Nervous chuckles bubbled up around the room.

"There's no doubt that NATO and the United States rely heavily on advanced technologies to achieve their war-fighting aims, and they have had some spectacular successes."

Sevrov pulled up another video. "We've all seen the videos of laser-guided drone munitions destroying nests of Islamic fighters. The West believes that technology is the key to everything, including warfare."

Sevrov paused for effect.

"But I will remind everyone in this room that every war the Americans have lost—Korea, Vietnam, Somalia, and, yes, Afghanistan—has been lost to *technologically inferior* opponents."

Sevrov watched heads around the room nodding in surprised agreement as that revelation hit home.

He flashed two more images: a B-2 stealth bomber in the sky and another of a smiling, toothless, and bearded Taliban fighter holding his battered AK-47.

"Seventeen years after invading Afghanistan with their billion-dollar bombers and lasers and drones, who is still in charge of the Afghan countryside? The illiterate peasant with his two-hundred-dollar rifle."

More heads nodded in agreement. Sevrov continued.

"I'm not saying that NATO and America aren't powerful military forces. They certainly are." For a moment, the humiliating image of NATO forces smashing the Russian invasion of Lithuania flashed in his brain. He pushed it aside.

"But even they will tell you they are powerful only because of their technological advantages, and they are only becoming more reliant on their technology.

"But what would happen to their vaunted military power if suddenly their radars and radios, satellites and lasers, strike fighters and helicopters, cruise missiles and missile cruisers, GPS and drones, were suddenly snatched out of their hands with the flip of a switch?"

The general pulled up a new slide, titled "Russian Strategic Doctrine: Radio-Electronic Combat."

"We have taken an entirely different approach from NATO. Whereas NATO sees the electromagnetic spectrum as a *means* of improving combat capabilities *in* the battle space, we view the electromagnetic spectrum *as* the battle space, and, perhaps, the most important one."

Sevrov then tapped a few keys on his computer keyboard, pulling up a live video feed of a handheld camera focused on a four-axled cab-over truck with stabilizer bars extended perpendicular from the open bed. EW troops scrambled over and around the green all-terrain vehicle, monitoring the vertical extension of a huge telescoping mast reaching straight up for the sky. The handheld camera swung over to three more identical trucks in a semicircle several hundred feet away. Their masts were already extended to more than one hundred feet.

"What you are witnessing here is the deployment of our Murmansk-BN electronic warfare system just north of your air base. Murmansk-BN is just one of several new systems we've brought into service in the last year. It has an operational range of three thousand kilometers, and is capable of locating enemy radio signals such as the American High Frequency Global Communications (HFGC) system and targeting the source. It is also capable of monitoring radio signals and even jamming them over that incredible distance."

Sevrov tapped another key and pulled up a picture of an American Civil War Confederate cavalry unit on the attack. "Some claim it was the southern Americans who first engaged in EW by deploying telegraphers with their advanced cavalry units who would 'spoof' federal troops with false orders, sending them to the wrong locations or reporting enemy positions that didn't exist." Sevrov smiled broadly. "Of course, our own troops have done much the same thing in recent operations, sending phony text messages and voice mails, confusing and frightening enemy combatants in our latest version of PsyOps."

Suddenly, cell phones vibrated and buzzed all across the room. As delegates checked their emergency text messages, a wave of laughter bubbled up. A few concerned faces frowned as well. Sevrov's team had crashed through the security architecture of their phones and sent them all a spoof text cracking an obscene joke at President Ryan's expense.

A few chuckles of admiration murmured among the Serbian officers.

An oil painting depicting a battleship engagement during the 1904–1905 Russo–Japanese War appeared on the screen. Sevrov continued.

"But without question, the first instance of radio jamming during war happened in 1904, when a Russian operator jammed Japanese radio signals during a bombardment of Port Arthur. Of course, radio jamming was practiced in World War One and perfected in the Great Patriotic War by all sides."

Sevrov tapped more keys. Another live feed came up showing a BAZ-6900 series cab-over truck, another four-axled transport, but this one was enclosed. A three-dish array deployed on the back end of the roof rotated in a slow circle.

"This is the Krasukha-4 jamming station with a three-hundred-kilometer range, designed to neutralize airborne radar systems like the E-3 Sentry AWACS and the E-8 Joint STARS. It is also capable of attacking low Earth orbit (LEO) systems like the Lacrosse/Onyx radar-imaging reconnaissance satellites and, of course, UAVs like the Reaper. And these are just a few of the many new systems we're deploying now, including handheld devices and aerial drone systems."

Sevrov surveyed the room again. He had their attention for sure now, particularly the Republika Srpska delegates.

"Without question we are years, even decades, ahead of NATO in EW weaponry, deploying systems that will utterly deny NATO's C4ISR capabilities with a virtual flip of the switch. Flipping that switch will render them electronically blind, deaf, and dumb, completely disrupting their battle plans.

"And one last thing, perhaps equally important. All of these systems, and others detailed in your briefing books, also provide impenetrable defenses for our own forces against NATO's inferior EW capabilities.

"In short, our doctrine provides total electronic support, protection, and attack resources for all of our tactical and strategic operations. As you can clearly see, our Radio-Electronic Combat doctrine is both a sword and a shield, and my government is proud to extend both to our Slavic brethren throughout the region."

Sevrov shut his laptop and cast a glance back up at the portraits of old Serbian generals hanging on the wall. He swore they were smiling at him.

General Sevrov set his controller down, then stepped out from behind the lectern, raising his opened palms, and smiling like a kindly uncle.

"Questions?"

18

CENTRAL BOSNIA

The driver squinted his weary eyes through the fog of cigarette smoke in the truck cab. The dark figure in his headlights stood in the two-lane asphalt road far ahead, waving a red flashlight.

The driver tapped the brights. The figure in the road was clad in black and masked, with a rifle slung behind his back.

The driver's heart fluttered for a moment. The Croatian Mafia was active in this part of the country, and truck hijackings weren't uncommon. He wasn't sure if he should try and speed past the guy—or maybe run him over.

But before he could decide, his headlights caught the white fluorescent POLICIJA patch blazoned across the man's chest, and the driver's tension eased a little. He geared down and tapped the big truck's brakes with a short bark of compressed air.

The truck slowed to a crawl as the policeman leaped onto the running board, seizing the chrome handle assist on the side of the cab. He directed the driver onto a rutted dirt road that angled off into a deserted farm a few hundred meters from the highway.

The truck driver panicked again, but the tactical officer could easily shoot through the glass if he tried anything, so what was he to do?

When the truck reached the farmhouse, the cop signaled for the driver to stop and cut the lights, which he did, killing the engine and setting the parking brake with a final blast of air.

The driver's door flew open and the policeman grabbed a fistful of the trucker's stained soccer jersey, flinging him all the way down into the hard dirt with a crashing thud.

Before the driver could raise himself up, a knee in his spine forced him back down and a strong pair of hands wrenched one of his arms back. The driver felt something hard and sharp cut into his wrist with a zipping sound, and then his other arm was yanked into the same position, and the other plastic cuff was zipped into place. A hand shoved the driver's face into the ground and held it there for a moment, a silent command to lie still and be quiet. What else could he do?

The officer finally stood, relieving the pressure from the driver's back. He heard the man unsling his weapon and rack the firing bolt. Warm urine flooded the driver's oily trousers.

He was going to die.

The tall policeman raised a pair of bolt cutters and snipped the padlocks with a couple violent cuts. The shorter officer pulled the ruined padlocks off and the two of them lifted the handles and unbolted the trailer doors.

They pulled out their flashlights and scanned the contents.

It was a stack of cardboard boxes, eight high, marked ELEC-TRONICS and MADE IN CHINA.

The tall policeman climbed into the trailer and with a crash pulled down a box as the shorter one glanced over at their partner standing guard over the truck driver and watching the road.

The tall policeman pulled out his heavy combat knife and slashed open the top seal, revealing several smaller boxes of LED desk lamps with flexible necks.

The two exchanged a worried glance through their balaclavas.

The tall one pulled down another box, then stood on his toes and flashed his light toward the back of the truck. He turned around, his eyes beaming. He flashed a thumbs-up, then pulled down three more boxes to make room to crawl. He lowered his long arm and the smaller cop grabbed his hand and pulled, and soon the two of them were scrambling over a few rows of boxes to get to the real thing.

Behind the stacks of desk lamps were a dozen wooden crates about ten feet long. The shorter cop pulled off the balaclava, spilling out a wave of shoulder-length blond hair. The woman grinned ear to ear and flashed her light on one of the crates as the tall cop pulled his balaclava off as well, and started working the crate lid with his thick blade. The weak nails squeaked inside the soft pine as the knife levered up the lid. When his fingers could finally get purchase, the big man sheathed his knife and pulled the lid off with his hands and tossed it aside as the woman knelt down and yanked out the packing material. They were looking for 122-millimeter missiles.

Instead, they found a crate of cold rolled-steel plumbing pipe.

The woman—a GRU major—swore a vile curse in her mother tongue.

Russian.

Eighty kilometers south, a thirty-nine-foot-long Happy Times! tour bus was parked behind a line of trees, far from the empty highway. Eight men in pairs, including the "Greeks"—Captain Walib and Lieutenant Dzhabrailov—pulled heavy ten-foot-long wooden crates out from the wide luggage compartments beneath the bus's passenger cabin and loaded them onto a flatbed truck for the drive to the camouflaged storage building a hundred meters away.

19

I t was an informal meeting, if any meeting in the Situation
Room could ever be characterized as such, particularly with
the President and his closest advisers on hand—SecState
Scott Adler, SecDef Robert Burgess, DNI Mary Pat Foley, and
chief of staff Arnie Van Damm.

A regional map of the Balkans was displayed on one of the
big screens on the wall nearest the table, along with satellite
photographs of Russian forces in and around Belgrade, Serbia.

President Ryan had ordered up a buffet of salads and sandwich fixings for the late dinner gathering. He had a few things
on his mind that he wanted to get cleared up as soon as possible, and this was the only time Arnie could pull everyone together. With a hundred urgent national and global issues
clawing at his schedule every day, Ryan had learned to priori-
tize better than most.

But he'd also learned that the White House wasn't just a fire station, and his job wasn't limited to turning the hose on the nearest blaze raging out of control. Anticipation was one of his great strengths, born out of decades of analytical experience. Better to keep the fire from starting than to try to put it out. He'd also learned to trust his gut—technically, his limbic system—and his gut was boiling.

Ryan stacked a few slices of rare roast beef between pieces of dark and hearty pumpernickel bread slathered with Dijon mustard, serving himself after the others had filled their plates. Only DNI Foley helped herself to the kale salad with cranberries, almonds, and fig dressing, which she ate seated in a chair next to Arnie. SecState Adler and SecDef Burgess sat across from them, each sipping hot black coffee from a heavy ceramic mug bearing the presidential seal.

"Thank you all for taking the time out of your schedules and away from your families," Ryan said, taking the black leather chair at the head of the room. "I'm hoping this will be a short one." Ryan took a big bite of his sandwich.

"You mentioned two questions in your memo," Arnie said.

Ryan nodded, swallowing. "The first question I want to tackle is this Russian buildup in Serbia. My PDB this morning"—Presidential Daily Brief—"contained photos of Murmansk-BN EW vehicles deployed near Belgrade." Ryan hit one of the pictures on the big-screen monitor with his laser pointer. "I'm told it's part of their Slavic Sword and Shield military exercise. Are we convinced that's all there is to this?"

As the director of national intelligence, Mary Pat Foley oversaw the intelligence gathering and processing of all sixteen agencies in the IC, including the CIA. She didn't miss much, and even scanned Ryan's daily PDBs. "The Sword and Shield exercise is an annual event now—three years in a row.

This one is the largest one yet, and the most sophisticated. But we have no indication of hostile intent."

The SecDef set his coffee down. "It's a massive training exercise for Russian, Serbian, and Belarusian Spetsnaz units. It's the wrong mix of forces to launch any kind of sustained cross-border strike, if that's your concern, Mr. President."

"Key word 'sustained,'" Ryan said.

"Noted," the SecDef agreed.

"Spetsnaz are their best troops, and the EW equipment they've deployed is top drawer. Some say better than ours," Ryan said. "Interesting combo. Putting their most advanced equipment that far forward is a helluva security risk for them. They must really want to make an impression."

"They do," SecState Adler said. "They're feeling the pressure in that part of the world. Montenegro just joined NATO last year; Croatia and Slovenia are already members. Macedonia wants to join, and so does Bosnia-Herzegovina—except for the Republika Srpska. They all want to join the EU, even some Serbian politicians. The Russians are feeling encircled, and Serbia is the key to stopping the advance."

Ryan rubbed his chin. "Okay, let's assume all of this is to keep the Serbians in the fold, and that it actually works. That doesn't stop the rest of the cards from falling out of their hands. Their strategic situation will continue to deteriorate. So, what's the play here?"

"Restore their reputation," the SecDef offered. "They let NATO bomb the hell out of the Serbs during the war. Maybe this is their way to try and rehabilitate themselves with their Slavic brethren."

"National and ethnic appeals are very strong these days. Catalonia, Belgium, Brexit—the European Union is threatened by nationalism. It only makes sense for the Russians to play on that to their advantage," Mary Pat said. "While Europe is dividing, Russia might be trying to gather her Slavic children under her wing."

"I'm sure that's part of all of this," Ryan said. "But there's something more." He stood and stared at the images on the wall monitors. "You all know how these guys think. If they can't take a country outright, they like to stir up the pot."

"Which 'pot' are you talking about?" Van Damm asked.

Ryan pointed at the center of the regional map. "Seems to me that there used to be sixty thousand NATO peacekeepers over there to enforce the peace accords, but they're all pulled out now, aren't they?"

Adler shifted in his seat. "Down to about six hundred total for the whole area."

Ryan turned to him. "The Europeans were the ones who made a hash of that whole thing, and they're the ones who promised to keep an eye on it. What happened?"

The secretary of state shrugged. "Europe's always been that way. They never carry their full load, and they seldom follow through. As far as Bosnia's concerned, they didn't want to pay the price for continued peacekeeping operations, and their attention is drawn elsewhere these days."

"I thought the Europeans had a high representative over the entire Bosnian government—some joker who can pull crazy politicians and stubborn bureaucrats out of office, and implement laws or whatever else they need to do to keep the peace and make the government function," Arnie said.

"You sound a little jealous of this high representative guy," Ryan said, smiling.

"It would make things a lot easier around here if you had

that kind of power over Congress." Arnie's pale blue eyes smiled mischievously.

"No, thanks," Ryan said.

The secretary of state said, "The bottom line is that in recent years, the high representative has stepped back from any kind of intervention, in order to promote Bosnian self-determination."

"Which is just another way for the Europeans to say they don't want to be bothered with it anymore. But by pulling out those peacekeepers, they've created one hell of a power vacuum," Ryan said. "And the Russians, like nature, abhor a vacuum."

The President crossed over to the wall of monitors.

"There are recent reports of escalating violence in Bosnia, and the re-formation of ethnic militias," Foley said. "That fits your vacuum thesis quite neatly."

"It's a damn powder keg over there," Adler said. "Five hundred years of blood feuds and genocides. It's like the damn Hatfields and McCoys, but with IEDs and machine guns."

Ryan touched the Bosnian map. "The Russian New Gen warfare model fits this situation perfectly, doesn't it? They have the means, the proximity, and the natural target—an ethnically and politically divided country right next door to Serbia. Even if the Russians don't want to take Bosnia over, another bloody civil war in the heart of Europe will demand a NATO response."

"Tying up NATO forces for years, maybe decades," Burgess said. "Freeing the Russians up to pursue their interests elsewhere."

"And keeping NATO from any further expansion," Adler added.

The DNI shook her head grimly. "That's playing with fire.

After the last war, the Bosniaks aren't going to wait around for NATO to save them from Serbian attacks. They'll retaliate quickly and in force."

"There are twenty-five million Muslims in Europe who might rise up if NATO doesn't act swiftly enough, or if the Serb attacks are too vicious," the SecState added.

"Bosnia," Ryan said, processing a thought. He tapped the map again. "The cradle of modern jihad against the West. This is where it all began, twenty-six years ago."

Ryan turned around to face the long mahogany table, his prodigious memory kicking into high gear. "Osama bin Laden was issued a Bosnian passport at one time, and Khalid Sheikh Mohammed—the mastermind of 9/11—was granted Bosnian citizenship. Thousands of jihadis flocked from all over the world to fight in the war against the Western powers in defense of the Umma in Bosnia. Al-Qaeda learned its first battle lessons here before moving on to Afghanistan."

"We can't let that happen again," the SecDef said. "The radicals don't need another base of operations, particularly one in the heart of Europe. We need to stomp that out before it even gets started."

"So that's the Russian plan? Reignite a Muslim war in Europe?" Arnie said.

Burgess and Adler exchanged a worried glance as Ryan poured himself a cup of coffee.

"Maybe," Ryan said.

"Maybe?" Adler asked.

"The Russians aren't stupid," Ryan said, "and they're pretty good at history, too." He took a sip of hot coffee as he headed back for the map. "That's a lot of chaos, and it could easily spin out of control. Especially if the Serbs are suddenly on the bad end of the stick again. For the sake of their existing alliances and their credibility, the Russians would have to intervene."

"If ethnic Croats in Bosnia got caught up in all of that, Croatia might take advantage of the situation again, just like in the last war," Adler said. "They booted two hundred thousand Serbs out of Croatia in 1995. Some of their politicians have dreams of Greater Croatia just like many Serbs dream of Greater Serbia."

Ryan touched the map again. "Here. Sarajevo. Ring a bell, anyone?"

"Oh my God," Foley said. "World War One."

"Archduke Ferdinand and his wife killed by a Serbian nationalist, right in the heart of the city," Ryan said. "That was the spark that lit the fuse."

"Resulting in the collapse of three empires, including Russia's," Adler said.

"The Russians are a lot of things, but suicidal isn't one of them," Ryan said. "A civil war in Bosnia could turn into another clash of empires. Another world war."

"So you *don't* think the Russians are engaging in New Gen warfare over there?" Van Damm said.

The President sat back down, rubbing his face with frustration. "Hell, Arnie, I don't know. That's why I have all of you here. My gut tells me no, but I know we're missing something. I can feel it. What did Twain say? History doesn't repeat, but it often rhymes?"

He glanced around the room. "We need to keep a close eye on this situation. I'd like each of you to take another swipe at this stuff with your staffs and get back to me with your best ideas by the end of the week. I'm not in the mood for any surprises, Russian or otherwise. Understood?"

Heads nodded around the table as notes were taken on paper and tablets.

The President glanced back up at the map of Bosnia and its capital city. He knew his son was due to land in Sarajevo in the next several hours. He had to remind himself that Junior managed to survive a killer typhoon in Singapore last year.

But the fiery storm his son might be heading into now would be far more dangerous.

The President's thoughts about his son were interrupted by his chief of staff. "You said you had another question about the Russians."

"Yeah, but it's not exactly connected. My PDB this morning contained secondary confirmation of the report we received a couple of weeks ago about the Syrian Army strike on Idlib with thermobaric munitions."

"Deploying the new Starfire heavy flamethrower system," the SecDef said, "122-millimeter thermobaric missiles fixed on the new T-14 Armata chassis."

"Thermobarics? That's some nasty stuff," the DNI said. "Almost as destructive as a tactical nuclear strike, but without the radiation."

"I thought the Syrian government had a ceasefire with Al-Nusra," Arnie said. "Trying to stabilize the area."

"There was a ceasefire," Foley said. "Al-Nusra leadership got complacent, and the Syrians took advantage. Decapitated the entire senior council in one strike, including the emir."

"Just like those bastards to break a truce," the SecState said. He was a longtime opponent of the vicious Damascus regime.

"But damn smart," the SecDef said. He turned to the

President. "How does a Syrian Army operation tie into the Russians?"

"A Syrian operation, sure, but with Russian weapons, Russian training, and, I'd be willing to bet, Russian 'advisers' on the ground."

"Without the Russians, Damascus would've fallen by now. They're the reason a ceasefire with the opposition was even possible to begin with."

"But you're connecting what happened in Syria with what's happening in Serbia," Foley said, her face frowning with curiosity. "You think it's two sides of the same coin?"

"If the Syria situation starts to spin out of control, our attention will be focused there, and not on the Balkans," Ryan offered, tossing out a bread crumb. Foley picked it up.

"And if the Balkans heat up, we won't be paying attention to Syria."

SecDef Burgess added, "And it's not as if there aren't a hell of a lot of other things going on in the world right now."

"I see it now," Adler said. "The Russians are playing a little three-dimensional chess with us."

Ryan sighed, exasperated. "I can't shake the feeling there's another pair of hands at work here."

"Whose?" Foley asked.

"*Cui bono?* Who benefits?" Ryan asked, falling back on his Jesuit training.

"Al-Qaeda, ISIS, the Russians . . . even the Chinese and the NorKs, if all of our attention is diverted away from the Pacific," Burgess said.

"All true. But something tells me there's a missing piece, something obvious and right in front of our noses, if we could just see it." Ryan stood, buttoning his suit coat, signaling an end to the session. The others stood as well. He thanked them again for coming on such short notice as Arnie ushered them out the door.

"Anything I can do for you, boss?" Arnie asked.

"Maybe a couple aspirin, and a crystal ball, if you can find one."

Arnie smiled. "Back in a jiff with the aspirin. And that crystal ball is still on back order." He shut the door behind him.

Ryan reached for the phone to call his son but caught himself. It was six hours later over there and the kid was probably asleep.

Besides, Junior could take care of himself.

20

REPUBLIKA SRPSKA, BOSNIA AND HERZEGOVINA

The man was pouring himself a cup of hot tea when a pair of heavy boots clomped onto his front porch. Before he could set the pot down, his door rattled beneath the pounding of a thick hand.

The man assumed the worst. He pulled a nine-millimeter pistol out of a drawer and marched toward the door, holding the weapon behind his back. Just as he arrived, the hand pounded on the door again. He unlocked it and flung it open—

"Tarik?" the man said. "It's an honor—"

"Idiot! What are you thinking!" Tarik Brkić shouldered his way into the man's house, followed by two younger Bosniaks, dark and determined. They slammed the door shut as Brkić stormed toward the wide picture window, where a huge black AQAB—Al-Qaeda in the Balkans—flag hung. The banner bore the infamous white Arabic letters declaring the *shahada*.

The tall, burly Chechen snatched the black AQAB flag and balled it up before shoving it into the man's quivering hands.

"I don't understand."

Brkić had a full, wild red beard streaked with gray, and a voice cold and hollow like an empty grave. But it was the Chechen's milky white eye that struck terror deep into the man's soul, a brutal reminder of Brkić's terrifying war record.

"The whole point of hiding in the middle of the infidels is to remain invisible, and you go and hang that flag?"

"But I'm far from the road, and I'm proud to be in the jihad. The *kafir* Serbs never come out this way."

"Take your damnable pride back up north and gather with the others who are under constant OSA-OBA surveillance," Brkić said, stepping closer. "But if you do anything to jeopardize our work here again, I will personally make you a martyr for the cause."

The man bowed his head. "I understand. I am truly sorry."

Brkić laid a callused hand on the man's shoulder. "Zeal is good, but wisdom is better if we are going to win the day."

The man nodded violently, cursing his own stupidity. The Chechen felt his burner phone vibrating in his pocket. There was only one person who had his number, and never a reason for him not to pick up when he called.

Brkić signaled to his men with a nod, and the three of them headed back outside. When they shut the door behind him, he answered.

"Yes?"

"You did well," the electronically altered voice said. "But there is still much to do."

Anyone listening in on the encrypted line—an impossibility, his technicians assured him—would not be able to tell the gender, age, or nationality of either of them. But Brkić knew the caller well from years before, under the code name Red Wing—from a time when Brkić had another name, too.

"I'm following the plan, according to schedule."

"Perfectly, as far as I'm concerned. But my sense is that we need to move the calendar forward. Keep striking while the iron is hot. It's time for sharper measures."

The Chechen bristled. They had agreed to a plan and to a timetable more than two years ago. Thanks to their cooperation, Brkić had been able to smuggle in jihadi fighters from Tunisia, Egypt, Libya, Yemen, Morocco, and elsewhere, along with weapons and much-needed cash and drugs to finance their operations.

What Red Wing didn't understand was that Brkić had yet another plan, and another timetable, with an even larger agenda. But Red Wing could never know that. Red Wing wouldn't understand.

Worse, Red Wing would oppose it.

Red Wing was a reliable ally, but not a true believer.

Brkić still needed Red Wing's contacts and resources, but it was Allah himself who guided Brkić's steps now.

"What do you propose?" Brkić finally asked.

Red Wing laid out a new timetable. It was possible to carry it out, Brkić calculated, and smart. But it was also dangerous. If it failed or endangered his own, larger plan, he would kill Red Wing and fulfill the will of Allah instead. But for now, Red Wing was useful, and their smaller plan helpful for the cause.

"I will plan the next mission immediately," Brkić said.

"You are a great patriot, and a servant of the Most High."

Brkić found that in life it often wasn't possible to be both.

"His will be done."

21

SARAJEVO, BOSNIA AND HERZEGOVINA

Jack powered up his cell phone as the airport bus shuttled from the plane toward the small, dated terminal, an unpretentious glass-and-concrete building surrounded by low hills dotted with houses and pine-covered mountains beyond.

No point in wasting time, he thought. He scrolled through the list of names Gavin had sent him. A list of eleven blond, blue-eyed women in their twenties birth-named Aida Ćurić, all living in Sarajevo. Gavin even included photos from driver's licenses or other official documents, along with their contact information, but with the caveat that the Bosnian databases he found weren't always up-to-date and might not be completely reliable.

At least it was a good start, and with any luck, one of these women would be the adult version of the young girl in his mother's cherished memory. He actually looked forward to delivering his mother's letter to this woman, though she had forbidden him to read it in advance. She didn't say, however, that he couldn't hang around to see the woman's response. Jack knew his mother, and whatever she wrote would bless this Aida Curić person down to her toenails.

He owed his mother a lot—well, everything, actually—and she never asked anything of him, so, in a way, this was a blessing to him as well. The smile he'd see on her face when she got the good news and the "Nice job, son" he'd get would be worth whatever minor hassles he was going to face over the next few days. He just hoped this Aida person appreciated the gift his mother had given her and would somehow reciprocate, even if it was just a letter in response.

Jack fetched his one piece of slightly oversized luggage from baggage claim and passed easily through a largely disinterested passport check, then snagged a wad of local currency at an ATM in the lobby: Bosnian convertible marks, aka BAM.

Jack turned around and saw a twentysomething guy in a worn polo shirt and jeans, holding a handwritten sign that read JACK RYAN and scanning the lobby. They locked eyes and the driver smiled broadly.

"Mr. Ryan?"

"Jack, please." Jack stuck out his hand and the man shook it enthusiastically. "You are?"

"Adnan."

"Great to meet you, Adnan. Ready to roll?"

"Let me get your bag," Adnan said, reaching for the handle, but Jack waved him off.

"I got it, no sweat." He knew the man was angling for a tip, but Jack was always a good tipper and, like his dad, he didn't care for people making a fuss over him, whatever the reason.

"Okay," the driver said, nodding and pointing at the sliding-glass-door exit. The two of them headed out into the surprising heat of a bright September afternoon. Jack read online that it was always better to arrange for a cab or car service in advance. The locals often jacked up the price if you just showed up. This way, the price was set and not negotiable, and the driver knew where to go in advance, which, in this case, was an address for an Airbnb that Jack had found near the Stari Grad—the Old Town. After a change of clothes into something cooler, he'd start his search for Aida Curić, and maybe try to find a place that sold this *ćevapi* stuff he'd heard so much about.

Adnan popped the trunk on a slightly worse-for-wear silver Toyota sedan and Jack tossed his roller into it. Adnan's front passenger seat was crowded with boxes of used business books in German and Serbo-Croatian, along with a few English-language thrillers, so Jack climbed into the backseat.

Adnan threaded his way through Sarajevo's busy streets, crowded with mostly late-model cars, crammed public buses, and at least one Tito-era trolley car straight off the set of *Doctor Zhivago*. Like most urban centers these days, Sarajevo had a lot of trash on the ground and graffiti sprayed on the walls, Jack saw. Had it not been for the street signs, Jack might have thought he was in a working-class suburb of Rome or Paris.

"American, yes?" Adnan asked in a thick accent. He glanced at Jack in his rearview mirror.

"That obvious?"

"Your e-mail address tell me this." A battered Mercedes sedan stopped short in front of them as he spoke, his eyes on Jack in the rearview. But somehow Adnan sensed the trouble; he blasted his horn and swerved into another lane to avoid a collision.

"First time in Bosnia, Jack?"

"Yeah."

"What do you think?"

"So far, so good." Jack was grateful for the air conditioner even though it clearly needed a shot of Freon.

Adnan smiled broadly. "It's a beautiful country, with beautiful women and the best food. Yes, very beautiful."

"Can't wait to find out," Jack said, suddenly realizing his faux pas. "The food, I mean. I hear the thing to get is *ćevapi*."

"Yes, it's the best. We are famous for it. And cheap. The food here is very good prices for you Americans."

Adnan's phone rang and he picked up, chattering in Bosanski with the caller on the other end. Jack cast his gaze back outside. The people in their cars or walking the pavement seemed neither particularly well dressed nor desperately poor, and many of them were smoking, young and old alike. Like city dwellers everywhere, they had mostly unsmiling faces stress-hardened against the harsh realities of not enough wages and too-high rents. The anxious energy of the city radiated against the car's tinted glass like the rays of the sun.

Adnan hung up. "Sorry about that."

"No worries. Everything okay?"

"My mother. She's sick."

"I'm sorry."

"Not bad. Just a cold. But I worry, you know?"

"It's your mother. You should worry," Jack said.

Adnan smiled at that. "How long are you in Bosnia?"

Jack didn't particularly care to answer questions, especially from strangers, but this guy was a driver and just trying to make small talk.

Right?

"A week," Jack lied. He had no idea how long he'd be in town. He might even be leaving tomorrow if his luck held.

"Too bad. There is much to see, especially out in the country. Business?"

"Pleasure."

"Good. You Americans work too hard."

"What about you? Is this your full-time job?"

"Me? Yes. One of them. I also study German, and sometimes work at my father's shop, and sometimes clean windows. Whatever work I can get."

"Jobs are hard to get here?"

"More than forty percent unemployment here in the city. Very bad."

"Why so high?"

"People moving into the city from the country every day. But mostly, it is stupid government and corrupt politicians causing problems. Hard to develop industries and jobs when you pay too much in taxes and bribes to idiots like we got."

"Trust me, you don't have a monopoly on idiots," Jack said. "Your English is very good. You learned it in school?"

"Mostly on the Internet, playing video games. School not so good here."

"I saw your books in the front seat. You're studying German and business. Thinking about starting an importing company?"

"No. Export company. Starting with me."

"I'm sorry?"

"I want to learn enough German to emigrate. Eighty thousand Bosnians leave every year looking for work, especially in Germany. I have a cousin in Frankfurt, drives a taxi. Soon as I save up enough money, I'm going there."

"That's gotta be tough, leaving your own country to find work somewhere else," Jack offered.

"What choice do I have? You go where the work is. If I make enough, maybe come back."

Jack didn't know what else to say. Adnan was like millions of other people displaced by the crushing economic realities of globalism. Jack was lucky he was born in a country that still knew how to compete.

"How much longer until we arrive?"

"Ten minutes. Maybe."

Adnan kept weaving in and out of lanes, and even ran a few yellow lights. Not being on the meter put a fire under his tail, which didn't bother Jack at all.

He glanced back out the window and enjoyed the ride, absorbing as much detail as he could. There were plenty of small private shops and kiosks selling tobacco and convenience items but also chain shopping markets, department stores, and big banks, particularly foreign ones, as the taxi neared the city center. There were several mosques, their soaring minarets stabbing the skyline. He wasn't used to being in a Muslim-majority city. But he also saw a fair number of churches, Catholic and Orthodox, and he'd read somewhere that the city still had a vibrant Jewish community. No wonder Sarajevo was referred to as the "Jerusalem of Europe."

But there weren't any soaring skyscrapers or super-wide boulevards in the oldest part of the historic city, nor any cranes or signs of new construction. Sarajevo felt like an old suit: well tailored and serviceable but worn and tired. No new construction meant nobody was planning for a bright and expansive future. Maybe the lack of it was partly a function of the city's historical sensibilities, but more likely it meant this was a city without visionary leadership and, perhaps, without hope. Jack noticed as they crossed a bridge that the Miljacka River was barely a trickle in the wide, littered bed that marked the southern boundary of the Old Town.

Adnan turned and made his way to a narrow but unremarkable street flanked by low concrete buildings just tall enough to block the sun. Checking his Google Maps, he parked in front of a driveway leading to an alley, bordering a four-story apartment complex.

"Here we are," Adnan said. "Twenty marks, please."

Jack opened his wallet and pulled out his Visa card. Adnan frowned. "Cash is better."

"Your website said you took Visa and MasterCard."

"Sure, but cash is better." Adnan saw the skeptical look in Jack's eyes. "If you do not have the cash, I will take the card. But in my country, there's a seventeen percent tax on credit cards, and a three percent fee, so I lose twenty percent if I take the card."

Twenty percent? No wonder these guys were struggling. "No problem," Jack said, and pulled out a twenty-mark bill and tossed him another ten for the tip—which, according to the travel guides, wasn't necessary to do in this part of the world. But ten marks was about six bucks, and Jack figured Adnan was working his ass off just to keep his nose above water.

"Thank you!" Adnan reached for his door handle. "Let me get your bag."

"Just pop the trunk, will you?"

"Yeah, sure." Adnan shoved a business card into Jack's hand. "You need a ride, you call Adnan, okay?"

Jack pocketed the card and grinned. "Who else would I call?"

"Oh, one more thing I should tell you. There is no water in Sarajevo from midnight to five in the morning."

"Is there a water shortage?"

Adnan shook his head, grinning. "No, no water shortage."

"Then why?"

Adnan shrugged. "Who knows? But plan accordingly."

Jack pulled his bag out of the trunk, slammed the lid, and waved good-bye as Adnan pulled away. He turned into the alley and headed for his building. He hadn't noticed the Audi sedan parked at the end of the street, let alone the man in the loose tie and rumpled suit intently marking Jack's arrival, and even if he had, he wouldn't have known the man's name was Dragan Kolak.

22

NEAR TJENTIŠTE, REPUBLIKA SRPSKA,
BOSNIA AND HERZEGOVINA

Tarik Brkić's 4x4 Nissan quad pickup arrived at the camp at
the end of the dusty road, his driver heading for the camouflaged storage facility. A bearded Tunisian raised a palm
in half salute and smiled as the Chechen commander passed.

Brkić was pleased, despite the earlier call from Red Wing.
The Tunisian was one of a group of eighteen jihadi fighters
trained and equipped here in the last two months and heading
out for Germany later tonight, soon to be replaced with fresh
new recruits from Kosovo and Macedonia. The foundation was
being laid for an independent Muslim state in the heart of Europe, guided only by sharia law, and beholden to no one but
Allah himself.

But independence was not enough. Even Red Wing understood that. Such a state would pose too great a threat to the
European powers, a humiliating reminder of the Islamic flood

that nearly swamped Europe centuries before. NATO would crush it at the first opportunity. How to protect such a state? That was where he and Red Wing differed.

As for the rest of Europe, hadn't Islamic armies once invaded Spain and Portugal? France and Austria? Italy and Hungary? Bulgaria and Greece? Crete and Malta? Hadn't Muslim fighters stormed the city gates of Constantinople, Athens, Moscow, Vienna, Lisbon, and Madrid?

Brkić believed with all of his heart that former Muslim lands would be Muslim again, and sharia would come to all of Europe, either through demographics or, sooner, by force of arms, which he preferred. As a prolific father and a ruthless fighter, he was proud that he had excelled at both.

The Nissan pulled up to the storage building and parked next to a Happy Times! tour van just as Emir stepped into view. Brkić grinned broadly and signaled for the driver to stop. He leaped out of the vehicle and embraced the smaller Bosniak in a bear hug. They were related by marriage and by blood, or at least the shedding of it.

"Emir! You bring good news?"

Emir smiled, almost shyly. "Good news, yes, but even more than that. Come."

Emir steered the larger man through the opened sliding doors of the warehouse. It was too far from the nearest paved road to be seen, even with binoculars. It was further hidden by the small draw where it was built, and flanked on three sides by towering pines. As a precaution, the steel roof was insulated inside and out with natural materials to eliminate any kind of heat signature or optical detection from overhead surveillance.

Outwardly, the building appeared to be an oversized barn. It was large enough to hold several wheeled vehicles, service bays, welding equipment, an industrial forklift, tools, and, most important, a Bosnian Army BM-21 Grad multiple rocket launcher. Stolen during the confusion of the last war, it had been stored and maintained in secret by Brkić ever since.

The Grad and its variants were the most ubiquitous multiple rocket launch systems (MRLS) in the world, in service in more than seventy countries, from Afghanistan to Zimbabwe. Of Soviet design, the Grad had been around since the 1960s, and its ease of use, simple maintenance requirements, and enormous destructive potential made it one of the most effective artillery systems ever designed.

The gasoline-powered eight-cylinder 6x6 truck mounted a box launcher of forty 122-millimeter rocket tubes, and was operated by a three-man crew. The rockets could be launched from inside the cab or externally by a trigger on the end of a sixty-four-meter cable. The BM-21's primary flaw was its accuracy. The fin-stabilized "dumb" rockets were targeted with Cold War–era optical periscopes and collimators.

Originally designed as an area denial weapon to blunt massed armor and infantry assaults, the Grad system relied on large numbers of relatively inaccurate rockets and their high explosive payloads to overwhelm opponents. Over the years, the unguided rockets increased in range and accuracy with improved engines and more reliable propellants, but the Grad was never considered a precision weapon.

Until now.

The TOS-2 Starfire 122-millimeter missile featured a new and highly efficient solid-fuel propellant, which meant a larger payload without sacrificing range. Most important, computers onboard each missile provided laser and GPS guidance that adjusted the missile fins during trajectory, allowing for minimal but sufficient in-flight maneuver to ensure highly accurate targeting. All the BM-21 launcher had to do was fire the missile in approximately the right direction and the automated, computer-controlled guidance systems would take over.

Brkić's plans now hinged on the Syrian and the magic tricks he'd brought with him.

Emir and Brkić made their way past sparking arc welders and the clang of steel hammers toward the middle of the facility, where the BM-21 Grad vehicle stood.

"Aslan!" Tarik shouted.

The big Chechen lieutenant was standing on the launch platform. He whipped around at the sound of his name.

"Commander!" he called out, and jumped down onto the concrete floor.

The two men crashed into each other in a hard embrace, long-lost comrades in a too-long war.

"It's so good to see you again, Commander," Dzhabrailov said.

Brkić beamed with pride. "Your bravery and your patience have reaped a great reward."

Dzhabrailov shrugged. "It's for our people. How can I do less?"

Like most Chechens, the lieutenant despised the Russians, a long and bitter oppressor of Chechnya. After years of suffering under the Russian boot, the latest Chechen government decided to join forces with its stronger enemy, and many young Chechen fighters joined their ranks.

Many Chechens refused to serve with the hated Russian Army. But others, like Dzhabrailov, enlisted with an eye for both gaining combat experience and exacting revenge on their ancient enemy.

Dzhabrailov had met Brkić four years before when Brkić re-cruited him into his organization. Secured communications had enabled them to formulate their plan for the stolen missiles.

Brkić clapped him on the shoulder. "Come, my young lion. Show me this miracle you have brought."

23

Dzhabrailov led Brkić and Emir to the far side of the building, where they found Walib hunched over a workbench, a wisp of smoke curling up from a soldering iron in his hand. On the table beside him was a four-inch-diameter electro-optical turret for the hand-launched, eagle-sized Elbit Systems Skylark I-LE UAV, which stood assembled on another elevated table a few feet away, stolen from the Russian arsenal as well.

"Captain, I want you to meet my commander, Tarik Brkić."

The mustachioed Syrian turned around, a smudge of solder on his cheek. His eyes were black with fatigue, but his smile was genuine. Marrying the Grad's ancient launch platform to the portable fire-control computer he'd brought in the Pelican case was taking more time and energy than he'd anticipated. He was having to improvise quite a bit. The Grad's rifled launch tubes spun the rockets like a bullet to improve flight stability and accuracy. The trajectory of a rocket's flight and its ultimate destination were determined by elevation and azimuth angles, along with the duration of engine fire, warhead weight, distance, wind speed, and a dozen other factors. Fortunately, most of these factors were known and fixed, and the variables could be measured or calculated, and all of it accounted for in the brain of the fire-control computer.

"Commander, this is Captain Walib, the Syrian Arab Army's finest rocket forces officer."

Walib extended a small, confident hand. Brkić took it.

"Aslan has told me all about you, Commander."

"And he has spoken well of you, Captain," Brkić said. He broke into a grin and pulled Walib into a bear hug and clapped him on the back, then released him from his massive embrace but kept a firm grip on Walib's hand and a big paw on his shoulder.

The commander's good eye brightened. "Welcome to Bosnia. Thanks be to God for your safe travels. You have come very far."

"Without Aslan, I never would have made it."

"Without God, neither of us would have," Dzhabrailov was quick to add. The journey had taken longer than expected, partly to avoid the Russians, who'd managed to pick up their trail early on.

Brkić stepped closer to the workbench. "How close are you to completion?"

"I have everything I need, but the work requires precision and is time-consuming."

The big Chechen bent close to the soldered electrical components, examining them with his one good eye. "We only have nine days to prepare, and there are still other pieces we need to put in place."

"I have already checked out the flight systems on the Skylark. Of course, it's an Israeli unit, so it's in perfect condition."

"Israeli?" Brkić asked.

"They make the best equipment, so naturally the Russians buy their drones from them, or copy them."

"I thought the Americans made the best drones, like the Predator."

"Interesting that you mention the Predator. It was the first drone the CIA used in live combat reconnaissance, and the first place they flew it was in the Bosnian War. That experience is what began the modern drone revolution. But the Predator was invented by an Israeli engineer who emigrated to America to start his company. The Predator is a great machine, and Abraham Karem will go down in history as one of the great inventors."

Brkić's darkening face told Walib what the Chechen thought about Jewish engineers.

The Syrian pressed on. "The Skylark is a portable unit, hand-launched, quiet, and fully automated, with a three-hour flight time for its electric engine. Two men can set it up in the field and launch it within eight minutes."

"Shafiq has trained me how to do it," Dzhabrailov said, smiling. "I'm a drone pilot now, though in truth, the operation is mostly automated."

"What is the purpose of the drone?" Brkić asked. "We know the GLONASS coordinates of the target."

"Aslan will 'paint' the target with the onboard laser. The Starfire missiles are equipped with a laser guidance system, which is the most accurate guidance system available. It drops the CEP—circular error probable—to less than one meter."

"Practically a sniper rifle," Dzhabrailov said.

Brkić's white eye flared. "But lasers don't work in bad weather."

"The weather forecast is sunny and cloudless for launch day," Walib said.

"But weather changes, especially around here."

"In case there is a problem, each missile is also equipped with a GLONASS guidance system. Also more than accurate enough for our purposes, with a CEP of less than thirteen meters."

"Like Uber, but for missiles?" Emir asked.

Walib smiled. "Perhaps. But at least with these, you don't have to tip the driver."

"And what if the GLONASS system fails?" Brkić asked.

"Highly unlikely, sir."

"Humor me, Captain."

"Then there is an onboard inertial navigation system, computerized gyroscopes and accelerometers. No guarantees at that point we will hit the target, but even so, we will land close enough to cause enormous casualties."

"Computerized, eh? And what if that fails as well?"

"Three system failures? It isn't possible," Dzhabrailov said.

Brkić jabbed a finger on the larger man's chest. "In war, anything is possible, especially the unexpected."

"Your commander is right. Technology can fail." Walib nodded at the big green 6x6 truck. "I first trained on the Grad system. It's old technology, but reliable. The rocket motors are reliable and the fuel burn rates are known quantities. A straight launch with no electronic guidance systems at all will still result in a satisfactory strike. Think of it as a very long-range, very effective mortar system."

"We cannot fail," Emir said.

Brkić nodded, satisfied. "So everything is ready?"

"Not yet. The next thing I'm doing is taking the extra precaution to confirm that the laser wavelength on the Skylark's laser designator is synched with the laser-guidance computer onboard each of the Starfire missiles."

"Excellent. Leave nothing to chance. What else is there?"

"Once the missiles are programmed and synched to the portable fire-control computer, we should move the launcher to the location we talked about, much closer to the target. The shorter the range, the better.

"Once the launcher is fixed in place, I will need to make fine gun-laying adjustments to the launcher by hand, using the Grad's mechanical traverse wheels on the stabilized platform for azimuth and elevation in milliradians. It won't be necessary to be more precise than that; the laser and GLONASS guidance will more than make up for any mechanical error."

"It will be a Day of Judgment. A glorious victory for the Dar al-Salam," Dzhabrailov said.

"That is not for us to decide," Brkić cautioned. "All we can do is work, and pray." He turned to Walib, and pounded his narrow shoulder. "But thanks to you, the work will be easier, and the prayers lighter."

"There is a reason why God brought the two of you together," Dzhabrailov said. "Your vision, Commander, and your expertise, Captain. How can we fail?"

"*Inshallah*," Emir said.

"As soon as we have all of the missiles, I can finish the other work."

Brkić frowned. "What work is that?"

Walib pointed to the open Pelican case on the floor. It contained the portable fire-control computer he'd also stolen from the Russian armory.

"With that unit, I can preprogram the exact coordinates and elevation of the target on each missile, which is critical. In my studies at the Russian artillery academy, they taught us that back in 1999, during the Yugoslav wars, the American GPS-guided JDAM bombs slammed into the Chinese embassy in Belgrade because the wrong targeting coordinates had been inputted."

Brkić grinned. "So, the Americans make mistakes?"

Walib shrugged. "At least, that was the Americans' official explanation. Of course, other sources indicate it was intentional, because they believed the Serb White Tigers were being directed out of that building."

"Fortunately for us, our target is permanently fixed, and its exact geo-coordinates are widely available on the Internet. No accidents are possible as far as the GLONASS targeting system is concerned, let alone the laser."

"Excellent."

"The computerized fire-control system also allows me to perform hardware and software checks before launch. So far, everything I've tested has been in perfect working condition, so I anticipate no problems with the other units when they arrive."

"If you need anything, come to me directly," Brkić told the Syrian. "You are the top priority. Everything we have is yours."

"What I need most is time," Walib said. "And the rest of those missiles."

"Of course." Brkić turned to Emir. "Walk with me."

Brkić and Emir exited the warehouse and headed for the trees for privacy. When they were out of earshot, the Chechen asked, "When do you expect the next shipment to arrive?"

The small Bosniak shook his head. "Tomorrow night."

"And the rest?"

"The day after, or perhaps two."

"I don't like these delays," Brkić said.

"It can't be helped. The rumors of Russians in country aren't just rumors."

"SVR?" Brkić asked, incredulous. The Russian version of the CIA.

"Perhaps. Perhaps not. I myself spoke with a driver who was stopped only last night."

"Names? Faces? Anything we can use?"

"Only that he heard Russian spoken." Emir grinned. "He still reeked of his own urine. He thought for sure they would kill him."

"I'm surprised they didn't." Brkić scratched his beard. "Did you contact your friend in the police? Tell them about these Russian spies running around? That might help our cause."

Emir shrugged. "Our police friend laughed. A murdered truck driver? Yes, that would get things moving. But a stopped truck, with no one injured and nothing taken? Who cares?"

"But they're Russians on Bosnian soil."

"These Russian devils are smart. Keeping a low profile gives them freedom of movement, and keeps the police disinterested."

"How did the Russians even find out about this?"

"We don't know." Emir shrugged again. "Of course, someone could have told them."

"Who? Walib? The Syrian?"

"We don't really know him."

"But Aslan swears by him, and I swear by Aslan. Besides, if it was the Syrian, what is there for him to gain?"

"To track us down, disrupt our operations. Kill our leadership."

"Then we would already be dead, wouldn't we? He's here." The Chechen pointed a scarred finger toward the distant road. "And the Russians are still out there." He shook his head. "No, it was God who brought us the Syrian and his missiles, not the Russians."

Emir nodded submissively. "Yes, of course."

"Do whatever you must to get the rest of those missiles delivered here, and tell me when they arrive."

Emir nodded. "God's will be done."

24

Gerry Hendley sat at his spotless desk in his top-floor office, squinting behind his reading glasses as he scrolled through the minutes of the latest European Central Bank meeting from the Bloomberg news feed on his desktop.

As director of one of the most successful privately held financial services firms in the world, he had the responsibility of staying on top of global macroeconomic news, but he employed an army of talented analysts to handle the day-to-day tactical decisions of stock trades, arbitrage plays, and other client services.

The former senator liked to dress the part of the financial mogul whether in the office or not, but today he was headed for lunch with the ranking minority leader of the Senate Finance Committee, an old colleague and bridge partner. For the occasion he wore a crisp, starched white dress shirt with French cuffs and a blue silk tie. To complement his full head of perfectly coiffed silver hair, he wore a silver Rolex watch, sterling silver medallion cuff links, and a matching silver tie bar, all offset by a charcoal-gray, pin-striped Brooks Brothers suit.

A soft knock at the door caught his attention.

"Come in."

The door pushed open and Gavin Biery stumbled in, holding his iPad in his trembling, overcaffeinated hands. His bloodshot eyes were rimmed with exhaustion after an all-nighter fueled by a steady flow of Monster drinks, peanut M&M's, and Cheetos. Wrinkled beige chinos and a crumb-dusted blue polo rounded out his disheveled-casual ensemble.

"Hi, Gerry. You sent for me?"

Hendley suppressed a smile. He hadn't hired Gavin for his sartorial splendor, but rather for his impeccable brain. Gavin was the IT manager for both Hendley Associates and The Campus, and also Gerry's best hacker.

Gerry set his reading glasses down and pointed to the overstuffed chair in front of his desk. "Pull up a chair and take a load off, son."

"Thanks." Gavin smiled weakly and fell into the leather wingback, ignoring the springs groaning under his weight.

Gerry put his computer to sleep. "I saw your e-mail. Somewhat cryptic, but it sounded urgent."

"I don't know about urgent. Interesting, maybe."

"You've got my attention. Shoot."

Gavin shifted around in his chair. "So, is Jack still going to press charges against that Elena Iliescu woman?"

"Last time I talked to him, yes. Can't say that I blame him, especially after the ice-chest revelation."

"Yeah, that was creepy, for sure. Did she press charges against him yet?"

"Strangely, no. I just got off the phone with the lawyer we hired for Jack. She thinks Iliescu is holding off, hoping that Jack will drop his charges against her."

"A Mexican standoff," Gavin said. Then he caught himself. "Is it okay to say that?"

"Who the hell knows anymore." Gerry leaned forward on his desk. "Why don't you fill me in on the details of your e-mail."

"So, just like the Slovenian police told Jack, the woman is squeaky clean. No priors, no Interpol notices, not even a ticket for jaywalking. I mean, I don't know if jaywalking's a crime over there, I've never been to—"

Gerry waved a grandfatherly hand. "Go ahead, son, get on with it."

"Anyway, I wanted to double-check her background myself, and so I broke into the Interpol network—"

"You what?"

"No worries, I've done it before, and I'm buried behind a Tor browser and a couple remote VPNs."

Gerry sighed. His IT director might as well have been chattering in Urdu, with all of his technical mumbo-jumbo. But that's why he hired Gavin in the first place. He was the best. He could hack into virtually any computer, anywhere, and hide from just about anybody.

"Go on."

"So I checked the retinal scan she has on file with Interpol, the one that gets checked when she passes through EU customs."

"And?"

"All clear."

"But you said you found something."

"Don't ask me why, but I got a bug up my nose, and I decided to pull up the retinal scan Jack sent me from the crime scene."

"And?"

"And the funny thing is, the scan Jack sent doesn't match the Interpol scan."

"How can that be?"

"I can think of a couple things, but it all boils down to the fact that somehow she's managed to get her actual retina scan to convert to a clean dummy file within the Interpol system that makes her look like Mother Teresa. Which made me think, of course, that maybe she isn't, especially since Mother Teresa was Albanian, and not—"

"Please, Gavin. Stay focused. I've got a lot on my plate today."

"Yeah, sorry." Gavin yawned like a hippo. "Sorry, I'm running on fumes."

"No worries."

"So, where was I?"

"The real versus fake retina scan."

"Oh, yeah. So, that isn't easy to do, spoofing a major database like that. Somebody's got some chops—or insider access."

"Interesting."

"The next thing I decided to do was take another run at her in some of the other databases I have access to."

"Such as?"

"It's better if you don't know. I mean, legally."

"Humor me."

"Well, I took a gander at TIDE. She isn't listed there."

"How the hell did you break into TIDE?" Gerry couldn't believe it. The Terrorist Identities Datamart Environment was one of the most highly classified databases in the intelligence community, shared by the CIA, FBI, NSA, and every other alphabet agency he could think of.

"I'd rather not say. But it's what you hire me to do."

"You're right. So, what did you find in your other searches besides TIDE?"

"Nothing to write home about. She always came up squeaky clean. She's some sort of a consultant. Lots of international travel, lots of airline and hotel miles, mostly in Europe. I checked her tax records. She has a steady income, but with irregular bumps. Some kind of bonus structure is my guess."

"You got her tax records?"

Gavin shrugged. "Sure. No big deal."

"Did you find out her favorite brand of toothpaste?"

Gavin frowned and pulled up a screen on his tablet. "I didn't realize you needed that. Let me see if I can find it."

"I'm joking, son. Sorry to interrupt your train of thought. Please continue."

"So, I started digging into the consulting firm she works for. Again, clean, nothing unusual or suspicious, except that the firm sometimes billed for work with one particular company with a Jersey office."

"You mean the state, or the country?"

"The country."

"A banking haven," Gerry said. "One of the Ten Dwarfs."

"Exactly. So I dug a little further on that and got the names of the board of directors of that Jersey company, and one of them is a British citizen. Well, I have access to an MI6 back door you probably shouldn't know about. It turns out that this director fellow is suspected of being somehow connected to an organization known as the Iron Syndicate."

Gerry frowned. "What the hell is the Iron Syndicate?"

Gavin shrugged. "Can't say exactly. MI6 was referencing it in regards to Afghan heroin, Libyan MANPADS, and human trafficking in Malawi. But they didn't have anything else."

"Holy cow. A global criminal enterprise that large and I've never even heard of it."

"I kept digging around but couldn't find anything else. CIA, DIA—all dead ends. So I put some bots together a couple hours ago and sent them off into the Net on their own to bird-dog this thing. They haven't turned up anything yet, but I hope to get something by the end of day."

"'Hope'? That doesn't sound like you."

"That's what's freaking me out. These Iron Syndicate guys are good at hiding secrets. Like, government-level good."

"You think this Iron Syndicate is a foreign agency?"

"Not really. More like a private outfit would be my guess. But given the quality of the OPSEC—"

Gerry sat up. "Rogue foreign intel officers?"

"Rogue or retired. Or both."

"What would connect heroin, arms, and human trafficking?"

"Money," Gavin said. "It's all lucrative stuff. That's why I think it's private enterprise, not some kind of government-sanctioned thing."

"You 'think'—but you're not certain?"

"Intel agencies have done the same kind of thing, even worse. So I can't be sure."

"You're right. We can't be. But Jack's still connected to this somehow, through Elena Iliescu."

"Yeah. She wanted to kill him."

"A personal vendetta? Or a hired hit for the Iron Syndicate?"

Gavin scrolled through his iPad again. "I mean, judging by her travel schedule and her income stream, I'd say she was definitely a professional hitter."

"Hired to hit Jack?"

"Again, I can't be sure at this point. But I broke into her cell network, and of course I have access to Jack's."

Gavin pulled up a screen with a video graphic and slid the iPad over to Gerry.

"Jack said the cops told him she'd driven in from Trieste, so I tracked her cell phone starting the day Jack was in London, eleven days ago. You can see her movement around Trieste, and, by the time stamp, you can see she picked up and headed to Ljubljana the day after Jack left London."

Gavin reached across the desk and swiped the screen for Gerry, pulling up a new video.

"And here you can see Jack's cell pinging in the city, and hers. Notice how closely she stays next to him—got within a hundred feet of him a couple times."

"So she was definitely tracking him," Gerry said.

"No question."

"And she followed him up to—where was it?"

"Kozjak Falls. And actually, she got there ahead of him by about two hours. Here." Gavin picked up the tablet and scrolled to another page and showed him.

Gerry examined the tablet. "She knew where he was going."

"Maybe she tapped a phone or got a bug planted somewhere. But it wasn't an accident she bumped into Jack up there." Gavin cleared his throat. "Perfect place for a hit, especially if she planned on beheading him. I mean, not that I've ever done that sort of thing."

Gerry leaned back in his chair, flipping through Gavin's tablet. "The place is pretty remote." He studied a police photo of the crime scene: picnic bench, ice chest, bone saw. "Let's assume you're right and this woman was hired to kill Jack. We need to find out why."

"She would know."

"And she isn't talking, at least not officially." Gerry sat up and reached for his laptop. "Maybe it's time to arrange an unofficial chat with Ms. Iliescu. Find out more about the Iron Syndicate, and why they ordered a hit on Jack."

"Should we call the Feds in on this?"

"No, we don't have proof of anything yet to give them, and we're still just making educated guesses. Besides, they're going to want to know my intel sources, and neither of us wants that."

"Agreed. So what makes you think she'll talk to us?"

"Assuming she is a pro, that means she's been hired by somebody for a chunk of cash. By not filing charges against Jack, she might be sending a signal that she's looking for more money."

Gerry woke up his computer and pulled up a list of phone numbers. "On the other hand, she failed her assignment, and that means she's in trouble with her employers, so my guess is she might be looking for protection. Either way, I know just the guy who can suss it out."

Gerry dialed a number, then held up a finger toward Gavin. "Excuse me for one second."

"Of course." Gavin's eyes drifted to the photographs of the ex-senator posing with presidents, kings, movie stars, and business titans over the years. The most prominent one featured Gerry and President Ryan, close friends for many years and cofounders of The Campus and Hendley Associates.

A few rings later, someone picked up on the other end.

"Dom? It's Gerry. I have an assignment for you. Might make a nice little vacation for you and Adara—and Midas, too, come to think of it. I'll set up a conference call from my end and fill in the details."

Gerry hung up and turned to Gavin. "Nice work, Gav. I'll keep you in the loop. In the meantime, keep digging around for whatever you can find on this Iron Syndicate."

"If the syndicate knows she failed her hit, you know they'll send somebody else for Jack."

"I told Jack that, but he says he's got something to finish before he can come back where we can keep an eye on him."

Gavin frowned with worry. "The fact we've never heard of these Iron Syndicate people makes me extremely nervous."

"I'm worried, too. That's why we've got to find out what's really going on and who's behind it."

25

Jack met the apartment owners briefly, a charming young Bosniak couple, both high school teachers, who showed him around the spotless two-bedroom apartment decked out in IKEA furniture and local art. They left him a set of keys and a couple maps, along with a small pot full of dark, rich ground beans and instructions on how to brew a cup of Bosnian coffee.

This was his first Airbnb rental, and he was extremely pleased. Half the price of a hotel, and twice as nice. The only bummer was that the building's garbage chute was located on the third-floor landing across from his front door. Fortunately, the smell didn't reach inside the apartment.

Jack changed into shorts and a linen flannel shirt and headed out, pulling on a pair of Oakleys against the bright sun. He was famished, but fortunately, his first "Aida" target worked at a restaurant with great TripAdvisor reviews in the Turkish part of the Old Town. It was about a ten-minute walk from his place. He was looking forward to stretching his legs and seeing Sarajevo up close and personal, and the part of town where he was headed was a pedestrian zone.

A few blocks from his apartment, he crossed the Latin Bridge heading north, stopping at the traffic light just as a battered trolley car came screeching to a halt. He glanced across the street and saw the sign on the building and it suddenly hit him. This was the street corner where Archduke Ferdinand and his wife were assassinated in 1914.

It was a dope slap, for sure.

Jack had studied World War I in high school. He'd watched the grainy film footage of soldiers swarming out of their trenches through barbed wire and mortar fire and into no-man's-land only to be machine-gunned down by the thousands, or gassed, or blown apart by concentrated artillery fire. Millions of soldiers and civilians were butchered in a war that served no purpose other than to lay the foundations for the next one, an even bloodier affair. All of that carnage that laid waste to an entire generation, all triggered by the pistol shots of a Bosnian Serb nationalist fired here.

Right here.

The assassination was one of the most historically significant events in the past two hundred years: the Russian Revolution, the collapse of the Austro-Hungarian and Ottoman Empires, the rise of the United States as a world power, the beginning of the end of the British Empire. Those fatal gunshots also gave rise to Lenin, Stalin, Mussolini, Franco, Hitler. The whole world crumbled in the earthquake that was the

Great War, and this place was the epicenter, where it all originated.

It was practically hallowed ground, wasn't it?

But as Jack glanced around, all he saw were locals marching off to work with cell phones stuck in their ears, frustrated car drivers, a couple old-timers shuffling aimlessly along, teenagers lugging book bags. Their faces were heavy with frustration or fear, or numbed with boredom and fatigue. Just everyday people, trudging through history as casually as they would through a shabby shopping mall.

The light turned green and Jack crossed with a woman who tossed her smoldering cigarette onto the street, maybe right at the place where nineteen-year-old Gavrilo Princip stood and pulled the trigger. To these people, it was all so ordinary and familiar. How could that be?

Jack stepped onto the curb and stood in front of the museum commemorating the terrible event. It was just a single room, occupying the bottom floor of a three-story building standing on the corner. He found a plain, simple inscription in Bosanski and English on an unremarkable stone slab on the museum's outer wall:

FROM THIS PLACE ON 28 JUNE 1914 GAVRILO PRINCIP ASSASSI-
NATED THE HEIR TO THE AUSTRO-HUNGARIAN THRONE FRANZ FER-
DINAND AND HIS WIFE SOFIA.

That was it?

Unbelievable, Jack thought. He'd seen Chevrolet ads with more emotion. It seemed as if the city was hardly trying to remember this tragedy. Or they were trying to ignore it. Maybe they didn't want to be blamed for all the inconsolable suffering and death that followed.

Jack was suddenly as depressed as he was confused.

He was tempted to check out the museum, but his gurgling stomach told him to wait until some other time. Jack turned and walked north. With any luck, he'd find the girl and a good meal all at the same time.

A few blocks up and Jack was formally in the Old Town, his Merrell Moab Ventilators clopping on limestone pavement stones smoothed by three hundred years of foot traffic.

Suddenly the grime of the working-class city behind him was transformed into a Turkish bazaar, the wide streets lined with shops of every kind selling jewelry, clothes, artwork, books, and food.

Lots of food.

And the streets were suddenly crowded, too, mostly tourists. Europeans, certainly, and Asians. But he also saw his first Muslim woman in Sarajevo covered from head to toe, her eyes alone exposed beneath her *niqab*, walking alongside a bearded Muslim man in Western slacks and a shirt. Were they locals? Tourists? He wasn't sure.

He passed by the wall of the Gazi Husrev-beg Mosque with a fountain on the corner where passersby stooped to drink water from a spigot with their cupped hands. Google Maps steered him left, and three minutes later he stood in front of a wrought-iron archway opening into a small courtyard between two buildings with wood tables and bench seating jammed with diners. Small, clear electric lights hung from the branches of trees overhanging the courtyard. Bosnian folk music played on the outdoor speakers, but it could hardly be heard over the laughter and loud, friendly banter of people having a good time.

There wasn't a breeze of any sort, and Jack felt a small trickle of sweat sliding down his spine as he stood there searching for a place to sit. The tables were crowded with plates of delicious-looking food and glasses full of wine and beer, and quite a few cigarettes. It was a good vibe and obviously a popular place.

He glanced through the open door of the air-conditioned restaurant interior and saw a standing-room-only crowd inside and no empty tables or even a space to stand at the busy bar. Even if Aida was in there, he wouldn't have the chance to talk to her.

"You want table? Over there," a waitress said, nodding her ponytailed brunette head toward an empty two-seater in the back of the courtyard while she balanced plates of lamb kebabs and fish. Her left ear was pierced with at least ten small hoops, and tiny blue star tattoos were clustered on her neck.

"Great, thanks. Is Aida Curić here?" Jack asked, but the waitress had turned her back to him and was delivering food to an eager table of hungry young Germans.

Jack made his way carefully through the choreographed chaos of flying waitresses, harried busboys, and shuffling tourists passing in and out of the restaurant. He kept his eye peeled for a pretty blonde with blue eyes. He assumed Aida was a waitress, but maybe she was a cook or tended the bar. Gavin's notes weren't that specific. He figured he'd order food and try again to ask whoever his waitress was about her after he ate. It was still early and he couldn't imagine this Curić woman would bail out of her shift before the dinner crowd got rolling and the tips started dropping, especially if she was a server.

Jack wedged past a bench with a fat Spaniard bulging into the walkway on one side and the gangly legs of a couple tall Finns on the other, then excused himself past three plus-sized women before dropping into the seat behind the small open table he was aiming for. He picked up the menu that was thankfully in English as well as a few other languages, and scanned the selections.

Where the hell was the *ćevapi*?

The waitress with the ponytail and the fishing tackle on her ear carried bottles of beer wedged between her fingers, dropping them off along the way before reaching Jack's remote location.

"You decide?" she asked with a harried smile.

"No *ćevapi*?"

"Not here. Ćevabdžinica Petica Ferhatović is best."

Jack assumed that was the name of another restaurant. He'd figure it out later. "What's good here?"

"Bosnian Pot. It's a kind of soup. Very local."

"Sounds good. And your best local beer, too. Please."

"Okay," she said as she snatched up his menu and scampered off.

Jack kept scanning the courtyard while waiting for his order, hoping to catch sight of Aida. He was too far back on the patio to see inside the restaurant. A few minutes later, a giant bowl of soup and a cold bottle of Sarajevska beer arrived. He dug into his bowl greedily, savoring the lean, spicy beef that practically melted in his mouth, along with the soft wedges of potato, sweet onions, and crunchy vegetables in the rich, red broth. It was really more like a stew than a soup. He washed it down with the smooth, drinkable lager that tasted especially good and even a little sweet chasing the soup's mild spices.

By the time he spooned up the last bite of soup his waitress had reappeared with another beer in her hand.

"How'd you know?" Jack asked.

She smiled, her eyes flashing with just a little bit more than professional interest. "You have the look."

"What look is that? A dumb American?"

"No, just thirsty." She set the beer down on the table. "Anything else you want, thirsty American?"

"Yeah, maybe you can help me. Is Aida Ćurić here tonight?"

Her interested smile suddenly faded. "Yes."

"Do you mind asking her to come over here?"

"She's busy."

"It's important."

She shrugged, resigned to her disappointment and clearly annoyed. "I will tell her."

Jack watched her bobbing ponytail disappear into the restaurant. A minute later, a pretty, young blonde appeared, followed by a man with a close-shaved head and a serious addiction to weightlifting and, quite possibly, steroids, to judge from the unnatural shape of his upper body.

The blonde approached his table. The man stood behind her, glowering at Jack over her shoulder. A few heads turned to watch the show unfolding.

The woman's piercing blue eyes narrowed, and her small mouth curled with a question. "You asked for me?"

"You're Aida Ćurić?"

"Obviously. Is there something you need?"

Jack ignored the Hulk behind her, his nostrils flaring. Jack had the feeling that if he waved his handkerchief the guy would start pawing the ground and charge him.

"I'm sorry to bother you, Ms. Ćurić. I tried calling earlier, but nobody picked up. My name is Jack Ryan, and I think I'm looking for you."

She frowned with confusion at the strangely worded statement. "Sorry?"

"I'm looking for a young woman about your age who was injured years ago in the war. Her name was Aida Curić and—"

"My birth name is Lulić." She nodded to one side, indicating the goon behind her. She raised her left hand and flashed a diamond wedding band. "My husband's name is Curić. So is mine now."

"Well, then you can't be the Aida Curić I'm looking for. Sorry to have bothered you."

"Anything else?" she asked.

"My check, please."

Jack drained his beer waiting for the check, leaving cash and an enormous tip for the trouble he'd caused and his slight embarrassment. He now realized this little adventure was fraught with a few more challenges than he'd anticipated.

At least the beer and the Bosnian Pot were good.

NEAR BIOKOVO, BOSNIA AND HERZEGOVINA

The small, idyllic farm was surrounded on three sides by gently sloping, forested hills and bounded by a burbling creek that ran all year except for the winters, when it froze. The traditional whitewashed one-story house appeared gray in the quarter moon, and the red roof tiles grayer still. The sturdy barn stood nearby, topped with cedar shingles slathered in moss. Part of the meadow was surrounded by a stack rail fence to accommodate three milk cows, and another part was a neatly groomed truck garden behind the house, plowed by a swaybacked horse now bedded down in the barn with the cows for the night.

The squad of black-uniformed men approached from out of the tree line, with red-checkered Croat militia CRUSADER KNIGHTS unit patches sewn on the sleeves. They carried suppressed AK-74UB long guns with night-vision optics, far more firepower than what they needed for this operation. But it wasn't the elderly Serb farmers inside the house they were worried about.

Tarik Brkić was kitted out like the others but didn't wear a balaclava. No need. He remained in the tree line one hundred meters back, and, thanks to his blinded white eye, used a Gen 3 night-vision monocular to supervise the operation.

He watched as flash-bangs flared and popped inside the farmhouse, and a moment later came the dull flash and muffled chatter of suppressed small-arms firing. The only scream that arose was snuffed out in another short burst.

Four of his men dragged the bodies onto the lawn and splayed them out in a row, a slaughtered choir robed in blood.

"Don't forget the note," Brkić whispered in his comms, staring through his monocular.

The ghosted green hand of his number two reached into a coat pocket and held the envelope high. The envelope and the letter inside both bore the dreaded crossed swords and red-checkered shield of the infamous Crusader Knights militia.

"Got it," he replied in Brkić's earpiece as he pinned the note to the old man's bullet-ridden nightshirt.

Brkić also heard three dull pops in his ear. Three more of his men in the barn had just dispatched the animals in short order.

But the crack of a branch behind him caught the big Chechen by surprise.

He whipped around, scanning the trees with his one good eye.

Three meters away, pale moonlight illumined a barefoot Serbian boy in nightclothes, staring at him, his wide eyes fixated on the Chechen's rifle.

The boy was about the same age and height as his own seventh son. He even looked like him.

The boy's eyes locked with his. Brkić recognized the horrified shudder. His milk-white eye did that to children, even the ones who knew him.

Brkić smiled, gesturing the boy forward with a gloved hand. "Everything is going to be okay."

The boy stood frozen in place, trembling. His terrified face grew brighter in the rising yellow light of a roaring fire far behind Brkić's shoulder.

But it was the scream of the burning horse that made the boy suddenly gasp.

The flickering catchlight of the fire danced in the boy's dark eyes in the clear German optics of the Chechen's rifle. A muffled pop and the spray of black blood behind the child's head ended his terror. His body crumbled to the ground like a puppet when its strings are cut, crunching in the pine needles where it fell, as the first of his men thundered up behind him.

"Who was that?" one of them asked.

"Time to go," was all Brkić said.

Ten minutes later they were in their vehicles and far away, long before the fire would even be noticed or reported.

Red Wing had called for sharper measures, Brkić thought, as they sped along the two-lane road. Tonight they had delivered, with evidence left behind to spread the tale of Croatian crimes, written in blood and lead.

And the corpse of a nameless boy.

Brkić prayed his parents would find him before the rats did.

Inshallah.

26

After his embarrassing first attempt at finding his mother's Aida Curić, Jack decided to try working the phones harder and avoiding personal contact. He came to realize that if a Bosnian appeared out of nowhere and walked into his office at Hendley Associates and asked if he was Jack Ryan, he'd be suspicious as hell.

Before he went to bed, he dove into his first three calls. They were nearly as awkward as the encounter earlier in the evening had been, but he played the bumbling American role pretty well, apologizing after every question and acknowledging that what he was doing was strange. All three calls were strikeouts, but he was encouraged. He showered and hit the sack early, determined to make a day of it tomorrow.

———

After a cup of steaming-hot Jocko White Tea, he made his first two phone calls for the day. They went faster and felt less awkward than the previous ones, and also resulted in two more names getting crossed off the list.

Six down, five to go.

He popped on the news and caught the local weather. Cool this morning, but it was going to be another warm and perfect day. No point in staying cooped up in the apartment. He decided he could make his calls from a breakfast joint just as well.

He'd noticed the day before that he was the only guy on the street wearing shorts. He wondered if that was a cultural thing or even a taboo. But then again, it was brisk this morning, so pants made sense and it made him look just a little more professional.

He found a TripAdvisor review for a place on the edge of the Old Town and dropped in. The small restaurant was crowded with people grabbing coffee and pastries to go. Jack spotted a seat by the window and beelined for it.

He took the advice of one of the TripAdvisor commenters and ordered a Bosnian coffee and a crunchy chocolate-hazelnut pastry called a *pita*. The doughnut-shaped pastry was phyllo dough, and the dense, gooey filling tasted like Nutella.

Full of fat, sugar, and countless carbs, the flaky pastry might have been the best damn thing he'd ever eaten.

Knowing he'd have to run at least an extra ten miles next week to burn off the additional calories, he passed on getting a second *pita* and instead ordered another cup of dark, rich

Bosnian coffee, smoother and less harsh than a full espresso, and sweetened with two small sugar cubes, Bosnian style.

Fortified with sugar and caffeine and happy to people-watch through the big picture window, Jack began his next round of calls.

The next Aida, number seven, was a harried bank clerk who assured him in no uncertain terms he had the wrong person, and number eight's mother informed him her daughter had immigrated to Australia two weeks ago. But he sounded like a nice man, she said, and she had a lovely daughter named Amina, who worked as a bookkeeper, and perhaps he would like to meet her?

Number nine was unemployed and living at home with her parents, and, unfortunately, she wasn't the one he was looking for, either, she said in the form of an apology.

The tenth call was not only nice but sympathetic and, even though she wasn't the woman he was looking for, offered her services to help him in his search. Jack thanked her but politely declined.

One Aida left.

Despite his failure so far, he was encouraged. Nearly everyone he spoke with this morning was not only nice but even understanding. He picked up the phone and dialed the number, but it went straight to voice mail in Bosanski. He hated leaving voice mails in his own language, let alone with such a strange request, so he hung up. He double-checked the address of her employment and discovered she worked in a bookstore just a few blocks away.

Jack paid his bill and tip with cash and headed out the door. Within twenty feet, he was out of the pedestrian part of the Old Town and walking down one of the main thoroughfares bisecting the capital city, Maršala Tita—Marshal Tito Street. Bustling with traffic and pedestrians, it felt like a downtown street of any large American city, except for the minarets in the distance and the noticeable lack of skyscrapers.

He reached the bookstore in no time, a modern European-style shop featuring children's books in several languages in the large picture window.

The young woman behind the counter greeted him with a warm smile. Her name tag identified her as Aida Curić as well as the store manager. A thick lick of blond hair peeked out beneath her fashionable pink patterned headscarf. She spoke softly and with an accent somewhat different from what he'd heard before, but she was extraordinarily polite and even interested in meeting him, possibly because no one else was in the store and she was bored.

After handing her his business card, he noticed that her left eye tended toward an outward drift—something that could've been caused by an injury. His hopes rose. This might well be the woman he'd been searching for. But he didn't feel comfortable asking the shy young woman about her lazy eye, and he was glad he hadn't when she informed him she had moved to Sarajevo from Izmir, Turkey, only in the past year.

She explained to him that there were as many Bosniaks living in Turkey as there were in Bosnia itself, and that Turks and Bosniaks both here and in Turkey thought more highly of one another than they did of Americans. She assured him she did not mean this as an insult.

He assured her he didn't take it that way and thanked her for her time, trying desperately to hide his disappointment behind his practiced smile.

Time to return to his apartment and regroup.

———

Jack marched back down the street past the corner of the assassination and caught himself almost missing it because he was running through options in his brain about next steps. Discouraged as he was that all eleven Aidas didn't pan out, he was more determined than ever to see if he could still find her.

But how?

It was six hours earlier in Virginia and way too early to call Gavin, but he had a couple ideas.

As he was crossing the Latin Bridge, it suddenly occurred to him that there was something else about Bookstore Aida that caught his eye. The lick of blond hair strategically located on her forehead was *very* blond. So much so, he wondered if it was natural.

By the time he jogged up the staircase two steps at a time and opened the apartment's heavy steel door, he'd already composed an e-mail to Gavin in his mind. After hitting the head and washing up, he opened up his laptop and logged on to the apartment Wi-Fi and Google-searched a factoid he seemed to recall about blondes.

He then composed the e-mail, first of all thanking Gavin for the outstanding list of names, which, unfortunately, didn't pan out, so would he mind putting together another list for him? This time searching for brown-haired women instead.

To drive home the point, he added a link to an article he found and explained to Gavin that a lot of young women who are blond when they're children find that their hair turns brown or chestnut just before they enter puberty. He signed off with "Let me know your thoughts" and "Thanks again."

Jack was a huge fan of Gavin's, even though the tubby IT

genius was kind of a smart-ass. He knew Gavin was covered up to his eyeballs in work, and he knew he was asking him to go the extra mile, but Gavin was his best shot at finding the elusive Aida Curić.

He hit the send button and went to the living room to check out the local TV, always a great window into any culture. He flipped through a dozen channels. They were all American programs, mostly reality shows, with a few familiar cop and medical dramas, all in English but with subtitles. No wonder everybody around here spoke good English. The only reality show he ever watched was on there, too: *Forged in Fire*, where bladesmiths and farriers competed to forge iconic combat swords from history.

But he hadn't come to Sarajevo to watch American television. He kept searching until he could find true local programming, and that was a news show. It wasn't in English and it didn't have English subtitles, but the shaky, handheld footage of covered bodies on the grass and cops swarming around what looked like the smoldering ruins of a barn told him all he needed to know.

Bad shit happens here, too.

27

Since Gavin probably wouldn't be responding for a while, Jack decided to venture back out and do some sightseeing, and finally find a place to grab some *ćevapi* for lunch.

Jack decided that the first place he wanted to check out was the assassination museum. He followed his familiar route to the Latin Bridge. From his Google search on the plane to London, he'd learned that Sarajevo was eighty percent Muslim, so he presumed that eight out of ten people he passed were Muslims. There were a half-dozen women in very casual headscarves like the one Bookstore Aida wore, but far more women wore nothing on their heads, and some were dressed scandalously. Same with the men: jeans, soccer shirts, polos. There was nothing to indicate their religious affiliations at all, save for the one old man he saw shuffling along, his hands clasped behind his back, prayer beads rolling absentmindedly through his fingers.

It was always exciting for Jack to find himself in a new country and a new culture. He tried to drink in everything he saw and encountered, down to the smallest detail. He was on vacation, not an op, but he was trained to be observant. Situational awareness was the first and best form of self-defense, and that meant being aware of one's surroundings and the people in them. As it turned out, that skill set came in really handy on vacations.

And though he couldn't be sure, the man in the sport coat and Ray-Bans seemed to be tracking him from a discreet distance, and doing so better than most.

Or maybe not. Sometimes his training made him paranoid.

Jack crossed the bridge and the traffic light and entered the modest little museum, paying about six dollars American at the small ticket window inside. He could stand in one place and glance around the room and see just about everything, but since he bought the ticket he decided to take advantage of the exhibits.

The subject matter covered more than just the assassination, depicting life in Sarajevo from 1878 to 1918. It started with a display of immaculate breech-loading rifles with ivory inlay from the nineteenth-century revolt against the Ottoman Turks. He proceeded on to some furniture displays, singing competition medals, famous mustachioed administrators, and other random "slice of life" presentations. What really caught Jack's eye were the two life-sized mannequins depicting the archduke and his wife in their regalia.

The only other people in the little museum were four teenage kids bowing and curtseying before the royal couple, half clowning around and, in a way, not. One of the girls politely asked Jack if he'd take a photo of them doing that again, so he grabbed her Samsung Galaxy phone and snapped a couple shots as they repeated their genuflections.

On the other side of the creepy mannequins was the glass-box display that he'd come to see. The first thing that grabbed his attention was the picture of the assassin, Gavrilo Princip, the nineteen-year-old Bosnian Serb who killed the couple and sparked a holocaust. The guy didn't look like a fiery revolutionary or a thoughtful ideologue or even very bright. Apparently, he was too short to be accepted into regular military service. There was nothing in his eyes or his stature or his looks that drew your attention. He was just an ordinary kid with a thin mustache and a bad haircut.

But unlike other teenagers his age, he had the blood of millions on his hands, or, at least, the blood of two people he considered oppressors. Maybe Princip read Jefferson just as Ho Chi Minh had—quoting Jefferson in stinging rebuke of his American enemies during the Vietnam War.

The Serbian assassin wanted what every nationalist wanted: freedom and independence for his people from the oppression of foreign powers. No wonder a lot of Serbs still considered him a hero. But to everyone else, he was just another terrorist.

The other thing that really grabbed Jack's attention was the pistol on display, with the claim that it was the weapon Princip had used to carry out the murders. What struck Jack was how completely unremarkable it was, almost primitive, even for those days. Jack knew enough about the actual event, with its multiple failures and incredible coincidences, to believe that God or history or some other force had decided that Ferdinand was supposed to die that day, no matter what.

Jack's moment of philosophical musing was interrupted by the phone vibrating in his pocket. It was Gavin. Having seen enough, he stepped outside into the warm sunlight.

"Hey, Gavin, kinda early for you, isn't it?"

Gavin yawned on the other end of the line. "I was just hot-dropping my frigate through a wormhole."

"Excuse me?"

"EVE Online, dude. You should play."

"Thanks for calling, Gav. You got my e-mail, I take it?"

"Sure did. Sorry that other list didn't work out. There were some real cuties. Any chance you at least got a date or two out of it?"

Jack laughed. "Not exactly why I'm here. But thanks anyway. So, do you think you can pull another list together for me?"

"Won't be a problem, but it will take a little while. I remember culling out a bunch of candidates from the original search because I was only looking for blondes. Shouldn't take more than thirty minutes, maybe less."

"Wow. That fast?"

"We aim to please."

"Shoot that to me as soon as you can. And thanks again. I really do appreciate it."

"It's for your mom, dude. No problem."

Gavin hung up and Jack pocketed his phone. That was really good news, Jack thought. But it also meant he needed to get back to his place. He'd have to do his sightseeing some other time, and his *ćevapi* would have to wait.

He turned and headed back for the Latin Bridge. It was a good thing there wasn't a tollbooth at this crosswalk, otherwise he'd be paying a fortune. It just proved how good the Airbnb apartment's location was.

Jack kept an eye out for the man in the Ray-Bans in his peripheral vision but didn't pick anyone up as he sped past knots of tourists and locals checking out the fruits and vegetables at an outdoor stand.

He turned off the main street and onto a narrower one, then left again onto the street facing his building, past a bar where two old men smoked cigarettes and drank beer in the sunshine. He turned the next corner into the little alleyway leading to the parking lot that fronted his entrance and turned sharply again and slammed his back against the wall of his building.

Listening.

The soft clop of leather soles on concrete stuttered nearer. A suit coat turned the corner—

Jack grabbed the heavily muscled man by the lapels and spun him around in a one-eighty, like a ballroom swing. The man's wide back slammed into the concrete wall and he *oof*ed as he hit, his Ray-Bans clattering to the ground.

"Who the hell—" But Jack was cut short by an unexpected elbow punch to his chest. It was weak because the man had no momentum behind the thrust, but it was hard enough to knock Jack's grip loose.

But before the man could throw another punch, Jack was already in counterattack mode, returning the favor of an elbow strike, but this one fired straight into the man's pockmarked face.

The man howled as the cartilage in his nose broke, gushing blood onto his shirt.

Jack pulled his arm back to launch a devastating strike with his right fist when a pistol racked behind his ear.

Oh, shit.

28

The Italian customs officer boarded the Gulfstream 550 in the FBO hangar at the Trieste airport, and after a cursory inspection stamped passports and wished everyone a good stay in his country.

Dominic "Dom" Caruso, Adara Sherman, and Bartosz "Midas" Jankowski deplaned without luggage. The director of transportation, Lisanne Robertson, a former Marine and the newest member of The Campus team, stayed behind, in keeping with her role as security for the plane and crew, though nobody believed that the sleepy port city posed much of a threat to anybody on this operation.

The three Americans picked up the rental van that Lisanne had arranged, and headed for Nova Gorica, just thirty minutes across the border. The Trieste airport was the closet one in the region to the small Slovenian city. Paradoxically, the quickest route was also the longest, according to the GPS, but even that "highway" was only a two-lane through mostly flat farm country, heading toward the mountains. They passed through a customs station without issue and arrived at the police directorate complex in Nova Gorica in less than an hour.

Gerry Hendley put Dom in the lead for this particular mission, though he had fewer years in the field as an operative than Midas, a retired U.S. Army Ranger colonel. Not that the rock-jawed snake eater couldn't break down an Iraqi insurgent or a Taliban fighter in a field interrogation under combat conditions, but as an FBI agent seconded to The Campus, Dom had the superior experience and qualifications to conduct a softer, civilian investigation. Normally, Gerry would have sent Ding Chavez or John Clark to head up an operation like this, but the two of them were in Pretoria, South Africa, on a consult with the "Recces"—the South African Special Forces Brigade. Dom was glad for the chance to show his leadership skills.

The goal today was to first meet Detective Oblak and discuss Jack's case and, after gaining his confidence, persuade him to arrange a meeting with Elena Iliescu to try to get her to open up about the attack and her possible connection to the Iron Syndicate.

Dom suggested Midas wait in the van while he and Adara made the first attempt. Two people, one a woman, would appear less threatening than three in a room.

A frosted-haired woman in a gray jumpsuit and wearing a photo badge sat behind the small security desk in the lobby, focused intently on her computer screen. Dom approached her with a big, friendly smile.

Dober dan—Good morning—were the only two words of Slovenian that Dom spoke, and he'd picked that up from

Google Translate only ten minutes ago. He'd found over the years that just saying hello in the local language broke the ice, especially with overworked bureaucrats.

The middle-aged woman glanced up from her screen with a sour look on her face, like somebody had double-dipped a chip in her guacamole.

"Dober dan."

Clearly his mastery of Slovenian wasn't up to snuff, Dom thought. So much for breaking the ice. He soldiered on.

"We have an appointment to see Detective Oblak."

"Your identity papers, please."

Dom and Adara handed over their passports. Dom included his FBI credentials in a separate wallet.

The woman scanned the documents, unimpressed. She handed them back.

"Let me check his log." Her red-lacquered nails clacked on the keyboard. A screen pulled up. She shook her head.

"Detective Oblak isn't here."

Dom stepped closer to the desk. "I'm sorry? There must be some confusion. He's expecting us." He wanted to add, "And we've traveled over four thousand miles to get here," but he bit his tongue. Quantico had taught him that little trick. "Keeps an agent from sticking his foot in his yapper," his training officer had explained.

"He's not available. He's out in the field."

"Perhaps you can call him for us? It's quite urgent."

The woman frowned an *Are you kidding me?* glance over the top of her reading glasses.

Adara smiled. "We wouldn't ask if it wasn't extremely important."

The woman sighed, picked up a cordless phone, and dialed. A man's voice answered on the other end. They chatted in Slovenian. Dom and Adara didn't understand a word.

The woman's eyebrows raised. She handed Dom the phone. "Detective Oblak will speak to you."

"Thanks." Dom took the receiver. "This is Dominic Caruso."

"Mr. Caruso, I'm sorry I missed our appointment in regards to Elena Iliescu. I'm at the hospital right now. Why don't you come over here and we can discuss the matter further."

"In the hospital? Are you okay?"

"I'm fine. Thank you for asking. It's Elena Iliescu you should be asking about."

"How is she?"

"She's quite dead."

"Dead? How?"

"It's obvious," Oblak said in a flat, even voice. "You killed her."

29

'm sorry, but I don't know what you're talking about," Dom said into the phone, glancing over at Adara. She was clearly concerned.

"When your office set the appointment to meet with me to discuss her case, you signed her death warrant."

"That's a serious accusation. Like you said, maybe we need to come over there and talk about it."

"I'll text you the address, Mr. Caruso. Meet me in the morgue. And please, drive carefully. The roads here are quite dangerous."

n their respective lines of work, Dom and Adara, a former combat medic, had seen plenty of corpses in their day, many of them in states of ruin so horrific they wouldn't dare describe them to their civilian friends.

But Elena Iliescu's lifeless body on the coroner's slab was pristine. Her firm, toned body was completely intact. Even her breasts were full and round, no doubt the result of skillful plastic surgery.

Rather than dead, she appeared to be just sleeping. Dom swore she'd wake up at any minute.

"The coroner will confirm the cause of death this afternoon, but the attending physician assures me it was heart failure, likely brought on by a catastrophic myocardial infarction. Iliescu was dead at the scene."

"Where was she when she died?"

"We put her in one of our safe houses, under police protection, as per her request."

"And I take it no one came in or out of the house?"

"Only the clinic nurse who was called in when Iliescu complained of a minor headache." At Dom's skeptical look he added, "We checked her out. That nurse has worked at that clinic for eleven years."

Adara pointed at the corpse. "She's in better shape than most Olympic athletes. She can't be more than thirty-five years old."

"Thirty-two, according to her passport," Oblak said.

"A heart attack for a woman this age and in this condition is highly unlikely," Adara said.

"Which is why you suspect foul play," Dom said.

Oblak shrugged. "It's quite a coincidence that about the same time your plane landed in Trieste, this woman was being pronounced dead, don't you think?"

"Which is why you accused us of killing her."

"Someone killed her and chose this time to do it. The only independent variable in this equation is you. Something about you coming here resulted in this woman's death."

"Well, we sure as hell didn't tell anybody we were coming. That leaves your people."

Oblak's jaw clenched. "And you're accusing me of divulging your arrival and your intention of meeting with this woman?"

"You, or someone in your office." Dom wondered if the Iron Syndicate might have had sources inside Oblak's organization.

Maybe the person was Oblak himself.

"Not possible," the Slovenian said.

"I wouldn't expect you to say anything else. But if I'm right, then you know you have a problem inside your department and you're going to have to deal with it."

Adara felt the heat rising between these two roosters. She decided to intervene before the feathers started to fly.

"Why do you think anyone would want to kill her?" Adara asked.

Oblak's rugged mouth broke into a thin smile. "I was hoping you might shed some light on the subject. Who, indeed, would have a motive to want to see her dead, a woman on the verge of filing charges against the man she claimed attacked her?"

"Jack Ryan had nothing to do with this, I assure you," Dom said. Jack was one of the best guys he knew, and not just because they were cousins.

"Ms. Sherman asked me why anyone would want to kill her. The term of art is 'motive,' and right now, the only person on the planet I'm aware of that might have any motive whatsoever is Jack Ryan."

"You don't really believe Jack Ryan tried to hurt that woman."

"Highly unlikely. But that's what we were investigating"— Oblak glanced at Elena's corpse—"until this happened." He turned back to Dom. "So tell me, why is an FBI agent getting involved in this case?"

"Officially, this isn't an FBI case. I just happen to work for them. Jack is a close friend, and he works for another friend of mine, Gerry Hendley. So does Ms. Sherman."

"Yes, Gerry Hendley. The former senator. Jack Ryan has many good friends, some in very high places."

"Yeah, you could say that."

"And for whatever reason, Elena Iliescu allegedly attacked him, and now she is dead." Oblak's eyes bore into Dom's. "Where does that leave me?"

Up shit creek, Dom thought. *Just like me.* He'd come all this way to try to find out Elena Iliescu's connection to the Iron Syndicate, if any, and why they wanted to kill Jack. He was prepared to cajole or bribe her with offers of protection or even cash to get answers, but now she was gone. His only hope at the moment was Oblak.

"Sometimes cases don't get solved. It's part of the business."

"True, but the case isn't closed yet, is it?" He glanced back down at the corpse. "Such a shame. A beautiful young woman, dead for no apparent reason."

Dom wasn't sure how much to confide in the Slovenian detective, particularly in regard to the Iron Syndicate—what little Dom actually knew. But there was something about the way Oblak presented himself. He was definitely not happy that the two of them were standing here with no apparent authority over a corpse that used to be his primary suspect and/or witness to an attempted murder.

Oblak might just be a local cop who resented the hell out of the arrival of an American FBI agent into his jurisdiction. God knows he got that kind of reaction when he encountered insecure or incompetent law enforcement back home, which fortunately wasn't too often.

Oblak didn't strike him as either insecure or incompetent, but then again, it was too early to tell. If he wasn't either of those things, then why did he resent their presence? Was he hiding something? Dom just couldn't be sure, and a silent exchange with Adara confirmed his own hesitation to divulge Iliescu's Iron Syndicate connection. Better not tip their hand just yet.

"You said that there was no one you could think of with a motive other than Jack. I can think of two more," Dom said.

"Enlighten me."

Dom pointed at the corpse. "The first person is her."

"You think she killed herself?"

"It's possible."

"With what motive?"

"The same as the other suspect."

"And who might that be?"

"I believe Jack when he said that this woman tried to kill him. Either she was doing it for herself or she was instructed to do so by somebody else."

"Instructed, or hired," Adara added.

"So your other suspect is Iliescu's unknown employer?"

"Logically, those are your only two choices."

"But I still don't have a motive for why she would kill herself, or why her employer would order her to kill herself or have someone else kill her."

"Sure you do. It's Jack. Or, technically, her failure to kill Jack. If her employer is anything like the Mexican cartels or the Russian Mafia, her failure to execute her mission would result in a far more gruesome death than one she might inflict upon herself. That, or her employer had her killed because she was in your custody and they were afraid she might betray them." Dom grinned. "But you already thought of all that, didn't you?"

"We may be a small country of villages, but we don't raise idiots, Mr. Caruso."

"Do you have any idea who might have hired her, or who wanted to kill Jack?" Adara asked.

"The only reason why I agreed to meet with you, and allow you to interview her, was to find the answers to both of those questions. My office has limited resources, and unfortunately, we've reached a dead end."

Or you're trying to find out what we know because you're on the same payroll as her, Dom thought. *And if you are, Detective Oblak, your life is at risk now, too.*

But trying to guess Oblak's motives was a losing game. Dom decided to throw the dice.

"Have you ever heard of the Iron Syndicate?" Dom asked.

Oblak shook his head. "No. What is it?"

Dom was pretty good at catching people lying. But so were most cops. Which was why cops were harder to catch at lying than just about anybody else, even other cops. Maybe Oblak knew more than he was letting on, but there was no way to tell from his body language.

"We don't know much. It's an international criminal enterprise. There's a very weak link between Iliescu and that organization. A friend-of-a-friend kind of thing."

"I can call my intelligence unit and put in an inquiry. Why would this Iron Syndicate want to kill Jack Ryan?"

"That's what we came here to ask her about." Dom looked at the corpse. "And she ain't talking."

"My advice to you, then, is to retrace her steps. She told us she had come from Trieste, which we have since confirmed. I can get you her address there." Oblak pulled up his phone to forward it.

"I don't want to step on any Italian toes," Dom said. Italian cops were as touchy as anybody else about outsiders intruding on their turf.

Oblak shrugged. "The coroner is driving up from Ljubljana. That means he won't be performing the autopsy until later this afternoon. Legally, I'm not required to issue a notice of death to the Italian government until the cause of death is confirmed. Depending on the bloodwork, that might be as late as tomorrow morning."

Dom's phone dinged. He checked it. Iliescu's Trieste address. If they left now, they could be there within the hour. Plenty of time to snoop around the place before the Italian police would even know they'd been there.

Interesting.

"That's awfully generous of you, Detective."

"Consider it a professional courtesy."

Yeah, or a setup, Dom thought. He was glad that Gavin had issued them untraceable phones, since Oblak had his number.

"I've handed out a few 'professional courtesies' myself over the years. I usually attach a string or two."

"You want to know my motive? I'll make it simple. I'm a patriot. I love my country as much as you love yours. Slovenia has survived countless occupations since the time of the Caesars, and yet we are still here. We know who we are. One people, one language." He glanced back at the corpse. "Now that we're part of the EU, our borders are open, and anyone can cross them, including our enemies, and I'm powerless to stop it.

Worse, I don't have the authority to cross those same borders and prevent it. It's a one-way street, and I don't care for it."

"So you're using us to do your dirty work."

Oblak smiled. "One courtesy begets another. So my 'string' is that if you find out anything about this Iron Syndicate or this woman's connection to it, I want to be informed."

"Fair enough. And maybe you'll let us know about the cause of death, and the time you call it in to the Italians."

"Fair enough."

Dom extended his hand. So did Adara. They shook. "We'll be in touch, Detective."

"And tell your large friend in the van to mind his speed limit. We're much more strict about that sort of thing in Slovenia than they are in Italy."

Dom hid his surprise. He didn't think they'd been under surveillance.

That's a good start, Dom thought, as he climbed into the van.

Or maybe Oblak was just handing them over to his Iron Syndicate connection in Italy, waiting to find a way to throw them off the trail, or worse.

Either way, Trieste was the next stop.

Jack was in trouble, and this was their only shot.

30

SARAJEVO, BOSNIA AND HERZEGOVINA

Jack stared at his hands, silently fuming. He knew he was under observation by the camera unit shielded in a translucent dome in the ceiling of the small interrogation room. No point in giving anybody any ammunition to use against him. He glanced around the room for the umpteenth time, bored out of his mind. A desk, a couple chairs, industrial carpet, acoustical tiles on the walls. Not exactly a torture chamber, unless you counted annoyed frustration as inhumane psychological duress.

What was taking so long? It felt like he'd been in there for hours, but without his iWatch and iPhone, he couldn't know for sure. They'd been taken from him for security purposes.

The electronic lock clicked and the steel door swung open. Dragan Kolak, stepping past a uniformed guard, carried two cups of steaming coffee in his hands. The guard shut the door behind him as Kolak set the coffees down on the table and took the only open seat.

"Black coffee, yes?" Kolak said, not really asking.

"Thanks," Jack said, not really meaning it. He took a sip. Not bad. Agent Kolak was straight out of central casting for an American cop show: rumpled suit; loose tie; thin, graying hair, badly cut; and cheap leather shoes, slightly scuffed. Only Kolak wasn't a cop. He introduced himself as an agent of OSA-OBA, the Bosnian version of the CIA.

"Everything check out?" Jack had provided Gerry Hendley's direct contact information, along with his own passport and wallet containing his international driver's permit, an ATM card, two credit cards, and about a hundred dollars in Bosnian convertible marks. He knew Kolak had been running background checks since he'd last seen him.

"Your passport appears up-to-date and valid. So let's get down to business, Mr. Ryan." He blinked his overly large, sad eyes.

"The sooner, the better. I hadn't planned on spending my vacation in the basement of a security facility."

"Then perhaps you shouldn't have attacked my agent."

"He took the first swing."

"If my other agent hadn't been there, I wonder what else you would have done to poor Višća?"

"I was just defending myself."

"Quite skillfully, for a . . ." Kolak snapped his fingers, trying to prompt his memory. "Ah, yes, a 'financial analyst.'"

"You obviously believe me or you would've had me arrested—or whatever else your agency does with criminals."

"I believe what my agents reported—and lucky for you,

they're honest. But if I were you, I'd stay away from Agent Višća. He wants to return the favor of the broken nose."

"Tell him I'm sorry about that. And the shirt."

"So you came here for vacation? Tourism?"

"Yes."

"And what led you to pick Sarajevo as your destination? It's not exactly high on most Americans' lists of places to visit."

"I'm a student of history. Always wanted to come here. As your guys probably know, I was just visiting the assassination museum."

"We have a lot of history here, for sure, Mr. Ryan. And not all of it pleasant, as you must know."

"Very complicated, too."

"Just like my job here." Kolak took his first sip of coffee. "Your passport says you were just in Slovenia."

"I didn't stamp it myself, I promise."

"Another history tour?"

"Business."

"More 'financial analysis'?"

"As you already know, I work for an American firm, Hendley Associates. We were hired to do some work for a company in Ljubljana."

"Yes, I've confirmed both. And yet you found yourself in the remote mountains near Kozjak Falls."

Jack stiffened. "Where I was attacked."

"And yet the woman you say attacked you is the one who winds up in hospital."

"Self-defense."

"Self-defense? And yet you're not the one in hospital. You're really quite the violent man, aren't you?"

"I don't go looking for trouble, if that's what you mean."

"And yet it comes seeking after you wherever you go. A pity."

"Are we done here?"

"Just a few more questions, if you don't mind."

"You have until I finish my coffee. Unless you plan to arrest me."

"No. Nor do I plan to have you deported, nor charged with espionage, nor tossed into a rendition facility far from the prying eyes of your government, all of which is in my power to do."

"In that case, what do you want to know?"

"What is your interest in Aida Ćurić?"

The question caught Jack by surprise. He hoped it didn't show on his face. How could the man know about that? Well, obviously, they'd been following him. But why?

"I'm not sure that's any of your concern," Jack said.

"Aida Ćurić is a citizen of my country, and it is my sworn duty to protect the people and constitution of Bosnia. And when a violent foreign national enters my country to hunt down one of my fellow citizens? Well, that's very much my concern."

So much for keeping a low profile, Jack thought.

"Well, when you put it that way, I kinda see your point."

"So I'll repeat the question, Mr. Ryan. What is your interest in Aida Ćurić?"

The best lie, Jack knew, was one that contained the most truth. But any lie at this point might put him in harm's way, and sitting here, he couldn't quite figure out what advantage there was in lying to Kolak at all.

"Technically, I'm here on an errand for my mother."

"Your mother? What kind of mission are you running for her?"

"Mission? No, it's more like an errand. I'm making a delivery. A letter."

"What kind of letter?"

"Just a letter from my mother to Aida. She knew I was going to be in Slovenia, and she asked me to come down here to find Aida so that I could give her a letter she wrote to her."

Kolak leaned forward, his elbows on the table.

"And how does your mother know Aida Curić?"

"When Aida was a little girl during the war, she received a bad eye injury. My mother performed surgery on her. She lost contact with Aida over the years, and asked me if I could find her. She wanted to know how Aida was doing after all this time, and to let Aida know that she was still thinking about her."

Kolak sat back in his chair, rubbing his chin, his face lost in thought.

Finally, he said, "As incredible as your story sounds, I am still inclined to believe you, Mr. Ryan."

"Then I'm free to go?"

"Why not?"

Kolak stood. So did Jack. Kolak handed him a business card.

"If you run out of resources in your search for Ms. Curić, feel free to contact me. Perhaps I can be of some assistance."

Jack was confused. Why would Kolak want to help him find Aida? He slipped the card into his pocket.

"I appreciate that. If you'd just let me get my stuff, I'll get out of your hair."

"Follow me." Kolak opened the door. "Just one favor, if I may. When you find her, would you mind letting me know?"

"You're telling me that you won't be tracking my every step?"

Kolak shook his head. "I don't see any reason to. Besides, my department is, how do you say, short-handed? My resources are better deployed elsewhere."

"So why do you want to know when I find her?"

"Just curious. It's a fascinating story."

Kolak flashed a smile full of crooked teeth.

Jack and Kolak shook hands in front of the OSA-OBA main building, a drab, unremarkable structure on a modest, narrow street just up a long, steep block north of Maršala Tita.

A half block east, a remote camera positioned behind the one-way glass of a third-story apartment window recorded the handshake.

The camera software triggered an alarm on a laptop a half kilometer away.

A woman, an officer in Russia's Main Intelligence Director-ate (GRU), glanced up from texting on her phone, noting the image capture. Her hazel eyes were light brown today. Depending on her mood, they could also shift from gold to pale green.

"Who is it?" A Russian man's voice from the kitchen. He was preparing a pot of tea.

"It's our boy, Dragan Kolak."

The facial-recognition software automatically logged name, place, and time. But per their protocol, she manually logged the same data into another database on a separate computer.

Their sources pegged Kolak as a central figure in the Bosnian security services. They just weren't sure whose side he was playing for. Part of their job was to find out. More important, they wanted to know if he knew where the stolen thermobaric missiles were, or at least who had them.

Finished, she returned to the image capture. Kolak headed back into the building, but the man he shook hands with was walking toward the camera. She dragged the red camera target reticle to the scowling, bearded face. The target reticle flashed three times, indicating it was searching for the man's identity. A moment later, it turned back to solid red.

A rare miss.

She froze the live video feed long enough to capture the man's facial image as a still photo, then saved it to the Search Alert file.

Her partner leaned over her shoulder, setting a steaming cup of tea down by her elbow just as Jack turned the corner, heading back toward the main drag. The camera tracked him until he disappeared.

"Who's that?" He pushed his wire-rimmed spectacles closer to his eyes for clarity. The aroma of cigarettes and cinnamon in her hair made his mouth water.

"A friend of Kolak's, perhaps."

"Name?"

"None."

The man leaned closer to Jack's saved image. "How is that possible?"

"Beard, mustache, dark eyes. Perhaps not distinctive enough for the algorithm."

"Perhaps."

He stood erect again, sipping his tea. Facial-recognition technology was advancing rapidly, but it was still limited by one significant fact: "Recognition" was a comparative exercise.

The quality of existing images in the search database, or the lack of them, ultimately determined the software's success.

She scrubbed the video backward, capturing the footage of Jack walking toward the camera until the turn. She saved the clip and loaded that into the system as well.

"Gait capture will help us keep an eye on him. And whoever he meets with might give us a clue to his identity."

"Send it along to Khodynka." He was referring to GRU's main headquarters in Moscow, a run-down, nine-story glass tower affectionately known as the Aquarium. "Maybe they'll have something on him."

The woman tapped more keys.

"Done."

PLOČE, CROATIA

Beneath a clouded quarter moon, the Greek-registered *Aegis Star* sat low in the water on her twenty-meter beam, anchored in the small cove just beyond the mouth of the port of Ploče, the second busiest on the Croatian coast. The ship wasn't scheduled to unload its cargo until mid-morning the following day. A warm breeze chucked the cold Adriatic tide against the rusting blue hull, its deck illumined only by dim navigation lights on the bow and stern. The bridge was dark.

The low hum of an electric outboard motor cut to silence as the FC-470 rubber-hulled Zodiac combat craft drifted to a halt at the stern.

Ten Russian KSSO operators scrambled silently up the aft ladder carrying only suppressed pistols on secured holsters and plasti-cuffs. The KSSO was Russia's newest and most effective special operations unit. It was led by an eager young lieutenant who believed that an operation was only as good as the intel that drove it.

Having trained for this kind of mission previously and possessing both the ship's schematics and its crew manifest, KSSO made short work of securing the vessel. They first subdued the lone night watch on deck with a blow to the back of his skull, and then bound and gagged the rest of the sleeping, unarmed crewmen in their bunks, including their captain, a fat, flatulent Greek who reeked of ouzo and stale tobacco.

Twenty minutes later they were belowdecks, breaking open the last of thirty-two ten-foot-long wooden crates in hold number three. The lieutenant swore prodigiously as he yanked off his balaclava and called his commander on an encrypted satellite phone.

Another dead end, he reported.

No thermobarics.

No defectors.

Where the hell are they?

31

After his interrogation by Kolak, Jack returned to his apartment. He opened up his laptop and found an e-mail from Gavin on the secure Hendley Associates website. True to his word, Gavin had revised his search list and provided Jack with the names of twenty-three brunette Aida Curićes.

That was a lot of Aidas, and only forty-eight hours to check them all out before his flight back to Dulles.

He spent the rest of the evening mapping out the location of each new Aida. His intention was to call as many as he could, but when all else failed, he would attempt a personal contact. He was running out of time.

Like his father, Jack was a bulldog when it came to finding something, or someone, he was looking for. His mother jokingly called it a mild form of OCD; his dad preferred the less clinically precise term *stubborn*. So did Jack.

The next morning, Jack went back to the same breakfast restaurant as before and ordered the same chocolate-hazelnut *pita* and two cups of Bosnian coffee. Why not? He was still on vacation. The only difference this time was he wore a ball cap to help prevent facial capture by any surveillance cameras. Kolak had spooked him.

Fortified again with sugar and caffeine, he decided to take an extra precaution and found an electronics store, where he purchased a prepaid phone. He was certain that his iPhone was secure, but somehow Kolak had figured out what he'd been up to. The use of a local phone with a local number might make his prospective Aidas more likely to pick up, too.

Kolak's promise to back off rang hollow to Jack, considering the fact that he was apparently using him to find Aida, which didn't make much sense. With his resources, Kolak could find anybody, or at least had a better shot at finding somebody in Bosnia than Jack did. And why in the world would he be interested in the same Aida, unless Kolak was telling the truth and he was just as intrigued by the story as Jack was?

Jack wandered over to a small park in the middle of the Turkish part of the Old Town. He found an empty bench not far from a chess game. The enormous "board" was painted on the concrete in gray and white squares, and the giant pieces ranged from shin-high pawns to thigh-high kings.

There was a gallery of old men sitting on benches close to the action, smoking and kibitzing as a thirtysomething guy in a sport coat lifted a pawn and took out the horse-headed knight of a silver-haired gent in a red-and-gold Adidas tracksuit, much to the gallery's delight. Jack shook his head. From where he sat, the move seemed a strategic blunder.

Keeping one eye on the spirited game, Jack began smiling and dialing in his hunt for the next Aida. He felt like a retiree playing nickel slots in Vegas, certain the next pull of the handle would hit the jackpot.

Four calls in, that certainty began to fade.

His fifth call went straight to voice mail, and, according to his map, her place of business was just a few minutes away on foot. Abiding by his new search protocol, Jack decided to head over there. It also gave him an excuse to see some more of the Old Town.

He passed a large metal statue of a naked male figure on a pedestal in the middle of a small rose garden, in full sight of a towering, onion-domed Orthodox church. The figure looked like he was doing pull-ups on the shattered longitudinal axis of an open globe. His face pointed to the sky, but his polished bronze Johnson headed in the other direction. Jack read the inscription: "Multicultural Man Builds the World." Jack shook his head. He wasn't into modern art.

Jack walked east on the narrow pedestrian lane past the Orthodox church, then turned left for half a block until he bumped into the wider pedestrian street, Ferhadija. It was lined on either side with restaurants and shops, with quite a few wares on tables and stands along the walkway. Jack wandered along with the crowds of tourists, stopping occasionally to inspect a few places, half looking for presents for his mother and younger siblings, half conducting an SDR—surveillance detection route. Kolak had said he wouldn't put a tail on him, but Jack wasn't exactly the trusting type. The incident with the Romanian woman still had him on edge as well.

Most of the wares Jack found in the shops were touristy

knickknacks: gauzy scarves, bronze teapots, postcards, beaded purses. He checked the labels, expecting to see MADE IN CHINA stamped everywhere, but in this part of the world, Turkey had the corner on cheap stuff.

A few minutes later he found himself back at the fountain on the corner of the Gazi Husrev-beg Mosque, where people were still lapping up the cool water with their cupped hands. There were more hijabs and fully covered women here, and bearded men in traditional garb, than he'd seen anywhere else in the city.

He walked past the open gate of the mosque grounds and caught a glance of men and women segregated on either side of the elevated, rug-covered porch, praying on the outside. Still others in the courtyard were washing their feet before putting their shoes in the tall cubbies farther up. Clearly there were more tourists than worshippers entering the compound. A large knot of Russians wearing earphones listened to their guide yammering into a microphone, leading them through the gate. Jack followed them in.

The same smooth, tightly fitted stones on the walkway led him into the wide but modest courtyard. As a Catholic, Jack wasn't completely sure how he felt about this place. The men and women praying up front seemed sincere enough, and God alone knew when Jack had last been in a church to pray.

On the other hand, he thought about the long and troubled history between his faith and theirs, a history too often characterized by blood and death. The European Crusades were a counterattack against the invading Islamic armies that swept throughout the Middle East and deep into the heart of Europe.

But that was ancient history, as a sign nailed to a tree in the courtyard confirmed. The sign displayed a stylized drone with a red slash through it, wordlessly proclaiming: "No drones."

Jack smiled at the anachronism and headed back out of the gate toward his destination.

32

Jack crossed through the pigeon-jammed and tourist-crowded square of the Sebilj, an eighteenth-century wooden fountain, beautifully carved and topped with a metal dome like a mosque. He waited at the light for the sea of cars and buses to pass before crossing the street and back out into the bustling part of town. He walked past eclectic styles of buildings: some Western European–inspired, others more Mediterranean, and still others unremarkably modern and utilitarian. Sadly, most were marred by graffiti.

He followed his Google Maps directions until he reached a bus-wide alley and turned in, walking past a few storefronts and restaurants to a courtyard and the glass doors of the building he was searching for: the Happy Times! Balkan Tours office.

A bell hanging on the door tinkled as Jack entered the tiny lobby. A young woman with dirty-blond hair stood behind the counter, glasses perched on her nose. She glanced up from a book she was reading at the sound of the bell.

Could it be her?

"*Dober dan*," the woman said. Smile lines radiated against her soft brown eyes.

Nope. Not her.

"Are you here for the two-o'clock tour?" she asked.

"Afraid not. I'm here to see Aida Curić."

The woman frowned. "I'm sorry. She is not here at the moment."

"Is there a way I can reach her? It's important."

Her frown hardened. "Excuse me, please."

The woman disappeared behind a closed door and shut it behind her. Jack heard muffled voices. A moment later, it swung open and a man appeared. He was short and athletically built, with sparkling, dark eyes and an infectious, bearded smile.

"May I help you, sir?" Emir asked.

"I'm looking for Aida Curić."

"She is not here at the moment. Is there something I can help you with? Arrange a private tour, perhaps?"

"No, nothing like that. I'd just like to speak with her."

"What do you want to talk to her about, may I ask?"

"It's private."

Emir's eyes narrowed like a cobra's just before a strike, his smile frozen.

"She's not here today, but I can leave a message for her."

"When will she be back?"

"I don't know."

Jack wasn't sure why this guy had his back up, but he figured he'd better change tactics. He pulled out his wallet and handed him a business card. "Honestly, it's no big deal. I leave town tomorrow. A friend of mine asked me to look her up and to give her a letter."

Emir studied the card. "You can leave the letter with me if you like."

Jack forced a smile. "I appreciate that. It's just that I have to make sure it's really her. That's why I need to meet her."

"I will give her your card and your message. Is there anything else I can do for you?"

"No, but thanks for your time."

The sparkling shine returned to Emir's eyes.

"Of course. We are here for you, anytime."

Jack could feel the smaller man's gaze boring into the back of his skull as he headed out the door.

"Swing and a miss," Jack whispered to himself. Number five of twenty-three was probably a no-hitter. Time to push on.

He pulled out his phone to call the next Aida on the list, hoping for the best.

TRIESTE, ITALY

Dom called ahead to Lisanne after forwarding Iliescu's address to her, a hotel in Trieste, asking her to book a room for Adara and him at the same place, ideally on the same floor as the Romanian's.

"I guess I'll be sleeping in the van," Midas said with a wink after Dom hung up.

"We won't be spending the night. Just need the room reservation for cover. Besides, you Ranger guys are tough. I'd bet a night in a van wouldn't be the worst place you ever slept."

"Not by a long shot," Midas said, and laughed.

Dom directed the retired colonel to take them back to the FBO hangar and the Gulfstream. The airport was on the way to the city center, where the hotel was located. Besides the pistols and ammo they had stored in well-hidden shielded storage lockers, the Hendley Associates aircraft possessed several hidden items of particular use on field ops. Dom needed to grab one of them, and he called ahead to Lisanne to retrieve it. When they arrived, Lisanne greeted them at the hangar door.

"I hope you don't mind, but I did a little research," Lisanne said. "You're in luck. Your hotel uses Onity locks."

"Damn lucky."

"I downloaded Gavin's Onity program into the Arduino microcontroller. It's ready to go."

"Thanks."

Dom shouted a greeting to the two Gulfstream pilots on the way to the cabin ladder. First Officer Chester "Country" Hicks and the captain, Helen Reid, were cleaning up at the open sink in the maintenance bay after performing a thorough inspection of the aircraft.

"Where to next?" Reid asked.

"No telling where or when," Dom said. "I hope you guys brought a deck of playing cards."

Hicks laughed. "Never leave home without 'em."

Dom followed Lisanne into the cabin. The item Dom had requested sat on the polished rosewood table in a plastic case about the size of a paperback, along with three holstered SIG Sauer P938 Micro-Compact nine-millimeter pistols and extra mags. The single-stacked, 6 + 1 SIGs were built for concealed carry, not combat operations, but were handy enough in a pinch. Better a peashooter in the pocket than a .45 in the truck, his twin brother, Brian, had always said.

Where did that come from? Dom asked himself. Man, he missed that guy. Dead for too many years.

Dom snatched up the plastic case Lisanne had retrieved but passed on the weapons.

"I'm not expecting any trouble. Besides, if we get pulled over for any reason, we'll be on the dry-pasta-and-tap-water diet for the next five years if we're caught with those things."

"I thought you Italians liked pasta," Adara said.

"I do, with candlelight and violins in a fine restaurant, not in some graybar hotel."

"Your call," Lisanne said. "Just giving you options. One more thing." She pulled out two wheeled suitcases and set them in the aisle.

"For the two of you. If you're checking in, you need to look the part."

"Good thinking." Dom checked his watch. "We gotta roll."

Midas parked the van on a side street just off the wide and stately Piazza Unità d'Italia, near the small boutique hotel.

Dom and Adara showed their passports to the vivacious thirtysomething Italian woman behind the counter, the spray of freckles on her pretty face a perfect complement to her mop of brown curly hair tied off in a fashionable pink bow. In flawless English she gave them instructions about their room and informed them about the magnificent buffet breakfast available tomorrow morning. Dom's mouth watered as she described it, saddened to know he wouldn't have the chance to partake. As they left the lobby, they heard the woman on the phone chatting in crisp German.

Unfortunately, their room was booked two floors above Il-iescu's, but at this time of day, and with the perfect weather, nobody seemed to be around anyway. Inside the small but well-appointed room, Dom broke open the small plastic case and removed Gavin's device, slipping it into his coat pocket.

Moments later, with Adara standing guard, Dom gently knocked on Iliescu's door. No response. *Good.*

He removed the device from his pocket and slipped the socket connector into the magnetic lock's DC rechargeable power socket, and in less than a second the Arduino micro-controller, loaded with Gavin's capture software, grabbed the lock's own stored key code and opened it.

"Voilà," Dom said, pushing the door open with his shirt-sleeve to avoid leaving prints. He was careful to leave the mul-tilingual "Do Not Disturb" door hanger in place as well. He nodded to Adara. "After you."

Adara brushed past him and into Iliescu's room as Dom pocketed the lock-picking device and shut the door quietly be-hind them. He wasn't sure if the hotel monitored the door locks of its guests to keep track of room occupancy for the maid service. He hoped not.

Judging by the condition of the room, he thought it had been ransacked. Empty liquor bottles, unmade bed, dirty clothes on the floor. But apparently Iliescu was just a slob.

"I'll check the bathroom and closets," Adara said, snapping on a pair of gloves.

Dom was pulling on his gloves, too, nodding at the bed-posts. "Note the silk ropes affixed to each bedpost, counselor." He pointed at a collection of male prosthetics on the night-stand. "And for your edification, please observe—"

"Gross. Let's get on with it. I'm getting the willies."

"So did she, apparently." Dom smiled.

"Double gross."

Fifteen minutes later, they had scoured every corner, drawer, shelf, and container.

Nothing.

No weapons, no electronics, no clues.

"Not even a secret decoder ring," Dom said.

"Now what?"

Dom glanced around the room and thought of another tasteless joke, but the serious look on Adara's face told him to cool his jets. They were a committed, fun-loving couple when they weren't at work, but out in the field she was all business. That was part of their deal. Her work ethic was just one of the reasons she got promoted to field operative from the position Lisanne now occupied so skillfully.

Instead he offered, "Let's get back to our room and call Gavin. Maybe he's got an idea."

Back in their room, Dom and Adara called Midas, then the three of them jumped on a conference call with Gavin and Gerry on Adara's encrypted phone. Dom laid out the dead-end situation they now found themselves in.

"Gavin, I had this crazy idea. You pulled up Iliescu's flight schedule, so we know the cities she's been to. Any chance we could collate a list of those cities from the last year with a list of unsolved killings and suicides that occurred within seven days of her arrival?"

"Yeah, sure. But it would take a while. Problem is, people

die every day in big cities. Even if we placed her in temporal proximity to some of those deaths, we wouldn't know which ones she might be connected to. We'd be pushing on a string."

They batted around several more ideas, all of them leading to more dead ends. It was possible to trace Iliescu's movements, but that didn't get them closer to linking her to the Iron Syndicate, or to the reason for the attempt on Jack's life.

Exasperated, Midas asked Gerry, "You said we had some intel from MI6 on the Iron Syndicate. Some guy on the board of a company connected to those jokers?"

"That's right."

"Any chance we can get hold of that guy? Shake his tree a little bit?"

"There's too big of a chance we'd be pissing into the Brits' punch bowl," Gerry said. "Who knows where their investigation is or how they got that intel. We might be compromising one of their sources."

"So how about we read them in on what's going on? Get them to shoulder some of this weight?"

"Technically, MI6 doesn't know we exist, so I'd have to go through official channels. Mary Pat Foley, most likely. But if Gavin's right, the Brits don't know anything more than we do at this point, and blowing this thing up into an international incident without anything to go on is only going to cause more problems without solving any of them."

"Why not just order Jack back home? At least we can protect him here," Gavin asked.

"Jack's due to fly back tomorrow anyway. He's pretty good about protecting himself. Besides, he's determined to finish what he's started."

"And even if we get him home, there's no way to keep Jack

safe short of locking him up," Dom said. "And that ain't gonna happen."

Midas chimed in again. "What we need is the long-term solution: find these Iron Syndicate bastards and take them out."

"Agreed," Gerry said. "Easier said than done for an enemy we can't identify or locate or, in fact, confirm even exists.

"Gavin, is there any way you can take that list of known cities Iliescu has visited, and try to figure out some kind of pattern of movement? Maybe she's on a circuit, making regular stops at certain times of the year? Coordinate that with her bank deposits? That sort of thing."

"It's worth a try. I'll get right on it."

"And I'll keep thinking about the MI6 piece. There might be something to that. I just need to figure out what it is and how to go about it."

"What about us?" Dom asked. "What can we do?"

"Sit tight, put up your feet. We won't be sending you back out until tomorrow at the earliest. Trieste is a beautiful little city. Go enjoy it. I'll be in touch."

The conference call ended. Dom reached into his pocket and handed the key card to Midas. "You keep the room. We'll take the van and grab the others and find somewhere to stay."

Midas shoved the key card back into Dom's hand. "No way, kid. You two relax. Uncle Midas will take care of the rest."

Adara started to protest, but Midas cut her off.

"I know. You're both pros. But tonight, you're off duty. So take advantage of it while you can. In our line of work, tomorrow isn't guaranteed."

33

PANČEVO, SERBIA

Serbian troopers fast-roped from the Mil Mi-8 "Hip" single-rotor helicopter hovering low over the ministry building as the gunfire chattered throughout the seven floors beneath.

The chopper roared away as the last pair of boots hit the roof. On the street below, the first captives emerged from the front entrance, prodded forward by short-barreled AKS-74Us of the civilian-clad Serbian special ops fighters.

The captain in charge of the building assault radioed in over the speakers on the observation deck. "Objective achieved, Colonel!"

Lieutenant Colonel Maksimović, the commander of the Serbian 63rd Parachute Battalion, picked up his comms. "Well done, Captain. Congratulate your boys for me. We'll muster in fifteen minutes for a debrief, and prep the exercise again."

"Yes, sir!"

The tall Serbian colonel was genuinely pleased. The exercise couldn't have gone any better. That was fortunate, given the two Russian officers standing next to him watching the live video feeds.

Colonel Smolov, HoRF—Hero of the Russian Federation—commanded the Russian 45th Guards VDV (Airborne) Detached Spetsnaz Brigade. A distinguished combat veteran, Smolov was also in charge of the Slavic Sword and Shield training exercise today.

As part of the Special Brigade of the Serbian Army, the 63rd was one of the elite Serbian Spetsnaz units, a mirror image of the Russian 45th Guards. Not only was the Russian commander a personal hero of the Serbian colonel, but the Serbian's future military career depended upon today's evaluation by Smolov.

The man standing next to him was equally intimidating to the tough Serbian parachutist. Colonel Denisov was a lean, bespectacled GRU staff officer rumored to have spearheaded the deployment of a malware Android app used by Polish tank officers for fire control. Thanks to Denisov's operation, the Russians were now tracking the exact whereabouts of all 247 Leopard 2A4 main battle tanks in the Polish arsenal.

Denisov was also known to be one of the principal architects of the New Generation warfare strategy, and a personal favorite of the Russian president. The GRU was by far the largest and most effective Russian intelligence service in both field agents and combat operatives, dwarfing the more famous FSB and SVR agencies, with which they competed for resources and political favor.

Colonel Maksimović wasn't sure why a man of Denisov's

stature had been invited at the last minute to observe this relatively minor exercise. It only added to the Serbian's anxiety.

"Your men are well trained in CQC," Denisov said. "You should be pleased."

"Colonel Smolov deserves most of the credit, sir," the Serbian replied. "It's his training regimen we follow."

"Nonsense. These are your men and they obey your orders," Smolov insisted.

"Thank you, sir. They're good men. It's an honor to lead them."

Today's exercise was intended to take down an "unnamed parliamentary building," but everybody in the observation post knew exactly what that meant. The practice facility had been reengineered to fit exact blueprints of the actual target building just across the border.

Denisov turned to the Serbian commander, the disastrous report from Croatia and the empty cargo ship still on his mind.

"How soon could you mobilize the rest of your battalion, Colonel?"

The tall Serbian grinned. "Twenty-four hours, maximum, sir."

Smolov frowned, curious. No such mobilization had been scheduled. "An impromptu training exercise for the Serbians, Colonel?"

Denisov smiled. "What else would it be?"

SARAJEVO, BOSNIA AND HERZEGOVINA

Jack hardly noticed the stink of the garbage chute outside his door as he entered his apartment. He kicked off his shoes in the foyer and fell onto the living room couch with a yawn and a sigh. It wasn't as if he'd been humping a fifty-pound ruck up the side of Mount Rainier or doing wind sprints at the beach on Coronado Island. But a long day of cab rides, failed phone calls, and often tense, suspicious encounters left him emotionally spent. He'd run through the entire second list of twenty-three names that Gavin had sent him. Three were no longer in country, and the two he left messages for hadn't called him back yet, nor did he expect them to.

Now what?

He could give overworked Gavin another call and ask him to generate yet another list, but he doubted the IT whiz had any more Aida cards up his digital sleeve. Besides, Gavin had actual work to do as the man in charge of all things computer-related for both Hendley Associates and The Campus.

His other option was to cancel his flight back home and keep hunting for other clues in the public record, or just keep his fingers crossed and hope the émigrés came back home or the ones he left messages for would call back.

The only problem with that was the text Gerry had sent an hour ago. `Glad you're coming home tomorrow. A lot going on. Need you back ASAP.`

So with his two lists exhausted, no prospects for a third, and his boss breathing down his neck, it was clear to Jack it was time to get packed and head for the airport tomorrow.

He'd tried, hadn't he?

Sure, his mother would be deeply disappointed—not that she'd ever say anything. In fact, she'd tell him how grateful she was that he'd tried his best.

And failed.

The *and failed* was the snarling demon inside Jack's head. He couldn't stand the thought of failing at anything.

What would cut him the deepest was the hidden disappointment his mother would undoubtedly feel when he told her the bad news that he couldn't find little Aida. His mother never asked him to do anything for her. She was the most self-reliant person he'd ever known. As a physician, she was always doing something for others, sometimes risking her health and even her life to save peoples' eyesight. The idea of letting her down was almost too much to bear.

But he didn't really have a choice. Staying here another couple days or even another couple years wouldn't change the likely outcome. Aida Curić, his mother's young patient from so many years ago, simply didn't exist. And he had important Campus work to do, as well as his work as a financial analyst at Hendley Associates. He was a good worker, and a good soldier.

But he was also his mother's son.

He was so lost in his thoughts that he actually jumped when he heard a knock at the door. He was expecting his landlords to drop by for an inspection before he flew out tomorrow.

Jack padded over to the door in his stocking feet and opened it.

Oh.

Not his landlords.

34

Jack's jaw dropped, just like in the cartoons. Standing in front of him was one of the most beautiful women he'd ever seen.

And maybe one of the angriest.

Jack didn't care. Her thick, chestnut shoulder-length hair and full-figured beach body would have caught his attention any day of the week, but her startling blue eyes absolutely gobsmacked him.

She must have liked what she saw, too, because the harshness in those magnificent eyes softened. She might even have blushed a little.

God knows he felt a jolt racing through him, from the nape of his neck all the way down to his . . .

Toes.

Standing behind her in the tiled hallway was a slopeshouldered slab of meat, with a shaved head and a closely trimmed beard, staring daggers at him.

The woman gathered her wits. Her softness disappeared. All business now. "You are Jack Ryan?"

If you're looking for me, yeah. I mean, hell, yeah!

"Yes, I'm Jack Ryan," he said evenly.

"My name is Aida Curić. I understand you were looking for me."

"Yes, I was. I mean, I am."

In a million years, Jack never would've connected her grainy driver's-license photo, which Gavin had sent him, to that perfect face.

"Please come in."

"No, thank you. What is it that you want from me?"

"Nothing, I promise. I was trying to find you in order to give you something."

"A letter?"

"Yes."

"From whom?"

Good English, Jack thought. "My mother."

"Why would your mother want to give a letter to me, a perfect stranger?"

Mr. Clean shifted his stance, his glowering eyes still fixed on Jack. From where Jack stood he couldn't see a weapon on the man, unless you counted the two seventeen-inch guns hanging from his wide shoulders.

"You and my mother may have met many years ago when you were a child. She's an ophthalmologist, I mean—"

"An eye surgeon. Yes, of course. Go on."

"She performed an eye surgery twenty-six years ago on a little girl named Aida Curić who was injured in the Bosnian War, and saved her eye. She knew I was coming to the region and asked me to see if I could find Aida and give her a letter she wrote to her."

"How do you know I was the little girl?"

"I don't. That's why I was asking all over town and looking for every Aida Curić I could find. But you'd know. I'm sure you'd remember something like that."

Aida's eyes narrowed. "Let's say that I do remember. What does she want from me?"

"Nothing, I promise. She never forgot you and just wanted you to know that. I haven't read the letter, but that's what she told me. Can I get it for you?"

Jack watched the wheels turn behind her eyes. She offered a slight smile. Finally, "Yes, of course."

"Won't you come in?" Jack glanced over her shoulder. "Your friend, too."

"All right."

She whispered something to Mr. Clean in Bosanski. He nodded and stepped back into the hallway, facing the stairwell, folding his hands in front of him as Aida shut the door.

Aida didn't budge from the little foyer. She saw the look on Jack's face.

"My friend is concerned. It's a difficult time these days for Bosniaks like me. You understand the politics of my country? The history?"

"A little. More than most Americans, I suppose." Thanks to Rojko Struna's mini-lecture on the drive from the Ljubljana airport, Jack reminded himself.

"Can I get you anything?"

Aida shook her head. "No, thank you. It's late."

"Then let me get that letter."

Jack dashed to the bedroom and pulled his mother's letter from a suitcase pocket. He hurried back, suddenly aware of his socks as he slid a little on the polished tile floor. He glanced down at his feet and wiggled his toes.

Aida stifled a giggle.

Jack handed her the blank envelope. His mother was clever enough not to use official White House stationery. She wasn't trying to impress Aida, just communicate with her.

Aida slipped an unadorned fingernail beneath the sealed flap and opened it. She pulled the folded letter out but didn't open it. She glanced up at Jack, and then back down to the letter. Jack saw in her eyes the tug-of-war between suspicion and curiosity.

Curiosity finally won out.

She opened the letter carefully, as if it were an ancient manuscript. Her eyes swept back and forth as she read, her frown softening into a little smile. As she reached the end, she touched one hand to her mouth, her eyes misting.

"You said you haven't read this?"

"No."

"It's quite beautiful." She brushed a fingertip against the corner of one of her almond-shaped eyes. "May I keep this?"

Jack smiled. "Of course. It's yours."

"Thank you. And please thank your mother for me. It was very kind, and very thoughtful of her."

"If you'd like to tell her yourself, you can reach her here." Jack handed Aida a plain business card with his mother's P.O. Box address. She took it.

No wedding ring, Jack noticed.

"Thank you. I would like that very much."

"Are you sure you don't want a drink or something?"

"I have to get back, but thank you. And thank you for taking the time to find me and for delivering this."

Jack shrugged. "It was no big deal."

"When do you go back to the States?"

"Tomorrow, actually."

Aida's shoulders slumped. "Oh, that's too bad. I would have liked to show you my city."

"Well, it's not a problem to change my plans."

"Really? That would be wonderful. Can you come back to the tour office at ten o'clock tomorrow?"

"Sure. That would be great."

"Wonderful." She put her hand out.

Jack shook it. A firm grip. Their hands lingered for a moment longer than he expected.

More electricity.

"See you tomorrow, then."

She turned and opened the door, whispered something to her man as the two of them disappeared down the stairwell.

Jack shut the door.

What was he going to tell Gerry?

He'd promised his boss he was flying home tomorrow, but that sure as hell wasn't going to happen now.

35

At ten o'clock the next morning, Ambassador Topal sat at the head of the table in the conference room of the Islamic Peace Studies Center (IPSC), built with funds from a religious organization based in Ankara, Turkey.

Lining both sides of the conference table sat several Bosniak Islamic religious and community leaders. Two of them were bearded imams from conservative mosques in the suburbs. All of the others were decidedly moderate in their views, including two women, one in a silky blue-and-yellow headscarf and the other one, the IPSC director, wearing no head covering at all.

Topal had called this morning's brief meeting. Recent polls showed the upcoming Unity Referendum was plummeting in the polls because of the recent ethnic violence. Without a strong Bosniak voter turnout in favor of the referendum, it was doomed to fail. The purpose of today's meeting was to shore up the support of those assembled and of their respective constituencies before attending his next event.

There was one empty chair at the table that concerned the ambassador. He would look into that later.

"We feel that we have a religious duty to show the world we can live in peace with Catholics and Orthodox, as well as Jews and people of every faith—or no faith at all," the director said. "The Unity Referendum is vital to the exercise of that sacred duty."

Several heads nodded around the table.

Topal radiated a grandfatherly smile. "I applaud your ecumenicism, Madame Director."

One of the imams spoke up. "We cannot allow the Unity Referendum to become a mutual suicide pact."

"No, of course not," Topal said. "My government would be the first one to oppose it if I thought that Muslim interests were in any way compromised."

The imam placed an open palm against his chest. "Of this we have no doubt."

"Thank you," Topal said. The man's mosque was one of hundreds destroyed in the war by Serb and Croat forces, and one of the many rebuilt with money from Ankara. Topal had personally approved this imam's reconstruction project.

The headmaster of the largest private Islamic primary school, another facility built with Turkish funds, spoke up. "The government must redouble its efforts to stop the anti-Muslim violence we've been reading about."

Topal nodded again. "I have received assurances that everything is being done to monitor the situation. But my sources also tell me the violence has been directed against other communities. Small acts of retribution."

"Big fires begin with small sparks," the other imam said. His mosque had been rebuilt with Saudi money.

"Which is why we must always take precautions and remain vigilant, even as we work for peace," Topal said.

More heads nodded.

"Turkey is the hope of all Muslim nations, and President Özyakup is the father of the Umma," the first imam said. "We are not afraid to work for peace because we know you are not afraid to fight for us."

The Turkish president also said that every mosque was a barracks in his radical youth, Topal reminded himself. Özyakup had gone to great lengths in recent years to position Turkey as the new caliphate for the Muslim world. He was engineering an Ottoman Empire revival, including the restoration of historic Ottoman symbols, artwork, and buildings in Turkey and throughout the region. Özyakup even brought back Ottoman-styled uniforms to the presidential palace guard. State maps were being subtly republished to include areas formerly under Ottoman rule, and Turkish military and economic aid were spreading across the Middle East and even to Muslim Africa.

"Let us pray it never comes to that," Topal said. "Peace is always better than war, and peace is the way of the true Muslim. But as the prophet said—Peace be upon him—'He is a true believer who protects his brother or sister, both present and absent.'"

The two imams began applauding and the others quickly joined in. Topal smiled, crinkling his owlish eyes, seemingly embarrassed by the display, waving his hand to quell the collective enthusiasm.

Inwardly, he was shouting with joy.

The clapping stopped as he stood.

"Please forgive me, but I have another engagement to prepare for. I urge you all to do your utmost to encourage your people to vote for the referendum, and for them to encourage their neighbors to do so as well. The future of all Bosnia and of Bosniaks depends upon it. If the referendum fails, then Bosnia fails, and who knows what will happen after that."

"You can count on us," the director said.

And with that, the meeting ended.

Jack arrived at the Happy Times! office at exactly ten a.m. Emir stood behind the desk, greeting Jack with a forced smile.

"Welcome back, Mr. Ryan."

"Is Aida here?"

"She will be with you shortly. Can I get you a bottle of water or something else?"

"No, thanks. I'm good." Jack had skipped his standard morning *pita* chocolate-bomb breakfast and opted for a plate of fried eggs, pork sausage, and fresh fruit, and a couple cups of dark Bosnian coffee.

The office door behind the desk opened and Aida appeared. Jack almost forgot how beautiful she was, despite having spent half the night thinking about her. In tight jeans and a fitted but modest blouse, her figure was even more pronounced. Their eyes locked for a moment, and they both smiled.

Emir caught this. "We should get going," he said, stepping out from behind the desk.

"No need. I'll take him myself," Aida said, still staring at Jack.

Emir's constant smile faded. "But it might be better if I'm with you."

"I think Jack can take care of us both," she said. She turned to Emir. "Don't you have the ten-thirty tour?"

"I called Ibrahim. He said he can take it."

"Ibrahim needs a break." Her voice lowered. "You keep it."

Emir tensed.

Aida approached him. Emir's head lowered, like a dog bowing before its master.

"They asked for you specifically." Aida lifted his chin with her finger. He gazed up into her eyes. "You're the best, and they know it. And so do I."

Emir smiled and nodded. "I need to fuel the van." He turned to Jack, the smile still plastered on his face, but his dark eyes betrayed him.

"Enjoy your tour, Mr. Ryan."

Jack returned the menacing stare with a grin.

"Oh, I will. Trust me."

Emir pushed through the glass door with its tinkling bell without responding.

"Ready to take a little walk?" Aida asked.

Jack smiled. "Sounds good."

The GRU officer with the hazel eyes heard the coded *ding* on her laptop, signaling an encrypted e-mail from her superiors at Khodynka. The subject line read:

RE: Identification Subject #102459-BiH

She opened the file, along with the attached video clip of Kolak and the mystery man her facial-recognition software couldn't ID two days prior.

Her eyes skipped the preliminaries and found what she needed most:

Subject Identity: JACK RYAN, JR.
GRU Status: PERSON OF INTEREST

She was reading the details when her partner appeared over her shoulder, his cheap cologne more pungent than usual.

"Anything interesting?"

She turned to him with a smile. Her instincts had paid off. "Very."

He noticed her eyes had turned pale green.

"Tell me more."

36

Jack and Aida crossed the busy street and entered back into the Old Town.

"Where is your bodyguard?"

"Ibrahim is not really a bodyguard. He's just tough-looking. He's actually quite gentle, unless you provoke him."

"I'll do my best not to."

"I only brought him with me last night because I didn't know who you were. My work is controversial, so I took a precaution."

"How is the tour business controversial?"

"I run a refugee aid organization. It's not exactly popular."

"I assumed you owned the tour company." At least, that's what Gavin's notes indicated.

"I do own it. Emir runs the daily operations, but it's mine. He's also my number-one tour guide, but I have many others."

"Owning your own business is difficult, I imagine."

"It is, but I'm not afraid of hard work. Besides, it gives me financial independence." She shot him a sly glance. "No need to rely on a man to put a roof over my head."

"When did you start the company?"

"I didn't. The company was my father's. I was studying to become a medical doctor when he died, so I inherited it."

"I'm sorry for your loss."

"Thank you. He was a good man."

"Tell me about your refugee center."

"We just opened it last year. In a poor country like Bosnia, people resent refugees taking up scarce resources, even Muslim refugees."

"Why? Bosnia is Muslim majority."

"Yes, but it's also majority unemployed, or nearly so. Another legacy of the war. Here we are."

They stood in front of the corner fountain at the Gazi Husrev-beg Mosque, which Jack had seen twice before. As usual, people were drinking from the flowing spigot. Along with throngs of tourists shuffling by, there were more traditionally dressed Muslim men and women. One of the women was completely covered, exposing only her wide, dark eyes, which stole a glance at Aida.

"I didn't realize there were so many people of fundamentalist faith here," Jack whispered, not wanting to offend.

"Those are mostly visitors from Muslim countries. We are becoming quite a tourist destination for them."

Jack glanced up at the skyline. The secular buildings in this part of town were two or three stories at most. But from where he stood he saw three towering minarets: the one here at the fountain, and two others, denoting the locations of other mosques in the area. From what he'd seen so far, Sarajevo appeared to be a secular Western city. But there were so many historically significant Muslim sites in such a close area, Jack could see why people of strong Islamic faith would be drawn here.

"So, fundamentalism isn't a big deal in your country?" Jack asked.

"It's definitely growing, but most Muslims are like me. Islam is more of an expression of our culture and our identity, not a daily religious practice."

"Same with a lot of Catholics in America," Jack said, referring to himself.

Aida nodded at the streaming fountain water. "The tradition is that if you drink from the fountain, you will someday come back to Sarajevo. And the water is delicious."

Jack took the cue and waited behind a bearded middle-aged man in a skullcap before lapping up a few quick sips of the surprisingly cold and refreshing water.

Aida was clearly pleased by the gesture. "Would you like to go inside?"

"I already stopped in."

"Then let's keep going."

They strolled west along the wide, paved walkway of Ferhadija that Jack had traversed a couple times before, but Aida pointed out the best shops, and places of historical interest, which he had missed entirely.

What really intrigued him, though, was the number of smiles and waves and friendly nods that came Aida's way as they walked. It seemed like everybody knew her, including the ones with the obviously forced gestures. If he didn't know any better, he'd have sworn she was the mayor of Sarajevo, or at least this part of it.

Aida pointed out the directional arrows in the pavement stones as they stepped over them, indicating that they were leaving the Turkish side of the city and stepping into the Hapsburg side, the part of Sarajevo built during the Austro-Hungarian Empire. The old-world charm of the Ottoman side of the city suddenly gave way to more modern façades of glass and concrete, many of them large foreign banks and chain stores. It felt like they'd passed from one world to another in just a few steps.

"The one thing I haven't seen in this city are babies or little kids in strollers. Well, except for the tourists."

"An interesting observation, Jack. You're exactly right. Like the rest of Europe, our demographic profile is collapsing. There's an old saying: 'Where there is no hope, there are no children.'"

"Why isn't there any hope?"

"Here we are," Aida said.

They'd stopped in front of a Swiss chain clothing store.

"What am I looking at?"

Aida pointed at the plaque on the wall listing the names of twenty-six people. "All killed by a Serbian artillery shell. Look." Aida pointed at their feet. The pavement was marred by holes, almost like a flower. A large one in the center and smaller, irregular ones radiating forward from it. All of the holes were filled with a faded red resin.

"That's called a Sarajevo Rose. It marks the spot where the shell exploded, killing people. There are dozens of them all over the city as a kind of memorial."

Jack felt bad. He'd stepped on at least two of these since he'd been here, including this one, not even really noticing. But he saw that the Sarajevans walked over it without noticing, either.

"A shell from the siege?"

"Yes, when the city was cut off for over fourteen hundred days, the longest siege in modern European history. We were starving, thirsty, suffering. And then there were the snipers, and of course, the shelling."

Jack imagined living in a modern American city surrounded and shelled for years. These people must have been overwhelmed with feelings of anger and helplessness.

"The war is why there's no hope?"

"The Serbs did more than just kill and wound our bodies."

"There must be a lot of resentment toward the Europeans as well for letting it go on for so long."

"Yes. We are quite cynical these days about Europe. A bitter past, an uncertain future."

"Those memories of the war are still with you, aren't they?"

Aida nodded. "Yes, of course, though I was quite young." She darkened with a bad memory.

Jack waited for her to share more, but she didn't.

"We are all epicureans now, here in Bosnia," she suddenly said with a smile, willing away the darkness. "As you can see by the people passing by, we're all smoking and drinking and eating way too much because today we live and tomorrow we may die in another mortar attack."

"The war ended twenty-three years ago," Jack said. "Haven't most people been able to move beyond it?"

"The fighting stopped, yes. But not the war. Not its root causes. Nothing has healed the lingering mistrust and animosity. It's hard to find peace when there is no justice for the nearly forty thousand dead Bosniaks."

"What do you mean, 'no justice'?"

"Of course, I wouldn't expect you to know our history. But it boils down to this: Almost nobody was prosecuted for war crimes against us, and nobody at NATO or the UN was held accountable for letting the genocidal war go on for years. And when we were finally winning the war against our enemies? Despite the NATO arms embargo against us? Then NATO threatened to bomb us, so a 'peace' was forced down our throats to protect our enemies."

"I can understand why Bosniaks are still angry and still dealing with it."

Jack wanted to add, *But you can't undo the past.*

Aida searched Jack's eyes. "Perhaps you do understand. But you should also know that some of us still have hope, at least a little." She smiled. "And where there is hope, there is nothing that cannot be accomplished."

She checked her watch, then flashed him another smile. "Let me show you why."

MOSCOW

The middle-aged GRU intelligence analyst stared out of the open third-story window of his modest apartment toward Dubki Park, smoking oily Iranian tobacco, grateful the tram wasn't rattling down the middle of the street this cool evening or, worse, bothersome children weren't playing outside.

He was waiting for confirmation that an electronic Bitcoin deposit had been made in his account. The Iron Syndicate's digital "wanted poster" on the Dark Web site he frequented had offered an extremely generous reward for any information that could be provided. Bitcoin was the Dark Web's preferred currency, because of its anonymity, but the analyst insisted on it because he put no faith in the fiat currencies of the world's central banks.

He was surprised when his reward was doubled after he provided both the man's stolen image and its geographic meta-data to the Iron Syndicate account.

That told him the wanted man was, indeed, wanted badly, and the syndicate was known to pay both well and on time. Still, both his job and his life were hanging in the balance if his treason were to be discovered by his superiors at GRU head-quarters. On the other hand, his gambling debts and a drug-addicted girlfriend were significant drains on his meager government salary.

To his great delight, the analyst had been the duty officer when the identification request from Sarajevo came in, and he was the one who personally confirmed the identity of Jack Ryan, Jr., with a seventy-eight percent positivity score.

If Ryan was wanted by both the Iron Syndicate and the GRU, he was fucked either way. Might as well make a few Bit-coin off the man's corpse while he could, he reasoned, inhaling the last deep draw of bitter smoke from the nub.

His computer chimed: "Transfer Complete." He grinned, and flicked the spent butt into the street below.

Time to call his woman and celebrate.

37

SARAJEVO, BOSNIA AND HERZEGOVINA

Aida led the way by foot in a fast, ten-minute walk to a cul-de-sac at the end of a nearby side street. A large crowd had already gathered in front of the newly built three-story building with a banner in the Bosnian national colors of blue, white, and yellow proclaiming "Bosnia Youth Technology and Sports Center." Half of the crowd waved little Bosnian flags, but easily a third waved red Turkish national flags.

The Turkish ambassador, Kemal Topal, stood at the top of the entrance steps, flanked by school-aged children and several local politicians. He was just finishing up his speech.

Jack turned to Aida, whispering. "He sounds like he's running for office."

"The ambassador is a remarkable man."

"You know him?"

Aida just smiled.

T opal laid his hands on the heads of two small children propped beside him.

"The future of Bosnia stands on either side of me. The twenty-first century belongs to them, and the twenty-first century is a technological century. These children will dream technology dreams, and thanks to this center, they will help bring about advances in medicine, robotics, and artificial intelligence, which will change how we live, and how we live together."

Applause broke out among the crowd, and the kids on the steps, too.

"But boys and girls need strong bodies as well as strong minds. Life isn't all books—excuse me, tablets—and math equations. That is why we are also providing state-of-the-art exercise equipment, as well as martial-arts training, dance, and cardiovascular conditioning, what we used to call 'football.'"

His grandfatherly smile launched another wave of clapping.

"My government is deeply honored to sponsor the construction and equipping of this magnificent new facility." He turned to the adults around him. "And we offer our sincerest congratulations to the mayor, the minister of education, and all of the others who have worked tirelessly to make the dream of the Bosnia Youth Technology and Sports Center a reality for all children in Sarajevo—Serbs, Croats, and Bosniaks. Thank you!"

The Turks in the crowd roared their approval, applauding wildly, and were soon joined by the rest.

Topal scanned the audience, noting who was in attendance. His eyes fell on Jack and Aida standing in the back. He whispered in the ear of one of his bodyguards, who nodded and waded into the crowd.

———

Aida turned to Jack. "What did you think about the youth center opening?"

"That was the hope you were talking about."

"You have no idea how significant this is. Do you know there are schools in Bosnia where the kids are all separated? One floor is Croat, one floor is Serb, and the third floor is Bosniak, all learning the exact same subjects but taught separately. They even play in separate yards. What kind of message do you think that sends to those kids?"

The Turk bodyguard approached them. "Excuse me, but the ambassador would like to speak with the two of you."

Aida and Jack exchanged a look. Jack shrugged. "Sure, why not?"

The bodyguard led them back through the chattering crowd devouring the free snacks and beverages provided by the Turkish embassy, and through the doors of the center and into the foyer.

Ambassador Topal dismissed the bodyguard with a friendly nod.

"Aida, I'm so glad to see you here," he said, beaming, extending his hand.

Aida shook it. "Congratulations, Your Excellency. This is a wonderful project. I'm so glad it was completed. Ambassador Topal, this is my friend Jack Ryan."

Topal shook Jack's hand. "Mr. Ryan, it's a pleasure to meet you."

"Thank you, sir. It's a pleasure for me as well."

"An American accent. Is it East Coast? Washington, D.C., perhaps?"

"Close." Too close, Jack thought. "I live and work in Alexandria, Virginia."

"Just across the Potomac." Topal smiled. "I apologize for sounding like the class know-it-all. I was stationed at the Turkish embassy in Washington many years ago. It is a great and historic city. It was a good posting, despite the summer heat. Tell me, Mr. Ryan, what kind of work do you do?"

"I'm a financial analyst for the firm Hendley Associates."

"Hendley? I once knew a senator by the name of Gerry Hendley."

"One and the same. He retired from public life and started the firm." Technically, Gerry lost his bid for reelection after his emotional collapse following the death of his wife and three children in a car wreck, but Jack didn't feel the need to fill in that tragic detail.

"Senator Hendley is a fine man. If you work for him, you must be one as well. Please tell him I said hello."

"I certainly will, sir. May I ask how you and Ms. Curić know each other?"

"Ambassador Topal arranged for the funding of the Peace and Friendship refugee center. Without him, my work there wouldn't be possible."

"Nonsense, Aida. You were already doing the work. We were proud to partner with you."

"Thanks to the ambassador and people like him, Bosnia will have a great future."

Topal turned to Jack. "Aida is a fine administrator, but an even greater soul." He paused. "So, tell me, Jack, what brought you to Sarajevo?"

He stole a glance at Aida before answering. "Sort of what

you said about D.C. Sarajevo is a great and historic city, and I always wanted to visit it."

"And I see you found the perfect tour guide."

"She has great reviews on TripAdvisor, for sure."

"I use her company for all of my new staff, to orient them to the city, the history, and the culture. There is simply no one better."

"You are too kind, Your Excellency," Aida said.

One of Topal's aides signaled for his attention. Topal turned to Jack and Aida.

"I'm sure you two have better things to do. I just wanted to say hello."

They shook hands again, but before leaving, Topal said to Jack, "You must stop by my office before you leave."

"Thank you. I will."

"Please be sure to greet Senator Hendley for me. And let him know about all of the good things you're discovering in this wonderful country."

"Yes, sir."

Jack and Aida headed back out onto the street, each even more impressed with the other than they were before.

"Hungry?" Aida asked.

"Sure."

"Have you ever had *ćevapi?*"

"No, but I'm dying to try some."

"I know the best place in the city. Let's go. My treat."

38

The waitress set the platter of *ćevapi* in front of Jack. The aroma of the sizzling beef sausages and grill-charred bread triggered his inner, slavering wolf. Aida ordered a half platter of the same.

Not sure how to attack his plate with the available utensils, Jack waited for Aida to demo the long-awaited delicacy. She tore off a piece of flatbread, forked one of the finger-sized sausages onto it, and piled a little mound of finely minced sweet onion on top.

Jack followed suit. He thought he might cry for his culinary joy. The grilled minced-beef sausages were mildly spiced, the wood-fired bread was smoky and savory, and the raw onions provided a sweet, crunchy heat. The dish was simple but perfectly combined in its flavors and textures. In his travels around the world, Jack had found that "peasant" food was usually his favorite. Poor people could never afford the expensive ingredients of "haute cuisine" and so had to find a way to coax the maximum amount of flavor out of their simpler fare. This *ćevapi* was the food equivalent of an exquisite Ansel Adams black-and-white photo.

"What do you think?" Aida asked between delicate bites.

Jack was working a mouthful of food like a hyena devouring an antelope carcass. He took a swig of Austrian bottled water to wash it down. The restaurant didn't serve alcohol.

"Unbelievable. I've heard about this stuff. Had no idea how good it could be."

"It's the best *ćevapi* in the city, and believe me, there's a lot of good *ćevapi* in Sarajevo. I'm glad you enjoy it."

The place was packed, inside and out. When they arrived Jack didn't think they'd get to eat. But Aida approached one of the servers, and before she said a word, the server dashed into the back. She emerged with a busboy carrying a small table and two chairs, setting them up outside near the side entrance, where several other customers eagerly consumed their lunches.

Jack was halfway through his feeding frenzy when he saw Gerry's phone number appear on his silenced iPhone. A moment later a "Voice Message" alert appeared. Apparently, Gerry had read his text that he wasn't going to be getting on that plane for D.C. today.

Ten minutes later, Jack popped the last fragments of bread, onion, and beef into his mouth and polished off his water.

"Ready for the rest of the tour?" Aida asked.

"Can't wait."

The server approached the table along with a middle-aged man, who looked like the owner, greeting Aida with a deferential smile in their native language.

"Everything was good?" he finally asked Jack in his halting English.

"I can't imagine anything better. Incredible."

Aida opened her purse to pay, but the owner waved her off with a magnanimous shrug and words Jack didn't know but completely understood. Aida thanked him, and the two of them headed back to pick up the van at the Happy Times! tour office.

Aida navigated the crowded street traffic in the Volkswagen T5 tour van like a New York ambulance driver, skillfully weaving and accelerating as conditions required. Jack watched the little arrow on the dashboard GPS screen changing lanes in real time, too. They passed Sarajevo's first of only two McDonald's and, later, the presidential building. The buildings on this side of the city were definitely more modern and taller.

"I noticed quite a few Turkish flags in the crowd this morning at the youth center," Jack said.

"Hundreds of thousands of Turks live in the Balkans, and twelve million people of Balkan origin live in Turkey. Turks are popular here."

"It's all a little confusing."

"Of course it is," she said with a smile. "It's history."

She pointed at a huge, multistory Holiday Inn. "That was built for the 1984 Olympics. You can see pictures of it online when it was burning during the war."

"Yeah, I've seen them. Terrible."

A little farther along, Aida asked, "Have you heard of Sniper Alley?"

"No."

"We're in it. Google it sometime." She pointed at the surrounding mountains. "Serbian soldiers were up in those hills and in the skyscrapers, shooting at civilians as they ran through town, dodging bullets to find food and water during the siege. Of course, the whole city was a Sniper Alley. This is just where the journalists got shot at."

They left the city center, passing apartment buildings, offices, and light manufacturing facilities.

"Ever heard of Srebrenica, Jack?"

"The place where the massacre happened?"

"Eight thousand Muslim men and boys slaughtered by the Serbs."

"Are we going there now?"

"No, too depressing. If you want, I can make other arrangements with one of my guides for you. There is also a museum in town dedicated to it, and you can see many documentary videos on YouTube as well."

Jack wanted to get to know her better. He knew that the war was important to her understanding of the world and herself. He just wasn't sure how far he could probe. Since his mother was also a part of her story, he hoped she might let him in, at least a little.

"Was your family connected to Srebrenica?"

"Every Muslim is connected to it."

"I'm sure. But I mean, did you lose family members there?"

Aida shot Jack a sideways glance, keeping one eye on the traffic. "What the war did to my family is hard for me to talk about."

"Sorry. I didn't mean to—"

"No, it's good to talk about it. Maybe later, okay?"

"Sure."

"But today I want you to understand how the war affected the whole country. If you understand what happened to all of us, then in a way you understand what happened to my family. Does that make sense?"

"Yeah, it does."

"What the Serbs did at Srebrenica is unforgivable. They still won't even admit it happened, which makes it even worse."

"In your mind, is it safe to say that the war and all the things Bosniaks suffered were caused by Serb nationalism?"

"No, not at all. During the war, we were also attacked by the Croats. They're no better than the Serbs."

Aida made a turn off the main road. "The Ustaše were Croatian fascists who cooperated with the Nazis during World War Two. Croatia engaged in ethnic cleansing during the Yugoslavian wars, and Bosnian Croats fought us just like the Serbs for a while."

"And now the three of you—Bosniaks, Croats, and Serbs—are trying to live together as a democracy."

"Yes, with Croatia and Serbia as neighboring countries. We've been doing it for over twenty years. I'm just not sure how much longer it can last. There are nationalist forces on all sides agitating for a breakup."

She made another turn onto a small country road.

"I read about a Unity Referendum coming up soon?"

Aida smiled. "Yes, because there is always hope. Sure, there are many bad Croats and Serbs, but there are also bad Bosniaks, yes? But there are many, many more good people on all sides than bad. We're hoping the referendum will be a big victory over the bad guys who want to start another civil war."

Jack watched a Lufthansa regional jet arc low across the windshield on approach to the airport.

"Will the referendum be enough to prevent it?"

Aida turned onto an even smaller street crowded with

parked cars. "What did Burke say? All it takes for evil to triumph is for good people to do nothing? But we have to do something, or at least try, don't we?"

"Of course." Jack noticed the Sarajevo airport several hundred yards away.

"And yet, NATO and the EU did nothing to stop the war once it began." Aida found a spot to park and killed the engine. "And that's why we're here."

39

Aida led Jack past the knots of tour groups inside the Sarajevo Tunnel of Hope Museum, pointing out the exhibit of IEDs and land mines planted in the grass, and the display of mortar and artillery shells that hung like wind chimes at the entrance to the tunnel itself.

She led him crouching through the short span of timber-framed tunnel and out to the other displays depicting the tragic and heroic efforts of Sarajevans in crisis and under siege.

But the main point she wanted to drive home was on the other side of the cyclone fence. She pointed at the airport where Jack had landed a few days before.

"Sarajevo was completely cut off by the Serbs who occupied the surrounding hills. But here at the airport was where the UN and NATO planes landed with their food supplies instead of the guns and ammunition we needed to fight."

"I think I read that the West was worried about the war escalating. They were trying to keep guns out of everybody's hands, not just the Bosniaks'."

"And yet the Serbs and Croats had tanks and planes and all the ammunition they needed to fight, didn't they?"

"Yeah, I guess they did."

"But at least we had food." She led Jack over to a glass-enclosed display. "See? We received American military rations from the Vietnam War." She smiled. "Very generous, yes?"

Jack read the label: 1963. He was embarrassed.

"Wow."

"We received powdered chocolate, but no sugar. Flour, but no eggs. My mother used to pick hazelnut leaves off the trees to make dolmas because there weren't any grape leaves. It was a very hard time, and all of it could have been prevented . . ." Her voice trailed off.

Jack finished her thought. "If only good men had not stood by and done nothing."

It would've been a tough call for any NATO government, he thought to himself. Wage war to stop a war? With the Russians next door?

It wasn't unreasonable for NATO to try and tamp the fire down first with an arms embargo and hope it went out by itself.

Unless, of course, you were a Bosniak living in Sarajevo in 1993.

As a student of history, Jack understood NATO's reluctance. But he imagined himself as a Bosniak standing here with a family nearly starving to death in the city behind him. He knew he would be as angry today as Aida obviously was if he had experienced the war the way she and her family had.

Tough call. For the umpteenth time, he was glad he would never be president.

"In 1984, the whole world was cheering the Sarajevo Winter

Olympics," Aida said. "Ten years later, when it really mattered, who knew we were suffering?"

After the Tunnel of Hope Museum, Aida drove him to the seventeenth-century Jewish cemetery located on the slope of Mount Trebević.

"After Spain expelled the Jews in 1492, many of them sought refuge in the Ottoman Empire, and many located here. It's the second-largest Jewish cemetery in Europe, with nearly four thousand headstones and sepulchers."

Many of the stones were toppled and damaged. "The war was here, too, wasn't it?"

"Yes, we fight even among the dead. Unexploded mines and bombs weren't removed until years after the war. It's safe now."

Safe but neglected, judging by the graffiti on some of the stonework and the trash in the grass.

Aida then drove Jack to a high point in the pine-covered mountains overlooking the city, a sea of red-tiled roofs in the sprawling valley down below. She pointed out the Serb positions, and from here Jack could clearly see the advantage their guns would have had over the terrified civilians below.

She next took him to the nearby abandoned Olympic bobsled track, now a graffiti artist's wet dream of tubular concrete and colorful spray paint surrounded by tall evergreens. It was actually quite beautiful in its own unique, postapocalyptic anarchism. He ignored the FUCK RYAN—USA splattered in red spray paint on one of the support columns, though it couldn't be missed. Aida was courteous enough not to point it out, even though she surely saw it. He wondered what her reaction would be if she knew how closely connected he was to the slander-ous jab.

Jack would have liked to meet the poet laureate while he was rendering his aerosolized thoughts, to offer him a few choice adjectives of his own as he lifted the lad into an ambulance.

Aida pointed out the bullet and shrapnel scars on the bob-sled run. "Our forces used these heavy concrete tubes as ele-vated bunkers."

"Such a waste."

"Yes, but by then, what else were they good for?"

"How do you get beyond all of this?" Jack asked as Aida drove them to their next destination. "Even if every war criminal went to jail and every politician apologized, it wouldn't bring back the tens of thousands of people killed."

"You're right. If we only look to the past, we can never move forward as a nation. But because we still haven't dealt with the real causes of the war, I'm afraid we're doomed to repeat the same mistakes."

"I thought you had hope."

"I do. There is a bright future for my country. I'm just not exactly sure how we get there."

They rode along for a minute when Aida suddenly popped Jack on the arm with a friendly tap, trying to change the som-ber mood.

"Enough of all of this depressing war talk! Let me show you why my city is the most beautiful in the world, and why it will be great again."

They spent the rest of the day taking in the best Sarajevo had to offer, indoors and out. They wound up back in the Old Town, browsing through the shops of Aida's favorite local artists.

As they passed one of the shops, Jack saw a phrase stenciled in black block letters on the wall. It seemed completely out of place and yet the owner didn't remove it: *Samo nek' ne puca.*

Jack pointed it out. "What does it mean?"

Aida grinned. "You have to understand our dark humor. It's a saying that came out of the war, but it applies today. You know, with the high unemployment and corruption, all of our other troubles? The joke translates to something like 'Our lives totally suck and aren't worth living, but at least nobody is shooting at us.'"

She led Jack into a small gallery of handmade jewelry and art. She picked out a pair of handmade bronze earrings crafted from thin strips of antique coffee urns, etched with designs and studded with two small stones. The woman placed them in a small, cleverly folded box of her own design and handed it to Jack.

"What's this?"

"For your mother," Aida said. "My gift to her."

"She'll love these."

"I know she will." Aida smiled. "I have excellent taste."

She reached into her purse, but the gallery owner refused to take her money despite her repeated attempts. Aida finally relented and they headed out.

They ended the afternoon at Baklava Ducan, run by a couple young guys with a passion for culinary tradition. "The best in town," Aida assured Jack, as they were served coffee and the Bosnian version of baklava. The Greek—or was it Turkish?—dessert was usually a cloying, honey-soaked stack of crunchy phyllo, but the pieces he tried here had far more subtle flavors and a softer texture that practically melted in his mouth. He predicted a world of hurt for himself when he finally got back to early-morning PT in Alexandria after this bout of sweet indulgence.

But it was so worth it.

Aida never once mentioned anything personal about the war again after the bobsled run, though it was never far from Jack's mind, and there was a sadness descending on both of them, knowing that the day was nearly over. He hated the idea of leaving Sarajevo, in part because Aida's love for it had now taken hold of him as well. But he hated the idea of leaving her even more.

Still, he had a job to do back home, and his goal of finding her and delivering his mother's letter had been completed. Two more unplayed voice mails from Gerry told Jack it was time to push on.

They finished their coffee and baklava, but this time Jack insisted on paying the bill. The owners initially refused until a subtle nod from Aida completed the transaction.

They stepped outside into the setting sun, just as the melodic call to evening prayer echoed above them.

"I'm sorry if I bored you with too much history today, Jack. You Americans are fortunate because you always look toward the future."

"Your history is fascinating. I wasn't bored at all. I'm looking forward to coming back soon."

"It's too bad you're leaving tomorrow. I wish we had more time together."

Jack hadn't expected that. "I'd like that, too. How about dinner?"

"I'm sorry, but I have much work to do tonight at the office. I still own the tour business, and tomorrow we have a new group of refugees coming to the center."

"Can I come and see it tomorrow?"

"I thought you were leaving."

"Let me check in with my boss and clear it with him."

"It's nothing glamorous, Jack. I'm sure you'll be bored."

"I want to help out, if I can."

She sized him up and down again. "Come if you want. Or not. Either way, I hope your mother likes the earrings."

"Trust me, she will."

"You have my number. I'll be in the office until late if you change your mind."

She extended her hand. Jack took it. Neither bothered to let go. The heat in her hand matched the warmth of her eyes.

"I'll call you later either way."

"Ciao, Jack."

"Ciao."

Aida turned and walked away, confident that Jack's eyes were fixed on her every step as she disappeared into the crowds of tourists.

She was right.

40

When Jack got back to his apartment, he threw a load of laundry into the tiny washer/dryer combo unit in the kitchen. He had to Google instructions for it. Apparently, you needed a degree in electrical engineering to operate one of these things. As near as he could tell, it was going to take at least six hours to finish a load. He was down to his last pair of skivvies, the jeans he was wearing, and a faded Arcade Fire concert T-shirt, so he had to do it. Flying back to D.C. in dirty clothes wasn't an option.

Shit.

Flying back to D.C. period isn't what he wanted to do. He couldn't stop thinking about Aida. Yeah, she was a looker, for sure. But there was something else about her. Smart, compassionate, committed.

Well, yeah. And freakin' hot.

Lucky for him, he was able to extend his stay at the apartment because it wasn't booked for another five days. The place was so good and the rent so cheap, he grabbed all five, partly as a favor to his struggling young landlords, and partly so he could stop thinking about it. It was a great place at half the price of a fleabag motel in Virginia, but Virginia was home and where his job was, and so back to Virginia he needed to go.

Oh, well.

After tossing in the load, he pulled out his phone to face the dragon, but to his pleasant surprise the two voice mails that Gerry had left weren't royal ass-chewings, only pleas to call him when he got the chance. It was six hours earlier in Alexandria, and despite the coffee and baklava, Jack was hungry and knew he wouldn't get the chance to eat *ćevapi* again, so he headed back to the same restaurant.

He dialed Gerry's number while he was walking. His boss picked up on the first ring.

"Hello, kid. Glad you finally called. I was getting worried."

"No worries. I was out of pocket today."

"I thought you were supposed to be on that flight back today. What happened?"

"Nothing. I just decided to extend my trip another day."

"Still haven't found that girl?"

"Actually, I did."

"And you gave her your mother's letter?"

"Yep."

"Great, so you'll be on the first plane tomorrow, right?"

Jack crossed the Latin Bridge. He was about to tell Gerry about his decision to stay at least one more day, but there was something in Gerry's voice.

"Why do you ask? Has something come up?"

"I'm just concerned about the Slovenian situation."

"Did that woman finally get around to filing charges against me?"

"No, Jack. She's dead."

"What? How?"

The light turned green and Jack marched past the assassination corner without noticing.

"Heart attack. She was under police protection at the time, still recovering from the adult spanking you gave her."

"Why was she under police protection? The cops knew I left for Sarajevo."

"She said she was afraid you'd come back to hurt her."

"That doesn't make any sense. Either she was crazy or she was afraid of somebody else coming to get her, and used me for an excuse to get protection."

"Bingo. The Slovenian cops suspect foul play. She was murdered or committed suicide. Either way, we think she might be a gun monkey for an outfit called the Iron Syndicate. Mean anything to you?"

"Never heard of them."

"We're dry on our end, too, but we're shaking a few trees—gently. Still can't confirm anything."

"Then there's nothing to worry about."

"It's the fact we can't confirm one way or another that's got me worried, son.. If they exist and we're having this hard of a time finding them, they're a serious outfit. And they're gunning for you."

"I'll keep my head on a swivel," Jack said, hearing Clark's raspy training voice shouting in the back of his brain. "But I'm not worried."

"Just be damn sure to get on that plane tomorrow, will you?"

Jack arrived at the restaurant. "Gotta run, Gerry. I'll be in touch."

"Text me when your butt's in the seat, okay?"

"Got it. Ciao."

"What?"

"See you soon."

Jack hung up and searched for an open seat.

There weren't any.

J ack waited for a few minutes, and found himself scanning the crowd more closely than he otherwise would. If that woman really was a hired hitter and she was dead, whoever paid her would send somebody else. But how would this syndicate know he was in Sarajevo?

The same way they knew he was in Ljubljana.

Yeah, these guys have resources. But like Gerry said, nothing was confirmed. And if they really were out there, they were as likely to come after him in the States as here. And he wasn't one to hide.

Jack caught sight of a tall Muslim man in a traditional cotton tunic and pants pushing a stroller, followed closely by a woman dressed head to toe in black, only her eyes showing where the *niqab* barely parted. They entered the restaurant directly.

A funny thought struck Jack. How does that woman eat in a restaurant? Does she slip the *ćevapi* sausage up underneath her robe? And what about spaghetti or a hamburger? Or does she expose her face when she eats in public?

A moment later, a man and woman got up from a group table just outside the door. Jack figured out they were seating family style, at least at dinner, so he slipped over in that direction, asking with pointed gestures if it was available. To judge from the smiles and nods he received, it was. He took a seat.

Just then, the burqa-clad woman and her husband passed by Jack, exiting the restaurant with takeout boxes full of food and a happy toddler babbling in the stroller.

Burqa problem solved, Jack noted.

His *ćevapi* arrived hot and was just as tasty as he remembered. It didn't take him long to devour the meal. But he enjoyed it a little less than he had before, because he found himself keeping one eye on the passing crowds as he ate. Jack imagined an assassin's bullet plowing into his skull with his mouth full of sausage and onions. Not a pretty picture.

Other than that, Mr. Ryan, how was the ćevapi?

For some reason, though, he wasn't scared. More like annoyed that someone wanted to ruin his vacation. Gerry wanted him to tuck tail and run back home. That was the smart play, he had to admit. The Slovenian cop Oblak knew he was coming here, and, strangely, the Bosnian cop, Kolak, knew it, too. Someone wanted him dead and followed him to Slovenia. Someone else could be here in Sarajevo, right now, for the same damn reason.

Leaving made a lot of sense.

But he couldn't get the image of Aida out of his mind. If he left tomorrow, there wasn't a chance in hell he'd ever see her again. His last two failed relationships proved that.

But if he got his brains blown out like a Sarajevo Rose on the limestone pavement, that would cramp his dating life as well.

Helluva dilemma.

Well, Clark always said, a dumb guy thinks with his head, and a smart guy thinks with his brain.

True that.

Jack peeled off enough Bosnian marks to pay the tab along with a generous tip and headed back out onto the street,

ducking into a crowded souvenir shop with two exits. He purchased a blue-and-gold Dragon ball cap—the Bosnian national
soccer team—and switched it out with the one he was wearing,
which he stuffed in his waistband and hid beneath his shirt. He
headed out of the second exit, keeping the corners of his eyes
glued to the window glass across the street to see if he was being followed.

He continued his SDR for another thirty minutes, alter-
nately wearing one hat and then another, always careful to
keep his face pointed away from any surveillance cameras that
might be around, including the ones on ATMs.

Satisfied that he wasn't being tailed, and feeling just a little
stupid for being paranoid, he dialed Aida's number, hoping she
hadn't changed her mind.

He'd just have to figure out what to tell Gerry tomorrow
when he wasn't on that plane.

Fuck the Iron Syndicate.

41

NEAR TJENTIŠTE, REPUBLIKA SRPSKA,
BOSNIA AND HERZEGOVINA

Brkić listened carefully to Red Wing's electronically altered voice, but he still couldn't believe what he was hearing.

"It's extreme, yes. I agree," Red Wing said. "But necessary, if we want the referendum to fail."

Brkić still wasn't sure about Red Wing's order. It hadn't been part of their plan. But their plan so far hadn't entirely worked, either. Extraordinary measures were called for now, if they were to succeed.

Red Wing was right, even if it was for the wrong reason. Red Wing was often right, Brkić reminded himself. He'd known the man for a long time. Shed blood with him.

Red Wing had even saved his life.

That meant something, didn't it? More than the money and the weapons and the networks he provided. A debt that Brkić could never repay.

And yet, Brkić had other loyalties.

And another plan.

He was glad he'd never told Red Wing about it, or the missiles. Their alliance was one of mutual convenience, an arranged marriage. But this new order reminded Brkić that Red Wing's loyalties were not his own in the grand scheme of things. How could they be? Red Wing was neither Bosnian nor Chechen.

"Yes, you're right. It must be done."

"Excellent. You are still following the protocol?"

"A new phone every day. Yes, of course."

"Call me when it's done."

Brkić ended the call and tossed the phone into the crackling burn barrel that was keeping the night chill away. The phone popped in the fire, sending a burst of sparks floating up into the dark pine branches above his head, triggering a memory of another forest years ago, when his name was still Rizvan Sadayev.

POLJANICE, BOSNIA AND HERZEGOVINA, 1992

Sadayev heard the sputtering twin air-cooled radial piston engines low in the cloudy night sky long before he saw the plane. The twelve hundred feet of narrow dirt road servicing the small village saw double duty tonight as an airstrip for the rugged warhorse, a converted Vietnam-era Douglas C-47, a faded Greek air cargo company logo painted on its bullet-riddled fuselage.

A radio call from the plane was the signal for him and five other vehicles to turn on their headlights to illumine the road, a thin thread of hard-packed dirt wending its way between villages tucked between the thick swaths of forested hills and wide, grassy pasturelands of the Bila Valley. Central Bosnia was still a Muslim stronghold, but was under siege by Serb and Croat forces.

Sadayev was a junior commander in a unit of foreign jihadis in Bosnia—*bosanski mudžahidi*—fighting independently from the Bosnian Army. The other foreign jihadi fighters in country were organized by the Bosnian government into the El Mudžahid, a unit they kept under their tight control.

Sadayev's unit wanted no such control.

The plane landed with a heavy bounce and came to a hard-braking stop just short of the tree line. They began unloading the first crates of weapons, food, and ammunition before the engines had feathered to a stop.

The agent bringing the much-needed supplies jumped out of the cargo area and greeted Sadayev with a firm handshake. He identified himself only as "Red Wing," but his reputation as a fighter and his recommendation by trusted friends were all the credentials he needed. Sadayev introduced him to the other commanders in his unit—two Tunisians, four Saudis, a Libyan, and a fellow Chechen.

"Where are the other planes?" Sadayev asked.

"Delayed." Red Wing smiled as he pointed at the bullet holes stitched into the aluminum fuselage. "We were lucky to get through."

"We have an operation that begins in forty-eight hours, and the Serbs have tanks. Our weapons are useless against them." The Chechen was dismayed. The vintage American plane carried only seventy-five hundred pounds of cargo.

"I brought what you need, for now. The rest will be here within the week."

"*Inshallah,*" Sadayev said. "God willing."

Red Wing smiled. "Yes, of course."

Sadayev wasn't ungrateful. The UN arms embargo served only to cripple the Bosniaks' ability to resist their murderous neighbors. Illegal arms shipments from the Libyans, Saudis, Turks, and others gave their Muslim brothers a fighting chance. Rumors were the German BND supplied embargoed arms to the Croatians, and the Serbs could always count on Serbia and the Russians.

Without men like Red Wing, the Bosniaks were doomed. But Sadayev was under no illusion. Red Wing fought against the Western powers, but Sadayev and his men fought for Allah.

But such is God's way, he thought. To use unbelievers to accomplish His will.

"We'll discuss your operational plans later, my friend." Red Wing clapped Sadayev on his broad shoulder. "I have an idea you might appreciate."

He turned around and helped unload the next crate out of the door. Sadayev and the others joined in. It would be light in a few hours.

Two days later, a four-wheel-drive Bosnian Serb Army BOV-30 armored personnel carrier skidded to a halt in a cloud of dust. Its twin-mounted thirty-millimeter guns on its rectangular turret swept the village square in an ominous arc, scanning the small, neat Bosniak houses for resistance.

Nothing.

A moment later, a Serbian sergeant emerged from the cupola and scanned the area with his binoculars.

All clear.

He lowered himself back down and radioed the convoy commander. His ten-ton high-speed scout vehicle did double duty racing ahead of the column, confirming that neither mines nor enemy forces were located on the road or in the village.

They would stay put until the convoy arrived and dismounted infantry cleared the houses. Even if the civilians had fled, the village would have to be razed and the wells poisoned before they moved on to the next Bosniak enclave.

The Serb column rumbled down the dirt road, flanked on the left by a thick band of pines fifty meters away, and a wide, grassy meadow on the right, stretching more than a kilometer to the woods.

The lead tank in the column was an M-84, a Serbian-produced variant of the Russian T-72, with a 125-millimeter smoothbore autoloading gun and a three-man crew, including the convoy commander, a captain in the regular Army of the Republika Srpska.

Both the captain and his gunner stood in the hatches despite the threat, however unlikely, of sniper fire. The cramped, uncomfortable turret was a particular torture for the six-foot-tall captain, especially when buttoned up. The turret's primary purpose wasn't crew comfort, but rather to house the tank's autoloader, an ingenious Soviet design that reduced the crew size by twenty-five percent.

The autoloader could generate up to eight shots per minute, cycling the separate carousels of both charges and projectiles into the cannon's breech in a seamless mechanical motion.

When the autoloader operated, the captain felt like a midget riding inside a giant semiautomatic pistol, as toaster-sized propellant charges and arm-length explosive rounds clunked through the mechanism just inches from his shoulder. The crew compartment carried thirty-nine rounds of HEAT, armor-piercing and HE-frag shells.

Even when the gun wasn't firing, the vehicle at cruising speed echoed with the deafening roar of the tank's grinding steel tracks and the relentless V12 diesel engine. Pitiful electric fans hardly blew away the fumes, let alone the heat. The captain's TKN-3 primary optical sight and two episcopes were barely adequate under combat conditions, and practically useless otherwise. Better to ride the hatch and risk getting shot than stay hot, blind, and deaf for hours for no good reason.

The captain confirmed his scout's radio report and gave his gunner a thumbs-up. He turned around for another visual check on the convoy behind him. Thirty meters behind was the first of five FAP 2026 six-wheel-drive trucks loaded with heavily armed Serb White Eagles militia infantry, already infamous for their brutality against Muslim civilians. At least a third of the militia platoon were felons recruited straight out of prison, valued for their insatiable appetites for violence and mayhem.

The last vehicle in the convoy was another M-84 tank. It would be dark soon. If the village really was empty, they'd bivouac there tonight, and head out first thing in the morning after destroying it. Then they would proceed to assault the next village in the valley. With any luck, they'd cleanse the entire district of Muslims within the week. Poorly equipped and led, the Bosnian Army had put up virtually no resistance in the area.

You could hardly even call it a war, the captain mused, with forty-one tons of steel rumbling beneath him. His frontal armor could withstand direct hits by 105-millimeter tank guns and TOW missiles, neither of which the Bosniaks possessed in this region.

His tanks were invulnerable.

42

The Chechen Sadayev crouched at the base of the pine tree, the heavy bulk of the RPG-29 "Vampir" rocket launcher supported on the folding tripod behind the pistol grip. At this close distance he could've tracked the lead Serb tank through the iron flip sights, but his eye was pressed against the rubber cup of the magnified PGO-29 glass optics for extra accuracy.

His finger slipped from the guard to the trigger.

And squeezed.

The pulled trigger ignited the electronic fuse of the PG-29V, a 105-millimeter tandem rocket with a shaped HEAT charge capable of penetrating 750 millimeters of homogeneous armor, far thicker than the frontal composite sloped plating of the M-84 tank, let alone its far thinner sides.

The gunner whipped around in his hatch at the familiar sound of the rocket motor launching in the woods to his left, and gazed in horror at the long plume of exhaust racing toward his tank.

The shaped HEAT charge slammed into the thin steel wall behind the wheels. The eruption produced a hypersonic jet of molten metal and flaming gases, cutting through the twenty-millimeter steel hull like a plasma laser, incinerating the driver's atomizing corpse before his first scream.

The thirty-nine rounds of ammunition stores inside the hull ignited in a near-instantaneous chain reaction. The lower torsos of the gunner and commander were sheared away by the overpressure and shrapnel, but their upper bodies were still intact as the flaming turret cartwheeled high into the air before tumbling into the road with a thunderous clang.

The Serb tank commander in the rear of the column ducked instinctively back into his hatch when he saw the plume of rocket smoke racing out of the woods at the lead tank, shouting orders at the driver to break right, away from the trees.

The gunner, meanwhile, took the opposite tack and threw himself off the turret and onto the road, about the time a second HEAT round slammed into his vehicle. His act of cowardice saved his life, at least for another three seconds, when the white-hot shrapnel of the exploding tank shredded him like creamed chipped beef as he screamed in the dirt.

Some of the panicked White Eagles dove out of the trucks as they lurched off the road in a cloud of diesel fumes away from the nearby woods, racing for the relative safety of the tree line on the far side of the lush, green meadow.

Automatic-rifle fire erupted from the woods behind them

now, kicking up turf around the lumbering vehicles as they swayed and bounced on the soft grass.

WHAM!

Three of the trucks plowed into buried land mines. Flesh and canvas and steel erupted in a cloud of screams and boiling fire.

The remaining two trucks slammed their brakes just in time. The survivors leaped out of the cargo beds and bolted for cover as a hail of 7.62-millimeter bullets stormed into them, fired by the line of shouting mujahideen, rifles up, faces twisted with pious joy and battle rage as they charged out of the trees toward the broken Serb column.

Suddenly, a line of twenty-millimeter shells stitched across the surging wave of jihadis, breaking them open like clamming knives, spilling their butchered torsos into the pine needles in a spray of blood and shattered flesh.

The rotors of the Serb SA 341 Gazelle helicopter beat the air as it whirled around for a second pass with its GIAT M621 twenty-millimeter cannon, but its cabin-mounted 7.62-millimeter machine gun started pouring on the fire toward the trees. More jihadis fell as the Serbs gathered their courage, opening fire from prone positions across the road in the tall meadow grass.

The French-built Serb aircraft with its enclosed Fenestron tail rotor assembly swooped in a broad arc overhead to regain altitude and to draw a bead on the tree line.

Sadayev felt the overpressure of the metal-jacketed 7.62s buzzing past, cutting tree branches above his head and smashing trunks behind him.

CRACK!

A round slammed into the tree he lay next to, stinging the left side of his face, his left eye blinded with his own hot blood. He wiped it away with his hand as he pressed himself into the dirt and pine needles, waiting for the Serb volley of fire to cease. When it did, he jumped to his feet, pulled out his pistol from his leg holster, and shouted orders to his men to follow him to glory.

He bolted out of the tree line, keeping the flaming lead tank between himself and the Serbs in the far meadow, but as his feet hit the dirt he heard the sickening whir of a twenty-millimeter chain gun far above him. He glanced up just in time to see the rooster tail of dirt a hundred yards away racing toward him, cutting down more brothers in their tracks.

Sadayev shouted, *"Allahu akbar!"* knowing that his death was a blink away, until a speeding finger of smoke reached into the sky, smashing the Gazelle in a crushing, fiery fist.

Sadayev shouted again as the flaming wreckage tumbled toward the earth, his good right eye tracking the smoke trail back to its source on the ground.

Red Wing lowered the 9K38 Igla "Needle," a Russian MANPADS—man-portable air-defense system. He stood completely exposed in the middle of the road, dust kicking up all around him from Serb bullets fired in his direction. Sadayev nodded his thanks as Red Wing tossed the Igla aside and pulled out his own pistol, following Sadayev toward the Serbs in the meadow at a full run.

The surviving Serbs knelt in a line in the dirt of the village square, close enough to the smoldering wreck of the BOV-30 scout vehicle to smell the burnt flesh inside.

Wounded in battle or bleeding from their brutal interrogations, the seven White Eagles struggled to stay on their knees, their hands clasped behind their heads and their uniform collars secured by the hands of the Saudi and Tunisian jihadis standing behind them.

Sadayev nodded his command. His left eye was heavily bandaged and his tunic blackened with his own dried blood.

Seven razor-sharp serrated blades flashed in unison above the Serbians' heads, and the seven jihadis shouted *"Allahu akbar!"* as one. To the Serbs' credit, none of them wailed like women, Sadayev noted, as the blades opened up their throats and hot blood spewed into the dust. But they all struggled as the sharp blades continued their gruesome work.

Minutes later, the severed heads were set on a wall and several of Sadayev's men posed smiling and laughing next to their grimacing trophies. They held up a black AQAB flag between them for a picture. A Jordanian shouted encouragement as he snapped photos with his thirty-five-millimeter film camera.

"I understand the brothers have carried out similar operations against the Orthodox in the east," Red Wing said, watching the other fighters cutting off the White Eagles unit patches from the corpses' uniforms.

"We mujahideen are the sword of Allah. Our Bosniak brothers haven't the stomach for such things. But with more weapons, we will prevail against these Serb wolves, even if the sheepish brothers won't join us."

"What will you do after you win the war?"

"It's good country here. I will take a Bosniak wife. Perhaps even change my name. Raise up an army of sons to keep the land and raise the flag over all of Europe someday."

"I have no doubt you will prevail, my friend. But if you should lose? Then what?"

Sadayev laughed. "The same! We never lose. We only wait." He clapped Red Wing on his shoulder. "You are a good fighter. We can use you here. I wish you would stay."

"There are as many wars to fight as there are trees. I go where I am needed."

"Like a bird, flying to your next branch. Where to next?"

Red Wing only smiled. He wasn't at liberty to say.

Sadayev understood. "Perhaps we will meet again. In this life, or the next. *Inshallah*."

"Yes. In this life, or the next. But this life would be better for both of us, eh?"

43

Brkić's unmarked panel van straddled the narrow asphalt lane, blocking the only road leading to the restaurant overlooking the river.

Through his Gen 3 night-vision monocular, he watched his men gathering in the trees above the restaurant, guns at the ready, faces masked. Bloodstained White Eagles patches were sewn to their camouflage uniforms, trophies from an earlier war.

The same war, Brkić corrected himself. Twenty-six years and counting.

Or was it five hundred?

He swung his monocular down to the dining area, a covered porch with candlelit tables and a spectacular daytime view of the rushing turquoise waters of the Drina River down below. Each table was crowded with hungry, happy wedding guests.

The bride and groom's table stood at the end, their backs to Brkić's night-vision device. Even from here he could smell the bitter tang of cigarettes and the smoky-sweet aroma of grilled beef wafting in the soft breeze.

It was a festive, joyous gathering, judging by the laughter and wide smiles. Heaping plates of steaming food and ice buckets full of beer and champagne were shuttled from the stucco two-story house across from the dining structure to the guests by servers in dark slacks, silk vests, and red bow ties.

Brkić lowered his monocular, preparing to give the order.

He paused.

These were Sunni Muslims, like himself, celebrating a wedding. The joining of two families in the presence of God. This was a sacred time, a holy thing, wasn't it? He had no qualms about shedding the blood of *kafir* Serbs and Croats. But this? Wasn't everything he was planning designed to bless and save these very people?

Several champagne corks popped all at once to cheers and clapping down below, followed by the tinkling of long-stemmed fluted glasses, a reminder to the fervent Chechen that these were secular people for whom Islam was a mere cultural expression with no more meaning than a guide for manners. If they had faith at all, it was weak, and tempered by the pagan culture that surrounded and infected them.

Red Wing was right. This was a hard thing, but necessary. The plan to save his people from the predations of the Christian West must move forward. Tonight, these Muslim people of such little faith would bring glory to Allah in their unwilling martyrdom.

Brkić raised the radio to his mouth, gave the first order, then the second, unleashing the fires of hell.

Ten kilometers away, a small charge of C-4 plastic explosive decimated the unoccupied blue-striped POLICIJA van parked next to a roadside bar.

The two officers on duty that night were inside. This was their regular stop in the middle of the shift, to consume their free meal of flaky beef-stuffed *burek*s and strong coffee to get them through the rest of the night.

They dashed outside at the sound of the thundering explosion, the catchlight of the wrecked and burning van dancing in their eyes.

The firelight blocked the sight of the two masked White Eagles militiamen in camouflage stepping out of the shadows, but they caught the flash of their suppressed pistols. Both Bosniak cops crashed against the cinder-block walls in a spray of blood from the force of the slugs slamming into their unprotected chests.

They crumpled into a heap where they fell, and White Eagles death cards were shoved into their gaping mouths.

Brkić watched the unfolding mayhem as gunshots sparked inside the dining porch and echoed inside the restaurant. He barely heard the radio confirmation of the police assault above the plaintive screams of the wedding party. Men begging for their lives were shot in the mouth as their women were dragged outside by the hair to suffer the brutal frenzy of unleashed animals.

He checked his watch. Another fifteen minutes would be enough to finish the assault. His men had orders to spare the lives of the women but not the men. They had already cut the one phone landline they could find, and a portable cell-phone jammer in his van would take care of any guest who might try to call for help.

Red Wing would be pleased that his loathsome orders had been carried out tonight.

But soon Red Wing would discover that he wasn't in charge after all, when his world burned to the ground.

44

ida picked Jack up the next morning at his building. He met her at the curb. She was driving the same Volkswagen T5 Happy Times! tour van they had ridden in yesterday. She greeted him with a smile, obviously glad to see him.

She was as beautiful as he remembered. Maybe more so. It would be well worth the verbal ass-whooping Gerry would be handing him sometime later today for not getting on that plane.

"I'm so glad you decided to come."

"Me, too," Jack said, as he climbed into his seat.

Thirty minutes later they were up in the pine-covered hills surrounding Sarajevo and pulling up to the entrance of the refugee center with a banner proclaiming PEACE AND FRIEND-SHIP CENTER! WELCOME! in Bosanski, English, and Arabic. It hung from the newly installed cyclone fence that surrounded the refurbished facility. The dated buildings were mostly made of rough-hewn logs and stacked stone, recently repaired with concrete, and were laid out in orderly fashion on relatively flat, open ground surrounded by trees.

"What was this place?" Jack asked as Aida pulled through the front gate.

"It was a summer camp for the League of Socialist Youth. It was abandoned years ago, after the socialists evaporated. It's perfect for our needs. Let me show you."

She parked the van and led Jack into the first log-and-stone building, the medical clinic. Inside, there were examination rooms, a nurses' station, and doors marked X-RAY, LAB, and the like.

"We renovated the original, adding some basic medical equipment. We can perform routine health, dental, and eye exams, X-rays, and bloodwork."

"No surgeries?"

"No. We can send them to the hospital in Sarajevo for an emergency. These people have all been screened earlier for serious illnesses back in Greece or their point of entry. We're just taking care of basic needs like fevers, coughs, headaches, small cuts—that sort of thing. And to make sure big issues weren't missed earlier."

Aida introduced Jack to a nurse passing by with a chart in her hand, and then a young female doctor who appeared with a hijab-clad mother and her young daughter. Aida knelt down and cooed with the shy child, provoking a wide smile from the mother and the child when she offered the girl a piece of candy from her pocket.

They spent another few minutes meeting other staff, along with several more patients, all women in hijabs and their young children. The staff clearly respected her, and the patients all adored her, especially the children.

Jack was impressed.

She was pleased that he was. "There's much more to see."

She led him to the rest of the camp, almost a village unto itself: a large kitchen and dining area, an administrative office, an education building, sleeping quarters for families and singles, along with storage and maintenance sheds.

Aida explained that when the refugees first arrived, they were processed through the administration building, where they were enrolled for whatever Bosnian or international financial aid they qualified for.

Next, they were assessed in their health, education, and employment status, and finally assigned sleeping quarters.

"The Peace and Friendship Association that sponsors this place also generously supplies a monthly stipend for the first six months they are here. Many of the people coming here are surprisingly well educated and professional: doctors, lawyers, accountants. But they're willing to do any kind of work to survive."

"Where are all the men? I've only seen women and children," Jack said, as they walked around the camp. The women appeared to be from all over the Middle East, to judge from the wide variety of ethnicities, but all of them were covered to one degree or another.

"For the men who can find regular employment, we use our tour vans to run a shuttle from the refugee center to the city. But for the others who are still in transition, we operate a small furniture factory a few kilometers from here, and sell the furniture to help support the center, while giving them something meaningful to do and the chance to learn a new trade."

"Why do you use your tour vans?"

"It's one small way my company can help, and save the center the expense of hiring an outside firm."

"It's amazing what you're doing here. How many people can you accommodate?"

"At full capacity we can serve two hundred people. The idea is to move people in and out of here as quickly as possible, depending upon their employment status. Most families move on within two months of arrival." She looked around. "It's not exactly a five-star hotel, but I think it is rather pleasant."

"I've been in worse places, believe me."

"You? I think you are one of those rich one-percent Americans I keep reading about."

"Hardly. Not that we were ever poor when I was growing up. My parents work very hard, and raised us to do the same."

"Good. Then let's put you to work."

Jack smiled broadly. "That's why I'm here."

Aida dropped Jack off in the kitchen and pointed him at a giant stack of dirty breakfast dishes. Without batting an eye, Jack rolled up his sleeves, washed his hands, and filled up one of the big sinks with steaming hot water and sudsy soap.

"I will check on you later," Aida said, heading back to the clinic.

When she did check back an hour later, not only had Jack cleaned and dried all of the dishes, he'd swept and cleared the dining hall, and he was just finishing up scrubbing the toilets.

"I am impressed, Mr. Ryan. You know how to work."

"What else do you need done?"

Aida dragged him from building to building. The two of

them worked together, cleaning, moving, and stacking as the need arose. Aida was as willing as Jack to get her hands dirty. There was a kind of friendly competition between them.

In a storage room full of donated clothes, the two of them sorted and folded for an hour, sharing stories about their childhoods and their parents. Jack found that he did most of the talking, thanks to Aida's endless questions; he was still careful to avoid divulging his father's true identity.

"But American doctors make a lot of money, yes?"

"Compared to some other people, yes. But not millions. At least, not my mom."

"And your father, the bureaucrat? People in government here steal so much money, and they get very rich, very fast."

"Some of our politicians are crooked, too. It's amazing how many 'poor' congressmen become millionaires while in public service," Jack admitted. "But there are more honest people in government than not, and my dad is one of those."

They folded the last shirts and Aida led them outside. Jack nodded at a group of kids kicking a soccer ball around, laughing and shouting.

"My company, Hendley Associates, has a charitable foundation. You should apply for one of their grants. This would fit in perfectly with Gerry's vision."

Aida's eyebrows lifted. "The senator, yes?"

"Yeah. Now, that's a rich guy. But he worked hard for it, and he came by it honestly *after* he left office."

"You admire him."

"Yes. He's like a second father to me."

As if on cue, Jack felt his phone vibrate in his pocket. He was sure it was Gerry. He ignored it.

Aida smiled coyly. "Then I can count on you to put in a good word for us with your foundation?"

"Sure. Excuse me a minute." Jack bolted off to the soccer game and jumped into the middle of it.

Aida saw Jack laughing and smiling as much as the kids. She decided to join the game, too, and a few minutes later, more kids came out to play.

Jack was a big hit. When lunchtime came around, the children begged him to sit with them, and of course he did. The rest of the day went the same way, with Jack helping teach an English-language class, and peeling potatoes back in the kitchen. Whatever needed to be done, he did it, working shoulder to shoulder with Aida.

It was a total contrast to his normal life, not that his life could be considered normal by any stretch. He was proud of what he did back home with The Campus and Hendley Associates.

But he had to admit he hadn't been this happy in a long time.

They were back outside playing with the kids again when Aida checked her watch.

"There will be another bus arriving here any minute. We should greet it."

"Let's go."

They left the kids and their teacher kicking a soccer ball around and headed for the front gate just as a gleaming black Audi A8 sedan pulled up to the front office. The driver's door opened and a suited chauffeur leaped out, then opened the rear passenger door. Ambassador Topal unfolded himself from the sedan and stood.

"Ambassador, it's so good to see you," Aida said.

Topal smiled, the corners of his eyes crinkling beneath his steel-rimmed glasses. He stretched out his hand. "My dear Aida, hard at work as usual, I see." He glanced at Jack. "And I see you've recruited another volunteer." He extended his hand to Jack. "Good to see you again, Mr. Ryan."

"Please, Your Excellency. It's just Jack."

"What do you think of our little oasis?" Topal asked.

Aida explained, "The ambassador is the chairman of the Peace and Friendship Association. He has raised nearly all of the money from private contributions in Turkey for our facility."

"It's a wonderful place, and a very generous thing you are doing for these people."

Jack saw over Topal's shoulder that a giant Happy Times! tour bus was making a wide turn from the road toward the gate. Jack felt a tug on his shirtsleeve. An eight-year-old girl, dirty-blond and green-eyed, stared up at him, smiling.

"Please, Jack? Come play more?"

Jack shrugged and said to Topal, "I think I'm being drafted into service."

"Then you should serve, as any good soldier does," Topal said, smiling.

The little girl began pulling on his sleeve with both hands like a one-man tug-of-war, giggling hysterically.

He turned to Topal. "You want to join us?"

"I'm sorry, but my old knees won't allow it." He shook Jack's hand again. "Enjoy your game. I still want you to come by my office sometime."

"It might have to be the next trip. But thanks."

Jack turned and sped away with the little girl, who shouted in Arabic to her cheering friends waiting for them on the field.

Topal watched Jack resume his play as the bus's pneumatic brakes barked with a whoosh of air. He turned and whispered to Aida out of the side of his mouth.

"What is Jack Ryan doing here?"

"I told him to stay away."

"And yet here he is."

"He's a good man. I'm not worried."

"A good man? Yes, perhaps he is. Which surprises me. Your taste in men tends to run toward the opposite." Topal removed his glasses and pulled a handkerchief from his suit pocket to clean them.

"My taste in men is no concern of yours."

"Everything about you concerns me these days."

The bus door finally opened, and the first refugee stepped out, a bearded twenty-five-year-old Tunisian male in jeans and a T-shirt. He shaded his eyes from the sun with one strong hand. He was followed by others just like him.

"This is not a good time for distractions."

"I'll do as I please," she said. "And Jack pleases me."

Topal finished wiping his glasses and put them back on, along with an affected smile.

"Let's go greet our new friends, shall we?"

45

When Aida finished processing the new refugees, she stopped by the kitchen, where Jack was helping prepare the evening meal.

"Time to get you back to your place, Jack. I'm sure you need to get packed for your flight."

"I don't have much to pack. I'm happy to stay longer if there's anything more I can do."

"Actually, I need to get you home so I can get back to my office. I have more paperwork to do tonight. Taxes are due."

Jack tried to hide his disappointment. "Okay, sure. Let's go."

Aida pulled up to the curb at Jack's building just as the sun was beginning to set. The call to prayer echoed outside from the nearby mosque, beautiful and hypnotic, even muffled through the Volkswagen's glass.

"You did wonderful work today, Jack. I really appreciate it."

"I wish I could have done more for you."

"Perhaps when you get back to the States, you could spread the word. We can always use more donations."

"You should come back with me. You'd sell it better than I could."

She set the parking brake. "Don't tempt me."

"I am tempting you. I could introduce you to some heavy hitters."

"Heavy hitters?"

"Big-money people who love to donate to causes like this. I might even be able to convince my dad to look into some kind of federal money or something."

"Your father must be a very important bureaucrat."

"I'll tell him that. Better yet, tell him yourself."

"Someday, I would like to visit your country. But now is not the time."

Jack heard the finality in her voice. He didn't want the day to end. "Man, I'm hungry. How about dinner?"

"I'm sorry, but I can't. I really do have a mountain of paperwork tonight, and tomorrow I'm leaving for Dubrovnik."

"I've heard it's a beautiful city."

"You have never been there?"

"No. But I'd like to someday."

"Too bad you're flying home tomorrow." She lowered her eyes. "If you were staying longer, I would take you there, and on the way show you more of my beautiful country."

Jack's heart raced. Music to his ears. But he had checked his cell phone earlier in the day. Three texts from Gerry, all with the same message: "Call me." It was time to get home and get back to work.

Right?

"Why are you going to Dubrovnik?"

"I need to pick up some things for the medical clinic. I can make the drive in a day, but if you came, we'd do it in two days like on one of my tours, so I can show you some amazing things that you may never see again."

"I can change my plans."

Aida brightened. "So you'll come?"

"It's for the refugees, right? How can I say no?"

While Jack was packing his underwear for the trip, Aida was in her office working on her books when Emir stormed in.

"You're taking him to Dubrovnik?"

"Sure. Why not? He's never been there."

"Is that . . . wise?"

"I have to make the pickup anyway. Now I'll have company."

"I don't like it." Emir's sulking face betrayed him.

Of course you don't, my sweet cousin, Aida thought. "It's only a courtesy. His mother is a surgeon. This is an easy way to repay her kindness to me."

She pitied Emir, and he knew it. That made him feel even worse.

Emir's face hardened. "It's shameful."

"Stop being so old-fashioned. We'll be in separate hotel rooms. It's only a kindness. I'm taking him on the same boring tour stops we've both done a thousand times."

"It doesn't look right."

"What do I care what it looks like? I do as I please."

"How do you know he's not a spy?"

Aida laughed. "A spy? Why? Because he's an American? Yes, I see it now. He's a CIA assassin!" She laughed again.

"Do not mock me, woman."

Aida recoiled inwardly at Emir's tone of voice. She'd never heard it from him before. Normally, she wouldn't take that from anybody, but his ego was wounded, and she cared for him, though not in the way he had hoped for since they were children. She never felt guilty about that. In fact, she used it to her advantage. She decided to forgive him the insult this one time.

She pointed at the QuickBooks screen on her computer. "Do you see that? That's what Jack does all day. He's a financial analyst—a numbers cruncher. He's no spy. Believe me, I'd know."

"It's too risky, even if he isn't a spy."

"This life we live is full of risk. This is a small one, at most. And Jack may help raise money for the refugee center." She smiled at the irony.

"Then I will go with you. You need protection."

"That isn't necessary. You have responsibilities here. We'll be fine."

"I insist."

Aida stood. "You're being a fool. It's you who should be ashamed."

Emir's hands trembled slightly, but he didn't speak. A moment passed, and he willed his body to relax.

She yanked open a drawer and pulled out a bottle of The Macallan single-malt whiskey along with two glasses.

"Have a drink with me, like we used to do, back in the old days." She coaxed him with a teasing smile. "Before you got religion."

"Be careful with that man," was all he said before he turned and headed for the door.

"Emir—"

The door slammed shut behind him.

Not good, Aida thought. *But he'll get over it.*

46

Jack and Aida left early the next morning in the Happy Times! Volkswagen tour van. The traffic in Sarajevo was heavy but cleared up as soon as they passed the city limits heading west.

Jack wore a pair of jeans and a Polo shirt. Aida was equally casual in form-fitting Lululemon yoga pants, FK Sarajevo soccer jersey, and Ray-Ban aviators. Jack watched strands of her thick hair dancing in the air of the open driver's window.

Stunning.

They drove southeast about thirty miles through forested mountains to their first destination. According to the dashboard GPS display, they were coming into a little town named Konjic.

"Do all of your vehicles use GPS?" Jack asked.

"None of our drivers need it for directions, but it's a great way for Emir to keep track of vehicle locations, distances traveled, gas mileage, and that sort of thing."

Aida parallel-parked on the main drag, directly in front of a magnificent stone bridge spanning the wide Neretva River. She yanked on the parking brake and smiled. "Let's check it out."

She led him to the center of the bridge and a commemorative plaque above the central pylon, written in Turkish and Bosnian. Jack deciphered enough to figure out that the bridge was built during the reign of the Ottoman Sultan Mehmet IV in 1682. Aida filled in the rest of the details.

"Illyrian tribes first settled here two thousand years ago, but others may have been here much earlier. The Old Stone Bridge was destroyed by retreating German forces in 1945, but it was finally rebuilt in 2009 by Turkish engineers using the exact same seventeenth-century building techniques and materials."

"I'm betting the Turks don't rebuild Hapsburg monuments," Jack said. Smart advertising on their part. A great way to display their generosity and promote their cultural hegemony all at the same time.

"Not that I'm aware of."

Jack took in the picture-postcard view, a real Rick Steves moment. They could just stop here and be done, as far as he was concerned.

Aida took his hand. "Let's keep going. There's so much more to see."

Their next stop was Tito's Bunker, a surrealistic trip back into the Cold War. The nuclear bomb shelter was secretly built by the communist dictator for himself and three hundred handpicked companions to survive a nuclear strike and live another six months.

The people who ran the bunker now got the bright idea to not only preserve as much of the original furnishings and equipment as possible, but also to stage it with modern art exhibits throughout its many rooms, since the bunker itself was a strange kind of Brutalist art form.

After touring the bunker, they drove about seventeen miles

to the next town, Jablanica, which also bridged the Neretva River. About half of the drive was along the wide Jablanica Lake. Their destination was a large city park and museum, commemorating a famous victory by the Yugoslavian Partisan forces against the Nazis in World War II. A blown railway bridge, half collapsed into the river, was still in place.

"This is actually a bridge built and destroyed for a Yugoslavian war movie. But it looked so good and so real, the Tito government decided to leave it."

They jumped back into the van, the road generally following the track of the wide and winding Neretva River through tree-covered mountains. The sky was crystal-blue, warmed by a pleasant, late-morning sun.

The farther they drove, the more Jack fell in love with the people and the scenery, which at times was quite dramatic. It was another reminder to him how big the world was and how many fascinating places there were that he had yet to discover. A hundred generations of people he had never really thought about had lived in this magnificent country. Too many of them had died in the wars that plagued the area since the time of the Caesars.

But for all of the interest he was taking in the tour, he was mostly curious about the woman driving the tour van. She fielded every question he had about geography and culture and local delicacies. And while she was amazingly well versed in the history of the Ottoman sultans and the Hapsburg emperors, she remained politely evasive when he probed about her own personal history, which made her all the more intriguing. Still, he kept trying.

"So, you've never been married?" Jack's feet were up on the dashboard while Aida drove on the curving two-lane.

"No," she said with a smile.

"Why not?"

"I was going to ask you the same thing, Jack."

"I want to get married someday. Just need to find the right woman who has the time for a relationship."

"Do you have the time for one?"

"Ouch. I guess I'm kinda busy these days."

"And yet here you are, in the middle of Bosnia. Not so bad, is it?"

"Not bad at all."

"I'm curious. Tell me about this 'right woman' of yours."

Jack sat up. *This is getting interesting.*

"Smart is the most important attribute, after character. Beautiful is nice, but that comes from within. And, let's see. How about transparent?"

"Transparent? That's terrible!" she joked.

"Why?"

"A girl likes to keep a little bit of mystery about her. Don't men find that more interesting?"

"Depends on what the mystery is, I guess. What about you? Who is your Mr. Right?"

"That's easy. A man who loves his family. An honorable man. A man who works hard and provides for the ones he loves." She shot him a glance. "And a man who doesn't ask too many questions."

"Well, I guess that takes me out of the running, especially since I have one more. Do you want kids?"

"As many as possible."

"Me, too. Or four, whichever is less."

She laughed. "You have brothers and sisters?"

"Two sisters and a brother. The older sister is a neurosurgeon and a brainiac like my mom."

"And your father works for the government. A high-level bureaucrat, you said."

"That's what he'd call it, for sure. It's kind of an executive position."

"And your parents are still married?"

"A long time. They're even in love."

"How romantic. And rare, I think."

"It's a miracle."

"And you admire them."

"More than you know."

"That's nice."

And just like that, Jack felt the door shut. They were definitely connecting, but something happened. Did he say something wrong? No, he hadn't. But for whatever reason, she wasn't going to let this thing go any further. Jack couldn't blame her. He was just another American tourist who'd be moving on in another day or two.

And what was he thinking? There wasn't any way this thing was going to work between the two of them. He was grateful she'd shut this conversation down.

They rode along in a sad, comfortable silence for a while, Jack's mind turning to the world outside the windshield.

At around noon, Aida finally asked, "Getting hungry?"

"Yeah, sure." Jack was staring out of his window. Down below, the Neretva River rolled wide and slow between sloping, tree-covered hills.

"I know a place."

"You're the tour guide."

A few minutes later, Aida pulled off the two-lane asphalt and onto a dirt road threading down through the pines and toward the river. A hundred feet later, a chain barrier blocked the way down farther. She put the van in park, hopped out and unlocked the chain, then crawled back into the driver's seat and continued on.

A few moments later they entered a secluded clearing on the banks of the river, sparkling in the warm sunshine. Aida killed the engine.

"This place you know must deliver," Jack said, as he opened his door.

"I brought a little picnic for us. Hope you don't mind."

She opened the back hatch and pulled a blanket off a small ice chest hidden beneath it.

An ice chest.

Great.

She opened the ice chest. Bottles of frosty cold beer jutted out of the ice.

"It's Sarajevska brand. Hope you like it."

Jack pulled one out. "Know it well. Good choice."

"Thank you." Aida grabbed the blanket and a basket. "Follow me."

They set up beside the river in the leafy shade of a paper mulberry tree. She'd put together a spread of sandwiches, a Bosnian version of Greek salad, and fruit. And of course, the beer.

They ate mostly in silence, with a few stolen glances between bites and heaping servings of Jack's praise for the delicious food. The cold beer tasted great in the gathering heat, and the whispering river looked cool and inviting.

Aida finished her meal and her beer, and stood. "I'm going in."

She sauntered down to the water's edge, knowing that Jack's eyes were tracking her every movement. She stared at the light dappling on the river's surface for a moment before lifting off her blouse and dropping it by her feet. She kicked off her shoes and slipped off her yoga pants.

Jack's eyes drank in the curves of her body, a silhouette against the sunlight dancing on the water. A lacy bra and panties weren't much of a bathing suit, but that was fine by him.

Aida reached behind her back and unhooked her bra. Slipped the straps off her shoulders and turned around, then let the bra fall away.

"Will you be joining me, Jack?"

Uh, yeah.

They played and swam in the river, both naked as the day God made them. But Aida's play turned to something else altogether when Jack carried her back to the blanket and laid her down.

And Emir watched it all through his binoculars from high on the road, his eyes blurred with bitter tears.

47

ROME

The Hendley Associates Gulfstream jet was parked near a hangar on the far side of the General Aviation Terminal at Ciampino airport, smaller but more convenient than Leonardo da Vinci. By special arrangement, Ciampino operated 24/7 for Hendley aircraft, a critical advantage for short-notice missions like theirs. It was also closer to the city where Dom, Adara, and Midas were chasing down leads on Elena Iliescu and the Iron Syndicate, which presumably employed her.

Trieste had been a bust, and the closest thing to a thread of possible connection between her and the mysterious organization had led them here. Gavin Biery tracked down a cell-phone number that had received a call from Iliescu's phone the night before she drove to Trieste. The man's name was Renzo Castelletti, born in Florence, but lately shuttling quite frequently among Rome, Trieste, and Vienna.

At first they assumed the man was Iliescu's accomplice in

the attack on Jack, running intel or interference. But a more thorough analysis of Castelletti's phone records indicated something else. He was either a traveling gynecologist doing international house calls or, as Gavin reported breathlessly, "an honest-to-goodness authentic Italian gigolo," judging by the disproportionate number of women he spoke to and visited with on a regular basis.

Castelletti's cell phone was currently pinging off a cell tower near Rome's Westin Excelsior hotel. Gavin hadn't been given permission by Gerry to break into any private cell phones of people who weren't demonstrably guilty of any crime, but he was allowed to build an algorithm that allowed him to vacuum up cell-tower data and match it to simultaneous cell-phone usage. When two parties were both pinging on cell towers at the same time, Gavin's second algorithm sorted for length of phone call. When two calls lasted for the same exact length of time, he presumed they were speaking with each other. Gavin's magic math tricks, as Dom referred to them, led the team to the Westin Excelsior, where they would be arriving soon.

After refueling and inspecting the plane earlier, Lisanne sent the two pilots to a local hotel with a Hendley Associates account. She opted to stay behind for a few more hours, taking advantage of the onboard computer and satellite link. She needed to catch up on her paperwork and check for the necessary documentation and other arrangements for the three cities where Gavin thought they would be heading after Vienna, their destination tomorrow.

Lost in her work, she was completely unaware of the airport customs officer standing at the foot of the stairs.

"Mi scusi," he called up.

Lisanne glanced up from her work, a little rattled by the voice. But when she saw the young, handsome Italian in his crisp new uniform and armed only with a clipboard, she relaxed.

"Yes?"

"I need to inspect your plane." The officer stood in the cabin doorway now, flashing a disarming smile.

If she had been in a cozy little piano bar, Lisanne would have been flattered. Tempted, even. But she was on duty.

"We were cleared this morning."

"Sì, sì. But my boss, he says take another look. I'm sorry." He grinned and shrugged while flashing his hands. A gesture of infinite regret but also official inevitability.

He was awfully handsome. What would it hurt? She relented. "Knock yourself out."

"Grazie."

The man stepped in, consulting his clipboard. He pointed at the cockpit. "Okay?"

"Don't touch anything."

"Of course. Just a formality."

Lisanne turned back to her workstation. She sniffed the air. Whatever sweet, leathery cologne he was wearing was having its desired effect. She stole a sidelong glance at him. She was on duty, but she wasn't dead.

He cut a dashing figure in his uniform, for sure, from the top of his high-peaked cap to the bottom of his shiny, patent-leather shoes.

His shoes.

The wrong shoes.

Lisanne drew her SIG Sauer micro nine-millimeter from

the holster beneath the table, but she was too late. The man batted the pistol out of her hand and lunged for her throat. She let him in close enough to throw a fierce uppercut into his clenched jaw. It wasn't enough. His eyes watered as he grunted, but his powerful hands still found her neck.

She couldn't breathe, let alone scream, as his weight bore down on her, pinning her against the desk. She reached behind, her hands desperately searching for something, anything—

She jammed the scissors into his left ear. He screamed in agony and clutched at his wound, releasing her. She threw a hard elbow into his face, toppling him backward.

She turned and ran toward the back of the cabin, diving to the floor where she thought her weapon had clattered to a halt beneath one of the seats. She reached back until she finally wrapped her hand around the pistol's walnut-grained handle, then rolled onto her back into the aisle, flipping the thumb safety to fire.

But her bladed sights were pointed at empty space.

The Iron Syndicate assassin was gone.

What about the others? She had to warn them. She grabbed her phone and punched Dom's number.

No answer.

NEAR TJENTIŠTE, REPUBLIKA SRPSKA, BOSNIA AND HERZEGOVINA

"Slowly, brothers! Carefully!"

The Syrian captain kept a wary eye on the two big Bosniaks muscling up the first two-hundred-pound missile into the BM-21 Grad launch tube. The four spring-loaded stabilizer fins were strapped against the fuselage so that the missile could fit inside the tube, but as soon as the rocket motor fired, the straps were burnt away, and the fins deployed upon exiting the tube. A simple, analog solution to a complex problem. Russian design genius at its practical best.

Brkić could hardly contain his excitement watching the first missile loading, a bullet being chambered into an assassin's forty-round revolver. This was the first step on the journey that would lead to the end of the humiliation of his God and his people, first in Europe and then throughout the world. A journey Brkić would take without Red Wing's permission, because Red Wing was only an arrow in the quiver of the Almighty, whose plans were never thwarted.

True to his word to Red Wing so many years ago, Tarik Brkić—then known as Rizvan Sadayev—remained in Bosnia after the war ended, married a local Bosniak woman, and became a citizen of the Republic of Bosnia and Herzegovina, biding his time until the next opportunity to strike.

And that time was now.

When Red Wing contacted him with the plan to initiate a civil war to defeat the Unity Referendum, Brkić gladly accepted, on condition that Red Wing would give him access to his smuggling routes so that guns, drugs, and jihadi fighters could be brought into the region and transported farther north into Europe as needed.

Causing a civil war through false-flag operations was a tried-and-true tactic of governments everywhere; Red Wing's own government had done it successfully in Syria only recently. There was no question that Red Wing's plan would work, but to what end? A civil war would end in the partition of Bosnia—itself a creation of the Western powers, designed to keep Muslims in the region under control. Muslims across the Balkans could form a new, larger Islamic state in the heart of Europe. But what would happen then? At best, neutralization by NATO and Russia, fearing the contagion of Muslim self-governance across the Eurasian continent. Or worse? The extermination of Muslims altogether.

It wasn't enough for Bosniaks to free themselves, or for Muslims in the Balkans to unite. Red Wing's government promised to protect them, but it was clear that his government's ultimate goal was to control them.

The only way to protect Muslims from the two great power blocs was to destroy those blocs. But how? Even now, NATO and Russia were killing brothers all over the planet. Fundamentalist Islam—the kind Brkić practiced—was on the run.

Brkić knew that only NATO and Russia were strong enough to stop the other. His plan would result in a war between NATO and Russia, and such a war would result in the downfall of Red Wing's government as well.

The destruction of the great powers would pave the way for true Islam to take leadership of Europe first, and then of the world, and, ultimately, the world to come.

Inshallah.

ROME

The woman in the fifth-story corner window across the street from the Westin Excelsior had eyes on Dom, Adara, and Midas as they entered the hotel. She was on the phone with her contact in Vienna.

"Any minute now," she said, and smiled.

D om, Adara, and Midas strolled through the hotel like they owned the place, knowing full well that the crowded lobby was under constant surveillance by the ubiquitous security cameras tastefully concealed in the ceilings and corners throughout the building. That knowledge was strangely comforting to a team that didn't want to be discovered, because it was that security system that would enable them to complete their mission tonight. Gavin's remote search of the hotel security system two hours earlier had paved the way for them in two important ways.

First, thirty minutes before the team entered the hotel, Gavin "spoofed" the live camera feed, replaying footage from two hours prior. No one casually monitoring the system would notice anything but the usual anonymous traffic of guests and hotel employees circulating throughout the hotel. Nothing live was currently being shown or recorded, including the movements of Dom, Adara, and Midas.

The second way the hotel's own security system aided their efforts tonight was in locating their target. Hacking past the hotel's civilian-grade firewall was a piece of cake for the wily IT genius. With a picture of Renzo Castelletti in hand, Gavin's search algorithm easily traced the Florentine's steps from the lobby to the elevators and finally to room number 3407, where he was greeted by the registered guest, a large and welcoming middle-aged real estate broker from Franklin, Tennessee.

With that, it was simple enough for Gavin to secure the computer guest check-in file and recover the RFID chip code embedded in the woman's room card. He then sent that code to a MIFARE Pegoda II 13.56 megahertz RFID reader-writer device stored for just such a purpose on the Hendley Associates Gulfstream. Adara cloned three hotel key cards for room 3407 and passed out two to Dom and Midas before heading to the hotel.

The three of them exited the elevator on the third floor. The hallway was empty. Midas dialed the Florentine's cell number lifted from Elena's phone address book, and proceeded to walk past 3407 just as Castelletti's phone rang. That was all the confirmation they needed that he was still in there.

They doubled back and approached the room. Muffled groans and shrieks rumbled behind the heavy door.

Midas nodded to the room-service tray on the floor next to the door, littered with three drained bottles of Collalto Prosecco Brut, a heaping mound of shucked oyster shells, and a couple empty tins of Iranian caviar.

"They're not doing Bible study in there," Midas whispered in his comms. "I hope you kids don't blush easily."

Checking to make sure the hallway was still clear, they pulled on ski masks and gloves and pulled their weapons, then keyed the door and rushed in as quietly as possible, heading for the bedroom, expecting total surprise and no resistance.

They were half right.

Neither Castelletti nor the woman offered any resistance. They couldn't. Their naked corpses lay tangled in the blood-soaked sheets, their throats slit ear to ear. The fat woman's wrists and ankles were tied by silken cords to the bedposts, a silver and jeweled Venetian Carnevale cat mask still fixed to her face.

Adding to the macabre surrealism of the moment was the porn movie groaning and shrieking in Dolby Digital 5.1 surround sound on the bedroom's widescreen television.

Surprise.

Their only lead to Elena Iliescu was gone.

"Now what?" Adara asked.

Dom nodded toward the door. "We get the hell out of here—fast."

As soon as they cleared the lobby, Dom called Lisanne. He filled her in on the carnage they had found, and the loss of Castelletti, their only lead.

"Just glad you're okay," was all she said. "I was about to call in the cavalry." Dom and the others had silenced their cell phones for the op. She told Dom about the syndicate hitter and the stainless-steel earache she had given him.

"You okay?"

"I'm fine," the former combat medic said. "I'm keeping his hat for a souvenir."

On the drive back to the hangar, the four of them discussed options on speakerphone. The attack on Lisanne and the elimination of the Florentine meant they were on the right path. The only question now was: Stay put and try and flush the syndicate out, or move on?

The syndicate must have known that Lisanne had filed the flight plan for Vienna. Trying to kill her and possibly destroy the plane meant the syndicate didn't want them going there. Staying put was also inviting another attack, and probably not by an unarmed singleton.

So Vienna it was.

48

MOSTAR, BOSNIA AND HERZEGOVINA

After sating themselves on the riverbank, Jack and Aida packed up and continued the drive along the winding road. They paid more attention to each other than to the local scenery, Aida pointing out less and less until they reached Mostar, jammed with spectators for the Red Bull Cliff Diving competition from the city's fabled bridge, famous for local talent diving off it for cash tips from tourists.

Mostar was crowded and hot, and after a quick walking tour of the Old Town and a gander at the bridge jumpers, they headed to a four-star hotel for a light dinner and even hotter sex than before.

They woke up famished and attacked an amazing breakfast buffet of local meats, cheeses, specialty dishes, and just about anything sweet Jack could think of, along with strong black coffee and orange juice. Aida devoured two helpings of ratatouille, not Jack's idea of a breakfast dish. She listed the sites they could see as they left Mostar, including the sixteenth-century dervish *tekija*, a monastery built into the side of a cliff, and the Catholic pilgrimage city of Medjugorje, where the appearance of the Virgin Mary to six Herzegovinian children in 1981 was commemorated.

She then began describing the windy Vjetrenica cave, one of the largest in Europe . . .

But Jack hardly heard a word. He just fell deeper into her stunning blue eyes. He grabbed her by the hand, tossed the desk clerk an extra twenty-euro note for a late checkout, and took her back to their room.

They arrived in Dubrovnik, Croatia, in the early afternoon. Situated on the coast of the dazzling blue Adriatic, the gleaming white medieval city glowed beneath the sun. It reminded Jack of Minas Tirith from the *Lord of the Rings* movies. The only problem was that Gandalf—Gerry—had already sent him two anxious texts: Where the hell are you?

"Problem?" Aida asked.

"Just my boss. Wants me to cut my vacation short."

"You Americans work too hard."

Jack texted back. I'm in Dubrovnik. Perfect weather. Four more days, guaranteed.

Gerry wrote back. The girl?

Yup

Would I like her?

Yup

Your dad?

Yup

Your mother?

Yup X 2

Since nothing confirmed on our end regarding your situation and against my better judgment I'll give you four more days. But that's it. Check in daily and stay alert. Understood?

Understood

"All good?" Aida smiled hopefully.

"All good." Except for the fact there might be a secret international criminal syndicate trying to murder him. But he dismissed it. If there was a real problem, Gerry would have told him.

The tourist traffic was bumper-to-bumper across the 1,700-foot Franjo Tuđman Bridge, an ultramodern steel-cabled structure featuring a giant A-shaped pylon, a real contrast to the fitted, ancient stones of the Old Town.

They finally made their way to Lapad, one of the newer suburbs of the city, where Aida said she owned an apartment.

She pulled up to a small warehouse, its steel door shut. She called a number on her phone and a moment later the steel door was rolled open by a Croatian man in grease-stained gray coveralls. His eyes narrowed at the sight of Jack, but he didn't say a word as Aida pulled in and the garage door closed behind them.

"This will just take a minute," Aida said as she got out.

"No problem."

Jack watched Aida and the Croatian wander over to a pallet stacked with cardboard boxes stamped in Croatian he couldn't read but with medical symbols he recognized, including the Staff of Asclepius. Aida had told him the reason she needed to come to Dubrovnik was to pick up some medical supplies. He assumed it would be at a pharmacy or a hospital, not an unmarked warehouse in a semi-suburban neighborhood.

He watched Aida chatting it up with the expressionless Croatian, and what little he could hear of it was in a language he didn't speak. The man kept his heavy hands shoved into the pockets of his coveralls, his eyes shifting back and forth between Aida and Jack.

Aida turned around once or twice, offering Jack a wide smile while she kept speaking, and Jack returned it, but he got the sense the conversation was a little more heated than Aida was letting on.

Finally, the Croatian nodded. Aida pulled out cash from her pocket and counted off a number of bills that Jack couldn't make out. Apparently, it was enough. The stone-faced Croatian finally smiled and took the cash.

Aida came back over to the van and stuck her head in the window. "Ready to go?"

"Everything okay?"

"Sure. We'll just leave the van here. Parking on the street is no good at my place. It's not far."

"Works for me."

They pulled their two wheeled bags out of the back of the van as the Croatian rolled up the steel door again, shutting it behind them as they started up the steep concrete hill toward her apartment.

"So those were the medical supplies you came for?"

"Yes."

"There was a problem, though."

"Not a problem, a misunderstanding. All good now."

The diesel engine of a giant silver Mercedes tour bus roared in their ears as it passed by. Several white-haired tourists stared blankly at them out of their smoke-tinted windows.

The hill got steeper as they walked. It reminded Jack of a summer he had spent in San Francisco. The air here on the coast was cooler and there was a slight breeze. They passed several staircases climbing up to homes and apartments built on the hills ascending from the street. Jack was glad he wasn't on crutches or in a wheelchair living in this city.

"So, I'm curious. Why drive all the way to pick up the meds? Wouldn't it be cheaper to order them by mail? Fly them in?"

"Sadly, it's cheaper to do it this way. The clinic can't afford the—how do you Americans say it? The 'five-finger discount'?"

"You're worried about stuff getting stolen?"

"Sometimes high-value cargo gets 'inspected' by customs agents, and things disappear. And then there is the red tape, which magically disappears once a handful of cash appears. Or sometimes things get impounded and the shipment is never seen again."

"So, basically, you're smuggling."

"Well, yes. I suppose you could call it that."

"Isn't that illegal?"

Aida tilted her head. "Yes, of course. But it was illegal to smuggle black slaves on the Underground Railroad, too, wasn't it? Why should I let corrupt and greedy politicians rob poor refugees of the medicines they need?"

"I expect that kind of thing in the Third World, not Europe."

Aida stopped in her tracks, fighting a smile. "Oh, Jack. Are you really so naive? Do you think such things don't happen all over Europe? And in your country as well?"

"What do you mean?"

"How do you suppose so many billions of dollars' worth of drugs and smuggled people and guns and everything else illegal gets into your country every year? Do you think it could be done without bribing judges and mayors? Do you think there are no American border guards and customs officers on the payrolls of the Mexican Mafia?"

Jack should have known better. His grandfather was a Baltimore police detective, and Jack had heard stories over the years of all manner of big-city corruption and crime. He just thought—or, rather, hoped—those days were long past in his country.

They trudged along like Sherpas for another hundred yards and Aida stopped again. "We're here."

Jack glanced up the staircase. He'd skied on Colorado mountain slopes that weren't as steep.

Aida laughed, collapsing her telescoping bag handle. "If it's too much for you, I'll carry your bag."

Jack collapsed his handle, too, and snatched up her bag. "I've got the bags. Start climbing, Sir Edmund."

Seventy-seven steps later, they made a sharp left turn onto a landing, and then another right, and up yet another twenty-seven steps through a vine-covered archway gate. Aida pulled out a set of keys and opened the door on her front porch.

The apartment was small but clean, decorated with local art pieces, and full of comfortable and stylish furniture. Best of all, from her front porch was a view of the Adriatic Sea. A cruise ship was passing by, trailing a small wake, heading south for the Old Town.

"Can I get you something to drink before we leave? Water? Beer?"

"'Leave'?"

Jack was surprisingly exhausted from the arduous climb. Nearly two weeks without a serious workout and overindulging in rich food and carb-loaded beer hadn't exactly enhanced his physical conditioning.

"We're going to tour the Old Town. It's beautiful this time of day, and then I know a great place for dinner."

49

Jack and Aida took a Dubrovnik city bus to the Pile Gate in the Old Town and crossed over the moat beneath the iron bars of the portcullis, just like in an old Hollywood movie. They climbed up the stone stairs beyond the gate and paid for their tickets for the wall walk, and they strolled the perimeter of the ancient port citadel.

The wide, towering walls provided picture-perfect glimpses of the glassy Adriatic Sea, the sturdy St. Lawrence fortress just beyond the western wall, and the city's old battlements, Croatian flags snapping in the breeze. Tour boats, yachts, and cruise liners were at their slips or heading out, as rental kayaks bobbed up and down near the walls.

Directly below, Jack saw the smooth, tightly fitted stones of the city streets crowded with international tourists, Renaissance-era churches, and innumerable shops. He could definitely feel the Venetian influence on the architecture.

Aida explained that the Serbs bombarded the city at the

beginning of the war, and pointed out the original faded red roof tiles and then the newer, brighter ones that had been replaced after the shelling finally stopped.

"How long was the siege here?"

"It lasted from October 1991 until May 1992."

"Eight months? The casualties must have been terrible."

"Less than a hundred civilian deaths and less than two hundred military killed." She added dismissively, "That was *their* war."

They descended the wall into the city and she dragged him through the crowds to a few of her favorite shops, but she could tell Jack was less than interested.

"Something wrong, Jack?"

"I noticed a lot of *Game of Thrones* merchandise in the windows."

"They shoot some of the series in Dubrovnik. You can even take *Game of Thrones*–themed tours if you want."

"Don't get me wrong. The city is beautiful, but some of it feels like a Renaissance version of a shopping mall."

"Yes, I suppose you're right. But shopping is what tourists do, isn't it? And Dubrovnik is all about tourists."

"I guess I'm just not a big shopper."

"Hungry?"

"Starving. Where's that restaurant you were talking about?"

Aida smiled.

They raced back to her place and messed up her bedsheets with rigor before she ordered up a hand-tossed pizza from a local restaurant while Jack opened a bottle of fine Croatian red wine.

This was definitely Jack's favorite restaurant in Dubrovnik, but he wouldn't be posting about it on TripAdvisor.

———

While Jack and Aida feasted on their delivered pizza and red wine, the grease-stained Croatian bolted shut the last case of handguns in the secret compartment wedged into the undercarriage of the Happy Times! tour van. He then wiped on a couple handfuls of manufactured road grime to camouflage the compartment just in case an honest cop decided to put a mirror to the undercarriage at the border crossing. He slid out from underneath and dusted himself off, satisfied that the medicines were as well hidden as the guns. The van was ready to go now.

Time to find something to eat.

SARAJEVO, BOSNIA AND HERZEGOVINA

Cenk Yılmaz, an ethnic Turk, was happy.

The room he supervised was working exactly as he had designed it, humming with the murmur of excited young voices sharing ideas and the rapid clicking of computer keyboards.

As a former Facebook employee with contacts still working in Menlo Park, Yılmaz possessed an intimate working knowledge of the complex algorithms that drove social media trends across all the major platforms. He'd personally trained each of the fifteen men and three women working this evening, pushing out the next social media campaign he'd designed.

By his calculation, within hours, four hundred thousand Bosniaks would be raging at their computers and smartphones over the Muslim wedding massacre.

The talent in the room was divided into two distinct parts: the humans and the bots.

Over the past two years, Yılmaz had used his human engineers to create dozens of fake but prominent social media accounts of "ordinary" Croats, Serbs, and Muslims, primarily on Twitter, Facebook, Instagram, and popular Bosnian blogging sites. Several of the fake accounts had garnered tens of thousands of devoted followers across the country and throughout the region in both the Serbo-Croatian and English languages. No matter how hard the coding wizards in Silicon Valley tried, nobody had yet come up with software that could simulate the authentic engagement of actual human minds. These human-orchestrated accounts were the platforms where Yılmaz's important messages were first deployed. Any message put on them would instantly touch thousands.

But in order to get those messages to go viral and reach hundreds of thousands—if not millions—of people with sudden impact, his other, nonhuman team jumped into action.

Yılmaz understood better than most the Achilles heel of all social media platforms: They were their own worst enemy. Social media platforms were designed for the sole purpose of drawing as many eyeballs as possible to their sites in order to sell ads to advertisers.

Social media platform algorithms were always on the lookout for hot new trending topics and looking to point their consumers to those same hot trends, and in turn make those pages even hotter. The more popular the trend, the more eyeballs on the page and the more advertising money the platform could make.

The challenge for any blogger or poster was to find a way to get their blog or post trending. Technicians like Yılmaz knew the answer: Fake it.

Yılmaz's cadre of talented software programmers designed

and deployed social media bots. These bots—automated software programs—amplified each human post, "Like," and tweet with thousands of new software-generated Likes, posts, and tweets, along with retweets and reposts, making it appear as if an avalanche of interest and engagement was coalescing around the original human content.

Suddenly, "hot" trends manufactured by Yılmaz and his team became hotter and hotter as more and more people became aware of them, fueled by the social media platforms' own search algorithms. This created an exponential increase in social media attention for any news item Yılmaz was directed to exploit. He further capitalized on the situation by deploying commercially available analytical tools such as BuzzSumo and DataMinr, which identified and even contributed to emerging social media trends.

Using the carefully edited photos and videos he'd received from the Višegrad wedding massacre, Yılmaz deployed both his humans and his bots to begin a campaign to manufacture Muslim outrage, first in Bosnia, and then, he hoped, throughout the Muslim communities of Europe and, eventually, the world. The first Facebook post that started gaining viral traction ended with the hashtag *#remembersrebrenica*.

His main concern was that companies like Facebook had recently begun to take extra precautions against the governments and criminal organizations corrupting and hijacking their algorithms. But Silicon Valley paid scant attention to Bosnia and didn't deploy enough software-generated assets in Serbo-Croatian for shadow banning or any other defensive measures to be of any concern.

If Yılmaz was wrong he'd know soon enough, but he hoped

his phone call to his employer would be a pleasant one. Judging by the gruesome massacre images now being pushed out onto the Internet, Yılmaz understood the brutal consequences of failure for him and his team.

Red Wing was not a forgiving person.

50

The one place Jack wished he had seen on the way out to Dubrovnik was the dervish *tekija* overlooking the Bruna River. So, on their return leg, they left Dubrovnik in time to arrive at about noon to tour the sixteenth-century cliffside monastery, and then to sample the special trout at the nearby riverside restaurant. That left them enough time to get back to Sarajevo before dark if they kept moving.

A kilometer south of Blagaj, Aida and Jack spotted a Bosnian policeman standing in the road behind his unmarked car with a sign that read GRANIČNA INSPECKCIJA and waving a red flashlight baton, indicating where they should exit the road.

"My Bosnian isn't so good, but that looks like a customs inspection."

"Not a problem," Aida said. "Open the glove box, please."

Jack opened it and saw a folded stack of Bosnian marks in a money clip. He handed it to her as she slowed to a stop. She peeled off a large bill as she rolled down her window and spoke to him in their native tongue. But neither the sweet talk nor the cash had the desired effect, and the sour-faced policeman simply shook his head and pointed the baton in the direction of the exit.

Aida gave up, muttering under her breath, and headed down the dirt incline.

"So maybe it is a problem," Jack said. For a brief moment, he wondered if this might have been the Iron Syndicate hit Gerry had warned him about.

She shook her head. "More money, that's all. They're all greedy bastards."

She seemed confident enough, so Jack relaxed. The van kicked up dust as it rapidly descended toward the river, far below the highway above and out of sight of any passing traffic.

Jack turned around and saw the unmarked police vehicle following them down the same dirt path in their cloud of dust.

Not a good sign.

Two masked policemen in tactical gear stood down by the river where the dirt road ended. The tall one had a Heckler & Koch MP5 submachine gun on a sling. The shorter carried only a pistol on his hip. He pointed to a spot just in front of him, indicating where Aida should park the van.

"This doesn't look friendly," Jack said, wishing like hell he had his Glock 19 with him.

"Just scare tactics. No worries."

Unless these are hitters for the Iron Syndicate.

As Aida slipped the van into park, the tall officer crossed over to Jack's side and the short one approached Aida's window.

The other police car pulled up behind the van, blocking

their escape route, Jack noted, wondering if Aida was thinking about it.

The short cop yanked Aida's door open and jerked his head, indicating she should get out. The tall cop did the same on Jack's side and the four of them walked to the back of the van, where the third cop was already standing.

The short cop barked a command and Aida opened the van's rear doors. He glanced inside. Nothing but two pieces of luggage and a couple cardboard boxes. He ripped them open and found used baby clothes, which he flung out piece by piece like he was searching for something.

Nothing. He tossed the empty boxes back into the van, frustrated.

The short cop turned back to Aida, firing questions at her in Bosanski, starting with her name, which she repeated.

The short cop's voice got more heated with each one-word answer Aida gave, *da* or *ne*—yes or no.

Jack kept his eye on the other two cops, and their hands, touching their weapons. Their eyes shifted back and forth between Aida and him. Something was going down.

Finally, the short cop pulled a photograph from his vest pocket and showed it to Aida. He asked, *"Da li znaš Tarika Brkića?"* Do you know Tarik Brkić?

"Da. On je mehaničar. Ponekad radi za mene." Yes. He's a mechanic. He works for me sometimes.

The short cop nodded, satisfied with her answer. He shifted his gaze over to Jack. He asked Aida a question in her language. Aida translated for Jack.

"He wants to know who you are."

"Tell him I'm nobody."

"He won't like that answer. He wants to know your name."

Jack hesitated. But what choice did he have at his point?

"Jack Ryan."

The cop's eyes shifted to his taller partner standing beside Jack. They exchanged a few words. He turned back to Jack and stuck out a gloved palm. *"Pasoš."*

"He wants to see your passport, Jack."

"Yeah, I figured."

Jack reached for his back pocket. Two pistols snapped up, pointing at his head.

"Hey, fellas. Just doing what the man asked."

He handed the short cop his passport. The cop flipped it open. Read it. Handed it to the tall cop, who read it, too. He nodded at his short partner and pocketed it.

"I need that back," Jack said. "It's private property."

The short cop told Aida to keep translating. She did.

"He says your name is familiar."

"It's a pretty common name where I come from."

"He wants to know what you're doing in Bosnia."

"I'm a tourist."

"How do you know this woman?"

"She's my tour guide." He nodded at the Happy Times! van. "We're heading back to Sarajevo."

"Where did you come from?"

"Dubrovnik."

"What did you do there?"

"Toured the city."

"Anything else?"

Jack wanted to say something about the unbelievable sex he and Aida had enjoyed but held his tongue. This cop's fuse was lit. He was angry as hell, and Jack wasn't giving him what he was looking for. But then again, he was a little prick. Jack shot a glance at Aida, trying to lighten the moment. "You can tell him we ate at a great restaurant."

Aida frowned but translated it anyway.

The short cop suddenly got in Aida's face, shouting, *"Gdje su te jebene rakete?!"*

Aida startled and answered, *"Rakete? Nemam pojma o čemu govoriš."*

WHACK!

The cop backhanded Aida across the mouth. She whimpered and clutched her face with her hands.

"Hey!" Jack lunged toward Aida to block another strike, but the two cops next to him each grabbed him hard by his shoulders and yanked him back, shoving their pistols in his face.

The little cop grabbed a fistful of Aida's hair in his hand and pulled her close, sticking his pistol in her face. In his anger he slipped from Bosnian to the English he had been trying to conceal, *"I will only ask you one more time, you Muslim bitch! Where are those—"*

Behind them, a horn blared, stuttering and loud. The two cops next to Jack turned around with him still in their grip and saw a cloud of dust billowing on the hill road toward them as another Happy Times! tour van came careening down at full speed. Jack saw Emir at the wheel, pounding the horn with one hand and steering the van straight toward Jack and the two cops with the other.

The two cops raised their pistols to fire.

Jack launched both fists up and back, smashing each cop in the face with the back of his hands. They each got off shots, but the shock of the blows caused them to miss. The blows also loosened their grips on Jack just enough for him to fire his right elbow high into the tall cop's jaw with a sickening crack. The man dropped his pistol in the dirt and let go of Jack's collar as he reached for his broken jaw.

As soon as Jack's elbow struck the tall cop, he twisted right, driving the heel of his right hand into the car cop's temple, stunning him. Jack rabbit-punched him again with a closed fist just behind the ear until the man and his weapon fell to the ground as Emir skidded to a stop in a flurry of choking dust.

The short cop knelt in the dirt in front of Aida, clutching his ball sack, blood trickling out of his nose.

Aida pointed the gun at him. She was breathing heavily, but her hands were steady.

Jack turned in time to see the tall cop lunging for his weapon. Jack kicked his face like a soccer ball. The man's head snapped back. Knocked out cold, he collapsed in the dirt.

Without hesitating, Jack turned and launched another brutal kick at the other cop, who was reaching for his own weapon in the dirt.

He wasn't as lucky as his friend.

Jack's foot cracked the cartilage in the man's nose and broke his top front teeth. The man shrieked in pain and clutched his mouth, blood gushing between his fingers.

Emir grabbed both pistols out of the dirt and stepped over to Aida. "Are you okay?"

"Yes, of course. I'm fine."

"Me, too. Thanks for asking," Jack said, pulling the MP5 off the tall cop and retrieving his passport from the man's pocket. "Who are these jokers?"

"Serb Mafia," Aida said. "Trying to steal the medical supplies." She spat at the kneeling cop. "Pigs."

Jack patted down the unconscious cop. "This guy doesn't have any identity papers."

Emir pointed at the other downed officer. "Neither does this one."

Aida barked a command at the short officer, who shook his head. "None of these assholes do," she said. "Believe me, they're not cops."

"We should call the real cops," Jack said.

Aida shook her head, her eyes still sighting down the barrel of the gun toward the short cop, now glowering at her. "We can't."

"Why not?"

She shot him a confused look. "What if the police impound my van? I can't risk it."

The medical supplies, Jack remembered. Crap. Smuggled in illegally, but desperately needed by the clinic.

"What do we do with these guys, then? We can't just let them go."

He noticed Aida still hadn't lowered her weapon, and Emir still held two loaded pistols in his hands. "And we sure as hell can't shoot them."

"I have an idea," Emir said, shoving the pistols into his waistband. "You and Jack go on ahead, and I'll follow. In ten minutes, I'll pull over and call the police. We don't want to be here when anybody shows up." He looked at Jack. "Okay?"

"Okay."

Aida added, "Get some rope and some duct tape. We don't want them leaving before the police arrive."

"I'll take care of everything," Emir said.

"But call an ambulance, too," Jack said. "They're gonna need it."

51

W hy was Emir following us?" Jack asked. He drove the van.
Aida was still shaking from the encounter. She lit a
cigarette to calm her nerves. It was the first time Jack
had seen her smoke.

"I don't know. I told him to stay away."

"So why didn't he?"

"He's in love with me. Has been since we were kids."

"I hope he didn't see—"

She waved a hand dismissively. "I don't want to think about
it." She took another drag.

"So who was that guy in the photo? Brkić?" Jack asked.

"He's family. He married one of my mother's cousins, years
ago. As a favor, I use him to work on my vehicles sometimes."

"And what was the cop asking you about? He was pretty
pissed off."

Aida shook her head. "He wanted to know why we had not
paid our protection money."

"Did you owe him protection money?"

Aida blew out a cloud of blue smoke, ignoring the question. The open window whisked it away. "You know they were going to kill us." She flicked the butt out the window. "Fucking Serbs."

She turned to Jack. Her eyes were wet. She put her hands to her face. "I was so scared."

Jack's cage got rattled, too. He was deathly allergic to lead, especially the kind thrown at him at high velocity. He laid a hand on her head and stroked her thick hair.

"It's okay now. You're safe."

She glanced up through her tears. "Am I?"

"Sure. Why not?"

"You frightened me, Jack." She pulled her knees up to her chin and wrapped her arms around her legs.

"Why?"

"I saw what you did to those men. What kind of financial analyst knows how to fight like that?"

"I've been training in martial arts for a long time—"

"Bullshit, Jack. The way you handled yourself? No. What you did back there you don't learn in judo classes. You've done this before, haven't you?"

"I just wanted to protect you."

"Who are you, Jack?"

"I'm just a guy who can throw a punch."

She sighed, turned her face toward her window, and closed her eyes.

They rode along in silence the rest of the way, Jack following the prompts of the GPS tracker. He kept running the day's events over in his mind. He wished he spoke the language. There were a few English cognates, for sure, but they spoke so fast he could hardly pick out the words. Drugs? Guns? Money? He just didn't know.

The only word he thought he heard clearly was *rakete*. He supposed it must have meant "racket," like Mafia rackets.

Whatever it was, that Serb Mafia "cop" was sure pissed about it.

Emir pulled over twenty minutes later, after tying up the fake cops and shutting their mouths with duct tape. He picked up the phone and dialed a number, but not for an ambulance.

"Why are you calling me?" Brkić asked.

"We have a problem." Emir explained the situation.

"I'll take care of it. You make sure you keep an eye on Aida."

"There's something else you need to know."

"What?"

Emir told the Chechen about that fucking *kafir* American and his shameful use of Aida. But he added, "The American is leaving soon."

"The sooner, the better. For Aida's sake. And yours."

SARAJEVO, BOSNIA AND HERZEGOVINA

Aida had fallen asleep for the last hour of the trip but woke up when they hit massive traffic on the outskirts of town. She yawned and stretched, and glanced at Jack with a smile, brushing her tousled hair out of her eyes like a girl who had been dreaming pleasant dreams.

But her smile dimmed as she suddenly remembered what

had happened earlier. Jack could see the gears grinding behind her eyes.

Jack pointed at the GPS. Traffic lines were red everywhere. "What's going on?"

"These are Serbs coming in for the Orthodox Renewal service day after tomorrow."

"Yeah, I heard about that. Is it some kind of religious revival?"

Aida shook her head. "It's all just politics, believe me."

Jack noticed quite a few national license plates from Serbia in the traffic mix.

"I'm sorry for what happened to us back there, Jack."

"It's not your fault."

"Of course it is. I shouldn't have brought you with me on this run."

"I wouldn't have traded it for anything."

"And I'm sorry for what I said." She reached out and touched his arm. "I'm not scared of you. I know you'd never do anything to hurt me. I know you would always protect me."

"Yeah, I would. I'm kinda sweet on you."

That made her smile.

Jack hated to ruin that smile, but he had to clear the air. "You did pretty well with that cop today, taking him down and stealing his gun."

"I just kicked the guy in the nuts. Not exactly Bruce Lee stuff like you were doing."

"You handled his pistol like a pro."

Aida shrugged. "My father taught me how to use one when I was very young. He said he never wanted me to be a victim."

"Then he taught you well."

I wonder who taught him.

"Guns don't scare me, Jack. People do."

"Could you have pulled the trigger?"

"I protect the people I love."

Jack turned toward her. That four-letter word caught his attention.

She smiled impishly. "And I protect the people I'm 'sweet on,' too."

Jack followed the GPS onto the narrow street where his apartment was located. "So, what's the plan for tonight? Heck, I might even be able to bust out a dance move or two if there's a club you like."

"I'm sorry, I can't do anything tonight."

"But I'm leaving soon."

"Don't remind me."

"Did I do something wrong?"

She reached up and touched his troubled face. "No, my love. I'm the one who has failed you. I never should have opened up my heart to you. You have your life back in America, and I have my life here in Bosnia. It was a beautiful spontaneous fling. But it's over now, isn't it?"

"A fling?"

"What else would you call it?"

Jack shrugged. "I don't know."

"Were you planning on staying here forever?"

Jack shook his head. She was right. But he said, "You can come to the States with me." He didn't pretend to make a play about fund-raising.

"That's very thoughtful of you, but I have my work here."

"Work that almost got you killed today."

"It's nothing new. Someday, things will get better for us."

"What if they don't?"

"Then they don't."

"I don't want you to get hurt."

"How can you stop it?"

"Can I at least see you tomorrow?"

She shook her head. "I'm sorry, but I can't. A new group of refugees are arriving tomorrow. I need to be at the center."

"Then I'll come, too."

"That's not possible. This group is Syrian. They don't trust Westerners, especially Americans. I'm sorry."

She saw the hope dying in his eyes. He looked like a lost little boy. She took pity on him. "But tomorrow night, I can pick you up and take you to my place for a home-cooked meal. I bet you haven't had one of those in a long time."

Jack thought about saying, *Not since Mom made me dinner with Dad at the White House.* But he wasn't a name-dropper, and he wanted to win the woman over on his own merits, not his folks'. "Sounds great. What time?"

"I'll pick you up here at five after I finish at the center. Try to stay out of trouble until then, okay?"

"Okay. See you tomorrow."

Jack leaned over to kiss her good-bye. Their mouths lingered for a tender moment. He grabbed his suitcase and watched her pull away before heading up to his place.

He couldn't shake the feeling that something was wrong.

52

Jack jogged up the stairs to his apartment only to find a DHL delivery envelope lying against his door. It was addressed to him.

He entered his apartment, kicked off his shoes, and fell into a chair at the small dinette table. He opened the envelope and read the cover letter from Detective Oblak instructing him to sign the enclosed legal documents acknowledging that the case of Elena Iliescu was officially closed and he was no longer considered a suspect, nor did he have any legal standing in Slovenia against her since she was now deceased, et cetera, et cetera. Luckily, everything was written in English as well as in Slovenian. Jack didn't care about all of that, and he was happy to sign the documents and put it all behind him.

His mind turned back to the fake cops. He wondered why they didn't bother to carry any identity papers, even fake ones. Real ones would've been even better. He chided himself for not grabbing their pictures, retinal scans, and fingerprints with the apps on his phone. But why would he? They were Serbian Mafia, according to Aida. Not foreign operators. The Campus wasn't a crime-fighting outfit.

Still, something was bugging him. Those three cops were pretty rough customers. They weren't run-of-the-mill gangster types. Maybe they had service training. If so, Gavin Biery could have found them that way.

Gavin had saved his bacon back in Singapore by identifying a couple undercover Chinese special operators Jack had run into, by accessing a DoD biometric database. Fingerprints, saliva, hair, and even semen samples of foreign operators were acquired one way or another and stored for future reference. If any of those phony Serb cops had ever spit or combed their hair anywhere near one of these DoD operations, Gavin would have been able to ID him.

Didn't matter at this point. Those guys were in Bosnian police custody by now. The police would figure it out.

His mind turned back to Aida. The smell of her soft skin, the taste of her mouth. She was an incredible woman, and clearly they were connecting deeply.

More deeply than he'd thought possible.

But he had to admit that she was a mystery. She wasn't a trained operator, but obviously she could handle herself in a pinch. She said she was only trying to protect him. He could believe that.

He *wanted* to believe that.

He was crazy about her.

And she was crazy about him, too. He was sure.

It had been a long day. A helluva couple days. Time for some chow and a hot shower and an early evening to catch up on some long-needed rest. Tomorrow was going to be his last full day in Sarajevo, and then dinner with Aida.

If tomorrow was going to be anything like today, he needed to be ready for it.

PARIS

Vasilev's glass-enclosed "clean" room—suite, really—occupied the entire fifth floor of the private hospital, located in a late-nineteenth-century Beaux Arts building in the ultra-wealthy 16th arrondissement. From his bed, the old Bulgarian had a postcard view of the River Seine below, as gray and listless as freshly poured concrete oozing through the city.

His medical suite looked like a set from the old sci-fi movie *The Andromeda Strain*. The room was hermetically sealed and only select staff were permitted entrance onto the floor, and only when fully garbed in protective clothing and scrubbed spotless with the most powerful antibiotic cleansers. They adhered to BSL 3 protocols, just one step down from the biosafety level precautions the CDC would take when handling Ebola virus.

Vasilev's experimental CAR T-cell treatment was proceeding well, according to the doctors, even better than they had hoped. But his overall health condition was extremely fragile, and his immune system severely weakened after years of traditional cancer therapies. Every precaution was being taken to protect the crime lord from infectious diseases of every sort, even the most benign bacteria, until his body had a chance to recover its own natural defenses.

Vasilev was in a foul mood for a number of reasons, not the

least of which was the strict macrobiotic anti-cancer diet his idiot doctor required of him.

Who the hell can eat spelt and miso soup all day?

But it was his blood pressure that was threatening to kill him at the moment.

Behind the glass walls, Vasilev enjoyed every possible amenity, including an encrypted Amazon Echo Show, which he was using now while lying in his adjustable hospital bed, speaking with his number two, the Czech. The entire floor was vacated, even of staff, for the video call. One determined glance from Vasilev's soul-snatching eyes sent even his world-renowned doctors scurrying for safety on the floors below.

"My patience is running thin," Vasilev growled. "Why isn't Ryan dead?"

"Our first attempt failed. We're not sure why. But the loose end is tied off." The Czech stubbed out a cigarette in an ashtray offscreen. Gray smoke lingered in the air.

"And?"

"We're tracking him now, in Bosnia."

"Tracking him? You should be killing him."

"You said you wanted his head. That makes matters more difficult to arrange."

"Yes, Tomáš, his head. His head!" Vasilev pounded his mattress for emphasis.

The solemn Czech nodded curtly. "Of course. It will be done."

"When?"

"Soon."

"How soon?"

"As soon as is humanly possible. However, I do have good news about someone else."

"Tell me."

He did.

Vasilev chuckled. "Well done, old friend. Now finish the Ryan job."

"Everything is being coordinated, even as we speak. How are you feeling these days?"

"I feel fantastic. Of course, for seventeen thousand euros a day, I should. I could walk out of here right now on my own two legs. Something I haven't been able to do in a year."

The Czech allowed himself a small smile. "Then the treatments are even better than we hoped. Thank God."

"God? God has nothing to do with it."

The Czech's eyes betrayed nothing.

He couldn't agree more.

"I will report as soon as Ryan's head is in my possession. In the meantime, get better, old friend. We have much to do when you return."

The old Bulgarian nodded, shaking his jowls, which were pinking up nicely. "Worlds to conquer."

The Czech smiled again. "Indeed. Worlds to conquer." He lit another cigarette. Inhaled deeply.

Vasilev licked his yellowed teeth. He could practically taste the Czech's tobacco, one of many vices he sorely missed.

"And you, Tomáš? How is your health?"

"I feel fine."

"Good. If you want to keep it that way, get me Ryan's head before I leave this place, or I'll cut yours off myself."

Vasilev killed the transmission. His stomach gurgled like a fermenting beer cask. He called down for something to eat. Beans and brown rice, perhaps.

Anything but that filthy miso soup.

ALEXANDRIA, VIRGINIA

Gerry Hendley sat at his desk at Hendley Associates studying a piece of proposed legislation that the Senate Finance Committee was about to hold hearings on when his phone buzzed.

"Yes, Alice?"

"A call for you on line one. It's urgent."

"Thank you."

He picked up. A familiar voice. It was Jeremiah Morales, the head of the federal Bureau of Prisons, a man who owed his position to the ex-senator. They exchanged a few pleasantries, but Gerry could tell there was something on the man's mind.

"Out with it."

"Gerry, I'm sorry to tell you that Weston Rhodes is dead."

"Dead? How?"

"Hanged himself."

Gerry frowned with confusion. "That doesn't make any sense. Weston was only facing five years. He had a lot to live for."

"Some guys just can't cut it."

"Thanks for the heads-up, Jeremiah. My best to Meredith."

Gerry shook his head in utter disbelief. Weston Rhodes, the former senator and CIA field officer, was not a hero by any means, but not a wimp, either. And it wasn't as if he was doing time in the Hanoi Hilton like Admiral Stockdale. Rhodes had been located in the least restrictive wing of "Club Fed," the Federal Correctional Institution in Cumberland, Maryland. It was home to many white-collar criminals who posed no threat to themselves or others. Martha Stewart kinda crimes. Light duty, decent hours, no violence. It was a good gig, if you had to do time.

Rhodes was busted for his role in the Singapore affair that

nearly got Jack killed. He could've been tried for treason, conspiracy, and a number of other felonies that could've put him in for life or even snatched it away from him.

But one of Rhodes's K Street legal buddies bamboozled the federal prosecutor into a bench trial, and the presiding judge was a Yale alum who didn't see the need to recuse himself from the case despite having known Rhodes for more than thirty years. It was rumored that Rhodes had stashed a good deal of cash in an offshore account as well.

So why kill himself?

It couldn't have been about his situation. Perhaps it had something to do with how he got there in the first place. He was connected to a middleman, the conduit between the North Koreans and the operation to steal the quantum computing technology and the attempt on Jack's life. What was that guy's name? He couldn't pull it up. He called Gavin.

"Gavin, what was the name of that yahoo that was running Rhodes like a rented mule on the Singapore operation?"

"Zvezdev. A CIA SOG team found him—or at least parts of him—in a kimchi jar."

Gerry thanked him and called the director of national intelligence, Mary Pat Foley, a friend for many years. He had her personal number.

"We found him in Croatia. A Bulgarian. The rumor was he was connected to some kind of criminal syndicate, but we never got more than that. I'll forward the particulars of what we have."

"Thanks, Mary Pat. I might have to circle back to you on this."

"You have my number."

Bingo, Gerry thought.

Rhodes was connected to Zvezdev, some kind of syndicate mobster who wanted Jack killed but he winds up dead instead.

Zvezdev dead.

Rhodes dead.

And somebody connected to Zvezdev still wants to kill Jack.

Zvezdev is the key.

That's it.

Gerry's e-mail dinged. It was the Zvezdev file promised from Mary Pat.

He opened it and scanned it for details. Zvezdev was the link to everything. The Bulgarian had fled to Croatia to hide, and it was the place where he had been killed.

Gerry pulled out his encrypted cell phone and speed-dialed Dom.

"I'm forwarding a file to you guys right now. I need you to get over to Croatia, pronto."

53

Jack woke up with the alarm, refreshed and ready for a new day. He threw himself on the floor by his bed, banging out two hundred push-ups in sets of fifty before he even allowed himself to take his morning piss. Nothing like a sense of urgency to motivate the will.

It was time to get his head out of his ass.

Time to Get After It.

Nothing wrong with a vacation, but it was no excuse for letting himself go, and the last two weeks had been too much of a slide. After he took a leak, he thought about changing into a pair of running shorts and going for a run along the river. But he never saw any runners in the city and the sidewalks were crowded in the mornings, so he opted instead for four sets of twenty-five burpees.

He nearly puked his guts out, but he finally finished, gasping for air. Feeling a nice little pump all over his body, and a few aches he hadn't felt in a while, he padded barefoot into the kitchen to boil up enough water for his last bag of Jocko White Tea and fry a couple eggs.

After finishing up his breakfast, he turned on the English-language local news at the top of the early-morning hour. The two lead news items caught his attention.

The first was about the upcoming Serbian Orthodox Renewal service in just two days, and the growing excitement among Serbs in Bosnia and the region, with video clips of faithful Orthodox people boarding buses and smiling bearded priests packing suitcases. "Local officials are anticipating fifty thousand participants tomorrow, up from estimates of just thirty thousand a week ago," one commentator noted.

The second story featured the gruesome massacre of a Muslim wedding party three days before near Višegrad in Herzegovina, a region of the country through which he had passed with Aida on their trip to Dubrovnik.

The images were horrible and all too familiar to Jack, both on television and, unfortunately, in person. In catechism, the nuns taught him the theological concept of original sin, but life with The Campus proved to him it wasn't just a theory.

The grim newscasters introduced English-subtitled video clips of grieving families and Bosniak community leaders calling for swift justice against the murderous Serb White Eagles. They complained that the corrupt and incompetent government was either unwilling or unable to deliver it.

At least one Bosniak called for justice "to be taken into our own hands," and a raging imam called for jihad against the Serbs from his pulpit. A news crawl along the bottom of the screen read: *#remembersrebrenica is trending number one on Twitter in Bosnia . . .*

"Damn," Jack whispered to himself as he powered off the TV and headed for the shower.

Jack left his apartment with the prestamped DHL envelope addressed to Detective Oblak and a list of touristy things he planned to do: art galleries, museums, and churches. He wanted to get a better feel for the city and the culture. He'd really fallen in love with the country and the people he'd met, but a profound sadness dogged him. This nation had a long and painful history, and, it seemed, a dim future, barring some unforeseen development. Strong-willed, hopeful, entrepreneurial types like Aida seemed few and far between. There was no lack of human or natural resources in this beautiful country. It seemed like the only thing keeping it down was a culture of despair.

Jack found the DHL drop-off, then started his tour, marking off each spot on his list as the morning progressed. After visiting the Sacred Heart Cathedral with the giant metallic statue of Pope John Paul II out front, his stomach grumbled and he found himself back at his favorite restaurant, downing another plate of fire-roasted *ćevapi* and a bottle of sparkling water.

After finishing his meal, he checked his list, but he already knew what was next. The Galerija 11/07/95, with its permanent exhibit on the Srebrenica massacre, was the only stop he dreaded, thanks to Aida's warning. He seriously considered skipping it and going on to the Sarajevo Brewery Museum, but he knew he could catch that later.

He checked his GPS on his phone with a sigh and headed for the dark soul of the Bosnian War.

———

The Srebrenica exhibit didn't disappoint, if that was the right word.

Located inside a modern, minimalist gallery of light blond-wood floors and gray walls, it didn't sit right with Jack. The rooms were uncluttered and antiseptic, but the subject matter was messy and dirty.

It reminded him of his visit to Dachau years before, a single, perfectly preserved barracks building standing on well-groomed grounds without a speck of trash or disorder. No grimy, black soot or flaky ash to mar the barracks, no blood-soaked rags dropped in piles around the compound. The German exhibitors had removed all evidence of trembling, urine-stained fear and the groaning despair that boiled up from the merciless ovens.

The Galerija exhibit's most moving displays were the fifty-two-foot-long Wall of Death featuring the ages and names of the 8,372 men and boys killed by the Serbs, and the hundreds of haunting photos collected by the Association of Mothers of Srebrenica and Žepa.

Jack exited the Galerija utterly depressed. His soul thirsted for life the way a drunk craves a drink. He needed to see Aida. Now.

Before he lost his faith in the possibility of hope.

He turned the corner, heading for the exit, and saw a familiar pockmarked face.

Too bad.

A beefy man with bad acne scarring and a bandage across his broken nose blocked Jack's way out of the museum.

"Višća, isn't it?" Jack asked.

The man smiled beneath his broken Ray-Bans, Scotch-taped back together at the bridge. He was one of Kolak's goons, the one that jumped him just outside this building a few days ago.

The one that Kolak warned would want to get his revenge.

"Kolak wants you," the man grunted. "You come with me. Now."

The man wasn't exactly making a request. Jack weighed his options. Jack took him once before and could probably take him again. But the man's shoulder holster bulging beneath his coat was persuasive.

"Okay, Chuckles. But you're driving."

Jack reached for his phone—a little too quickly, apparently. Višća tensed, ready to throw a punch or pull his weapon.

"Just need to call somebody."

"No calls."

Jack's options hadn't changed. He stopped reaching for his phone.

"Am I under arrest?"

"Kolak. Now."

Jack shrugged.

Time to see Kolak.

54

Višća ushered Jack into Kolak's cramped, third-floor office at OSA-OBA headquarters and departed wordlessly. The gray industrial carpet was lightly stained, and the wood-paneled walls were mostly bare, save for the service commendation awards and shooting trophies.

At least this time it wasn't another basement interrogation room, but it wasn't much of an improvement. It looked like an abandoned set from *The Rockford Files*.

"Thank you for coming, Jack," Kolak said, standing up behind his desk and extending his hand. Jack took it firmly.

"Happy to be here."

"You are a gracious liar. Please, have a seat. Coffee? Water?"

"I'm fine, thanks." Jack took a seat. "And for the record, I don't have to be here. But I chose to come."

"Duly noted, and greatly appreciated. Of course, if you hadn't come in voluntarily, Višća was eager to encourage you."

"Yeah? How did that work out for him last time?"

Kolak laughed. "I like you, Jack."

"I doubt that's why I'm here."

"Just a few questions, if you don't mind."

"Sure. But a call would've worked just as well. I'm kinda busy at the moment."

"Of course you are."

The springs in Kolak's chair squeaked as he leaned back, folding his hands on his belly. "It's just that I like to be able to read a man's face when I talk to him." He tapped his cheekbone with his index finger. "The eye is the best lie detector."

"Fire away. And don't blink."

Kolak chuckled. "Funny."

He sat up with another orchestration of creaking springs and leaned on his desk. His round, rheumy eyes narrowed. "Three dead Russian nationals were found in an abandoned house last night, each shot once in the forehead."

"I'm sorry to hear that."

"My office was contacted. I reached out to a colleague at the Russian embassy. At first, he denied any knowledge about them. But an hour later, the deputy chief of mission called me, and—how do you say it? 'Tore me a new one.'"

"And this concerns me . . . how?"

"By the deputy's reaction, it was clear to me that these Russians weren't simply unfortunate tourists. But I already knew that."

Kolak folded his hands on the desk, his eyes searching Jack's face. "The strange thing is, they were wearing Bosnian police uniforms."

Jack felt the floor fall out from under his feet, but he kept his poker face. Could those have been the same jokers who stopped them on the road from Dubrovnik?

"No comment, Jack?"

"What do you want me to say?"

"Judging by their disguises, the deputy's reaction, and their summary executions, I'm quite certain these were Russian security operatives. SVR, FSB, perhaps even GRU. I'm leaning toward the latter. The deputy is a 'retired' GRU intelligence officer. A nasty fellow."

"Makes sense to me."

Kolak nodded. "So, you didn't know they were Russian?"

"How would I know anything about them? I never met them."

"But you did."

"I thought you said you weren't going to follow me around."

"I did say that, didn't I?"

"Yes, you did."

Kolak fidgeted with his knitted tie. "The last time we met, you said you were looking for Aida Ćurić. I take it you found her."

"You know good and well I did."

"I'm disappointed, Jack. I asked you to let me know when you found her."

"I guess it slipped my mind."

"Or other things were on your mind."

"Maybe."

Jack had to assume Kolak's spies had them under surveillance the entire time. He suddenly felt creeped out, and a little violated.

"And what is your opinion about Ms. Aida Ćurić?"

"My opinion is that she's the woman my mother wanted me to find, and I found her. Or, technically, she came to me."

"Interesting. Please go on."

"She's beautiful. She's smart. She loves her country. She's a great tour guide."

"A tour guide? Yes, of course. I'm sure she is very good at it. She knows the country extremely well. Her tour company travels all over the Balkans. Anything else?"

"Not that you need to know."

"Fair enough. For now. Let's get back to the Russians. You were traveling from Dubrovnik back to Sarajevo, yes?"

Jack nodded.

"And these three men pulled you over?"

"Yes. They wore Bosnian police uniforms, one civilian, two tactical. They diverted us off the main road and down to the river. Aida said they were really Serb Mafia, looking for a bribe."

"What time was this?"

"I'd say between two and three o'clock in the afternoon. I'm not exactly sure."

"Why did they target your vehicle?"

Jack shrugged. "I'd rather not say."

"Aida was smuggling 'medicine,' right?"

"You need to ask her. And I don't like your implication."

"It was medicine, wasn't it?"

"That's what the boxes said."

"Did you look inside one?"

"Why should I? I had no reason to doubt her."

"No, of course not. But perhaps it really was only medicine."

Kolak glanced at the ceiling, collecting his thoughts. "So they pulled you over, they demanded a bribe, you overwhelmed them somehow, and that's when you killed them."

Jack's eyes widened. "What? Wait, no. That's not what happened."

"Of course not." Kolak sat back again, smiling at Jack's discomfort. "So tell me what did happen."

"They pulled guns, I took two of them down—fists and feet only, no weapons. Aida disarmed the other one."

"Aida did? How?"

"She kicked him in the nuts and then cracked him on the nose. He was a little guy. Down on the ground by the time I turned around."

"Interesting skill set for a tour guide, wouldn't you say?"

"You should see my mother with an AR-15, and she's an eye surgeon."

"What happened next?"

"We tied them up and called the police to turn them in. When we left, they were very much alive."

"You tied them up, Jack?"

"No, Emir did. After we left."

"Emir Jukić?"

"Yes. Aida's cousin. He's the guy who actually runs the tour service, not Aida. She only owns it."

"He was traveling with you?"

"Apparently, he'd been following us. I didn't know that at the time."

"Interesting."

"You keep saying that."

"Everything you say is interesting to me, Jack. So tell me, who called the police, you or Aida?"

"Emir did. He told us to leave, and he'd take care of the phone call."

"Why not stay there with him and wait for the police to come?"

"Aida said we couldn't."

"Why?"

"She said the police were corrupt, and that they'd cause her big problems, and that she was scared of them."

"Of course she would say that."

"Was she wrong?"

Kolak shrugged. "Not entirely."

"What is that supposed to mean?"

Kolak sat up again. "In Bosnia, there are always three narratives for any given fact: a Croat narrative, a Serb narrative, and a Bosniak narrative. It's usually only those who aren't like you who can't be trusted."

"Can you blame her?"

"Who was it that said, 'We don't see things as they are, we see things as we are'?"

Jack knew that it was Anaïs Nin, but he didn't want to play along. "No idea."

"It doesn't matter. To continue, Aida said that these men who stopped you were Serb Mafia?"

"She did. We checked for identification, but they didn't have any, and they weren't offering any, so that explanation made sense to me at the time."

"Well, we know now they weren't Serb Mafia. Why do you suppose the Russians stopped you? Were they after Aida? Or you?"

"Why would they be after me?"

"Just exploring the options. Humor me."

"They searched the van, so my guess is they were after her, or something they thought she had."

"Not the medicines, obviously. Any idea what else?"

"None."

"Anything else they wanted from you?"

"They asked her about her uncle, Tarik Brkić."

"What do you know about Brkić?"

"Only what Aida told me. That he was related by marriage—her mother's cousin, or something. And he's a mechanic that does work for her sometimes."

"That's correct. I'm surprised she told you anything about him."

"Why is that?"

"Brkić is a man we've had our eye on for some time. He's a Bosnian citizen now, but originally he was from Chechnya. Nobody knows much about him. He keeps a rather low profile. The rumor is that he came over in 1991 to fight in the Bosnian War, though that was never proven. That makes him a person of some interest to us."

"And so is Aida, isn't she?"

"Why do you say that?"

"You wanted me to find her, and to let you know when I did."

"How does that make her a person of interest?"

"You already know who she is, where she works, where she lives. You didn't need me to find her, did you? You needed me to get close to her."

"Perhaps."

"Who's the liar now?"

Kolak laughed. "I said 'perhaps,' didn't I? Yes, you are correct. You're a smart fellow, Jack. I did want you to get to know her."

"Because you haven't been able to get anyone else close to her, which means you've tried to, which means you're interested in her."

"You should be an intelligence officer, Jack. You would make a good one. Or perhaps you already are?"

"Me? Hardly. Just a financial analyst."

Kolak smiled. "Of course. With Hendley Associates. We checked you out, remember?"

"Anything else you need to know? I have a plane to catch."

"Not until tomorrow morning, if I'm not mistaken. Vueling Flight 1405 to Rome, eight forty-two a.m."

"What else do you want from me?"

"Just a few more questions. You said that Emir Jukić made the call to the Bosnian police?"

"Yes."

"And you saw him make the call?"

Jack shook his head. "No, as a matter of fact. But Aida trusts him, and for what it's worth, we met up with him thirty minutes later. He didn't have any bloodstains on him or anything, if that's what you're getting at."

"I wouldn't suggest Emir killed those men. But perhaps he didn't call the police as he said he did."

"Or maybe he did. Maybe the police he called are the ones who killed those men."

"We checked with the local cops. They never received such a phone call."

"And you believe them?"

"Frankly, no. We accessed their phone records. No calls were made to the local station on the afternoon of that day."

"So you think Emir called someone else, and that's who killed those men?"

Kolak flashed another mouthful of crooked teeth. "Who can say?"

Jack checked his watch.

"Big date tonight, Jack?"

"Something like that."

"I hate to take up so much of your time, but just one or two more questions, if I may."

"Shoot."

"Tell me about your visit to the Peace and Friendship Center. What did you think about it?"

"I'm impressed that your government allowed it in the first place. With unemployment so high in your country, I wouldn't think you would want more immigrants."

"We don't. But it looks good to the pencil pushers in Brussels, and my government very much wants to join the EU. By taking in refugees, it solves a problem for Brussels, and makes us look more humanitarian for helping 'poor Muslims.'"

"You sound cynical."

"I'm a Catholic Croat. I'm sick and tired of always hearing about the suffering Muslims. I'm sure Ms. Curić filled your head with her propaganda about their unique victim status in our country."

"She told me about the Croatian-fascist Ustaše during the last war, if that's what you're referring to."

Kolak nodded. "Yes, of course she would. They were terrible, brutal killers, for sure. But I wonder, as she was giving you her history lesson, did she tell you about World War Two? About how Heinrich Himmler recruited not one but two entire Nazi SS divisions composed entirely of Bosniak Muslims? Judging by the look on your face, I imagine not. And if you want a real shock, Google the history of the German Nazis and the Muslim Brotherhood, the grandfather of all modern jihadis."

Kolak leaned forward again. "History isn't what we choose to forget, is it? If it weren't for the Catholic Poles saving Vienna from the Turks in 1683, we'd all be Muslims now, wouldn't we?"

"Can I go?"

"Yes, of course. But one last thing. I like you, Jack. I really do. And that's why I'm going to say to you that you are in the middle of things you can't possibly understand, including the three dead Russians."

"And yet, despite the risk to my personal safety, you were willing to use me to get close to Aida."

"A mistake on my part. I hope I have made it up to you by not telling the Russians that you and Aida were there."

"Why not?"

"If I had, you and Aida would already be dead."

"Thanks, I guess."

"Take my advice. Be sure to be on that plane tomorrow. Better yet, change your ticket and leave tonight if you can. You saw all of the crowds and the traffic on the way over here? Those are thousands of Serbs swarming into the city for the Orthodox Renewal service tomorrow. Sarajevo is a powder keg, and there are fifty thousand matches already lit and ready to be thrown."

"And if I decide not to leave tomorrow?"

"Have you heard the saying 'God must love fools because he made so many of them'?"

Jack stood. "Good-bye, Agent Kolak."

Kolak stood as well, and shook Jack's hand. "Good-bye, Jack. Please stay safe. And, if I may, stay away from Aida Curić."

55

OUTSIDE SARAJEVO, BOSNIA AND HERZEGOVINA

After processing the new batch of refugees, Aida swung by Jack's place and picked him up as promised. She drove him to her house out in the country, about fifteen miles west of the city, not far off the R442, another narrow, two-lane asphalt road.

"How was your day?" Aida asked as she pulled away from the curb.

"Went to the Srebrenica exhibit. Depressing as hell." He wasn't sure if he should tell her about the Kolak meeting yet. He was still processing it. "Yours?"

"It went very well. Syrians are such nice people. One of them is a dentist. I think he might stay and help us in the clinic."

They rode along in silence for a while.

"What's bothering you, Jack?"

"Nothing."

"I'm not sure I believe you." She rubbed his knee. "Tell me."

"I had a meeting today with a guy named Kolak."

"Dragan Kolak?"

"Yeah. You know him?"

"He's with Bosnian security. A Croat. A very bad man."

"He certainly knows you."

"What did he want?"

"Those Serbians that stopped us? He said they were actually Russians, and that they had been killed."

"What?"

"I told him that we left them alive, and that Emir called the police after we left. He was suggesting that Emir either killed those men or contacted someone who did."

Aida slapped the steering wheel, cursing in her native tongue. "That son of a bitch is a liar. Those weren't Russians, Jack. Don't you think I would know the difference between Serbs and Russians?"

"Yeah, sure."

"And why would he think that Emir wanted to kill them?"

"He didn't say. He was interested in Brkić, too. Said he was an ethnic Chechen."

"He is. So what? He's a Bosnian citizen."

"He knew that you were smuggling medicine from Dubrovnik."

"Did he say how he knew that?"

"No."

"Doesn't that tell you something?"

"No, what?"

"He knew about the medicine, he knew about the Serbs who were trying to rob us, he knew they were killed. But he blames Emir."

"What are you saying?"

"Kolak is dirty. They're all dirty. And Kolak is out to get me because of the refugee center. You see, anything that helps Muslims is a threat to Serbs and Croats and thieves like him."

Jack tried to put the pieces together. They still didn't quite fit. "There is another possibility."

Aida was focused on the hairpin curve spooling up the mountain. "What possibility?"

"What if Kolak is right? What if Emir and Brkić are somehow connected?"

"They are connected. They're family, by marriage. And sometimes Brkić does maintenance work on our vans and helps out with the tours. I told you that already."

"That's my point. I think Emir might be using your company behind your back for his own purposes, or to help Brkić do whatever it is he's into."

"That doesn't make any sense, Jack. If they did that, they would be working against me. Don't you think I'd know what was going on? Kolak is just using you to try and hurt me."

"Think about it. Emir runs the company day in and day out. He and his drivers travel all over the Balkans and into Europe. It's a perfect setup to run drugs or guns or, heck, smuggle people if they wanted to."

"No way. I'd know about it."

Jack laid a hand on her thigh. "I'm worried about you. There's something going on, and it might wind up killing you."

She stole a quick glance at him as she made another sharp turn. "Oh, Jack. What did I tell you? Bosnia is crazy, and it's hard for outsiders to understand it. Stay away from Kolak."

"I still think you should come home to Virginia with me tomorrow until we sort it all out."

"That's very sweet of you. But my people have been dealing with thieves like Kolak for five hundred years. We're survivors."

"I have friends back in Washington. They can do some research on this Kolak guy, and even Emir, if you want."

"You haven't talked to them yet about anything, have you?"

"No, not yet."

"Good, because there are things I would want you to check out for me first. But when you do, please be careful. I don't want you to hurt the center's reputation, or mine. The work is too important."

"I understand. I won't do anything to compromise you or the center."

"Thank you."

"But trust me, Aida. I'll get to the bottom of all of this, one way or another."

"I know you will, and I'm grateful."

Aida turned off the asphalt and onto a hard-packed dirt road that led through a copse of trees, opening up to a clearing. She slowed to a stop in front of her place. She nodded at the house.

"Let's forget about everything we talked about and just enjoy our last night together, okay?"

"Okay."

The main house was big by Bosnian standards, a two-story chalet style with steeply slanting rooflines, matching the pine-covered slopes it was planted against.

Inside, the chalet was as cozy as Jack expected, a real

mountain retreat with heavy leather furniture, woolen rugs on the hardwood floors, and old wooden skis and snowshoes on the walls. She asked Jack to make them a fire while she cooked, handing him a glass of The Macallan single-malt whiskey.

Thirty minutes later they sat at a thick wooden dining table, eating pan-fried sausages, onions, and potatoes flavored with a mix of spices that reminded Jack of the ćevapi, only hotter. The ice-cold beer matched it perfectly.

"I wish I wasn't leaving tomorrow."

"I hate it, too. Are you sure you have to?"

"Only if I want to keep my job." He took a swig of beer. "I checked my flight schedule while you were cooking and I reserved another ticket for you."

She took a drink of beer, smiling. "That's very thoughtful of you, but it's too soon, I'm afraid. Another group of refugees is coming in five days, and another a week after that."

"So you're open to the idea?"

"Open? Yes."

"Then come out in three weeks. You'll like Washington, and we'll figure this stuff out together."

She popped the last bite of sausage into her mouth. The fat glistened on the curve of her lower lip. "I've always wanted to visit America." She smiled as she chewed.

Jack had a few pieces of sausage on his plate.

Aida stabbed one of them and held it up in front of his mouth. "Hurry up and finish your dinner. You'll need your energy."

Jack bit the sausage off the fork. "Energy for what?"

She touched his hand, flashing a come-hither smile.

Jack didn't bother asking about dessert.

BRODARICA, CROATIA

Dom, Adara, and Midas stood with the operative from the Croatian Security and Intelligence Agency (SOA) a discreet distance away from the modest stone and red-tiled-roof home overlooking the dazzling blue Adriatic Sea. It was currently occupied by an Irish family on vacation.

"Zvezdev's remains were found here," the operative said. "Fermenting in a kimchi jar. But you already knew that."

"And no evidence of any kind was found?" Dom asked.

"Nothing useful. The few fingerprints we found were Zvezdev's, and those were mostly smudged. Someone definitely cleaned the place, but we think he wasn't here for very long, because he was on the run. I'm sorry you traveled all this way for nothing. Too bad you let your suspect in Slovenia get away."

"She wasn't *our* suspect," Dom said. "And she didn't get away. She was killed."

"By this so-called Iron Syndicate you referred to, yes?"

"With your permission, we'd like to stay a few days, ask around town. Maybe we can turn up something."

"I am instructed to extend to you every courtesy. However, I must be present at all times, especially in the event you question Croatian national citizens."

Adara frowned. "That's not how we like to operate."

Dom's phone rang. It was Gerry's ringtone.

"Hi, Gerry. What's shaking?"

"Change of plans."

56

NEAR SARAJEVO, BOSNIA AND HERZEGOVINA

Jack woke from a troubled sleep a half hour before the alarm and stared at the ceiling.

"What time is it?" Aida asked sleepily.

"Four-fifteen. Go back to sleep."

"What's wrong?"

"Still thinking about yesterday."

Aida sat up, spilling out of her sheet. She brushed the chestnut hair out of her startling blue eyes and smiled. "Only the good stuff, I hope."

She touched him.

He was ready.

She climbed on top of him.

He forgot his troubles.

After they finished, she pulled on a plush robe and padded into the kitchen to make a pot of strong Bosnian coffee and fry some ham while Jack checked his phone for messages. The one that caught his eye was from Gerry.

Be at the airport at 8 am sharp. No excuses.

Jack wondered what that was all about. Just a reminder for him to get there on time for his flight?

They ate, then showered. Drying off, Jack said, "Can you drop me off at the airport at eight?"

"I'm sorry, I can't. I have a meeting scheduled at eight-fifteen with a UN delegate, but I have to stop by my office first. Emir can take you."

"That's okay. I'll just grab a cab."

She crossed over to him and wrapped her arms around his neck and kissed him. "Emir is a good man, Jack. I trust him. You should, too."

"Yeah, sure. But he's also a busy man. A cab is easy."

"And expensive."

"But I'm a rich American, remember?"

"Hurry, then. We need to go if you want to get packed."

SARAJEVO, BOSNIA AND HERZEGOVINA

His orders came from the Czech directly just five days ago, confirming Jack Ryan's identity as well as his location in Sarajevo. The orders were explicit: Acquire the man's head, and do it without being detected.

It was the most insane hit he'd ever been assigned, but the bonus offered was irresistible.

Failure to fully comply with instructions would void the bonus. Worse, it meant he would be put on someone else's kill list.

It had been hell to actually locate Ryan because he was on the move, and harder still to track him, even when he was just in the city. He suspected Ryan was practicing SDRs, but if so, he did it so effortlessly that it was difficult to tell.

There had been only two prior opportunities to grab Ryan, and both would have resulted in collateral damage. But the assassin was infamously patient, and his patience paid off. Today presented an ideal opportunity. Probably the last one, too.

Ryan was his.

All he had to do was wait.

Aida pulled up in front of Jack's apartment building twenty minutes later than they had planned. The traffic pouring into town was the worst she had ever seen.

She didn't kill the engine.

"Good-byes are difficult, yes?"

"Yeah." He had a hard time holding her gaze. "You're not coming out in three weeks, are you?"

"I said I would try."

"Then I'll come back."

She touched his face with her hand. "That's not a good idea."

"Why not?"

"I've been trying to tell you, but you won't listen. Things are more complicated here than you can possibly realize."

"Then help me understand."

"Okay. Here is the most important fact. By being with me, you are endangering my work, and even my life."

Jack's eyes widened. "How?"

"You distract me, Jack. Others have noticed, including Kolak. The longer you are here, the harder they will work to use you, and to hurt me and the work I am doing, which is my life. The people that hate us will do anything, including kidnapping you, or worse. You saw what happened the other day. I care for you too much. I can't allow that to happen."

"I can take care of myself."

"I'm sure you can. But I'm not willing to risk it, or the work we're doing for the refugees. Do you understand?"

"No, but I guess it doesn't matter."

She leaned over and kissed him softly on the mouth.

"Good-bye, my love."

"Yeah. Bye," was all Jack could manage.

He stood in the street and watched her pull away, knowing he would never see her again. It hurt like hell.

Worse, he knew she was in trouble, and that he wouldn't be here to help her.

Jack jogged up the stairs, ignoring the stink of the garbage chute, and dashed into his apartment, running through a mental checklist of things to do before he left, starting with packing. The clock was ticking. But he wanted to clean the place up, too. Sweep, vacuum, put the dishes away, strip his sheets and toss them in the laundry. He didn't want to leave the apartment in worse shape than he'd found it in, partly because that was the way he was raised, and partly because he really liked the landlords.

He also needed the distraction. Helpless despair was crouching at his door. Better to forget everything and get the hell out of Dodge.

He headed for the bedroom to start packing. He flung the closet door open, glancing at the floor where his bag was stored. Instead, he saw a scuffed leather Oxford that wasn't his—

The heel of a hand bludgeoned Jack between the eyes. The

blow was blunted slightly when the man's arm crashed into the partly opened closet door, but it still hit home.

Bright lights flashed in Jack's eyes just as the pain exploded in the front of his brain.

He staggered backward a few steps as a dark-haired man in a janitor's uniform lunged out of the closet with an old-school leather garrote strung between his hands. As tall as Jack but thinner, the charging man thrust both balled fists into Jack's chest, knocking him backward against the far wall, stunning him again, and sending the hanging picture frames crashing to the floor in a shower of glass.

Reeling from the blows, Jack struggled to focus on the wiry man, who suddenly grabbed Jack's shoulders and spun him around with a powerful twist. Before Jack could catch his footing, he felt the thick leather thong wrap around his neck. The sharp spike of a knee against his spine corresponded to the vise grip of leather choking off his windpipe.

Years of CQC training dulled the panic welling in Jack's gut. He was just moments away from blacking out and certain death, but the limbic-system dump of pure adrenaline cleared his brain.

With his arms out of reach of his attacker's face, Jack's only recourse was to grab the leather thong and drop his body weight to the floor. The man's grip didn't falter, which Jack had counted on. The man stumbled forward as Jack's back hit the floor.

But now the man's head was just above Jack's, the perfect place for Jack to thrust his knee into the top of the man's skull with a sickening thud.

The man grunted, but his grip didn't loosen at the first blow. Jack kept pummeling his skull with a series of bicycle kicks, alternating his left and right knees, battering the man into semiconsciousness. His grip finally loosened enough that Jack could breathe a little.

Jack grabbed the leather garrote and pulled the man down to the ground next to him, where he rained a series of well-aimed elbow strikes just behind the man's temple, cracking the pterion, the weakest part of the human skull, where the frontal, parietal, temporal, and sphenoid bones all joined.

The man lost consciousness entirely, finally releasing his iron grip.

Jack unwrapped the garrote from his throat, struggling to breathe. He stared at the sudden swelling on the side of the man's head. The broken bones had ruptured the middle meningeal artery, exactly the outcome Clark's training had told him to expect. Jack was fighting for his life, and his training took over.

He stumbled into the bathroom to splash cold water on his face. That's when he saw the ice chest sitting in the bathtub next to a stainless-steel bone saw, a bottle of bleach, and a box of heavy-duty garbage bags.

A cold chill ran down his sore spine. Bad enough that someone had just tried to kill him, but the vision of his own head in that cooler made him shudder, and the idea that more than one killer—first the woman in Slovenia, now this guy—was trying to behead him and transport his skull to someone else made him realize his life really was in danger.

Who the fuck was this Iron Syndicate, anyway? And what had he done to earn their hate?

Jack splashed cold water on his face and checked his throat. Definitely red and a little swollen. If that guy had used piano wire, it probably would've cut his head off right then and there. To judge from the bone saw and heavy-duty garbage bags, the man was planning on doing his wet work inside the bathtub, and cutting up Jack's body into pieces and hauling it away in the bags, then cleaning up the DNA evidence with bleach.

Strange that he launched out of the closet the way he did, Jack thought. Normally you come after a guy from behind with a garrote. He must have surprised the shitbird when he opened the closet door.

Now what?

Well, he still had to pack.

But what to do with the asshole in his bedroom?

Jack stuck his head out of the front door to make sure no one was around, then hauled the wiry man by the shoulders onto the landing and heaved his slim frame headfirst into the garbage chute.

The man's body clanged inside the fetid metal tube as it hurtled toward the dumpster three stories below. The man was still breathing, but in the reeking filth he was about to land in, that might not be to his advantage.

Jack rushed back into the apartment and, having wiped the items clean of his fingerprints, went back into the hall and tossed the man's ice chest, bone saw, bleach bottle, and garbage bags in after him. He tossed the broken picture frames into a separate bag. The sound of their tumbling and crashing echoed in the tube.

Jack shrugged. Given the beaten assassin he'd tossed into the dumpster, the busted closet door, and the broken picture frames, Jack figured his Airbnb guest rating would probably suffer a few hits.

Time to go.

57

Tarik Brkić stroked his wide, bushy beard out of nervous habit as he approached the camouflaged launch area.

He'd just received a phone call from the brother stationed at the Olympic soccer stadium. The roads this morning were still jammed with cars and buses streaming into Sarajevo. According to the brother, a former Bundeswehr scout, there were already fifty thousand people in the stands. That was nearly double the number they had originally planned for.

But according to the news reports, today's event could draw as many as seventy thousand Orthodox, which the stadium in the past had accommodated for the visits of the *kafir* popes John Paul II and Francis.

Seventy thousand!

He scarcely could take it in. Such a gift from Allah. Was this His plan all along? To ensnare such a host? Was He not Al

MIKE MADEN

Mumit—the Deathbringer? Was this not in accordance with the will of Al Muntaqim—the Retaliator?

Still, Brkić worried. A hundred battles had taught him that some plans never come to pass because of the changing fortunes of men, weather, or circumstance. If there were already fifty thousand Orthodox in place, why be greedy? Why not launch now?

Brkić entered the launch area where Captain Walib was sitting in the cab of the BM-21, checking and rechecking his electronics.

"Brother, a question," Brkić asked.

Walib glanced up from his tablet. "Sir?"

"Tell me again of your rockets. How accurate will they be?"

"We have the exact GLONASS coordinates of both the launch vehicle and the target. The targeting computer is functioning as designed, and has acquired the coordinates. But it is the laser-targeting provided by the drone that will easily put our strike within one meter of our intended target. Our kill box—the stadium—is approximately three hundred meters by three hundred meters. We can't possibly miss."

"And if we launched right now, with fifty thousand on site already, what casualties do you anticipate?"

Open air, no place to hide. Perfect weather. It was a simple math problem. "Nine to twelve thousand dead, twelve to fifteen thousand wounded, many of whom will die of complications later. Many survivors will suffer permanent injuries—blindness, loss of hearing, loss of limbs, respiratory defects. It would be a decisive blow."

"And if that number should rise to seventy thousand?"

Walib shrugged. "Twelve to eighteen thousand dead, twenty

378

to twenty-four thousand wounded. And I am being conservative."

Brkić paced in front of Walib, stroking his beard, calculating. His organization, Al-Qaeda in the Balkans, or AQAB, would broadcast live video of the launch and blast social media with it, along with footage of the carnage afterward, mocking the Orthodox Serb heathen and their impotent Russian puppet masters. The worse the carnage, the more the Russians would be provoked.

And the more provoked, the more likely to intervene.

And with the forces of the Slavic Sword and Shield exercises just across the border, they had the means to do so.

Nine thousand dead would surely be enough to provoke them. But if he waited a few more minutes, it was possible that as many as eighteen thousand would perish.

But then again, planners like Walib always assumed the best-case scenario. What if there were misfires? Or a sudden gust of wind? If his casualty numbers were off by half? Two-thirds?

Yes, better to wait, especially if there were contingencies, Brkić decided. The more slaughter, the more likely the Russians were to intervene, and NATO to respond. The blood of the Orthodox would fuel the hellish fire that would be the next world war, and save the Umma from their suffering in Muslim lands at the hands of the *kuffar*. This would lead to the uprising of all brothers across Europe, and the final conquest of the world under the banner of Islam.

All he needed was a little patience.

A little faith.

Allahu akbar!

SARAJEVO, BOSNIA AND HERZEGOVINA

Jack packed and scrambled out of the apartment, reminding himself to send his landlords a text when he got to the airport, apologizing for not cleaning up and for the broken pictures and asking them to bill his credit card for damages.

He'd call Kolak after he arrived in the States and let him know about trash pickup. Bosnia and the United States had no extradition treaty, though Jack could reasonably claim self-defense if it came to that.

This time he was smart enough to grab a retinal scan of his intended killer, along with the man's fingerprints from apps on his iPhone. He also took the man's wallet with credit cards and ID, as well as his cell phone, so that he could get those to Gavin for further analysis. He also grabbed the man's car keys. Why pay for a cab if he didn't have to?

Down on the street he hit the key fob and a green Škoda sedan beeped. Jack opened the trunk to toss in his suitcase and spotted a gun bag. He zipped it open and found a Heckler & Koch MP7 machine pistol with iron sights. A sweet rig, firing a 4.6x30-millimeter round. The MP7 was one of Jack's favorite weapons to shoot.

He zipped the bag back up and tossed a blanket over it, hoping like hell the Bosnian police had no reason to pull him over and do a trunk check. If they did, it would be a guaranteed one-way ticket to the local hoosegow. But getting pulled over was unlikely on a day like today, when all of the cops would be tied up with the Renewal service at the soccer stadium, and the idea of having his own wheels appealed to him. He tossed his suitcase and laptop on top of the blanket, jumped in the car, and plugged the airport address into the dashboard GPS.

Fortunately, he was driving against traffic, so the road was relatively clear in his direction. The traffic flooding into town was clogged with vehicles flying all manner of flags and banners; variations of double-headed Serbian eagles and Orthodox crosses and sometimes both, much the same way American Christians melded church and nationalism together. What really caught Jack's attention was a flapping red-and-gold banner and the scowling Orthodox Jesus, his eyes dark and disapproving.

Thirty minutes later, Jack pulled into the short-term parking lot and found a spot on the far end. He killed the engine and grabbed his bags out of the trunk. He locked it and pocketed the keys, figuring he'd toss them into the trash inside the lobby.

He made a beeline for the glass doors of the small terminal, the familiar smell of jet fuel in the air and the sound of a turboprop revving on the taxiway suddenly putting him in a traveling mood. There was still enough time to make his 8:42 a.m. flight—but just barely. Before he crossed the parking lot his cell phone rang with Gerry's distinctive ringtone.

Jack was glad to get the call. He was finally at the airport, and that would make his boss happy.

The Gulfstream 550 was making its approach to the Sarajevo International Airport. Following the entry point and radar vector instructions from the air traffic controller, the pilot dropped speed and altitude toward runway 12, the only arrival runway at the small but efficient facility. They were still five thousand feet in the air, but descending quickly through the clear September sky.

"Man, looks like the 110 freeway before a Dodgers game,"

Midas said, staring out of the window. "I'd hate to be driving around down there today. What's going on?"

"The Eastern Orthodox Church is holding some kind of big outdoor religious service in a few hours, according to the local news reports," Adara said, powering down her laptop for landing. "Orthodox Christians from all over the region are showing up for it, including a bunch of politicians."

"Good thing we're just picking Jack up at the FBO hangar, then," Dom said. "No worries."

"And then home," Midas said. "I'm tired of this snipe hunt."

Emir pressed the SA-25 Verba ("Willow") MANPADS against his narrow shoulder with his gloved hands, his eye fixed to the sight. The Verba automatically acquired and tracked the low-altitude civilian jet, feeding target data to the onboard computer controlling the missile's multispectrum optical seeker.

Even if the small civilian aircraft carried anti-missile defenses such as flares, decoys, or laser systems like Sky Shield, the Verba's advanced seeker could discriminate between them and the actual target. The latest Russian anti-aircraft missile could take out high-flying, supersonic NATO warplanes and cruise missiles, making it the most feared portable MANPADS in the Russian arsenal. A low-speed, low-altitude civilian airplane like the one he was tracking was no match against it.

The Verba was just one of the many stolen gifts bestowed upon AQAB by the Syrian captain and his Chechen lieutenant, Dzhabrailov.

He pulled the trigger. The solid-fuel 9M336 missile roared out of its tube, launching the high-explosive 1.5-kilogram warhead at supersonic speed toward the hapless civilian jet. The missile trailed a long finger of white exhaust as it clawed its way into the air.

Within seconds, the warhead slammed into the aircraft's thin aluminum skin in a thundering explosion, shattering the fuselage in a fiery cloud of twisted metal.

58

Jack whipped around at the sound of the booming explosion of the Verba missile eighteen hundred feet above. Its arcing smoke trail pointed to its launch origin west of the airfield, a mile away, maybe more. The plane's burning wreckage plunged toward the earth, leaving a trail of smashed luggage and cabin debris fluttering in its wake.

"Dear God," Jack whispered, his eyes widening.

Broken bodies were tumbling through the sky, some still strapped to their seats.

One of those bodies should have been his.

He fought back a wave of nausea.

It suddenly occurred to him that Gerry's ass-chewing phone call in the parking lot earlier had just saved his life.

Gerry had instructed him to forget his Vueling flight and instead make his way over to the fixed-base operator hangar, where arrangements had already been made for the Hendley Associates Gulfstream to land and pick him up. Gerry warned Jack that Midas and Dom were instructed to put him on the

Gulfstream "by any means necessary." Jack had left the main terminal and come over to this private hangar to wait.

The Gulfstream was still ten minutes out. Then it suddenly hit him. He was supposed to be on that Vueling fight, but he'd purchased a ticket for Aida, too.

Maybe that missile was meant for her?

Jack grabbed his phone and punched in her number, but his phone rang with Dom's number.

"Jack, it's me. What the hell just happened down there?"

"Somebody took out a passenger jet. The one I was supposed to be on."

"You must be in some kind of shit, all right, cuz. Look, the air traffic controller just put us on hold. They're not allowing any flights in or out until they can assess the situation on the ground. We've got enough fuel to loiter for another forty minutes, but if it gets beyond that, we'll have to land somewhere else and then come get you by car."

"Dude, I gotta go—"

"Hold on, Jack! The whole point of us coming to get you was to get your ass out of the fire. Don't you go running back into it, or Gerry'll have my hide."

"Why did he send you all the way over here to pick me up, anyway?" Jack glanced at the burning black cloud mushrooming in the distance.

"He didn't send us just to pick you up. We're over in this neck of the woods chasing leads on this outfit called the Iron Syndicate."

"Yeah, Gerry mentioned it. Something to do with that crazy woman in Slovenia that tried to kill me."

"One and the same. Maybe they're the ones that fired that missile."

"Don't think so. They've got a thing about collecting my head."

"Unless they changed their thing."

"I gotta go."

"Stay put, Jack. We'll be there in a few."

"Can't wait. Track my phone if you want to find me." Jack killed the call and dialed Aida again. The phone rang until it went to voice mail.

"Aida, it's me, Jack. Call me back as soon as you get this. I need to know you're okay."

He hung up.

Jack wasn't clear in his own mind who had done it. Serb nationalists? The Mafia? The Russians? Maybe even Kolak? *Shit*, Jack thought. It was like the fucking Star Wars cantina around here.

They all had it in for her.

Jack called the refugee center. Another voice mail. He hung up, called the Happy Times! tour office. Voice mail again.

Jack's anxiety spiked.

Shit!

Now what?

He could drive to the tour office or the refugee center, but traffic was miserable going back into the city. No point in trying to navigate that if he couldn't be sure she would be at either location.

But her place out in the country was west of here, away from the traffic. That was his best bet. Chances were she'd turn up there eventually, if she was okay.

He patted the keys in his pocket, glad he hadn't tossed them into the trash yet, and ran back toward the parking lot, praying the Škoda hadn't been towed.

———

The Škoda hadn't been towed, fortunately, and Jack sped out of the lot as fast as he could without breaking the law, grateful for the Bosnian marks he still had in his pocket to pay the ticket to leave.

Jack hit the main road, heading west, driving the speed limit. He didn't want to get pulled over for any reason, let alone the MP7 that was now stashed underneath his seat, locked and loaded. He found an English-language news station on the radio. It was already reporting the jet crash.

"Authorities believe the Vueling Embraer E-170 aircraft was destroyed with a shoulder-fired anti-aircraft missile. As many as sixty-six passengers may have been on the flight, though the number has not yet been confirmed. No survivors are expected. The Serbian National Front for the Liberation of Bosnia and Herzegovina has claimed credit for the attack on social media sites . . ."

"Sonsofbitches," Jack said out loud, his anger boiling over at the Serb nationalists who could murder innocent people like that.

But in his head he heard Kolak's "three narratives" lecture again. Three sides to every fact. There had been a lot of local attacks by all sides lately, and all of them escalating. It was hard to tell the good guys from the bad guys.

Jack wondered if the Serbian National Front really was behind the attack.

Or if the SNF even existed.

He drove along in silence for a while, listening to the story repeat every few minutes. Nothing new to report, except for denials by Serb politicians and activists, claiming it was a false-flag attack by either Croats or Muslims, meant to detract from the Orthodox Renewal service later that day.

Were they telling the truth? Or covering their tracks?

Who knew in this crazy place?

Jack followed the little blue arrow on the dashboard GPS. Part of his PERSEC training early on with The Campus was to always memorize new locations, as he'd done when Aida drove him to her place yesterday. He thought he could have found it on his own, but the GPS was too handy to ignore on the winding mountain road.

He prayed to God that she was there, and that she was safe.

59

Twenty-five minutes later, Jack made the turn off the asphalt and followed the hard-packed dirt road toward Aida's compound behind the trees. He saw the top of the two-story chalet peeking above the pines and his pulse raced. Last night with her had seared itself deep in his soul.

When Jack's Škoda cleared the trees and entered the compound, he saw two vehicles, a black Renault coupe and Aida's Happy Times! Volkswagen T5 tour van.

Two bearded Bosniaks were loading heavy canvas duffels into the van. They glanced up when they saw Jack, their eyes flashing with concern. They exchanged a look, dropped their duffels in the dirt, and reached behind them—

Jack knew that move all too well.

He slammed the brakes, shoved the shifter into reverse, and crushed the throttle. The Škoda leaped backward at the first crack of pistol rounds.

Bullets spanged against the front grille and spiderwebbed the windshield as Jack navigated through the rear window, steering with one hand. Suddenly the rear window exploded into tiny glass nuggets, some of them hitting Jack in the face. Instinctively, his driving arm jerked and the Škoda swerved hard off the road and slammed into a tree.

BAM!

Front and side airbags exploded open as Jack was jerked hard and forward by the crash, slamming his face into one. He was slathered in talcum powder from the bag storage, and blinded by the big balloons of air. As he reached for his seat belt release, the passenger bag burst with a pop, punctured by a nine-millimeter round.

Jack grabbed the MP7 and rolled out of the driver's-side door, using it as a shield against the slugs thudding into the steel panel.

Jack dove and rolled for the nearest tree, racked the charging handle, then stood and took aim through the iron sights at the first man racing toward him. He unleashed a short burst, opening the man's chest like a reciprocating saw. The joule force of the speeding projectiles smashed against the Bosniak's upper torso like steel fists, clotheslining him. His feet kicked out from under him as his back slammed to the ground.

In the two eyeblinks it took to dispatch him, the other Bosniak had cleared the far side of the Škoda and taken aim at Jack. He got off three rounds from his pistol, splintering the bark near Jack's face, before Jack unleashed leaded fury, tearing open the man's throat and walking rounds up into his mouth in a spray of teeth and blood until the magazine emptied. The man was dead by the time he tumbled into the dirt.

Jack checked for more tangos, but none were visible. He popped open the trunk and fished around for another mag, but he couldn't find one. He tossed the useless rifle back into the trunk and slammed it shut.

His heart was racing, but not because he was afraid.

He had to find Aida.

Now.

Jack dashed past the ruined Škoda, keeping as close to the trees as possible for cover. He stopped at the clearing and knelt down, scanning the compound from nine o'clock to three o'clock, looking for more shooters, but there were none. There was no movement in the chalet windows, either, and the front door was open, just as the dead shooters had left it.

The Volkswagen van hadn't moved and no one was in it. Same with the Renault coupe. The two heavy green canvas duffels lay in the dirt where the Bosniaks had dropped them.

He knelt down to open one when he heard a woman scream.

Jack!"

The terrified scream came from inside, and it was Aida's voice. Jack bolted for the porch, slamming his back against the wall.

"Aida!"

No answer.

No gun. No knife. Nothing but his fists. If there was anyone else inside with a gun, he didn't stand a chance.

He didn't care.

Jack dashed inside, sweeping his eyes left, then right.

Nobody.

Just the heavy dining table where he and Aida had eaten dinner last night, an open laptop on top.

He listened.

Nothing.

No, wait.

Sobbing.

Jack ran for Aida's bedroom, kicking the door open. She lay on the bed, fetal, wrapped in a blanket.

"Aida!"

He rushed to the bed. Knelt down next to her, still sobbing. "Are you hurt?"

He rolled her over, carefully.

Aida's sobs slowed. Her face was covered in her thick hair.

"Oh, Jack."

He leaned over her, gently pushing her hair aside.

"Aida."

Her face broke into an aching smile.

And then a laugh.

"Oh, Jack. My beautiful idiot."

She jammed a Makarov pistol beneath his jaw, her wide blue eyes bright with mischief.

A pistol racked behind his head.

She laughed again. "You are so fucked."

Yeah. He was.

Idiot.

Jack was duct-taped to one of the low-backed wooden chairs from the dining table, from the middle of his shoulders to his elbows. Even his wrists were taped together, his palms touching as if in prayer, and his forearms lay helpless in his lap.

Aida sat at the table, tapping keys on the laptop next to a burner phone.

No wonder she never picked up her smartphone, Jack thought.

Emir carried a wooden crate, a chromed Colt 1911 .45 shoved into his waistband. "Last one." He nodded toward Jack. "And then we can go."

By which he means time for me to die.

He hardly cared. He was raging and ashamed, all at the same time.

She'd played him, big-time. How could he not have seen it coming?

Because I've been a damned idiot, that's how. Thinking with my head instead of my brain.

"I'll be ready," Aida said, as Emir stepped into the harsh morning light.

Aida stood and turned the laptop around so that Jack could see it.

"Do you know what you're looking at?"

Jack leaned forward as far as the duct tape would allow, squinting his eyes. "I dunno. The Depeche Mode concert?"

"It's a live video feed from our drone, flying high over the Olympic soccer stadium, hosting the Orthodox Renewal. All of those people down there are crowding in like sardines in order to receive the blessings of their priests. Well, we have another blessing in store for them." She checked her watch. "In exactly forty-two minutes, they're all going to die."

"Just like those innocent people killed on that plane?"

"Oh, no. These Serbs will suffer much, much more than they did."

"Why are you doing this?"

"I tried to explain it to you, Jack. But you're too American to understand." She pocketed her burner phone.

"I can't believe you killed those people."

She giggled coyly. "Me? I didn't. Emir is the one who pulled the trigger."

"But you ordered him to, didn't you?"

"Yes."

"To kill me."

"I had to. You became a loose end."

"And that's supposed to make me feel better?"

"I shouldn't think so. Especially since you're responsible for all of them dying."

"Kill him now, and let's go," Emir said, stepping back into the room. "The commander is waiting for us."

"You mean Brkić, don't you?" Jack asked.

WHACK!

Emir backhanded Jack. "Shut your mouth. You are not worthy to speak his name." Emir pulled his chromed pistol out of his waistband and pointed it at Jack.

Aida laid her hand on the barrel and pushed it down. "Not yet."

"What are you waiting for? Kill him now! He treated you like his whore." He raised his gun back up.

"Not yet. I want him to see history unfold before his eyes, and to know the part he played in starting World War Three. And then he can die."

Emir smiled at the thought. "Sure, why not?"

"Good. You stay here with him. I'm going to the site. When it's done, blow his brains out, then come."

She kissed Emir on the forehead and headed for the door. The small Bosniak was visibly shaken by the kiss, as if a thousand volts of electricity had been shot through his body. His resolve stiffened.

Aida stopped and turned, a dark shadow framed in the doorway, the blazing sun behind her.

"You Americans sicken me. Ignorant. Arrogant. Naive. You are all fools. But you, Jack Ryan, are the biggest fool of all." She laughed as she headed for her van.

Emir brayed like a mule.

The Volkswagen's engine fired up outside, spitting gravel as it sped away.

60

Emir pulled up a chair and sat in it, still a safe distance away from Jack's long reach, even though he couldn't do much reaching at the moment.

Jack glanced at the laptop. A countdown clock was running.

Forty minutes remaining.

What the hell am I going to do?

"You know she played you, too, right?"

Emir frowned. "What are you talking about?"

"You're never going to see her again."

Emir sneered as he shook his head. "You don't know anything, do you?"

"I know she's a lying bitch."

"Watch your mouth, Ryan."

"And if I don't?"

"Soon you won't be saying anything to anybody."

"And you're okay with this? Mass murder?"

"Murder? They are infidels who have butchered my people

for centuries. They slaughtered my family in the last war. Therefore, this is not murder. It is holy justice."

"I thought you belonged to the religion of peace."

Emir nodded. "When all men are Muslims, there will be peace. But until then"—his back stiffened—"there will be jihad."

"Except you guys kill more of each other than we do."

Emir spat on the floor. "The days of the filthy Shia are numbered."

"Until you clowns can figure out how to invent something useful like an internal combustion engine or a telephone, I wouldn't sweat trying to run the planet."

Emir wasn't biting. "Pathetic."

Time to step it up.

Jack turned his attention back toward the laptop. "Another forty minutes of this? Don't you have Netflix or something?"

"Always with the jokes, you Americans. But this is no joke. This is how the world you know ends in fire and blood."

"That's stupid. There isn't going to be a World War Three."

"It is the truth."

"How? A bunch of Serbs get killed. So what? Who cares? That's like a bunch of dead ragheads—"

WHACK!

Emir backhanded Jack again.

Just like Jack hoped he would.

"Watch your mouth, Ryan. Or you'll watch that screen without any teeth in your ugly head."

Jack shook off the sting. "Enlighten me, shit-for-brains."

Emir stood over Jack. "You Americans don't know history. You don't know anything! Except your filthy rap music and pornography."

"Don't knock 'em if you haven't tried 'em." Jack shifted beneath the stranglehold of duct tape.

Emir raised his hand to strike again and Jack shut his eyes, wincing, preparing for the blow.

Emir stayed his hand and laughed. "Not so tough now, eh?"

"Take off this tape and I'll show you."

Emir's eyes flared with hatred. He turned his back to watch the screen.

Being ignored wasn't part of Jack's plan. He tried another tack.

"Okay, so enlighten me. How does killing Serbs start World War Three?"

Emir turned back around. "Commander Brkić has thought of everything. We will claim responsibility for the strike, the Russians will invade, and NATO will fight Russia."

"What kind of strike? A bomb? Chemicals? Biologics?"

"None of your business. Just watch—and pray."

"Don't tell me to pray, you satanic little fuck."

WHACK!

Jack didn't wince that time, despite the welt forming beneath his beard.

"Shit, dude. That almost hurt. You hit like my little sister, only not as hard."

WHACK!

"C'mon, you little goat fucker. That's the best you got?" Jack roared with laughter. "No wonder you could never close the deal with Aida." He shook his head, grinning. "Man, that girl sure liked to—"

"Shut up!" Emir drew his big semiauto Colt and pointed it at Jack. "Time to die!"

"Oh, no, no, no, little fella. Aida said you had to wait until after the big show before you pulled that trigger."

"Pray to Allah he will accept you into His Paradise, infidel." Emir racked the slide. The heavy .45-caliber bullet already in the chamber ejected, bouncing on the floorboards.

"You dropped one, chief."

"No worries, Jack. Plenty more where that came from."

"I don't think a pissant like you can kill a man like me face-to-face."

"You're about to find out." Emir flicked off the safety.

"Sure, fire a rocket launcher, kill a bunch of strangers up in the sky. But up close and personal? Eye to eye? You don't have the balls."

Emir stepped closer, staring hard into Jack's eyes. "Just watch."

"See? You're afraid to get close. I mean . . . real close."

"I'm not stupid."

"Are you sure? How would you know if you were?"

Emir glanced behind Jack's back, checking his restraints. Then he stepped around behind the chair, keeping the gun pointed at Jack's head. He pulled at the duct tape and shook it hard to make sure Jack was still secured.

He was.

"See, dipshit? I'm not dangerous. I'm tied up like a sacrificial lamb. But this little lamb's got way bigger balls than you. Just ask Aida—"

WHACK!

Emir smacked Jack's skull with the barrel of the pistol. Lights flashed in Jack's eyes, like he'd been hit in the head with a steel brick, which he had.

399

Jack shook it off with a laugh. "Fuck you, douchebag. Get it over with!"

Emir stepped up and shoved the pistol in Jack's face, an inch from his nose.

Jack stared straight up the barrel, from the bladed front sight back through the square notch on the rear sight, all the way to Emir's raging eyes. The barrel trembled.

"Put it against my forehead, you little shit. Put it hard against my skull, if you have the guts. Then pull the trigger. But I bet you can't. You're too weak."

Emir jammed the barrel against Jack's forehead.

Jack felt the barrel's cold, smooth crown pressing into his skin. He pushed back harder. Emir's arm stiffened.

Jack's eyes bored into Emir's, his bearded face twisted into a smug, satisfied grin.

"That's better," Jack said. "You want that barrel nice and tight against my skull so the gun doesn't flip back and crack you in the face when it fires."

Emir's grin faded.

Something was wrong. *What was the American up to?*

Jack shoved his head forward, grabbing Emir's attention. "What the fuck are you waiting for, pussy? Your period?"

Rage flashed over Emir's face, but then it faded, giving way to a slow, wide grin.

His finger squeezed the trigger.

Nothing.

Frowning with confusion, Emir pulled the gun back to check it, racking in another round and—

OOMPH!

Jack launched his boot into the Bosniak's ball sack, crushing his testicles with the devastating kick. Emir dropped the gun, bent over, and grabbed his crotch.

Jack lunged up in a half squat as Emir bent over, driving his frontal dome, the hardest part of his skull, straight into Emir's nose, breaking it with a sickening crack and a gusher of blood.

Standing in a half crouch and still tied to the chair, Jack turned sideways and threw his entire body weight against the much smaller man. Emir lost his footing and stumbled to the floor. Jack turned and kicked the pistol, sending it skittering across the rough-hewn boards, then turned back around and kicked as hard as he could at Emir's head.

The toe of his boot struck home with a nauseating crunch. Emir howled with pain as he clutched his face, balling himself up to prevent another boot strike to his skull.

Just what Jack wanted.

Jack raised his size-fourteen foot as high as he could and stomped the side of Emir's head, driving it into the floor. He stomped again and again and again.

Emir flailed widely, kicking at Jack but missing, blinded by pain and his own gushing blood slicking the wooden floor like an oil spill.

Emir tucked one arm under his head to cushion it against the floor and the other on top to protect his ear, now partially torn off from the repeated boot strikes.

So Jack kicked him in the face again.

Kicked him so hard that Emir's head snapped back, collapsing the fragile anterior nasal spine just below his nose and smashing his brain hard against his skull, knocking him out.

Jack raised his foot one more time to deliver a killing blow to Emir's exposed neck, but he hesitated. He couldn't kill a helpless, unconscious man, no matter how miserable a human being he was. Chances were he was going to die anyway.

Emir was God's problem now.

Jack lowered his foot. He stood in his tortured half crouch over the bleeding figure, gasping for air, the duct tape still tying him to the chair like a crooked crucifix, but he hardly felt it for the adrenaline dump still surging through his blood.

Jack couldn't believe his luck. Shoving the barrel of the Colt against his skull had pushed the slide back just enough to engage the disconnector, putting the gun out of battery and preventing it from firing. It was a long shot, but the only one he could think of at the time to get out of this jam.

Now he had another problem.

How the hell was he going to get out of this damn chair?

61

Jack turned around and scanned the kitchen.

On the counter was a knife block, but he couldn't stand up tall enough to reach any of the knife handles. He thought about swinging the chair legs up high enough to sweep the knife block off the counter, but chances were he'd only bang into the cabinets. He didn't see any other sharp surfaces he could use to cut the duct tape with, either.

But then he remembered he really didn't need any.

Jack sat back down in his chair and steadied himself. He took a deep breath, leaned back as far as he could within the constraints of the duct tape, then jackknifed his upper torso down toward his knees as sharply as he could.

The duct tape split at the chair edges from the force of his thrust as neatly as if he had ripped it with his fingers.

He stood and shook his body to free himself from the remaining strands of tape, toppling the chair to the floor. He then raised his bound wrists high above his head, palms together, fingertips touching. He thrust his arms down sharply, driving his elbows hard against his sides for additional leverage. The duct tape around his wrists gave way easily, though it tore away the hair on his arms and left a little bit of sticky goo on the face of his iWatch.

He ripped away the remaining shreds of duct tape from his clothing before dashing over to Emir's motionless body. He felt for a pulse. He found one, barely. He checked for more weapons but found none, save another loaded magazine for the Colt, which he pocketed, along with a set of keys for the Renault and, most important, his own iPhone, which Emir had lifted from him previously.

Jack ran over to the laptop. Nothing had changed, but the countdown timer read just thirty-eight minutes now. He punched in Gavin Biery's number on his phone. Two rings and Gavin picked up.

"Hey, Jack, are you okay? I heard about that airplane—"

"I'm fine. Look, I need you to run a search for a Volkswagen van owned by a Bosnian tour company called Happy Times!, based out of Sarajevo. It's the only Volkswagen T5 van in their fleet."

"You got a plate number by any chance?"

"Sorry, no."

"What do I do when I find it?"

"It has a working GPS map guide. I need you to locate its GPS signal and track it for me."

"On it, Jack. Give me a few." Keys began clicking instantly over the phone.

"Thanks."

Jack set his phone on the table next to the laptop and put it on speaker. He knew he didn't have any legal authority to do anything, but if Emir was telling the truth, he had to find a way to stop whatever was about to happen at that stadium, and the only way he was going to do that was to find Aida, and find her fast.

Besides, she had to pay for those people she ordered murdered today.

So did Brkić.

He thought briefly about calling Kolak for assistance or even the local police, but at this point he had no idea whom he could trust. Besides, all of those people died this morning because of him. It was up to him to make things right, not pass off the responsibility to someone else.

He probably needed to read Gerry in on what was happening, but at this point, all Gerry would do was yell at him and tell him to get his ass back to the airport.

"Found it," Gavin said on the speaker. "I'm tracking it live."

"Can you send the track to my phone?"

"Doing it now."

"Thanks, buddy. Hey, one more thing. I've got a laptop I'm staring at. We need to find out what's on it, and what we're up against."

"Send me the local IPv4 address, and I'll mirror your machine. Is it Windows 10?"

"Yeah. Just give me a sec." Jack found it easily and read it off to him.

"Thanks, Jack. I'll take it from here." Keys starting clacking on the phone speaker again.

"Gav, we need to hustle. How long will it take?"

"Not sure."

A second later, the cursor arrow moved remotely on the laptop screen. "I'm in, Jack. What am I looking at?"

"A live video feed from a drone looking down at the Olympic soccer stadium in Sarajevo."

"What's that countdown counter for?"

"In thirty-seven minutes, that stadium is going to be destroyed. I need you to find out exactly how."

Gavin pulled up another window remotely. It displayed a video of a middle-aged man in camouflage, holding a short-barreled AKS-74U and sitting in front of a black AQAB battle flag with white Arabic letters that spelled out the *shahada*. The man's full, wild red-and-gray beard was offset by a white cloth prayer cap, but it was his milky white eye that drew Jack's attention.

"This is all in some crazy language, Jack."

"*Bosanski*," Jack said. "Bosnian."

"I'll run my AI translator. It's good at real-time audio."

More windows popped up as Gavin worked; some were documents, and others were video frames.

"So how long?" Jack asked.

"As long as it takes."

"I can't sit around here waiting."

"Use your iPhone as a local hotspot, connect it to the laptop via Bluetooth, and then I can stay connected to the machine through your phone wherever you need to go. I'll call you if I find anything."

"Perfect. I'm going after that GPS locator you sent me. And Gav, don't breathe a word of this to Gerry. I'll tell him myself when we know more."

"Sure thing, Jack. And good luck."

"Thanks. I'm going to need it."

62

Jack jumped into Emir's Renault. He set the open laptop on the passenger seat, then took an extra minute and synched his phone with the Renault's Bluetooth audio so that conversation with Gavin would come through the car's audio speakers. He then set his smartphone on the dash so he could more easily follow the GPS signal from Aida's Volkswagen.

Jack punched the gas and headed out of the compound, Emir's Colt in his lap.

Jack followed the blue GPS arrow on his phone generated by the signal coming from Aida's Volkswagen. For the most part, he was just following the two-lane E73 north and west as through the contour of the mountains. She was ten minutes ahead of him and making good time, heading higher into the pine-covered hills. They seemed to be the only two vehicles on the road.

"Jack? I found something," Gavin's voice said over the car's audio system. "It's a video scheduled to go out to social media at ten-sixteen a.m. local—that's just thirty-five minutes from now. Some guy named Commander Brkić issued a fatwa against all nonbelievers and Crusaders."

"Is that the guy with the blind eye?"

"Yeah. Says he launched the thermobaric missiles that killed thousands—past tense, because the video hasn't gone out yet."

"Thermobarics. Holy shit. What's the delivery system?"

"Can't be sure. But there's footage of masked fighters standing in front of a Soviet-era BM-21 Grad rocket launch system flashing victory signs and waving a black flag. It's basically a six-by-six truck with a box launcher on back. According to Google, it holds forty 122-millimeter ballistic missiles."

"You think it's possible he has one in his arsenal?"

"The BM-21 is the most deployed missile-launch system in the world, and the Bosnian Army has had them since Tito's days. So yeah, it's credible. Only thing is, something doesn't make sense."

"What doesn't?"

"That launch system isn't known for being real accurate. I did a quick check of the stadium measurements. There's a good chance a lot of those missiles won't land inside it."

"But a lot of people will still get hurt."

"Still not the kind of casualties he's promising on that video. He obviously thinks his system is more accurate."

"How?"

"I haven't figured that out yet."

"Maybe he's bluffing."

"This guy doesn't look like a bluffer to me," Gavin said. "And why brag about it if it didn't, or doesn't, happen? Then he looks like an idiot."

"Good point. Let's assume he's telling the truth. We need to figure out how he plans to pull it off."

"Can I tell Gerry what's going on now? He's been breathing down my neck."

"He's at the office? At this hour?"

"Just arrived ten minutes ago. He's been after me to try and reach you."

"I'll call him right now."

"Good luck with that, Jack. You're not exactly his favorite person at the moment."

"Thanks for the heads-up."

Jack rang off, then dialed Gerry's phone. He picked up after the first ring.

"I've got a funny feeling you're not at the airport," the ex-senator growled.

"Worse than that, we've got a situation."

Jack read him in on the video and possible missile strike.

"Good God Almighty, Jack. This is a nightmare scenario. We need to start an immediate evacuation."

"Bad idea. Whatever asshole is watching the video feed will see it and order an immediate launch. Besides, the city is jammed. You couldn't empty that place out if you tried."

"Damn it, you're right."

"I'm on the way now to shut it down—if I can locate it."

"I don't know how you managed to step in front of this stampede, Jack, but you've got to find a way to stop it."

"With only thirty-five minutes left until the launch, I can't promise you I'll get it done."

"I'm calling Mary Pat Foley now to fill her in. Keep me posted. And for the love of God, watch your six, will you?"

63

WASHINGTON, D.C.

The dreaded three a.m. phone call had been a talking point in nearly every presidential campaign for the past twenty years, a metaphor for the gut-wrenching, unexpected national emergencies that usually cropped up at the most inconvenient moments.

The clock read 3:41 a.m. when President Ryan's cell phone rang. He picked it up from the nightstand, yawning. His wife stirred. "What's wrong?"

"Nothing, hon. Go back to sleep."

But Dr. Cathy Ryan knew better, having received a few early-morning emergency eye surgery phone calls herself over the years. Nobody called at this time of the morning for either of them unless it was a blood-soaked catastrophe in the making.

"I'll put on a pot of coffee." She dragged a comforting hand across his shoulder as she shuffled past him toward the kitchen, yawning.

Ryan smiled, grateful for the amazing woman sharing his crazy life.

"How bad is it, Mary Pat?"

"As bad as it gets."

DNI Foley filled him in on the events of the last twenty-four hours as relayed to her by Gerry, and the ticking clock winding down toward Armageddon with the Russians. The civilian aircraft had been blown out of the sky just a few hours before, but because no Americans were on board, the President wasn't notified, even though his son apparently had been the target.

"Mr. President, if Jack can't find those rockets and take them out . . ."

"Yeah, I know. We need to get the Russians in on this ASAP."

"We don't have a lot of options right now."

"Hell, we don't have any, since we don't even have a target at this point. Right now, it's all up to Jack."

The first call President Ryan made was to his chief of staff, Arnie Van Damm. Arnie was a veteran of as many three a.m. phone calls as he was, because Arnie was the first person Ryan always called at a time like this.

"Arnie, you've got five minutes to organize a conference call with Scott, Bob, and Mary Pat. And patch it over to the Situation Room."

"What's this about?"

"No time to explain." Ryan checked his watch. *Shit.* He'd already burned four minutes. "And now we've got just thirty minutes to go."

"It'll take at least twenty."

"You've got five."

"On it, boss."

Ryan stood in the kitchen in a pair of faded Levi's, a thread-bare USMC sweatshirt, and a battered pair of Saucony running shoes, calling on the landline to the overnight White House operator.

"Get me Admiral Dean, Commander, U.S. Naval Forces Europe-Africa, head of the Sixth Fleet, based in Naples, Italy. I don't care if he's on the crapper reading Marcus Aurelius, I need him on the phone now. And patch it through to my personal cell. Understood?"

"Understood, sir."

"And then get me General Colgan, 31st Fighter Wing in Aviano, Italy. Same drill."

"Right away, sir."

Two options, maybe, he thought, as Cathy handed him a sealed thermal cup of steaming black coffee and a kiss on the cheek. He bolted for the door, shoving his Bluetooth into his ear, searching his mind for more options, trying to remember distances and maps and borders in a part of the world he hadn't thought about in a long time.

Some men panicked when a crisis hit, but Ryan's mind cleared and focused like a sniper's scope drawing a bead on a distant target. That ability made him a good marine officer and a first-rate CIA analyst when he was younger, but it served him best now that he was commander in chief. He stood on the edge of a perfect storm of bad actors, bad intentions, and bad timing.

Everything hung on his next decision, but he didn't want to make it until he heard back from his son, racing into the eye of that same perfect storm. As President, he was grateful a man like Jack was on the scene.

As a father, he was scared to death.

64

The bleary-eyed communications tech working the video teleconferencing (VTC) cameras and audio in the Situation Room yawned violently behind the control room glass.

Ryan thought she looked like she had just graduated from high school, but she must have been in her early twenties. She was damn good, patching in the live video feed from Aida's laptop onto one of the big wall monitors, as well as video teleconferencing with Arnie Van Damm, DNI Foley, and SecDef Burgess, all scattered across the country. She also patched in Jack on his phone, along with Gerry and Gavin, who were at the Hendley Associates office in Alexandria, before the first tray of coffee had arrived.

The countdown clock from the laptop displayed on the main monitor. Just twenty-five minutes until the rocket strike at the soccer stadium.

President Ryan stood at the head of the long table, leaning on it, his eyes fixed on one of the wall monitors.

"According to Gavin's brief, our best guess is that the launch platform is a BM-21 Grad MRLS like the one playing on your screens from the Brkić video. It's mobile as hell, and we don't know where it is at the moment.

"That box launcher holds forty 122-millimeter thermobaric missiles, with a maximum operational range of twenty-four miles. Let's assume half that distance, because these jokers don't want to push their luck. That means there's over four hundred and fifty miles of territory to search, much of it tree-covered mountains. How in the hell do we find it in the next twenty-five minutes?"

"USA-224 isn't due over that area for another eighteen minutes," Foley said. She was referring to the NRO's KH-11 Keyhole orbiting optical satellite. "Not that it would do much good in that terrain, if they're trying to hide it. SBIRS is geostationary, but that's only going to tell us when the rockets are launched."

"Assuming we do find it, our options for taking it out are limited, to put it mildly," Ryan said.

"F-16s out of Aviano would be my choice," Burgess said.

Ryan shook his head. "General Colgan says it will take thirty-two minutes before his Falcons can scramble and deliver a payload. That's seven minutes too late if I give him the go order right now. And the nearest carrier is currently on a NATO training exercise off the coast of Portugal, so naval aviation is out of the question. But according to Admiral Dean, we have a guided missile destroyer steaming approximately twenty miles off the coast of Croatia at this very moment."

"Tomahawks," Mary Pat Foley said.

"Precisely. From the destroyer's position to Sarajevo, the Tomahawk flight time is just under fifteen minutes."

"But we still don't have a target location," Arnie said. "We'll have to get it within the next ten—check that—nine minutes if we hope to prevent the attack."

Ryan's eyes narrowed. "There is one other option."

ON BOARD THE USS *GARZA* (DDG-116), ADRIATIC SEA, TWENTY MILES SOUTHWEST OF DUBROVNIK, CROATIA

The *Arleigh Burke*–class guided missile destroyer sat in the choppy waters of the blue Adriatic, its launch alarm klaxon blaring like an ambulance siren, warning sailors to clear the foredeck where the thirty-two cells of the vertical launch system (VLS) were located behind the five-inch gun.

One of the cell hatches burst open in a gush of blinding orange fire as the solid-fuel rocket booster of a GM/UGM-109E (TLAM-Block IV) Tomahawk cruise missile roared from beneath the deck. When it reached its cruising altitude of one thousand feet seconds later, the rocket booster fell away and the eighteen-foot cruise missile dipped perpendicular to the water's surface as its turbofan engine fired.

The Tomahawk—essentially a pilotless airplane—veered northeast, trailing white smoke in its 550-mile-per-hour flight toward the Croatian coastline.

The Tomahawk's terrain-hugging, object-avoidance navigation was possible because of its TERCOM (terrain contour matching) and DSMAC (digitized scene-mapping correlator), aided by GPS and INS guidance systems.

During terminal phase on target approach, the Tomahawk's onboard radar homing systems would take over.

Three seconds later, a second Tomahawk launched from

another VLS cell, following in the wake of the first, but taking a slightly different course, programmed to arrive at the same time. Redundancy was key for a mission as critical as this one.

The only problem was, neither missile had a target.

65

Jack glanced at the GPS marker on his phone. Aida's blue arrow had stopped moving. Thanks to the Renault's thrumming V6 engine, he made much better time than she did. He was close.

A few minutes later he pulled to the side of the road, where he couldn't be seen. According to the GPS map, the Volkswagen van was parked in front of a house set back from the main road. Beyond the house, toward the back of the property near a steep hill, was a newly constructed warehouse-style steel building. The whole compound was set in a clearing surrounded by trees.

Jack checked for passing traffic as he slipped his phone's Bluetooth earpiece on. No vehicles were on the road, so Jack grabbed Emir's chromed pistol, jumped out of the car, and dashed for the tree line.

Jack stood in the trees scanning the compound for movement but saw none. No Aida, no Brkić, and sure as hell no rocket launcher. Only the house with Aida's van parked in front, about a hundred feet away, and the big steel storage shed a thousand feet back.

He figured Aida must be in the house, but was anybody in the shed?

Come to think of it, that shed was big enough to hold one of the really big Happy Times! tour buses. Or an eighteen-wheeler.

Or a Grad rocket launcher.

If he went for the shed, Aida might slip away. But if he went for Aida, he might be sentencing thousands to their deaths if the rocket launcher was located in that shed and started firing.

He started to run toward the shed but stopped, his mind racing. Something about that live video feed had been nagging at him for the last ten minutes. He called Gavin.

"Jack, it's Gavin. I've patched you in on a conference call with Gerry and—"

"Jack, it's me," President Ryan said. "And a few others on VTC. What did you find?"

"I found the van, but no Aida, no Brkić, no rockets, and no launcher—at least not yet. But I've got an idea. Gavin, do you still have the live feed on your end?"

"Of course."

"I can see it on my end, too," the President said.

"That live feed," Jack said. "Doesn't it keep the exact same center point? Like the drone is circling around the stadium, but the center point never moves?"

"Yeah. Looks like a preprogrammed flight pattern," Gavin said.

"Sure. But maybe it's not just a video feed, either."

"What do you mean?"

"You said that Brkić thought he had a way to make those

rockets more accurate. If they were somehow laser-guided by that drone, that would do the job, wouldn't it?"

"Dang it! Why didn't I think of that?" Gavin blurted. "That drone probably is shooting a laser guidance beam, along with the video image."

"The Bosnians need to shoot that thing down," the SecDef said over Jack's phone.

"No!" Jack said. "Just the opposite. That drone is a link between the stadium and the launcher."

"Which means I can find the launch site by tracing the launch computer uplink to the drone, or the drone's video signal. Well, unless they're encrypted."

"Do it, Gav."

"Good work, son. Gavin will take it from here," President Ryan said.

Jack hung up, relieved that the launcher and rockets were taken off his plate. Now he could focus on finding Aida and Brkić and make them pay for their crimes.

Jack sped over to the front of the house and climbed the porch as quietly as possible, the big chromed Colt in his hand. He listened again. Thought he heard some noise inside, but he couldn't tell what. No voices, though. If it was Aida, she was likely by herself.

Jack carefully turned the unlocked door handle and gently pushed the door open, trying not to make a sound as he slipped inside.

He stood in a living room. There were two doors on the left, both open. One was an empty bedroom with bunk beds, the other a bathroom.

To his right was a staircase leading to the second story.

A closed, swinging door was on the wall opposite him. A kitchen, he guessed.

The living room was strangely familiar. He'd seen it before in the video Gavin had pulled of Brkić. A giant black AQAB flag was nailed to a wall, and the video camera Brkić used to record himself was still on its tripod in front of the folding chair he was sitting in when he made it. The only thing that was missing was the rifle—and Brkić.

The noise was louder now, coming from the other side of the swinging door in front of him.

Thumping. Zipping. Footsteps.

Jack stepped forward as softly as possible.

Right onto a squeaking board.

Shit.

Jack froze. Listened. Nothing.

Wait. In the distance. A sound, muffled. Music. Singing? He wasn't sure. Not in the house. Where? The shed, maybe? If so, it must have been loud as hell for him to hear it all the way in here.

A loose floorboard creaked on the other side of the swinging door.

Jack cocked his head, listening.

Suddenly, heavy footfalls stomped and crashed. Aida was running away.

Jack charged for the kitchen.

Three gunshots blasted through the door as he reached it, forcing him back.

He counted three, then kicked the door open. He charged in, gun up, ready to fire.

Nobody there.

LINE OF SIGHT

Just an old farm table with a few stacks of bundled euros on it, left behind in a rush.

Feet thundered down a flight of stairs on his right. An open door, leading to a stairwell.

He dashed to the open door, stopped. Cool, musty air rose up from the dank basement below. He ducked his head around the corner, pulled it back—

Three more shots rang out from the bottom of the stairs. Jack felt the overpressure brush against his face like an invisible hand. The rounds crashed into the wall to his left. He reached his hand around the corner and fired off three shots down into the dark, expecting to hit nothing.

He didn't. But they did the job. Reconnaissance by fire. Nobody fired back.

Five shots left in his eight-shot magazine.

He dropped down low and took another quick look. Nothing. Not even a sound.

He held his pistol in front of him as he descended, pointing down toward the bottom of the stairs. The musty smell grew. The stairs were still lit by the light from behind him. He was a backlit target here.

Jack moved quickly, sighting his weapon into the muddy black of the rest of the basement where Aida was. He wished he had night-vision goggles or a high-powered tactical flashlight.

He reached the bottom of the stairs, the foundation wall just a few feet in front of him.

He could barely make out another wall on his right, six feet away. He dashed over to it.

No, not a wall, exactly. More like shelving. In the dim light, he saw cases of American MREs, folded Bundeswehr camouflage uniforms, canned food, bottled water.

Jack felt his way along the shelf wall, listening intently. He heard nothing but the far distant music, and felt a faint, cool breath of earthy air brushing against his skin.

He reached the end of the shelving wall and found a doorway. He knelt down.

Aida was on the other side, her pistol pointed at the opening, ready to blow his head off.

From his crouching position, he reached his pistol around the corner and fired his last five shots, emptying the mag. His ears ached from the explosions stabbing his unprotected eardrums like ice picks.

The slide of the empty pistol locked open. Jack pulled the weapon back around, dropped the empty mag, slammed home his last full one, and racked the slide shut, chambering a round in just under two seconds. He'd done it enough times in training with his eyes closed and Clark firing a pistol next to his face that it was as natural a movement as breathing.

He listened again through his ringing ears.

Nothing.

She was either dead or one cool customer.

He didn't really care which.

Alive was good, because she would have valuable intel.

But dead would feel a helluva lot better.

Jack turned the corner with his weapon up, ready to shoot. She was gone.

66

Aida was gone, all right.

Right down the damn hole in the ground. A square steel trapdoor lay open. The cool air that brushed against him earlier was now almost a breeze. It smelled like wet dirt and wood. A tunnel. Lit from down below.

There was a wooden ladder, but Jack skipped it and made the five-and-half-foot drop, his gun at high ready. He thumped onto the hard-packed dirt, his boots nearly stepping on another packet of money that must have fallen out of whatever Aida was lugging around. He crouched to avoid the low timber ceiling and the naked bulb hanging by a wire just above his head. The walls were lumber, too. It reminded him of the Tunnel of Hope near the airport that Aida had shown him before.

He was glad for the lightbulb over his head. He hated the idea of running down here in the dark. Three shots rang out from the black void ahead. Wood splintered by Jack's head.

He swore bitterly.

Idiot!

The damn light only made him an easy target.

He smashed the bulb with his pistol before leaping for the dirt. He heard dull footfalls far up ahead.

Jack jumped to his feet and charged forward, still crouching to keep from knocking himself out on the timbered ceiling. There was no more light in the tunnel, and the crunching glass beneath his feet told him that Aida had been smashing bulbs as she ran. He'd HALO'd out of airplanes on moonless nights without batting an eye, but somehow running down here was a lot more frightening. He couldn't shake the feeling he was about to slam facefirst into something running full speed in the dark.

He must have covered two hundred feet in his low, crouching run before Aida's pistol roared and flashed at the dark end of the tunnel, its sharp retort muffled by the wood and dirt. Splintering timber cracked nearby and Jack dropped to the ground again, firing three shots back in the direction of the flashes.

Five shots left.

He heard Aida curse in the distance, and the sound of feet shuffling through the dirt. Jack listened again, and aimed his pistol in the direction of the sound. He fired three more rounds.

Only two left now.

But his last three shots had lit up the tunnel near where he was lying. He caught sight of a small alcove just a few feet up ahead on his right—a storage area, he guessed.

He belly-crawled as fast as he could to the alcove and rolled into it, bumping into what felt like more wood shelving. His ringing ears quieted enough that he could hear the music more clearly now, still muffled at the far end of the tunnel. Melodic male voices were singing a cappella in, what, Arabic? He couldn't be sure. The voices were joyous, upbeat, powerful. What did they call that kind of music? *Nasheed*, Jack remembered. Islamic hymns.

The kind of stuff that jihadis sang before going into battle.

It wasn't so loud that he couldn't hear Aida swearing and tramping ahead, though.

Where was she going?

She was running toward the music.

Jack rolled out of the alcove again and stayed on his belly, aiming his pistol forward with muscle memory, since he couldn't actually see anything. It was so dark he couldn't be sure his eyes were actually open except by blinking. He was hoping Aida would fire at him again and he could use her flash as a target now that he was ready for it, but none was coming.

If she reached that other trapdoor, she might get help. Or worse. He couldn't let her do that.

He had to assume that the miners would dig the tunnel as straight as possible to avoid wasting their energy, and if there was another trapdoor on the other side of the tunnel, that's what Aida would be moving toward. And that door would be straight ahead, too. All he had to do was to aim straight down the center of the tunnel, halfway between the floor and the ceiling. Two shots of .45-caliber lead in the square of her back would put her down easily. Drop her before she could reach the ladder.

Jack sighted the pistol in the blinding dark, hoping he was aiming dead center. He started to squeeze the trigger.

He stopped.

Aida would know that his only hope of hitting her in the dark would be to shoot dead center.

Jack angled his pistol left, toward what he imagined was the far-left corner, and fired twice. He pointed right and fired again. His pistol locked open after just one shot.

Out of ammo.

He listened. All he could hear was the muffled music.

And gurgling.

He dropped his empty weapon, jumped up, and scurried forward in a low crouch, weaving just a little in case she was aiming in the dark, too, but in the cramped space he had little hope of dodging anything like a bullet, especially as he got closer to the sound.

He reached for his phone just as he heard feet kicking hard in the dirt in front of him. He dove for the ground. The kicking and gurgling sounds suddenly stopped. Jack held his breath. He listened again in the smothering dark. Only the distant, muted music.

He crawled forward on his elbows until his left hand hit something and he recoiled, freezing in place. He listened again. Nothing. He reached his left hand out. Felt around. Touched hard rubber. He flinched back. Waited. Reached out again. It was the sole of a shoe. He pulled up his phone and touched the flashlight feature.

His eyes ached from the bright light. He shined it at the shoe. It was Aida's foot, all right, attached to her corpse. A half-open duffel lay by her side, along with several stacks of cash scattered on the dirt floor. He moved closer. Her body lay against the left tunnel wall, her throat torn open by a .45-caliber slug, which practically decapitated her.

The bulb in the phone formed catchlights in her lifeless blue eyes.

He checked the time on his iWatch.

It was 10:08 a.m.

Seven minutes to launch.

A t 10:08 a.m. local time, the first Tomahawk arrived at its last GPS waypoint, five miles due west of the Sarajevo airport terminal. It slowed its speed by half. This latest cruise missile variant was capable of loitering over a battlefield like a regular aircraft, and able to retarget via its two-way satellite control and GPS targeting systems.

Not having the luxuries of either knowing the target location in advance or having the time to wait to launch, President Ryan decided to put two Tomahawks in loitering mode over an unpopulated area near Sarajevo. He hoped to God that Jack and the rest of The Campus could locate the BM-21 Grad launcher before 10:15 local.

In the event the target couldn't be acquired, the Tomahawks would be redirected back out to the Adriatic Sea and their explosive payloads detonated harmlessly. Croatian and Bosnian air traffic control were notified about the Tomahawks' unannounced "training mission" and their flight paths just before launch, as were their respective governments. Ryan believed it was always better to ask forgiveness than permission, especially in a crisis situation.

Given the flight time to and from the final waypoint, it was estimated each Tomahawk had approximately seventy-two minutes of loitering time.

Far more time than was left.

67

He fished around in Aida's pockets and found her cell phone and took it, then snagged up her pistol to replace his own.

His boots squished in the oozing gore near her head in the narrow passage as he sprinted away in a crouch to the other end of the tunnel.

A hundred feet before he reached the ladder he heard Gavin's desperate voice crackling in his Bluetooth.

"Jack! I . . . reach . . . can't . . . signal . . . launcher!"

"Say again." Jack was near the ladder now.

"I can't find the drone signal! I don't know where the launcher is!"

"I might."

"Where?"

"How much time before launch?"

"Just under seven minutes. We have two Tomahawks on station, ready to go. We just don't have a target."

"Tomahawks can use GPS coordinates for targeting, right?"

"Sure. Why?"

"Can you link my phone GPS to the Tomahawks?"

"Huh. Maybe. I don't see why not. It will take a few minutes."

"We don't have a few minutes."

"I'll call you when they're linked."

Jack stood at the ladder, nearly breathless. The metal trapdoor was shut. He climbed up the five and a half feet and stood at the top of the ladder and listened for a moment. The muffled jihadi *nasheed* music he had heard earlier now thundered above the steel plate.

He pushed gently on the trapdoor, just enough to get a view. The music roared in his ears now. Big truck tires were in front of him, and beyond them the steel walls of a metal building erected on a slab of reinforced concrete. The shed's front and rear doors were slid open. He also saw a spool of cable. At the end of the cable, hanging down from the side of the truck for easy access, was a box with covered safety switches.

A manual launch trigger? Jack wondered.

Jack checked his watch. Six minutes to go.

He looked to his right and saw a big man in camouflage standing outside the building entrance, his broad back to Jack. He was holding an electronic device in his hands, supported by a shoulder rig, his head bouncing to the *nasheed*.

Jack glanced up at the forty-box rocket launcher on the back of the truck, angled ominously toward the sky. Above the launcher, the camouflage netting that served as the roof was rolling back. Jack shifted his gaze. He saw a smaller man in a camouflage uniform standing in the far corner, turning a hand crank.

"Gerry, are you there?" Jack whispered.

"Yes, Jack. Go ahead."

"I see the truck."

Gavin crackled on his earpiece. "Jack, the Tomahawk is now targeted on your phone GPS."

"Jack," the President said. "Leave your phone there and get the hell out. That Tomahawk will be there in ninety seconds. Clear as far away as you can."

"Roger that—"

Bullets suddenly spanged against the metal trapdoor and slammed into the floor, stinging Jack's skin with jagged shards of concrete.

Jack flung the trapdoor wide open as he aimed Aida's pistol at the man in the corner, firing off two rounds even before he drew a bead. The first shot punched the man in the gut, the second through the heart. He thudded onto the floor on the far side of the truck, cracking his skull, but he was already dead.

Jack scrambled out of the hole and toward the big man up front, who was lunging for a rifle propped against the wall near him. Jack aimed his pistol at the man's head and pulled the trigger.

Misfire.

He racked another round. The gun locked open. The misfire was the last cartridge.

Empty.

Jack swore and sprinted hard at the larger man, swinging the pistol in his hand like a hammer at the man's skull, but the big Chechen lieutenant raised his rifle with two hands like a blocking guard and blunted Jack's blow. A stinger of pain shot up Jack's arms and his useless pistol clattered to the concrete.

The *nasheed* roared in Jack's ears. He could barely hear his dad's voice shouting, "Jack! Get out of there, now!"

Jack grabbed the Chechen's rifle with both hands, pumping

his legs as hard as he could to drive the bigger man hard against the steel wall.

The Chechen laughed, flashing wide teeth beneath his hairless upper lip. He thrust his massive skull like a cannonball at Jack's face.

Jack whipped his head to one side, avoiding the head strike, then whipped his head back to crack against the side of the Chechen's face. But Jack's strike was too weak and did nothing except shoot a bolt of pain through his own skull.

As if on cue, they both launched a series of hard, nasty kicks against each other, still wrestling with the gun between them. Jack's shins screamed with pain with every blow he got and every one he gave.

Jack twisted his arms right to throw the bigger man off balance, but he barely budged. The Chechen countered by thrusting the butt of the gun with his left hand toward Jack's gut. Jack countered him by pulling the butt hard toward him, using the man's own strength and momentum against him. Jack twisted sideways as he pulled, finally throwing the larger man off balance and toward the hard floor.

As the Chechen fell he fought his instinct to catch himself with his hands, and instead held on to the rifle for dear life. His greater weight pulled Jack down with him, and the two hit the concrete at the same time. The Chechen crashed onto his back and Jack fell on top of him, still clutching the rifle, as the music screamed in their ears.

Jack thrust a knee into the Chechen's groin. Dzhabrailov grunted in agony but still managed to twist the rifle hard enough to pop Jack in the jaw with the stock. The sharp crack of pain loosened Jack's grip for a second, but not enough to give way.

Exhausted, both men kept trying to use the gun as a bludgeon against each other while throwing knees and head butts, but the strikes were weaker and weaker. After another failed swipe, the bigger, stronger Chechen changed tactics and began pushing with his legs and rolling his shoulders to drag Jack slowly back toward the manual launcher, just a few feet away.

"Jack! Sixty seconds! Run!" his father shouted.

Over the din of the *nasheed* music Jack felt more than heard the thundering beat of helicopter blades in the air. So did Dzhabrailov. The Chechen kicked and rolled harder, inching inexorably closer to the manual launcher.

Jack tried to drag his boots against the concrete and pull back with his arms, but the larger man was too strong. He had to change gears.

Jack lunged to his feet to try to use his legs to leverage the rifle out of the man's powerful hands. Jack couldn't stand up straight, and in his low crouch he was off balance.

The wily Chechen took advantage of it.

He shoved his boot into Jack's gut and lifted him up with it as he pulled the rifle down to his broad chest with a berserker shout, levering Jack up in the air and over the Chechen's head in a classic judo *tomoe nage*.

Jack held on to the rifle, crashing hard on his back on the concrete, which knocked his breath out, stunning him.

The Chechen had the tactical advantage now. He let go of the rifle, rolled over, and leaped to his feet. The Chechen's left foot stomped on the rifle, crushing Jack's knuckles against the floor. Dzhabrailov planted his heavy right boot square into Jack's chest to launch himself over Jack. He stretched out his long arms to grab the launcher dangling just beyond Jack's boots.

Jack saw what he was doing and snagged the man's foot and ankle with his aching hands. The Chechen fell hard, and short of the launcher, crashing between Jack's legs, screaming with rage.

The rifle was just inches from Jack's face, but he had to let go of the Chechen to get it, and if he did, the jihadi would squirm forward the few inches he needed to hit the launcher before he could shoot him.

"Jack! Thirty seconds!"

If he let go now, he could make a run for it and save his neck.

But then all of those people would die.

If he held on, the Tomahawk would take care of everything.

And it would cost him his life.

He knew what he had to do.

Jack tightened his grip, straining every muscle to hold the Chechen back, the man's legs kicking furiously against Jack's desperate grip.

Dust and air pummeled Jack as the black EC-635 Eurocopter touched down, its whining turbines hardly slowing.

Jack twisted around just enough to catch a glimpse of Kolak racing from the chopper toward him, a pistol in his hand.

A pistol pointed at Jack.

68

OLYMPIC SOCCER STADIUM, SARAJEVO,
BOSNIA AND HERZEGOVINA

Ambassador Topal was given the honor of sitting on the raised dais next to the Catholic bishop of Sarajevo and other distinguished guests of the Orthodox Renewal liturgy.

The officiating senior clergy wore fantastical silken white robes hand-embroidered with silver thread, and large jewel-encrusted hats shaped like crowns. Their large crosses of silver and gold hung around their necks on thick chains, and they carried ecclesiastical instruments in their liver-spotted hands. The neatness of their finely gilded vestments was offset by the wild enormity of their scraggly gray beards.

The clean-shaven Roman Catholic bishop seated next to him, in contrast, wore a simple black cassock, with a bright red sash and a matching red skullcap. Not that the Catholics couldn't be every bit as colorful in their garish robes and golden accoutrements, but today at the Renewal they avoided competing sartorially with their Eastern brethren.

The only real difference between senior Roman Catholic and Orthodox clergy that Topal had ever observed was that Catholics shaved their faces. As far as he was concerned, their doctrinal differences were irrelevant because their religions were *kafir*.

As one of just three Muslims in the distinguished guests' box, Ambassador Topal felt a particular gratitude for his invitation. He knew quite a few of the local Orthodox clergy, and most of the Russian and Serbian politicians in attendance.

The mood so far was both festive and solemn. Crowds of faithful were still streaming into the stadium, waving nationalist flags and religious banners, packing in like sardines.

His security chief informed him the official count was now just above seventy thousand and rising, the largest stadium audience ever.

Topal nodded, satisfied.

He was proud to be part of this historic day.

A day to be remembered.

Jack felt the rapid-fire bullets brushing past the top of his skull.

The Chechen's back ripped open in a hail of jacketed rounds and his heavy torso slumped.

Kolak grabbed Jack by the arms, lifting him to his feet.

"Jack! Let's go!"

The two men sprinted for the chopper at full tilt.

"Fifteen seconds!" the President screamed in Jack's ear.

The rotors sped up and the skids lifted as Kolak leaped first into the cabin.

Jack thundered up as the Eurocopter rose to four feet. He jumped with every ounce of his failing strength.

His upper body thudded into the deck as he reached for the seat struts bolted onto the floor, but his legs were still hanging out. The copter thrust straight up and around. The centrifugal force started dragging him out of the door, but Kolak grabbed Jack's shirt and belt, helping Jack crawl inside as the chopper's nose thrust upward, clawing for the sun.

"Everybody strap in!" the pilot shouted.

Jack and Kolak fell into their seats, literally, and buckled up. Jack knew they needed to clear the area before those warheads—

A blinding white light erupted beneath the climbing Eurocopter, screaming for altitude.

But they weren't high enough.

The thermobaric munitions burned away the oxygen in the surrounding atmosphere, creating an enormous vacuum, robbing the rotors of their lift capability. The chopper bucked and yawed as the pilot fought for control in the turbulence.

Just as she stabilized, a concussive wave slapped the thin-skinned aircraft hard, hurling it toward the ground.

69

The President sighed with relief as the applause and cheers rang out from the VTC monitors in the Situation Room.

"And still over four minutes to spare," Arnie said, smiling. "Not bad."

The second Tomahawk was still providing a live video feed of the thermobaric explosion. The entire compound was leveled, and whatever wasn't destroyed was burning.

"We have a problem, Mr. President," the Russian president said.

Ryan's relief disappeared. "What problem?"

"My intelligence chief just reviewed the Tomahawk video feed. It cannot be determined with certainty, but it appears that there were forty rockets on the launcher."

"Yes, that is correct. Why is that a problem?"

"It is a problem because eighty thermobaric rockets were stolen."

President Ryan turned to his chief of staff, whose shocked face mirrored his own.

Where the hell were those other missiles?

"Jack? This is your dad. Come in, please."

No answer.

"Jack? Jack?"

"He's not responding, sir," the comms tech said.

"Keep trying, please," Ryan said.

"Mr. President, what do you suggest?" the Russian president asked again.

"One moment, please," Ryan said. He put the Russian on mute, the only person on the VTC who wasn't part of his inner circle.

"Any thoughts, people?"

"Another launcher?" Admiral Dean offered.

"Maybe," Ryan said. "But we have no indication of that."

"Or we just missed the other forty missiles. Maybe they were stacked in that building where we couldn't see them," Arnie said.

"Or maybe they're being saved for a future operation," Foley suggested.

"No. Whoever planned this attack only had one launcher, and they had one giant opportunity. I know what I'd do with an extra forty warheads if I couldn't launch them." Ryan un-muted the Russian president.

"President Yermilov, I have a suggestion. But there's no time to waste."

"I'm listening."

"Contact your man in Belgrade, Deputy Commander General Sevrov. And do it now."

70

Dželko sat by himself in the Happy Times! bus. His thirty-seven passengers, all bearded Orthodox clergy in simple black cassocks, were inside the stadium, participating in the Renewal service, while he remained parked near the facility, waiting for their return.

Or so they thought.

Thanks to them, entrance into the heart of the sports complex had been arranged, and the parking space next to the stadium preassigned by a senior Bosnian prelate.

He checked his analog watch again for the tenth time in the last minute. In a few seconds it would be 10:16. Brkić had been explicit, and his commander's words were sacrosanct.

Where were the rockets? They should have arrived by now. They should have exploded.

Something was wrong. His orders were clear. Still, he

needed clarity. He picked up his cell phone to call Brkić, but the phone was dead.

He glanced outside his windshield. He noticed other people struggling with their cell phones.

The *kuffar* must have killed the cell-phone signals.

No matter. He knew his duty.

He pulled a remote control switch out of the storage tray in the console. It was connected wirelessly to the forty detached thermobaric warheads hidden in the luggage compartment of the bus.

Džeko closed his eyes, took a deep breath, and prayed the *shahada*. "I testify that there is no God but Allah, and Mohammed is His Prophet. *Allahu akbar!*"

Džeko jammed the remote with his thumb.

Nothing.

He opened his eyes. What happened? He pressed the button again, and again, and again. Nothing. The batteries must be dead, he decided.

Or something else.

No matter.

Džeko reached for the glove box. Inside was a yellow handle. All he had to do was pull it to manually detonate the charges. He flipped open the glove box just as bullets shattered the bus's giant windshield and tore into his skull and upper torso, killing him instantly.

Outside, a knot of Russian and OSA-OBA operatives charged toward the bus.

With comms dead, they flashed hand signals and cleared the way for the demolition experts right behind them.

71

SARAJEVO, BOSNIA AND HERZEGOVINA

Two days later, there was a knock at the front door of Ambassador Topal's private residence. He glanced up, puzzled, in his silken robe and pajamas. Who would come calling at this time of night?

He shuffled over to the marbled foyer in his dress slippers and opened the door.

"Jack? What are you doing here?"

"You always told me to stop by before I left. Here I am."

"It's rather late." Topal glanced past him, confused.

"I gave your security team the night off, if that's who you're looking for."

"I don't understand," Topal said with a self-effacing smile.

"Invite me in and I'll explain."

Topal waved him in. "Please. I'm all ears. Something to drink?"

"I'm fine, thanks."

Topal pointed Jack toward the garish living room with its overstuffed red velvet couches and gold silk chairs. It was a room worthy of a sultan.

"Cigarette?"

"Those things will kill you," Jack said, taking a seat. His face was still scratched and bruised from his brawl with the Chechen.

Topal sat on the couch. "First of all, congratulations on stopping Brkić and his plot. You're a hero."

"I don't know about that. I was just trying to keep another maniac from murdering thousands in the name of Allah."

"An unfortunate desire among too many fanatics these days."

"Did you know Brkić?"

"No, not directly. I've heard of the name. It's common enough." Topal leaned forward. "I thought you were already back in the States?"

"I'm extending my stay a few more days. I have some things I want to clear up before I leave. That's why I'm here."

"Obviously you want to clear up something with me. How can I be of assistance?"

Jack slid a cell phone across the ornate rosewood-and-brass coffee table that separated the two of them. Topal picked it up.

"What is this?"

"That burner phone belonged to Aida." Jack smiled. "I pulled it from her corpse."

"Aida is dead? How?"

"I shot her."

Topal shifted uncomfortably on his couch. He'd misjudged the young American.

"That's quite unfortunate, Jack. I'm sorry to hear it. But what does all of this have to do with me?"

"We didn't find any burner phones on Brkić, Emir, or anybody else. Just that one, on Aida."

"I still don't see the connection to me."

"Funny thing about that phone. It's got a voice scrambler and encryption software. Real high-tech. Mil-spec, actually, according to my guy."

"So you weren't able to pull anything off of it?"

"Not yet, but my guy is real good. He'll crack into it eventually."

Topal's even smile betrayed his relief.

"No offense, Jack, but do you have a point? It is rather late."

Jack nodded at Aida's phone. "Judging by that phone, we figured your outfit must have been practicing some serious OPSEC. We're guessing your people were using and tossing these things just about every day.

"But the problem with OPSEC is that there are a lot of moving parts. Your people did a good job destroying their burner phones. But we decided to dig a little deeper. And you know what we found out? Brkić must have destroyed all of his burner phones, but he kept using the same Iridium GO! satellite hotspot for all of his calls. Can you believe it? He must have been a cheap bastard."

"You've lost me, Jack."

"My guy—his name is Gavin, by the way, and he's *really* good—did a search. He found a connection between you and Brkić."

"A connection? How?"

"Do you have any idea how many times Brkić used that hotspot to connect calls to a cell tower right next to your embassy and residence?"

Topal smiled, setting Aida's phone back on the table. "None whatsoever."

"Almost as many times as his hotspot connected to cell towers near Aida."

"All coincidences, I'm sure. There are few cell towers in the area. And as you know, Aida and I had a close relationship, thanks to the Peace and Friendship Center. And I also believe she hired Brkić occasionally as an auto mechanic."

"So why would they speak on burner phones?"

"I have no idea."

"Let's not play games. You and Aida were closely connected, and Aida and Brkić were connected. With these cell-tower records, we know you and Brkić were connected, too."

"You're talking about statistical probabilities, not actual phone calls." Topal glanced at Aida's phone. "You can't prove anything."

"Not in a court of law. At least, not yet."

Jack reached into his pocket, pulled out a spring-loaded Benchmade Infidel knife, and flicked it open.

"But I have enough evidence to satisfy my own conscience. So, Ambassador, tell me why you were part of this plot to murder thousands of people or else I'm going to spill your intestines all over that velvet couch you're sitting on."

Topal sat back, swallowing hard. "I have diplomatic immunity."

"Like I give a shit." Jack flashed the blade. "Last chance."

"Truthfully? Yes, I was using Aida and Brkić, but only to disrupt the upcoming Unity Referendum."

"How were you using them?"

"I supplied resources to them. Cash, mostly. Especially to Brkić, so he could foment civil strife."

"You mean civil war."

"Yes. I suppose that was the goal in Brkić's mind, now that I think about it," Topal said, extending the lie. "But my government would have intervened before things got out of hand."

"He was behind those terrorist attacks over the last few weeks? The rape of those girls? The wedding massacre?"

"All him. I told him to just agitate. Not kill."

Topal hoped his lies were convincing. His orders to Brkić had been explicit, but how could Jack know that?

"And the rocket attack on the Orthodox service? What was your role in that?"

Topal bolted upright. "Nothing whatsoever. That could have caused another world war—the very thing my government is trying to prevent. We're looking to create stability in the region, not crisis. Besides, as you know, I was at the Renewal service. Why would I want to kill myself?"

"So the rocket attack was all his idea?"

"Completely. I had no idea that he was planning it. I thought I was using him, but it turns out he was using me."

"I'm still confused. You just said you were for stability in the region. So why oppose the Unity Referendum? That would promote peace and stability in Bosnia."

"Bosnia is a historical miscarriage. These fools can't govern themselves. The local Muslims are secular *kuffar* and the Christians are all drunken nihilists incapable of holding a decent thought. Only Turkey and the New Ottoman Empire can establish lasting peace and stability in this part of the world, as it had in the glorious past."

"In other words, your plan was to destabilize the region in order to gain control over it."

"In order to bring a lasting peace," Topal corrected him. He

445

leaned forward. "You Americans should thank us. The next war between NATO and Russia will occur in the Balkans. We're your best hope of preventing it."

"But Turkey is part of NATO."

"Not for long. NATO is doomed to break apart, sooner or later. The European experiment is dying in the icy winds of a demographic winter, even as a generation of Muslim leadership is rising up all over the continent. Who is more naturally suited to lead this new reality than us?"

Jack shook his head, incredulous. "You think this is an episode of *Game of Thrones*, don't you? These are people's lives you're playing with, you sick son of a bitch."

"We've been playing this 'game,' as you call it, since the thirteenth century."

"Answer me one more question. Are you Red Wing?"

Topal's owlish face beamed with pride. "Yes. How did you get that name?"

"Aida's laptop. We cracked it open before her BleachBit was scheduled to run and wipe the disk."

Topal sighed. "'For want of a nail,' eh?" He pulled off his glasses and wiped them with a silk handkerchief, asking, "Have I satisfied your curiosity?"

"For now, yes. I'm sure the Bosnian government will want to ask you more questions."

"I will gladly make myself available."

Jack sat back, smiling. An uncomfortable moment passed.

"Anything else, Jack?"

Jack held up a finger, asking Topal to wait. He touched the Bluetooth in his ear. "Gavin? Yeah. Now? Good. I'll tell him." Jack rang off.

"You like social media, don't you?"

"It has its uses," Topal said.

Jack stood. "You might want to check your Twitter feed, and any other platform you like."

"Why would I do that?"

"Try it."

Topal reached into his pocket and pulled out his smartphone. He opened up his Twitter account. He frowned, then glanced up at Jack, frightened.

"Play it."

Topal tapped a button. His own voice played over the speaker, then Jack's.

"*Truthfully? Yes, I was using Aida and Brkić, but only to disrupt the upcoming Unity Referendum . . . I supplied . . . resources to . . . foment civil strife.*"

"*You mean civil war.*"

"*Yes, I suppose that was the goal . . . But my government would have intervened before things got out of hand.*"

Topal's face turned ashen. "How?"

"My man Gavin. Did I tell you how good he was?"

Topal leaned back in the couch cushions, utterly distraught.

Jack snatched up Aida's phone from the table as he headed for the door. He turned, grinning.

"Better watch your six."

72

Jack and Kolak stood in a small city park not far from OSA-OBA headquarters.

They were both silent, staring down at a small, weathered headstone marked AIDA CURIĆ 1989–1993. It was one of hundreds in the park, though not nearly as noticeable as most and, perhaps, the most pitiful.

"Here is your mother's Aida," Kolak said.

"I don't understand."

"The woman you knew as Aida Curić was actually named Sabina Kvržić. She was the only child of Samir Kvržić, the local head of the Bosniak Mafia. Aida's family ran a profitable and well-respected tour company before the war. Kvržić was high on the Interpol wanted list at the time. He saw his opportunity to steal the business and change identities when the war broke out.

"Aida was killed during the war after her eye surgery, and the rest of her family was murdered by Kvržić. The Kvržić family assumed the Curić family's identities, including Sabina, who took Aida's. When Samir Kvržić died of cancer, his only child, Sabina Kvržić, took over."

"The Aida I know didn't strike me as a jihadi radical."

"She wasn't. She was a criminal, pure and simple. She used the tour company to run drugs, guns, and illegals all over the region for years. Topal and Brkić were just her most recent customers. She was making millions serving both of them. It was brilliant."

"But she knew about the plan to start the war between NATO and Russia. Why would she do that?"

Kolak shrugged. "Scarcity is profitable. Mafias thrive in wartime."

"And still no sign of Brkić?"

"None. He's probably out of the country by now, but we've issued an Interpol Red Notice. That should turn up something eventually."

Jack pulled out his smartphone and took a picture of the grave for his mother.

"I never did thank you for taking out the garbage for me."

Kolak shrugged. "It was a small thing." The dead assassin had been incinerated along with the rest of the trash in the dumpster. "Anything else I can do for you, Jack?"

"You can thank Lidija again for saving my bacon. I was sure we were going to crash."

"She is my best helicopter pilot. I will pass your commendation along to her."

"And I've been meaning to ask you. How'd you know that Aida and I had been stopped by the Russians? Were you following us?"

Kolak lifted Jack's wrist and tapped his iWatch. "The same way I found you at the launch site. When I first interviewed you, I had my people put a software bug in here, forcing it to broadcast your GPS position to me at all times even though your watch indicated it wasn't doing so."

Jack fingered his iWatch. "Guess I'm going back to analog."

"Do you have any plans before heading back home?"

Jack nodded at Midas, Dom, and Adara, recently arrived from Croatia, where their Gulfstream had been diverted after the airport attack.

"I'm taking them to experience their first plate of *ćevapi*. Care to join?"

Kolak flashed his crooked smile. "Most definitely."

73

The Turkish embassy was a modern but modest four-story building on the leafy Vilsonovo Šetalište, a wide boulevard only recently converted to a pedestrian promenade. No cars or motorcycles allowed.

While normal citizens of the city were forbidden to drive motor vehicles on the tree-lined street, the Turkish embassy was allowed an occasional car on an "as needed" basis, and today was one of those occasions.

An armored Audi Q7 SUV pulled up to the curb in front of the white concrete, wood, and glass building. A two-story-tall Turkish flag, red with the white crescent moon and star, hung on the face of the building. It blocked some or all of the views of several street-facing offices. Topal's office, of course, was on the top floor, enjoying an unobstructed panorama of the promenade and the park across the street.

Moments after the Audi SUV pulled up, a Turkish security detail emerged, clearing a path to the vehicle. On an agent's signal, another security detail exited the embassy, surrounding the hunched figure of Ambassador Topal, wearing a Kevlar vest.

The Bosnian government had kept its promise to keep all traffic and protesters from the promenade and away from the Turkish embassy today. But the ambassador's security team wasn't taking any chances.

The social media firestorm kicked up by Gavin's edited tape of Topal confessing his crimes went viral—organically—on Balkan social media within hours. Topal was the most hated man in Bosnia at the moment, since Brkić couldn't be found.

Under a constant barrage of death threats, Topal's security team wasn't taking any chances on his short trip to the airport. He'd been called back to Ankara for immediate consultations with the foreign ministry after the recent social media revelations. Topal was related to the president, so he wasn't in fear for his life, but certainly his future in government service was in doubt.

His diplomatic security team ushered him swiftly into the waiting SUV. The team lead rode shotgun, while a grim senior officer from MIT, Turkish national intelligence, sat in back next to Topal. The driver punched the gas and the Audi rocketed forward.

Three minutes into the sixteen-minute drive, three bicyclists pedaling furiously along the promenade dashed out into the street, three abreast. The driver slammed his horn and his brakes, burning rubber and slowing to a violent stop to avoid killing the idiots. The bikers immediately scattered.

The Audi's stop was just long enough.

Ibrahim—Mr. Clean—had a clear line of sight from the third-story apartment overlooking the quiet street. He pulled the trigger on the RPG-7.

The heavily armored Audi was no match for the tank-busting HEAT warhead. The vehicle erupted in a cloud of shrapnel and fire.

Topal died instantly.

Not so the others.

74

SLAVKOV FOREST, EASTERN CZECH REPUBLIC

The old man's eyes opened slowly, awakened by the cold steel of a pistol barrel pressed in his ear.

"Nice place you got here," John Clark said, admiring the trophy heads and antlers on the walls. "Real rustic. Not all fancy, like some gilded Malaysian whorehouse."

Clark sat in a well-worn leather chair next to the Czech's large but simple bed. His hunting lodge on the wood-studded country estate had been built according to traditional methods, using local materials.

"Thank you, Mr. Clark."

"You know my name. Impressive."

"I know everybody in your line of work."

Clark leaned back in his chair. The old man had been hell on wheels in his youth, according to the few files Gavin had been able to dig up on him. But now the senior crime lieutenant was past his physical prime.

So was he, Clark reminded himself. But even in his eighth

decade, the ex-SEAL was still in better shape than this mook had ever been.

"If you know me, then you know I don't fuck around."

"Indeed, I do. May I sit up?"

"Sure. But keep your hands where I can see them."

"Of course." The Czech leveraged his long frame up against the pillows and the headboard. "I can't see without my glasses. May I retrieve them from my nightstand?"

"We're not here to watch home movies, chief."

"Then to what do I owe the pleasure of meeting the famous John Clark?"

"We have a little problem we need to sort out."

"And that would be?"

"Your organization has put out a hit on a good friend of mine. A fellow by the name of Jack Ryan, Jr. Sound familiar?"

"Too familiar."

"You don't sound happy about it."

"I'm not. The hit should never have been initiated."

"Good, then there won't be a problem calling it off."

"I'm afraid there is."

John leaned forward, his cold-blooded scowl turning even more so, though the half-blind Czech couldn't see it. "Why?"

"I didn't place the order. Vladimir Vasilev did. He's in charge of the organization, in case you weren't aware."

"He's in some hospital in Paris, dying. We were under the impression you were in charge."

"I'm the chief operating officer, yes, but he remains the CEO. And his last, dying wish is that Jack Ryan, Jr., should die before he does. I opposed the hit from the beginning, but alas, I couldn't prevent it. And I couldn't stop it, owing to certain organizational dynamics."

"'Organizational dynamics'? Be more specific."

"If Vasilev were dead and I were in charge, I would call off the hit in a heartbeat. I would even go so far as to kill Vasilev myself in order to take charge and end the hit, but if Vasilev dies of anything other than natural causes, my life is forfeit. But more to the point, if you kill me now, the next person in line after me would be responsible for carrying out Vasilev's order, and his life would be forfeit as well, all the way down the line, until Jack Junior is dead."

"A dead man's switch," John said. "That's a problem. But I have a funny feeling you might have a solution."

"Indeed, I do. But it won't be easy."

"Don't need easy. But it better damn well be good, or you'll wake up tomorrow with your brains blown out all over that feather pillow and a suicide note pinned to your pajamas. Those are my 'organizational dynamics.'"

75

Goran Fazli trudged through the snow crunching beneath his boots, cursing the bitter cold of a record early storm. His gloved hands were shoved into the pockets of his worn-out down jacket, a gift from an aid agency. In fact, everything the Macedonian immigrant wore this evening had come from a Swedish refugee organization, which collected used clothing from the generous souls in the city.

The fools.

Fazli had just left a clandestine meeting in a public housing complex in Rinkeby, one of the famous "no go" zones in Stockholm, where police feared to appear at all, let alone intervene, despite the government's denials to the contrary. He'd been walking for blocks, replaying in his mind the conversations he'd had with the others. It had gone very well.

The majority of residents in this part of town were foreign-born, as were so many other people in Sweden these days. The liberal government's generous open-door refugee policy had been particularly welcoming to persecuted Muslims like Fazli.

Fazli wasn't his real name, of course. For the past twenty-three years, he'd been known by another.

Tarik Brkić.

But, of course, that wasn't his birth name, either.

Brkić used forged documents supplied months earlier by Aida's Peace and Friendship Center to gain refugee status and to climb to the top of Sweden's immigration list. The center had also provided his credentials certifying him as a victim of persecution with no criminal record or terrorist affiliations. It even listed him as a skilled auto mechanic, which was actually true. This provided him immediate employment at a Volvo dealership in a refugee transition program in one of Stockholm's affluent suburbs.

Brkić blended in nicely at work with his shaved head, shaved beard, mustache, and Western clothing, including a pair of cheap H&M sunglasses he wore to hide his distinctively blind eye.

And when he couldn't wear his sunglasses? Well, it was evidence of the persecution he had suffered in life, wasn't it?

But Brkić hadn't picked Sweden because it would be easy for him to enter into it or to blend in with the locals. Sweden was a hunting ground for him now—a perfect one, really. It was another Yugoslavia in the making, with hundreds of thousands of Muslim Iranians, Iraqis, Syrians, Turks, Kurds, Somalis, Eritreans, and even Bosnians living in the Nordic country. Arabic was already the second mother tongue of Sweden, surpassing Finnish.

Brkić merely shrugged when he heard the BBC News report that the Unity Referendum had passed with a startling majority. He no longer cared. He was on a new mission now, and soon his wife and children would join him.

In the few short weeks he'd been there, Brkić had already successfully recruited seven members into his new organization, the Islamic Front in Sweden, and tonight's meeting with the Iraqi brothers would likely result in at least two more.

But now it was late and he was tired and cold, and it was still a long, miserable slog through the snow-covered streets to the nearest bus stop.

"Hey, you! White man," a voice called in Swedish from out of the alley. "Got a cigarette?"

Brkić didn't speak Swedish. He had signed up for language classes only last week, since most white Swedes spoke English anyway. Despite the language barrier, the menacing tone of the man's voice was obvious. Brkić trudged on, hoping that the glowing streetlamp up ahead provided enough light to deter the man who called to him.

Over the crunch of his own boots he heard the muffled rush of several feet speeding up behind him. Brkić whipped around.

Eleven lean, dark, angular faces confronted him. Somalis, Brkić guessed. Teenagers, mostly, glaring at him. A few flashed white teeth, like smiling wolves.

The tallest one of the group approached, his thin skull wrapped beneath an olive-drab Swedish Army winter cap, its flaps tied down around his ears and secured in a bow beneath the triangle of his chin. Thick flakes of wet snow began to fall, collecting on the brim.

"You don't belong here, white man. This is our territory. Pay the tax."

Brkić shrugged, feigning ignorance and fear. But his sharp eyes were sizing up the order of attack he had to make if he hoped to survive this engagement, starting with the leader first.

The leader stepped closer, his smile widening, gloved palms open to the sky in a gesture of peace.

"Just a little money, eh?"

One of the Somalis standing to his left howled with laughter as another barked like a madman, leaping around in the snow.

Brkić turned. More Somali voices called out from the upper stories of the buildings around him, shouting and mocking. Brkić glanced behind him. Another group of young men had approached him, equally menacing.

A heavy object, hard and angular, struck him in the skull, blunted by his thick woolen cap. Brkić reached up to touch his wound, his vision blurring. He turned around to see who'd thrown it, only to be greeted with a brick smashing into his face.

Light exploded in his good eye as his knees buckled. He tumbled into the snow, stunned like a steer before the slaughter.

A cold, narrow hand pressed against his face as a blade drew across his throat, severing arteries and muscle, cutting deep to the bone.

Brkić gasped for air, thrashing like a landed fish. His hot red blood gushed black and steaming into the snow under the harsh light of the streetlamp. His mind raced to find the words of the *shahada*, but they escaped him.

His heart failed as he bled out, surrounded by the frenzied chatter of a foreign tongue he could not comprehend.

76

Vladimir Vasilev woke up that morning beside himself with joy despite the freezing rain outside his window. Not only was he feeling better than he had in years, he had also greeted the day with his manhood tenting the bedsheets. He hadn't done that since he was a teenager.

The experimental CAR T-cell treatments for his cancer had been wildly successful, even better than the doctors could have hoped, let alone predicted. He had joked with his friend, the Czech, weeks ago that he might live forever. Now he was wondering if it was actually true.

His health was so good, in fact, that he was scheduled to be released early from his treatment regimen. Perhaps as early as next week, a month ahead of schedule. Yes, of course, regular visits for ongoing treatment and maintenance were necessary, his doctor assured him. But at least he would escape his sanitary life inside the glass aquarium, slurping miso soup and swallowing purified water.

Vasilev was so happy that he almost didn't notice the new nurse pulling on her protective suit outside the glass. His rheumy eyes caught the full curve of her breasts, the shapely turn of her fine ass, and the beguiling blond ponytail he'd love to wrap his gnarled fingers around.

The poor wretch was probably making less than sixty thousand euros a year. He'd offer her ten thousand euros for a quick ten-minute lay right here in the adjustable bed. Why not? And if she refused? He'd promise her a nightmare retribution.

Either way, Vasilev was determined to take advantage of his recovered libido. It wasn't his fault she was perfectly desirable and in close proximity.

His lust inflamed even more when he saw the two other shift nurses and the EKG technician leave their stations for a break. That meant it would be just him and her for at least thirty minutes, and probably more. These French people didn't value an honest day's work, but today that would be to his benefit.

He licked his fingers and smoothed out the thin hair on his motley scalp as the nurse passed through the secured enclosure, pushing a stainless-steel cart. A moment later, she was by his bed. Even behind her surgical mask, her eyes told him she was smiling.

"Good morning, Mr. Vasilev. Your regular nurse called in sick last night, so unfortunately you're stuck with me for the day."

Vasilev's loins tingled at the sound of her delicious American accent.

"I am in capable hands, I'm sure. Please, tell me your name—your given name. How do you say it? Your first name."

He laid a liver-spotted hand on the back of her thigh. The nurse didn't withdraw.

"That's so sweet of you to ask, Mr. Vasilev."

The nurse's bright eyes smiled again as she prepared a hypodermic needle for injection.

"You can call me Adara."